W9-AYP-957

RED LONDON

ALSO BY ALMA KATSU

RED WIDOW

THE FERVOR

THE DEEP

THE HUNGER

THE DESCENT

THE RECKONING

THE TAKER

RED LONDON

A NOVEL

ALMA KATSU

G. P. PUTNAM'S SONS
NEW YORK

PUTNAM
— EST. 1838 —

G. P. Putnam's Sons
Publishers Since 1838
An imprint of Penguin Random House LLC
penguinrandomhouse.com

Library of Congress Cataloging-in-Publication Data

Names: Katsu, Alma, author.
Title: Red london: a novel / Alma Katsu.
Description: New York : G. P. Putnam's Sons, [2023]
Identifiers: LCCN 2022052365 (print) | LCCN 2022052366 (ebook) |
ISBN 9780593421956 (hardcover) | ISBN 9780593421963 (ebook)
Classification: LCC PS3611.A7886 R435 2023 (print) |
LCC PS3611.A7886 (ebook) | DDC 813/.6—dc23
LC record available at https://lccn.loc.gov/2022052365
LC ebook record available at https://lccn.loc.gov/2022052366

Printed in the United States of America

1st Printing

Book design by Kristin del Rosario

For Jim Burridge,

the best storyteller of all of us

RED LONDON

CHAPTER 1

LONDON

It starts after midnight, when most harrowing and horrifying things seem to take place.

Emily Rotenberg has been in bed for about an hour but is still awake. It takes her hours to fall asleep these days, no matter how hard she tries. And she has tried everything to fix the situation, but nothing works—not a dreary book, not prescription pills. Not even a couple glasses of wine.

Emily has no reason to believe that anything was different about this night. After all, she lives at the most desirable address in London. That's what the newspapers say, anyway: the way the media fusses over The Bishops Avenue you'd think God himself lived there. She read about the mile-long stretch just north of Hampstead Heath years before she met her husband, Mikhail, breathless stories in the color Sunday magazines when she was a little girl. It all sounded so grand, like something out of a fairy tale, and she would wonder what it would be like to live there.

She doesn't have to wonder anymore. A huge mansion on Billionaires

Row is one of the things her husband, a Russian oligarch, has given her. Though she would say that the only thing of worth he's given her are the twins, Kit and Tatiana, asleep in the adjacent wing.

Mikhail is home. She knows this, even though he is not in bed with her. The fact that he's home is by no means a given: as often as not he spends the night without her at the Knightsbridge apartment, his in-town residence closer to business associates, but tonight he is in the house they share. He is downstairs somewhere in the rambling mansion, still awake. The man is famous for never sleeping. When they were dating, Emily used to joke that he was secretly Count Dracula, that he slept during the day and rose refreshed and ready for an evening of wining, dining, and dancing. Though she knew that he'd been working because she saw the evidence of it in the news. He seemed to have a finger in every pie in Russia, not to mention his international interests. Mikhail Rotenberg is a machine for making money.

She hears a muffled noise toward the back of the property. That in itself is a rarity worth noting, but they do live in London, albeit a quieter, sleepier area to the north. It is a Saturday evening—technically, Sunday morning—so you can't rule out the occasional odd bit of noise. Only a curmudgeon would complain on a Saturday night.

What happens next, however, *never* happens.

There is a burst of gunfire.

She bolts upright in bed. It's just a couple shots but that sound is unmistakable. *Pop, pop, pop.* While Emily was not wealthy growing up, she came from an upper-class family. She has been to her share of hunting parties, spent many an autumn weekend slogging through the woods of a family friend's Scottish estate, a rifle in her hands, once she was old enough to participate. She wasn't a bad shot. The father had proclaimed her a natural, marked her forehead with the bright vermillion blood of the deer she'd taken down.

The gunfire tonight is nothing like the quaint old hunting rifles she'd used for pheasant or grouse. These first shots are deceptively quiet, however. Nothing like what will happen next.

She's reminded immediately of a murder on Billionaires Row she'd read about. It took place almost four decades ago, a foreign businessman shot dead in his home on New Year's Eve. What made the case so fascinating is that it didn't fit the usual pattern for home robberies. The robbers locked the wife in an upstairs bathroom instead of killing her alongside the husband. The gun used to kill the man was one of those tiny ladies' pistols, the kind that was designed to fit in an evening bag, and—curiouser still—the bullets were made of *silver.* This last bit makes the whole thing ludicrous, as far as Emily is concerned. They had to be decorative or a conversation piece, unless the man was suspected of being a werewolf. Somehow, the wife managed to escape from the bathroom and run for help, but the assailants were never found.

Because the wife survived, there were rumors that she was involved—of course. Even when a woman is the victim, she can't escape suspicion.

That infamous house is a few doors down. It was eventually sold and now, predictably, stands empty, another of these absentee owners who only comes to London once or twice a year.

It's the peculiar sound of the gunshots that make Emily think of the unsolved case she'd read about. *Is that what the ladies' handgun sounded like, soft and dainty?* Emily can't help but wonder.

Her first, wishful thought is that it has to do with one of the neighbors. Some have their own security, just as they do—though, unlike the Rotenbergs, the neighbors' security tends to amount to nothing more than one or two personal security guards. One for the husband, maybe one for the wife and children. The bodyguards are discreet and professional, almost always former military. Many are Israeli, the preferred source for security at the moment—though Mikhail uses Russians, of course. The Rotenbergs have more security than most of their neighbors, but that's only to be expected, given who Mikhail is and his special circumstances. Igor Volkov, their chief of security, lives with them. *I like to keep my important people close* is how Mikhail explained it to Emily when they first started dating. She'd never known anyone as wealthy as Mikhail, so she took the otherwise bizarre situation as a given, assumed that all rich people had a clutch of people following them like a comet's tail. Volkov is an old family friend, to hear Mikhail tell it, and he has been with Mikhail from the very beginning. He is only a few years older than Mikhail but looks a hundred times tougher. Tall and wiry, and covered with scars. One circles his left eye, the circumference of a beer bottle. Like most Russian males, Volkov went right into the army after school. In contrast, Mikhail, due to family connections, avoided conscription and went to college, where he started to build his business empire.

Who else is on duty? she wonders. There are always three or four twitchy young Russian men at the mansion. Emily is never told their full names and refers to them by Anglicized nicknames she gives them. Tonight, it is Leo, Max, and Mikey.

Then comes the second round of shots, much closer to the house and altogether different in character. They must be automatic—something the police will confirm later. Short bursts of fire—*bang, bang, bang, bang*—much louder now.

Emily trembles. *What is going on?* she asks, even though deep inside, she knows. Has always been expecting this, if she is honest with herself.

Her first thought is of her babies in the children's wing. Alice Wilkinson is with them, of course, her bedroom next door to the nursery. It is her responsibility to get up in the middle of the night when one of the children coughs or cries or is wakened by a bad dream. But, given the circumstances, it doesn't matter that help is in the same room with them. A nanny isn't enough: *Emily* has to be with them, to make sure they are all right.

It's funny, the stupid things one does in a moment like this. She takes a few precious seconds to put on a dressing gown. In her defense, what she is wearing is rather sheer and hardly the kind of thing you want to be caught in when armed gunmen descend on your home. She hopes, as she yanks on the dressing gown and ties the belt, that she will be locked in one of the bathrooms. Maybe it is only Mikhail they want.

The house is dark. Why hasn't anyone turned on the lights? Have the burglars cut the power? You hear of robbers doing that sort of thing. Where is everyone? Igor, undoubtedly, has gone to check with his men. Two are supposed to be posted at the back of the estate, but it is ominously quiet back there. Perhaps Igor is taking Mikhail somewhere safe. Where is Mikhail? You'd think he'd be on his way to check on his wife and children but there is no sign of him. Still, she tells herself that he is coming for them and pictures him running down the hall, running toward them, as though she could will it into being. She thinks, too, of Westie—Arthur Westover, Mikhail's funds manager—arguably more important to Mikhail than his wife. Maybe her husband is taking a moment to make sure *he* is safe.

As she stumbles down the dark hallways, she curses Igor. Isn't it his job to make sure there are plans for exigencies like this, for exactly this sort of thing? They have active shooter drills in primary schools, for god's sake, but since moving in she cannot remember being told what to do in the case of emergency. This seemed like a huge oversight on the security chief's part.

It is then Emily remembers the panic room. *Of course* there is a panic room in this giant, sprawling behemoth of a house; with his typical foresight, Mikhail had had it installed when he'd acquired the place over a decade ago.

Emily hurries through the halls, her dressing gown fluttering around her like a shroud, as she makes her way to the next wing. Noises drift up from the great open foyer in the middle of the ground floor, commands issued in Russian (naturally: it is always Russian) that she doesn't understand. Still, she recognizes the voices. Igor's mostly. Strangely, Mikhail is silent and he is *never* silent. Where is he?

She has just crossed the main hall when she hears breaking glass below, high and bright and jangly. To Emily, the sound of breaking glass is one of the scariest in the world. It means that they—whoever "they" are, though she has a good idea—have reached the house and successfully breached the outer defenses. The invaders are about to come inside.

Surely, we'll hear sirens soon. This is London, after all. Even though the houses here sit on several acres, sound travels, especially loud, angry sounds like gunshots. Their neighbors will have heard and called the police immediately. That is, if the guards hadn't alerted the police already. (But would they, given that their damnable Russian pride is on the line?) Either way, the police should arrive any minute. All Emily has to do is get the children to the panic room.

She arrives at the unlit nursery to see Miss Wilkinson standing between Kit's and Tatiana's tiny beds. She looks utterly distraught, unraveling from indecision.

The children seem to still be asleep. Emily doesn't want to jump to conclusions about Miss Wilkinson's grasp of the situation. Children can be such heavy sleepers at this age.

"What in the world is going on?" the nanny asks in a loud, frightened whisper.

What does the silly girl think is going on? Surely, she can't be that naïve. She knows whom she works for. "I'll take Tatiana, you take Kit and follow me," Emily says, not bothering to answer the question. Had either she or Mikhail told the nanny that there is a panic room in the house? Probably not. No sense scaring the girl.

Emily picks up her daughter. She snuggles instinctively against Emily's chest in a drowsy half sleep, burying her face into her mother's clavicle. Drinking in the warm, soft baby smell of her daughter, Emily nearly breaks into tears. To think bad men with weapons are converging on the house at that very minute . . . Coming for *them* . . . The children are innocent. She's innocent, for that matter. Isn't she? Emily thinks again of the dead businessman's wife, locked in a bathroom, forced to shimmy down a drainpipe. There had been no mention of children in the newspaper stories.

She runs through the hall, Tatiana clutched to her chest. Two-year-olds are heavier than you might think. Kit is even heavier than his sister, and Miss Wilkinson, a slight thing, struggles to keep up. Emily probably should've taken Kit, she realizes in hindsight, and left the smaller Tatiana to the nanny, but she'd acted on instinct. She always worries more about Tatiana because she is the girl. Emily knows how hard the world can be on the fairer sex.

The panic room sits on the ground floor next to the kitchen. It is not a family kitchen, not the sort of well-decorated, lived-in room you see in magazines. It's a big industrial place, more the domain of staff, like a modern Downton Abbey. They'd put the panic room there, she supposes, because it was easiest for the builders. She'd been in it once: Mikhail had shown it to her shortly after they were married. He had been leading her around the huge mansion that had become her home. Showing her all the nooks and crannies that he didn't show most people: his second office, the *real* one with its documents' safe, and the armory in the basement where his bodyguards kept their auxiliary weapons. "God willing, we'll never have to use it," he'd said as they stood in the panic room that night.

There was no panic room in Downton Abbey, she is certain.

Now here she is in the dark with her daughter in her arms, ready to activate the heavy steel doors for the first time, with only the nanny for company. Where is Mikhail?

"Let's go in," Emily says to Miss Wilkinson, whose teeth chatter like she'd seen a ghost. It's understandable, under the circumstances, but a bit surprising, nonetheless. She'd struck Emily as quite no-nonsense when she'd interviewed her.

Wilkinson reads her employer's mind. "What about your husband? Shouldn't we wait until—"

"I'm sure he'd prefer that his children be made safe," Emily says, snapping a little. She is more desperate than she first thought to get behind those bulletproof walls and seal the door. Hand hovering over the keypad, she notices that the gunfire has stopped—for the moment, anyway.

"Would you really close the door without me?" Mikhail's deep voice is beside her, cutting through the darkness. Suddenly, he is standing next to her with Igor behind him holding a gun high, cradled in two hands. Surprisingly, in that moment, Igor seems very nervous. She's never seen him betray even a hint of nerves, and her stomach drops to her feet. It must mean they are in real trouble.

"Thank god you're safe." Emily presses her face to her husband's chest as best she can while holding a child in her arms. She wants to shout at him—*Where were you?*—because she is afraid and it would be an easy way to vent her fear, but she knows it's better to look like she'd been worried and frightened without him. Tatiana mewls slightly, like a kitten fighting to remain asleep.

A radio crackles to life somewhere on Igor and he steps away, the better to hear. Mikhail begins to shepherd her and Miss Wilkinson into the panic room. His demeanor hits Emily as all wrong. He is angry rather than seriously frightened. Whatever is bothering him, however, he clearly is not about to discuss it in front of the nanny. Emily knows that much about her husband.

Mikhail looks from Kit, now awake and blinking owlishly at his father, to the sleeping Tatiana and then to his wife, and Emily is grateful for this rare, tender moment. She trusts that means everything will be okay. Then he steps over to a control panel, a large, awkward thing affixed to the wall. He presses the touch screen once to light it up, then holds a finger above a prominent red circle on the screen, the button that would send the room into lockdown.

She realizes in that second that he never taught her how to use the control pad. Perhaps he'd assumed she'd never need to use it—or was it because he didn't want her using it on her own? Maybe he considers it *his* panic room, which she and the twins are welcome to occupy only with *him*.

Where does this strange, uncharitable thought come from?

Mikhail is ashen and grim. He is shaken up. His house—which is definitely his castle, Englishman or no—has been breached. They both understand that, considering his position, this violation can mean many things. The implications must be running through his head.

Someone wants you dead, Mikhail.

Before he can press the button, however, Igor is back and at Mikhail's elbow, walkie-talkie in hand. "I was just informed that the police have arrived. The intruders left when they heard the sirens." Mikhail and his chief of security step aside to confer before he releases Igor to go speak to the police, who are ostensibly rustling around on the floor above them. When he turns to Emily, he looks greatly—but not completely—relieved.

She starts toward the hall. She wants to get the children to the nursery. Tatiana is heavy in her arms; the twins are awake now and fussing to be let down.

He draws her aside. "Let the nanny take them upstairs. You and I must talk."

Emily resists. "They'll be upset. They'll have questions. I need to be with them."

"That's the nanny's job. You can go up in a minute, but right *now* we need to talk."

She does as he asks. She always does. A lump forms in her throat as she watches Miss Wilkinson lead her children away. The sight of another woman caring for her children in that moment tears her heart in two. *Never again.*

Mikhail steps close so he can whisper, even though it is unnecessary. There is no one else around. They are alone.

"Igor told me that two of the guards are dead. They've taken the third one to the hospital." Mikhail says this without emotion, as though he's rattling off sports scores he's heard on the radio. The news stuns her like a blow to the head and she thinks of the young men she saw earlier that evening, heading out to take their places behind the house. Which ones will she never see again?

"Who attacked us tonight?" Emily asks tearfully. It hits her all in that moment, what almost happened. *The wife locked in the bathroom, shimmying down a drainpipe to escape.*

"I don't know. We'll find out."

"The police—"

"The police are useless in this sort of thing. Igor will find out. He has—resources."

"*This sort of thing?*" That confirms it, as far as she is concerned: this is no ordinary robbery or home invasion. This is Mikhail's chickens coming home to roost. His very particular, high-stakes, deadly chickens.

Tonight was supposed to be a reckoning. They are being called to account for their sins and misdeeds. Mikhail's are so much worse than hers, even if you only count the ones she knows about. There are more, she is sure, and much worse. But whatever Mikhail is guilty of, he went into it with his eyes open, knowing full well what he was doing. He knew the world he was becoming part of. He knew its peculiar rules, its unforgiving players.

But she did not have that benefit.

Oh, she may have had an inkling. She had her suspicions, Mikhail being who he is. But she let them remain suspicions. The things that remained unspoken between them could fill a canyon.

Would he have told her, if she'd asked?

Does it matter? She hadn't.

All she had known was that she was deliberately choosing evil. How evil, how bad it really was, she didn't want to know.

That didn't mean it wouldn't catch up to her at some point. There had to be a price for all this luxury, all this ease.

Mikhail breaks into her self-pitying thoughts. "Don't speak to the police. They'll want to talk to you, but just tell them you need to see to the children."

Emily feels a spasm of anger pass through her, but she knows she won't act on it, no matter how tired she is. "You don't have to tell me, I'm not an idiot—"

"They would've stopped you and you would've spoken to them. I know you, Emily: so eager to please." He says the last part with an amused bitterness. Funny, that's what she thought he liked about her, her eagerness to make him happy. "*I'm* telling you not to tell them anything. I'll be right behind you, and I'll make it clear to them that you're not to be bothered. This is my affair."

His words are numbing, like taking a pill. They take the fight right out of her. "Of course."

They can hear the police on the floor above, the crackle of their walkie-talkies, unfamiliar voices mingled with Igor's. The children will be terrified. She needs to get to them.

As they start up the stairs, she cannot resist asking. Even though she knows he doesn't want to be confronted, not yet. She whispers, "*He's* behind it, isn't he?"

Mikhail stops in his tracks. He gives his wife a hard and incredulous look, as though he can't believe she's asking him this. That she has the nerve.

Yet, behind it, there is a hint of fear. Emily has never known Mikhail to be afraid—why should he? He's always been the one to hold all the cards. But tonight, he is afraid. Viktor Kosygin, the new president of Russia and arguably the most powerful man in the world, is behind this and, if that is the case, it is all over. They aren't safe and they will never be safe. There is no running, no hiding. No panic room will be sufficient to protect them.

Tonight, they've been lucky. He's gotten a reprieve, Mikhail seems to understand. But what happened tonight is just the beginning.

The worst, they both understand with absolute clarity, is yet to come.

CHAPTER 2

Lyndsey Duncan pads across the carpeted floor of her darkened Vauxhall apartment in search of the TV remote. Vauxhall isn't a quiet neighborhood, even on the backstreet where Lyndsey now lives. Traffic sounds waft up from the road, punctuated by the occasional bray of laughter or shout from a half-drunk restaurant-goer stumbling his way to the Tube station.

It's a lovely apartment, with high ceilings and plastered ornamental bits and heavy curtains, but it can't help but feel strange, like she's mistakenly wandered away from her own life. Because it is nothing like the apartment she left back in Washington, D.C.—or, technically, Tysons Corner, Virginia. The long-term hotel for business travelers, with its generic sheets and pots and pans, the place that was supposed to be temporary until she found a new apartment.

She settles into the velvet cushions on the couch, absently toying with a heavy tassel hanging from a corner of a pillow. Her eye wanders, as it has been prone to do these past few days, because the apartment's appointments are luxurious and beautiful and so different from what she knows. The more she looks, the more she finds. Take this wallpaper, for instance: heavy and satiny to the touch, with tone-on-tone swirls on an ivory background. She can't imagine how much it must have cost per roll. She can't believe she gets to live in such a swanky place.

Flickering images tug her eyes back to the TV screen. It's three a.m. and she's awake: lingering jet lag has left her off-balance. Maybe she's subconsciously searching for news of home, of the familiar, because nothing in London is familiar to her. She doesn't know why she watches the news late at night before going to bed. It isn't as though it is going to help her fall asleep. You might think being a news junkie led to her career in intelligence and perhaps it did, because it has been a lifelong habit, something she's done since she was a teenager and not just when she went, rather unexpectedly, to work for CIA. But did it make her want to have some part in world events?

She can't say that's the case.

She's been in London all of two weeks, relocated from Washington, D.C., to start her new job. She's been given a different kind of cover to facilitate this assignment and a new cover means a different routine. It's all new to her, from when she reports for duty in the morning until she's back across the threshold of her flat in the evening. She must live her cover, comporting herself differently in public, in her whole outward-facing life. She must internalize the security routine at the location that serves as her office here in London. Those first hectic, disorienting days when everything has been turned upside down have been a blur; but they are behind her now, and she had been looking forward to a quiet weekend.

Until she sees the news.

"We're getting reports of an armed break-in at one of the houses on Billionaires Row," a blond BBC news anchor says breathlessly. She's trying to appear professional, but Lyndsey, a behavioral analyst, sees faint but telltale signs that she's excited. Her eyes widen; she leans forward in her chair. Behind her there's footage of a dark street illuminated by the blue lights of a half-dozen police cars. The scene is utter bedlam, with knots of uniformed police standing in consultation, police tape stretched across the open gates that flank the drive, all stark in the glare of camera crews' lighting. It looks like a major disaster has taken place.

Lyndsey has heard of Billionaires Row. How could you not? It's one of the most famous streets in the city. Its proper name is The Bishops Avenue. Located in London's northern stretches, near Hampstead Heath—a lush urban oasis of forest, once the hinterlands of London beset by highwaymen. The street is now a run of swanky mansions owned mostly by absent mega-wealthy.

"The attack took place at the home of Mikhail Rotenberg, a Russian businessman who has made London his principal residence for the past decade . . ." Lyndsey's ears perk up at the name. It's vaguely familiar, but then again, all Russian names seem familiar. She's worked the Russian target at CIA for most of her career. It's the reason she's been sent to London: she's to be the handler for Dmitri Tarasenko, a highly placed asset in the Federal Security Service of the Russian Federation, or FSB as it's more commonly known. It will be easier for Lyndsey to meet with Tarasenko if she's based in Europe, and the expectation is that Lyndsey will have to meet frequently with their devious new Russian asset. She'll need to stay on top of him to make this mission a success.

Lyndsey had told her boss, Kim Claiborne, the new chief of Russia Division, that Tarasenko was too dangerous to be trustworthy, but he dangled a prize too tempting to refuse: he would help them bring in General Evgeni Morozov, the senior Russian officer responsible for the murder of a CIA Chief of Station a decade earlier. The seventh floor of Langley had wanted Morozov badly; the Agency could not let a cold-blooded killing like that stand. They would've gone to the ends of the earth to hunt Morozov down, but he'd immediately retreated to Russia and hadn't set foot outside of its borders since. When Tarasenko's offer was accepted, he made it clear that he would have no one as his handler but Lyndsey. Which made it impossible for her to decline the assignment.

In exchange for her sacrifice, Claiborne is making things as pain free as possible, starting with an office far removed from the politicking at a hot spot like London Station.

Claiborne also promised a free hand. This meant a lot, as Lyndsey had gotten seriously burned at her last assignment, a mole hunt that turned out to be much more than it seemed at first glance. It had all been a scheme set in motion by her former boss, who had been willing to sacrifice her to get his train wreck of a career back on track. The experience left Lyndsey with a strong distrust of management at Langley, even Claiborne, though she hadn't done anything to make Lyndsey mistrust her.

Yet.

"Rotenberg is one of many Russian expatriates who have made London their home in the past twenty years and is thought to be the wealthiest." *When does "rich" become "wealthy"?* she'd once asked a financial analyst at headquarters. *When you lose your place counting the zeros* was his dry reply. "Rotenberg owns Omni Bank, the largest private bank in Russia. He's reportedly close to Russian president Kosygin," the news anchor says, her voice getting higher. Perhaps the woman gets turned on by oligarchs.

Or perhaps it is Kosygin who excites her. He excites a lot of people, but not for the right reasons. In the aftermath of the Ukraine fiasco, which led to the ouster of Vladimir Putin, Viktor Kosygin stepped in. The West heaved a collective sigh of relief. Kosygin said the right things: that he respected the international order, that he wanted things to go back to normal. But in the uneasy silence following Putin's disappearance, people have begun to wonder if there isn't reason to worry. For one thing, Putin has well and truly disappeared: no one knows where he is. Kosygin is another KGB alum, not as well-known as Putin. One of Putin's nemeses, in fact, to hear him tell it. Kosygin had been biding his time.

Have they traded a bad man for an even worse one?

Next, a second reporter joins the anchor. He seems to be too young to be as smug as he appears. He begins providing background, perhaps to explain things to viewers clueless about London's Russian problem, or perhaps just to pad out the segment, as it doesn't appear they have any new information. "London has been a haven for wealthy foreigners for a long time, but in the past decade the number of Russians has swollen," he says in a posh, nasal accent. "Following the 2008 global economic downturn, the government relaxed policies regarding foreign ownership of property as a way to bring in money, even if it meant turning a blind eye to where that money came from. High-end real estate became a popular way to launder dirty funds," the reporter says confidently to the blond anchor.

"And why is that, Sean?" she asks.

He doesn't break his smirk. "Well, London real estate will never lose value, will it? There isn't a safer place anywhere in the world to put your money."

Lyndsey turns the sound down on the TV. This isn't exactly a new story, the Russian invasion of London—so much so that in the 2010s, the city became known as *Londongrad*, its more expensive communities overrun with Russian arrivistes. Arguably, the authorities started to reevaluate what they'd done after the 2018 poisoning of Sergei Skripal, a Russian military officer turned spy for the British, when the Russians showed their true colors. By then, the average British citizen had started to wonder if they'd made a deal with the devil.

Russia's attack on Ukraine in 2022 cemented that view in most Brits' minds. Whitehall decided to get serious against the oligarchs—well, at least against the ones with irrefutable ties to Putin. Brits woke up to the fact that wealthy Russians owned a good portion of their country estates and football teams. Assets were seized and bank accounts frozen, visas revoked, and a few high-profile Russian businessmen were kicked out of the country. There were still plenty of Russians left, but they knew to keep their heads down—which made tonight's very public dustup all the more intriguing.

Lyndsey's fingers reach for her laptop to do a little headline surfing, to see what she can find out about Mikhail Rotenberg. If he is a high-profile oligarch, he should be protected, like being a made man in the Mafia. Who would try to steal from a Mafia don? It would be suicide—unless something's changed behind the scenes.

As the news anchor scrambles for something to say—Sean has left the scene by now; the poor woman obviously has come to the end of available material and yet the director won't cut away—Lyndsey can't help but wonder what's really going on at Billionaires Row. Even a complete bungler wouldn't accidentally break into the home of one of Kosygin's favorites. It's no rookie mistake, but what does that leave? A personal vendetta? It's not unconceivable: despite what Kosygin says about respecting other sovereign states, his predecessor had a long reach and little compunction about breaking another country's laws. The Skripal poisonings proved that.

Will Langley look into tonight's robbery? She's pretty sure it will. She feels confident that something will lead back to Moscow. Nonetheless, she will hear nothing until Monday, when she returns to work. That is life for an intelligence officer: breaking stories on the news may lead to a new task, or intelligence may have been days or weeks ahead and what you see on TV is the aftermath.

Anyway, she is busy on the weekends, trying to establish a baseline. A normal life. Weekends mean a trip to the corner market for sundries, doing laundry in the tiny combo unit in her kitchen that takes forever to dry her clothes. There is still unpacking to be done, even though the big shipment of her belongings won't arrive for a few more weeks. She plans to take more walks through the neighborhood to familiarize herself with street names and landmarks, because that's part of the job. She must know the area like the back of her hand. Good tradecraft is woven into the fabric of her life, like going to the gym and watching cheesy romance movies and sudden cravings for Chinese dumplings at midnight. She also must practice surveillance detection, though she is pretty sure no one is tailing her.

It is too soon for that. She should not have surfaced on anyone's radar.

Not yet, anyway.

In Washington, Lyndsey's commute was a slow crawl through a perpetually tangled snarl of traffic, hours wasted behind the wheel of a car while listening to podcasts or books on tape. Here, it is a pleasant walk from her apartment building to an office in a row house. The lease would reveal that it's rented by the U.S. government. To the outside world, it looks like a commercial building with nothing to give its true nature away except, perhaps, the serious assortment of electronic locks on the front door. Still, it's plausible. The owner could just be paranoid, or perhaps it's something the insurance demands. From the signage, you'd think it held three small businesses, one on each floor: a law office, a small public relations firm, and something that hinted at import-export. The entrance is like an air lock: to get inside, you must punch a code into the keypad and wave a badge over a sensor to open the second door. Then it's a quick jog up one flight to another door controlled by another keypad. Cameras in the corners record your every move and transmit it to unseen minders.

Her office is a monk's cell, barely big enough for a desk and an extra chair in the unlikely event that she has a visitor. She sets down her coffee and powers up the computer before hanging up her coat. She is pretty sure she is the only one on the entire floor, the hour a bit early for the three others she has met. None of them knows the particulars of each other's assignments. They're all here as lone operators. This is the smallest shop she'd ever worked from, a tiny outpost used for special projects. Some officers might worry about being outside the Station, not for security reasons but because that's where the action is, the focus of the Agency's activities in country. But as far as Lyndsey is concerned, the less interaction with the Station, the better. Claiborne had understood this, given what had happened to Lyndsey during her posting in Beirut, and had made it clear that the Chief of Station wouldn't interfere. "Though it wouldn't be a bad idea to get on his schedule for a quick visit. Give him a chance to get to know you. So, he'll be able to put a face to the name," Claiborne had advised during Lyndsey's last visit to her office, days before she got on the plane to Heathrow.

That can wait until tomorrow . . . or the next day. Right now, she should be focusing on Tarasenko. Dmitri Tarasenko, senior FSB officer. Tarasenko the war criminal, the nightmare of South Ossetia. He will be a tricky one to control: wily as a fox, deadly as a lion. And he's working for them under duress: he was caught during an operation on U.S. soil and offered to flip in exchange for his freedom. He said he'd only help them get Morozov because he was tired of being under the old man's control, unpredictable as that was. She should be figuring out how she is going to control this unrepentant and potentially treacherous beast, not letting herself be distracted by the news.

Still. Her mind flits back to the images on the TV, blue police lights bouncing wildly off the three-story mansion; and she cannot shake the feeling that her path is going to lead her to that mansion, that her life is somehow fated to become entangled with the people who live there.

Lyndsey is about to push it completely out of her thoughts when the special cell phone lying on her desk, the one that she was given the day she departed Langley, beeps an alert.

CHAPTER 3

Lyndsey picks up the phone and taps through to the message app. The encoded message reads: *Whatever plans you have for this afternoon, cancel them. We need you to sit in on a meeting for us with the cousins at Vauxhall Cross at 2 p.m. Details to follow.*

Lyndsey didn't expect to get any invitations to meetings at MI6 headquarters. She is here undercover, after all, working on a very sensitive and important mission that's personal to CIA. Not something it will share with MI6 unless absolutely necessary.

She's not part of London Station for a reason. For the headquarters of a spy agency, Vauxhall Cross is incredibly open and accessible, squatting as it does beside Vauxhall Bridge, surrounded by the swirl of London life. It's been featured in the James Bond movies, for goodness' sake. Compared to Langley, which is tucked away in northern Virginia woods like a nunnery, Vauxhall Cross is practically begging to be the backdrop of selfies and YouTube videos. A nightmare for anyone undercover.

Langley's request gives her pause. She won't be able to just go waltzing in: if any adversaries were watching her, they would wonder what business a woman who ostensibly works in a cute little PR firm has with Her Majesty's foreign intelligence service. Lyndsey wonders if she even looks the part or if she's too serious, too no-nonsense. Tall for a woman, and athletic like a marathoner. She dresses soberly in neutral tones to avoid calling attention to herself and surely that is a mistake: someone who works in PR would dress more expressively, with more flair. Then there's a steeliness in her eyes: these are eyes that have seen too much for her years. A pair of sunglasses will help with that. There's no escaping the need for a surveillance detection route, hours spent running around to throw anyone who might be following off her trail. And, at the end of the two-hour dry-cleaning run, she can't just saunter in. She'll have to be brought in wearing a disguise.

In this case, she will need to take various modes of transportation around the city. Under normal circumstances, the walk to Vauxhall Cross from her cover office would be fifteen minutes. But she decides to first take the Underground and then a double-decker bus to carry her far, far away. She spends the time looking through windows at the passing scenes of London, on the alert for signs of watchers on her tail—checking reflections in the glass, looking for suspicious activity. A face she's seen once already. Someone parroting her moves, getting up when she steps off the bus. She stops at a café for coffee, the waitress curling her lip slightly when Lyndsey turns down her offer of tea. She'll never get used to the way they drink it here, with milk.

As she lingers over coffee, Lyndsey hopes that whatever the meeting is about, it is sufficiently important to be worth the trouble. She's eager to get started with Tarasenko. There's a lot to do, from testing the communications channel they've set up with him to setting a routine with her people back at Langley. She'd just contacted him to set up their first meeting—nothing more than a test drive, to see how he is settling into his new role as asset to CIA and traitor to his country—and is waiting to hear back. She's worried now that he's free, he's going to forget his promise or worse, that he's told the FSB and they're working out a way to run him as a triple agent. The permutations for treachery are nearly endless.

Mostly, however, she is getting used to working on her own. She's never worked outside of headquarters or a station. Normally, she spends her day in the company of fellow spooks and has a support system of reports officers and technical staff and someone back in Virginia to remind her about mandatory training classes and the like. For all the annoyances of working in an office, it has its benefits, too. There is the comfort of being surrounded by people in the same boat as you, who must navigate a secret life while dealing with family and friends. There is also the security of knowing you are behind a virtual—if not actual—barbed wire fence. That you are protected. Sitting in her office in the pretend PR firm on a commercial street, she feels exposed. Vulnerable. There are a few security measures in place but they wouldn't last long if they came under attack, not like armed guards and checkpoints made of metal and concrete. The cameras are designed for catching clues in the event something happens, not for preventing bad things in the first place. The only defense she has, really, is anonymity. You're protected best if no one suspects you of anything, if everyone thinks you're just another everyday working stiff.

When Lyndsey is pretty sure she's lost anyone who could've possibly been following her, she gets into a cab. The back seat is roomy enough for her to slip into a light disguise—tying a bright scarf around her hair like a glamourous starlet from the fifties, swapping her jacket for a thin red trench coat that she's been carrying in a large black tote—before switching to an Uber. It's the second car that takes her to the meeting. The Uber driver takes her to a parking garage, where she waits a couple beats before hopping into a car sent by MI6. "Ready to go, miss?" the driver says as Lyndsey pulls off the scarf and trench coat and dons a pair of very dark sunglasses. He takes another circuitous route to the big, conspicuous building on the embankment, zipping at the last minute down a ramp that leads to an underground garage.

She's inside. She pulls off the sunglasses.

Lyndsey breathes a sigh of relief when her car is met by a pleasant-looking young man in an ill-fitting suit. "Miss Duncan? I'm to escort you to the meeting," he says when she steps out of the blue Ford Fiesta. What the car lacks in comfort, it makes up for with ubiquity. What is more uncomfortable, however, is the outfit she'd slipped on behind the tinted windows of the back seat for the last leg of the journey. Dark brown wig, a smear of different colored lipstick, and a brightly colored cardigan. Her regular suit jacket and heels are packed all the way at the bottom of that voluminous tote bag.

"This way, Miss Duncan," the young man says as he takes off at a brisk pace. He doesn't offer his name.

"Do we have time for a quick pit stop? I'd like to get out of this outfit," she says, resenting only slightly that she has to ask.

"What? Of course . . . I'm afraid the meeting starts in a few minutes . . ." He trails off, clearly implying that if they are late, it is her fault.

She stands before a sink as she pulls off the pieces—wig, dowdy cardigan—and tries to smooth her hair. Her tote bag sits at her feet, over-stuffed like a boa constrictor that had just swallowed a pig. A tissue takes care of the lipstick, though it leaves a slight tinge on her lips.

Her heels click against the stone floor as she exits the ladies' room. "All set," she says to the young man.

He takes her to a conference room just down the hall. A few people are still trickling in, stragglers in the hall just like her. He holds the door open for her.

A handful of people mill restlessly around the table, a forest of upright men and women in suits and somber dresses. A low hum of chatter provides background noise, albeit with accents that are already sounding normal to Lyndsey's ears after only a few weeks in the country. There is a strict protocol to seating at these meetings: those with a speaking role or representing their office have a place at the table while extra bodies and junior officers take the seats flanking the walls. Lyndsey knows she is to sit at the table: she'd been directed to attend on behalf of Langley. Though it is a bit of a mystery as to why someone from the Station hasn't been sent, which would be normal protocol.

She is tired and just wants to sit but that's impossible, given the milling throng. But at that moment, someone pipes up, "Shall we get this meeting started?"

That voice is familiar.

Like gnus at the watering hole at the first roar of a lion, the men and women dart nervously for seats. The crowd parts.

The man standing at the head of the table *is* familiar.

It's Davis Ranford.

Her heart does that funny, flipping thing in her chest, like it's jumped off a board suspended high above a pool. She and Davis were lovers when she was stationed in Beirut. Their affair was the trespass against Agency policy that was used to send her home. Close personal relationships with foreign intelligence are generally prohibited; but as with most things in the world of covert operations, it's flexible. Among the CIAs and MI6s of the world, there is no black and white, only endless shades of gray. If an affair could be used to the agency's advantage, there might be room for negotiation.

Someone *had* planned to use her indiscretion to his advantage. Her former boss, Eric Newman, had used the affair as an excuse to pull Lyndsey back to Langley to head up the hunt for a Russian mole, but the whole thing had turned out to be Newman's plot, a power play of the highest order. He knew CIA had hidden the truth from Theresa Warner: her husband hadn't been killed in an operation gone wrong in Moscow but was being held prisoner. Both Moscow and Langley had decided to bury the op and Richard's imprisonment for political reasons. Eric made sure Theresa found out Richard was still alive and she took the bait, as he knew she would, and offered to spy for Russia in exchange for Richard's freedom. She became the mouse while Lyndsey was the cat, neither of them knowing Newman was the rat pulling strings behind both of them.

As trespasses go, Lyndsey's wasn't one of the worst: many officers have affairs with foreign agents. At least Davis is British: they're considered practically American. Nonetheless, they haven't spoken or even texted in all this time—though neither of them had to be told this prohibition. It was expected. To contact Davis after she'd been told explicitly not to would only confirm suspicions and be grounds for immediate dismissal.

His eyes lock with hers. She sees no surprise there, however. He *knew* she was coming.

She smothers the flurry of emotions that rise in her chest and finds a seat. She misses the introductory remarks, however, as her head is a blur of thoughts. He'd obviously requested her presence: that explains why they hadn't sent someone from Station. Does he know that Claiborne told her it would be all right to get back in touch with her former lover?

He looks good. He hasn't changed a bit since she'd last seen him in Beirut. His hair is still a tangle of dark, barely tamed curls. He wears the same world-weary smirk, sits with the same insouciant ease. Being in the same room with him brings back memories (inconvenient given the time and place) of their days together. Evenings hidden in hotel rooms. Gin and tonics and spiced almonds, long talks about their respective careers. His dry wit; she'd never been with such a clever man. She squashes memories of touching his lean, athletic body.

He's at the head of the table, which means it's his meeting, and he's giving everyone equal attention—except, she notices, his eyes settle on her for a split second longer than elsewhere. That's a signal. He has something to tell her.

"We're here because of the attack on The Bishops Avenue. There hasn't been an attack like that—sizable, orchestrated—on a political figure in London in recent memory. The police are conducting an investigation, yes, but Whitehall is concerned that this wasn't merely an overambitious robbery attempt. They suspect something more sinister is going on, particularly given the unorthodox leadership change in Russia not too long ago. That's why the Americans are joining us at the table. Whitehall has called for this to be a *joint* task force." He nods in Lyndsey's direction.

A murmur ripples around the room as Davis gestures next to a young man sitting halfway down the table. "I'm going to turn the meeting over to one of our Russia experts, Parth Arya."

The young man stands. He's dressed in a suit the color of mouse fur, a pair of small round spectacles perched on his nose. There are papers spread out before him, and the young man touches them briefly, almost superstitiously, before beginning. "Two nights ago, at approximately ten p.m., there was an attack on Seventy-Eight The Bishops Avenue in the neighborhood of Hampstead Heath. I don't have to tell you, that's some of the priciest real estate in a very expensive city.

"The target was the home of Mikhail Rotenberg." Behind Arya, an image flashes onto the white wall. It's the portrait of a man in his mid-forties, though he could be in his early fifties. He has the deceptively smooth, ageless look of a man who has never done physical labor, has never been afraid he wouldn't be able to make the rent. His most notable feature is a high forehead—or maybe it's just a receding hairline—that makes him look exceptionally intelligent. Or that might be due to his piercing eyes. They are merciless, those eyes.

"For those of you not familiar with Rotenberg, he's widely believed to be the richest man in Russia. The 'in Russia' part is a mere formality, since he declared London as his official residency some years back. Nonetheless, he still appears every year on *Forbes*' list of the richest Russians.

"Rotenberg straddles the line between the old-school oligarchs and the new generation. He got his start in oil and natural gas, like the men who made their fortune exploiting Russia's natural resources when the Communist state fell in the 1990s. But he's also part of the newer class of oligarchs—Pavel Novikov, Stepan Lenkov, even Oleg Galchev—the ones who built their fortunes in media, hotels, and the like. They're ambitious, they're greedy, and they're remorseless.

"Today, Rotenberg's empire is pretty far-flung." More pictures flash by in quick succession:, aerial shots of bristling shipyards and huge, gleaming buildings in downtown settings. The crowd stirs restlessly in their seats. "He still has oil, but his crown jewel—the lynchpin of his empire and the reason he has been able to stay afloat all this time—is Omni Bank, the largest private bank in Russia. It's said that one out of every two Russians has an account with Omni Bank and it certainly handles the accounts of some of the largest corporations. Now, you may be wondering how he's managed to remain so profitable and active, when many of his peers have been reined in by the authorities, and the answer is simple: he has lent a lot of money to the Russian government. So much money, in fact, that Russian media used to jokingly refer to him as 'Putin's banker.'

Rotenberg appears to be just as accommodating with the new Russian president as well."

One of the younger men seated at the table clears his throat. "If Rotenberg is a known agent of Viktor Kosygin, how has he managed to remain in the U.K.? Why wasn't he thrown out of the country following Skripal, or Ukraine?" So many of Rotenberg's less-notorious countrymen were forced to leave after the brazen Russian attack on double agent Sergei Skripal, who was under Her Majesty's Government's protection at the time. Then there was the concerted effort after Russia's attack on Ukraine to go after the oligarchs with close ties to the Kremlin—for all the good that did.

"Thank you, Jones. First of all, to say he's a 'known' agent of Kosygin might be overstating it. 'Suspected' is more like it. And secondly, well, you've given me the perfect segue." Arya smiles knowingly as he presses the button on the remote. A new image pops up on the wall, the portrait of an attractive woman. In her early thirties, Lyndsey guesses. The woman is the proverbial English rose. Her complexion is the color of fresh cream, her eyes deep blue. She smiles shyly at whoever is taking her picture as she squints into the sun. Her golden blond hair is pinned back in a style that's meant to be elegant, but stray flyaways give her an air of ease. She gives the impression of a woman who prefers it that way, who will never be as buttoned-up as her mother would like.

"This is Rotenberg's wife, the former Emily Hughes. Daughter of Evan Archibald Hughes, the eighth Viscount Rampshead. The Hugheses are an old family, but an impoverished one, thanks to the fifth viscount, who made some disastrous investments. Emily and her future husband met at an art gallery, where Emily was working temporarily. They were married six months later." Arya clicks through a series of photos of Emily Rotenberg so varied that it could be an ad for a Barbie doll. There she is as a teenager on horseback in a somber black jacket and velvet hard hat, her face the picture of concentration. Now she's in a gauzy dress, walking on a white sand beach, sandals swinging from one hand. Then she is emerging from a shiny town car, sparkling in sequins, dressed for an evening gala. In each photograph, she is absolutely beautiful but also, Lyndsey notices, stands slightly apart from everyone else.

She is lonely.

"Because Rotenberg is married to a U.K. citizen, it would be hard to get him removed from the country. Not an easy win for the Criminal Finances Act, in other words. Not to mention the fact that, being one of the earlier oligarchs to come to London, he's had years and years to dig in. He's developed a lot of influential friends and business partners. He's bought many properties, invested in a number of U.K. ventures, and not all of it with dirty money."

"How do you separate dirty money from clean money?" someone toward the back of the room quips.

"In this town? Very, very carefully," Arya replies. A chuckle ripples around the table.

Davis raps his knuckles for attention. "Thank you, Parth. Now, I'd like to return to the matter at hand. The attack Saturday night. Can we come to a consensus as to what it means? Do we feel safe in saying Kosygin has something to do with the attack?"

A woman in a dowdy suit shifts in her chair. "We're assuming it wasn't a run-of-the-mill robbery or home invasion?"

"Nothing run-of-the-mill about it," a man sitting to her right mutters. "Five men, armed with automatic weapons, break into a home with its own known security detail? Two dead, one wounded?"

"Maybe Rotenberg is known for keeping cash or valuables in the house?" the woman counters. Still, heads shake. No one is buying it.

"We'll need to let the police finish their investigation, but for the sake of argument let's rule out a simple robbery," Davis says. "What's going on here, people?"

"I'd say it's a clear sign that Rotenberg no longer has favored status." The speaker sits across the table from Lyndsey. Heads turn to listen, mouths closed politely; apparently, he's respected in MI6, unlike the woman who made the "run-of-the-mill" comment. "Let's not be coy: oligarchs of a certain class are linked to the Kremlin. That's a known fact. Rotenberg's demotion is not completely unexpected: his support of Putin during the Ukraine business was decidedly lukewarm. He was one of the first to pointedly distance himself from Moscow. It was risky, and he was damn lucky that Putin's reign ended as abruptly as it did."

"It's almost as though Rotenberg knew it was coming," someone at the table cracks.

The respected speaker continues. "We've never seen an attack like this on U.K. soil against one of the Russians. When there's been a robbery, it's more of a smash-and-grab or a dustup in a nightclub. No, this is different. To go after the man in his own home, while his family is present. That's a sign of disrespect. The sheer audacity."

"Not to mention the difficulty," Arya adds. "That's Billionaires Row, a key area of concern for the police, given the concentration of high-value citizens residing there. Then there's private security: each of those houses employs their own army of bodyguards. That's a lot of firepower to maneuver around."

"Again—the police will give us an assessment on all that," Davis says. He points at the people gathered around the table. "I'm interested in knowing what this attack *means*. Who's behind it? A business rival? Someone Rotenberg's hurt in the past? And—let's give Millie her due—what if it was an actual robbery? Is it because there's something in that house that's valuable enough to take this kind of risk? We can't trust our assumptions . . ."

The man across from Lyndsey purses his lips. "I think we can assume it signals some kind of disruption to Rotenberg's relationship with Kosygin. Otherwise, no one would dare act against him. Look, we're still figuring out who Kosygin is, exactly. We haven't had years and years to study him, like Putin. He's a largely unknown entity."

"A senior KGB officer?" Davis scoffs. "How is that possible?"

"We have the surface stuff, the official record, that sort of thing. But we don't have the deep dirt," Arya explains. "We're working on that now. Trying to find someone close to him, turning over every rock. You know the drill. But nothing is as revealing as action. Every move he makes, he reveals himself a little bit more."

"Which is to say, we don't know what precipitated the attack. We have no idea." The speaker is one of the older experts on the team of Moscow watchers: that's what his expression tells Lyndsey. He and Arya, and probably half the people in this room, spend their days compiling copious amounts of intelligence on the activities of Russian president Viktor Kosygin. Information that—for the most part—comes from far away, is not anything they have seen with their own eyes or touched with their own hands. They read and interpret those tea leaves, write up reports, and brief Whitehall.

And now there has been this momentous event and it's a *surprise.* It has happened right in their midst.

Davis scowls gently. Lyndsey remembers seeing that same scowl in Beirut when he weighed in on which restaurant they would dine in that evening, or when they argued over the merits of a particular film director. It didn't mean he was angry, only that he was thinking. Many case officers were smilers, hiding their true feelings behind an easy, friendly grin. It was to put targets at ease: people tend to relax around someone who is smiling. But Davis had never been afraid of being hard to like. He didn't care if he made people uncomfortable.

"I want you to double-check—no, triple-check—*everything* you have on Rotenberg. Obviously, something's happened and we missed it." Cheeks color on some of the people around the table though it's understandable. It's been a year of momentous surprises, after all. After a disastrous attempt to steal another country, Russia's president disappears in the night, replaced by a new man the next morning. A man who is a cipher. The fortunes of one billionaire oligarch might've gone unexamined.

Davis stabs a finger against the tabletop. "All right, everyone, that's enough for now. Stand by for the police reports—I expect we'll get a preliminary one by the end of the day. I want your ideas as to what's going on with Rotenberg before you leave for home."

There is the usual shuffling of papers and side conversations between colleagues as the meeting breaks up, but Lyndsey remains in her seat. She can wait, she's in no hurry to make the long, convoluted trek back to her secret office. Undoubtedly, the same sweet young man who escorted her in will be waiting at the door to take her to the waiting Fiesta.

No, she's waiting to speak to Davis. She's pretty sure he has something to say to her; but even if he doesn't, even if she's mistaken, it would be weird to brush by him.

And, as harsh or unromantic as it sounds, they both want or need their careers more than they need each other. For her, it is the bitter truth. Men can't be depended on—she learned that from her own life. Her father died so long ago she can barely remember him. Her mother worked herself sick all through Lyndsey's childhood. At the end of the day, for good reasons or bad, you need to be able to take care of yourself.

Lyndsey hadn't counted on seeing Davis, and she certainly hadn't expected to feel this way, light-headed and even a tad giddy. She can remember every minute they spent together in Lebanon—they were her only happy ones. He was her lifeline at a time when she was being sorely tested. She'd been yanked out of Moscow Station after her big success landing her first asset, respected career FSB officer Yaromir Popov, after she'd been ordained a rising star on the Russia target, thrown into the deep end of a target she didn't know. She'd been fed to sharks who didn't like it when young women were too successful, who felt they needed to work a little harder for rewards but for whom no amount of hard work and sacrifice would be enough. She'd learned that already the hard way.

She'd known at the time that she shouldn't get involved with an officer from a foreign intelligence service, but everyone knew of officers who broke that rule all the time—though the ones who got away with it were typically men. Women case officers, if they were brazen enough to have affairs with foreign nationals, knew to keep it secret. But still . . . everyone had heard stories of case officers having affairs with their assets and with the wives of officers from rival services. Worse trespasses than hers, and unpunished. Lyndsey had honestly thought at the time that it wouldn't be a big deal.

But her assignment was curtailed and she was sent back to Langley to await a final determination on her employment.

In the conference room, Davis knows she is waiting for him but he's pinned down at his end of the table as others take turns speaking with him. It's the usual slow exodus: they want face time with the head of the task force or need to go over this or that hypothesis. See me, hear me. Davis's gaze flicks in her direction each time a conversation runs long. *I'll be with you in a minute.* Lyndsey dawdles as she collects her things, pretending to rifle through her overstuffed tote.

Finally, he is free. "Thanks for coming on such short notice." Davis stands next to her, looming over her. Or maybe it's just the effect he has, being tall and wiry.

She looks up to see him swallow. The faintest smile hovers on his lips.

"I assume there's a car waiting for you. Shall we walk and talk?" he says, gesturing toward the door.

The escort trails unhappily at a discreet distance, a few paces behind. As they walk down wide halls, heads nod in Davis's direction, which makes Lyndsey wonder about Davis's rank. He never talked about that in Beirut, but he might be more senior than he let on. Everyone seems to know him.

Even though Lyndsey is not short by any standard, Davis is still a good head taller. He leans toward her. "I'm so sorry I never got in touch after—the incident." He speaks at a whisper so that not even their chaperone is able to hear them.

So, he knows what happened to her. "Don't mention it," she mutters. They both are guilty of the same offense. No reason to belabor the point.

There is one thing she wants to know, however. "What happened after I left? Did you get in trouble, too?"

He smirks. "They called me in and politely read me the riot act. I wasn't sent home, though, not like you. They're making me suffer for it now; I've been home for about six months in a make-work assignment, until this came along."

She realizes there's one more thing she needs to ask him. They come to a standstill, forcing everyone to part around them, like salmon swimming in a crowded stream. The escort stands fifteen feet back, dragging the toe of his smart dress shoe in an arc on the floor.

She draws Davis closer. "I'm undercover here. I shouldn't have been told to take the meeting today. Did you ask for me by name?" That would mean that he knew she was in England but hadn't reached out and she's not sure how she feels about this.

The look on his face—oh, she's seen that before, too. One part exasperation and two parts guilt. She's known since the first time she met him that he is complicated, and it's never good to give your heart to a complicated man.

"I did. I'd heard you were in London, and I knew you'd be the right one for the job. But as long as you're here . . . There's something I should tell you." He takes a deep breath. "There's a reason I haven't been in touch . . ."

She wants to spare him. "We were separated so abruptly, and it was confusing at the end. You don't need to explain."

"But I do. We never got the chance to talk about where things were headed . . . and it would be natural to wonder if maybe we'd pick up where we left off in Beirut . . ." It's hard to read the way he looks at her: is he hopeful or cautious? Is he trying to figure out what she wants?

"I'm not seeing anyone at the moment, if that's what you want to know."

"But I can't. It's impossible now." He blurts out the words like he's been holding them in a long time. "You see, I'm back with my ex-wife. I moved into our old place four weeks ago."

Four weeks . . . Langley would've *just* approved her request for the move, all the better for her to keep an eye on Tarasenko. She should've contacted him as soon as she'd gotten news, but it hadn't been that important. Oh, it had fleetingly crossed her mind—*maybe we can get back together*—but she'd been so caught up in her own life, her career, that she hadn't acted on it. She'd assumed he'd be waiting for her like a figurine in a museum. One of the many things she'd packed away, thinking *someday.*

Davis looks down at his feet. "Now that I've come this far with Miranda, I can't back out on her, not under the circumstances. You understand, don't you?"

"Of course I do. It's okay, Davis. I'm happy for you."

"I'm afraid our timing is simply impeccably bad," he says as though he didn't hear her. He runs a hand impatiently through that unruly hair, one of her favorite gestures. "Should I *not* have asked for you to be on the task force? It's just that I know you're good at assessing Russians. What they're thinking, how they're likely to act . . . Do you want me to ask Langley to send someone else next time?"

A funny twist in her chest catches her unexpectedly. It's the thought of not seeing him again. "No, no . . . I can do it. I have time. I'm at the start of this new assignment. It'll be a little while before things pick up."

"Great. That's super." He squeezes her forearm, then pulls his hand away like he's brushed up against a hot stove. They must be careful not to slip into the past. "Good to have you on the team, then. And thanks for understanding. I'll be in touch."

CHAPTER 4

Lyndsey rips the mousy brown wig off her head in the women's room of a tea shop eight blocks from her office. It's the end of her circuitous two-hour return trip. She scratches her scalp vigorously. It feels so good . . . or maybe it's just a way to work off her frustration after speaking with Davis.

She's in a tight stall, and her elbows bang into the metal partition as she peels off her costume and tucks the pieces into her tote. She tries to smooth herself once again back into her real self, fuming all the while. Even two hours of subway, taxis, and hikes have not calmed her.

She would not have predicted, not in a hundred years, that Davis Ranford would get back with his ex-wife. Not after what he'd said about his life with Miranda. Well, maybe it would be more accurate to say insinuated—he'd always been a gentleman when it came to the previous women in his life, and this included his ex-wife. But it hadn't been flattering. He'd said the reason he'd spent most of his career overseas was because England wasn't big enough for the two of them.

But he'd also said he'd disappointed his family when he'd separated from her. *They're probably ecstatic now.*

She wonders if she's seen a photo of Miranda, even in passing. She thinks not. She imagines Miranda is nothing like her. She's probably closer to Davis's age. Lyndsey wants to imagine her chubby, with short red hair and modish glasses. Miranda probably wears black pants suits and outrageously modern (and expensive) coats, her overall look sharp as a hawk and about as forgiving. Nor can she remember if Davis ever mentioned what Miranda did for a living. Maybe she ran her own business, an art gallery or a high-end shop. Or she works at a firm as a soulless corporate lawyer. It doesn't matter what she does: Lyndsey dislikes her already. It's okay to dislike a strawman standing in for the real thing, a woman who is probably kinder and nicer than the one Lyndsey has constructed. She's being childish and unfair, and she's doesn't care. She's going to wallow in the shock, at least for a little while. She hasn't even dated since they'd been torn apart, though it's hardly Davis's fault. She'd been swept right into an assignment on return to Washington from Beirut, an assignment that had been messy and maddening. It had left her with no energy for friendship, let alone romance.

Looking into the mirror, she searches her heart. Things had ended abruptly, without closure. They'd had fun together and he'd been a much-needed diversion in Beirut, where she'd had serious problems with the Chief of Station and her coworkers. Too, overseas affairs are meant to be fleeting: like falling in love on summer holiday, part of the attraction is that it's temporary. You know it's doomed to end from the start.

Lyndsey stuffs her props into the big black tote bag and emerges from the stall before someone comes into the ladies' room and wonders what she's up to. Better for the room to be empty if you're going to come out of a bathroom stall looking different. Chances are no one would've noticed the cardigan-wearing woman who'd rushed in here, but why risk it?

She goes into the tearoom and takes a seat at a table by the door, then orders coffee and a scone. By the time her food and drink arrive, she's thinking more clearly. It's not like she has time for a relationship right now. She's just arrived in England. She has to get her life in order. She has a very important asset who's already proven difficult to control, whom she needs to get in hand.

She has plenty of things to worry about. Davis Ranford doesn't have to be one of them.

Once she is back in her office, there is no time for dillydallying. She must take care of first things first: contact Tarasenko to set up a meeting. It's an important milestone in the relationship between handler and asset. She'll make sure he understands everything that's expected of him, how to use any equipment, all procedures. But more, it provides an opportunity to set the tone for the relationship.

Lyndsey's first big asset, one that she landed years ago when she first started at CIA, was Yaromir Popov. Theirs had been a special relationship. The old Russian spymaster practically had been a father to her, though it probably wasn't unexpected for a girl without a father to spend the rest of her life subconsciously searching for a replacement. What *was* unexpected was that she'd find him not at CIA, not at the place where she worked, but among the enemy. And while she'd always remained cognizant of the fact that he was Russian, she firmly believed that he'd grown disillusioned enough with the FSB and with life under Kosygin's predecessor to have been a trustworthy asset.

The relationship with Dmitri Tarasenko will not be so cordial. The man is charming, yes, but he is also a war criminal, having coached Ossetian troops to commit atrocities against civilians when he was in the Russian military. He'd learned to be a masterful manipulator, a characteristic common to many who came from the KGB system. You deceived others—your coworkers, your neighbors, friends, and even family—to stay alive. She is certain that every minute they are together, he will be trying to play her. As far as she's concerned, it's a coin toss as to whether he'll deliver General Evgeni Morozov to Langley as promised. She has far less faith in Tarasenko than the rest of the team back at Langley, but then again, they aren't the ones sticking their heads in the lion's mouth.

She shakes out her hair again, feeling itchy after all that time under a wig, and shifts her weight in the chair. Lyndsey's having a hard time getting used to the strange conditions in the cover office. She is, for all intents and purposes, working by herself. She rarely runs into anyone else in the office, which occupies the entire floor of the townhouse. Containers of restaurant leftovers or the odd packed lunch appear in the refrigerator—here one day, gone the next—but never sees the people to whom the food belongs. Similarly, the doors to the other two offices might be open or shut, new knickknacks left on desks, a new framed picture propped on a computer monitor, but it's unclear whether these things belong to someone or are just office dressing. If the latter, someone is going to lengths to make it look like an ordinary office and for whom this charade is for, she doesn't know.

She leaves the door ajar and wakes up the computer to compose an email on the secret system hidden inside, the one that communicates with the Agency classified network through a series of increasingly narrow and restrictive gates. The email will be sent to Moscow Station, to the Chief of

Station, the man Claiborne has cautioned Lyndsey not to freeze out. He'd just started his assignment, an old Russia hand by the name of Dave Lemley. Lyndsey remembers Dave from her early days in Russia Division. Back then, he was a nice middle-aged man known for bringing in the best jelly doughnuts she'd ever tasted, but he was often away for years at a time on overseas assignments. She has to admit she really doesn't know him at all. He seems amenable enough to this odd setup with Tarasenko.

"Contact requested with WINDSPEAR"—Tarasenko's cover name, assigned by an office, a word chosen off a list—"to request meeting out of country within the next two weeks." Desired location: the Estonian capital, Tallinn. The city is easy enough for Russians to get to, and no FSB bureaucrat would bat an eyelash when Tarasenko reported that he would be going there for a quick getaway. There would be Russian watchers in the city, too, but no more than at other easily accessible European locations. This proposed meeting would give Moscow Station a chance to work out its signals with Tarasenko, too. It's like breaking in a brand-new car or training an adopted dog—though Tarasenko is no tame house pet, more like a pit bull just come from a lifetime of fighting to see his next day.

She gives a choice of dates that Tarasenko can choose from, but in reality there is really only one particular weekend that will work with this assignment to the Rotenberg task force. She sends a separate communiqué to Tallinn Station, letting them know that she intends to be operating in their neck of the woods. Next, she checks available flights: there are plenty, as long as she doesn't mind a change of planes in either Riga or Frankfurt, with the shortest route going through Latvia. Satisfied that there should be no problem with transportation at least, she closes her computer down, content to wait until Moscow Station contacts Tarasenko and relays his response to her.

She's walking to her apartment, wondering idly what to have for dinner and marveling at the lull in her work life (while knowing it won't last), when her cell phone buzzes. A message has come in on her favorite secure messaging app. She opens it up: it's from Theresa Warner, who is trying to reacclimate to life with Richard, just returned from Russia, after being freed by Lyndsey's investigation. A husband who had been a top CIA spymaster before his capture.

How is London? Hate to bother you but can we set a time to talk? I kept hoping this would work itself out and it would go away on its own, but things have gotten strange with Richard, and I need to talk to someone to make sure I'm not losing my mind.

CHAPTER 5

The next day, Lyndsey is sorting through logistics for the Tallinn trip—feeling guilty that she hasn't spoken to Theresa yet, hasn't had a chance to find out what she meant by her mysterious text—when her cell phone vibrates. This is her personal cell phone, not the special one that Langley gave her. This is another anomaly Lyndsey must get used to: carrying her phone into the office. That's a no-no in the classified world. Cell phones, the perfect little tool for spying with its camera and recorder, are not allowed inside secure spaces. Normally it waits in a phone safe outside the sensitive compartmented information facility, or SCIF, or out in her car. It still gives her a fright every time she sees it, thinking she's forgotten to leave it behind, but she can't argue that it's not convenient. Is this how the rest of the world lives, able to connect to the people in their lives anytime they wish? She's afraid that before too long, she's not going to be able to live without it.

She reaches across the desk for it and checks the screen. It's Davis's phone number.

Meet me for lunch? One o'clock at the Black Dog?

The Black Dog is a nondescript bistro a couple blocks over, nice and convenient. Davis obviously knows where she works. She assumes this is about the Rotenberg case. Davis cannot have changed his mind about seeing her, not after what he said yesterday. Oh, she knows that Davis is not incapable of a relapse. Most men can be fickle when it comes to their libidos. A bad fight with their wife, a bit of weakness over thinning hair, or a setback in the office and they might want to assuage their ego with whatever can be had the easiest, which is often a woman's attention.

She tsks, unsure when she became so cynical. It might be a side effect of the job, too much exposure to what people will do when they find themselves in a bad situation. They rarely take the high road or do the right thing. No wonder so many of the older case officers she's known are so jaded and ready to hang it up.

Nonetheless, given the situation she finds herself in, it would pay to be cynical. Davis can be a charmer. She doesn't want to make an embarrassing mistake. And she would be making it twice.

It must have to do with the task force. She can't refuse without a good reason.

She types *yes*.

She's walked by the Black Dog but never eaten there, just another pub on a busy street full of them. She does a short surveillance detection route in case someone is watching—hopping a few blocks over on a pretend shopping trip, looping back on the Underground—and wearing a light disguise.

The restaurant is small and nondescript, lots of mullioned glass and white tablecloths. A bald man behind the bar pulls pints and aproned waitresses shuttle trays of drinks. The air smells pleasantly of beer and mingled aromas of various foods. Davis's invitation didn't mention a reservation under assumed names (in Beirut he often used *Thomas Hardy* as his throwaway pseudo, which might've given a Lebanese maître d' a chuckle), and she wonders briefly if she should see if there is a reservation for a Mr. Hardy. But it's not necessary: Davis waves, already seated at a table toward the back of the mercifully nearly empty establishment.

"I recommend the sole," Davis says as she takes a seat. He nods at her deep mahogany wig. "That color suits you."

After a busboy has filled water glasses, she asks, "Why did you want to see me? Have there been developments?"

"We're still waiting on the full police report to come in, but the consensus among the team is that someone was sending Rotenberg a message. The leadership analyst is unaware of anyone holding that kind of a personal grudge against him. That leaves one suspect, the most obvious one, though we don't know why Kosygin would be angry with Rotenberg, especially since he appears to be all peace and love, at least if the TV talk shows are to be believed." From his smirk, Davis clearly doesn't believe it. "It could have something to do with Rotenberg's support for Putin . . . According to the analysts, Rotenberg lent Putin an ungodly sum of money for the Ukraine fiasco, against his better judgment. It costs a lot to annex another country. One expert put Russia's cost of supporting the Crimea at one-point-five billion dollars, and that's for last year *alone*. It's hard to find that kind of money under the couch cushions."

"But why would Kosygin punish Rotenberg for supporting Putin? I suppose there's a twisted logic there . . ."

"The analysts are looking into this. Maybe Rotenberg has been trying to keep Kosygin at arm's length and it's pissed him off. Maybe this is his way of making the lords swear fealty. I don't know. It's hard to imagine Kosygin could get far without the cooperation of the oligarchs, though. The KGB created them without knowing where it would all lead," Davis says.

"Maybe Kosygin is trying to recoup all that lost money for the Russian people? Maybe he really is a good cop?"

"There's the sunny optimist I knew in Beirut." Davis gives her a weak smile.

Business talk is paused when the waiter returns with Lyndsey's iced tea and a recitation of the specials. Davis gets the sole, though Lyndsey goes with a goat cheese salad and they send the waiter on his way.

"So, this could've waited for the next meeting of the task force. You didn't ask me to lunch to tell me this," Lyndsey says once they are alone again.

For a second Davis seems flustered, gathering his thoughts because the path forward is difficult. "I have a request. Something we'd like you to consider. We want you to go undercover. We want you to get close enough to Emily Rotenberg to assess whether we might be able to recruit her."

A bold move and not one Lyndsey expected to be on the table. "You want her to provide evidence against her husband?"

He picks up his wineglass and takes a sip, so small as to be unnecessary. *Buying time to think.* "Emily Rotenberg has always been a bit of a puzzle. Like most of the oligarchs' wives, she tends to be seen and not heard. There are rumors that the marriage is rocky and while that works in our favor, we can't wait for the normal vetting to run its course. That home invasion signals that something extraordinary is going on and we don't want to miss our opportunity—if there is one." His gaze flicks her way, holding hers. "You're good at this kind of thing, Lyndsey. You're known for it, after all." He's referring to her tremendous coup: recruiting Yaromir Popov.

Davis continues. "Vauxhall wants your expert opinion on the situation before deciding whether it's worth risking such a bold move."

"And would I do the recruitment, too?"

"You'd do the initial approach. We'd probably bring in someone else to be the handler, free you up for your primary assignment. But it'll depend on the situation."

It doesn't matter that she doesn't know Emily Rotenberg: that's how the clandestine business works. It's either magic or dark art, depending on how you look at it. They'll engineer an encounter and then it's up to Lyndsey to parlay it into a friendship, and maybe eventually a very specific kind of business relationship. Assuming the wife is amenable to an offer, Lyndsey will need to find out what Emily wants in exchange, at which point CIA and MI6 will decide if it's worth closing the deal.

They pause as the waiter approaches, plates in hand, and don't resume until he's left.

"That's sort of unusual, sending me in?" Which is Lyndsey's shorthand way of asking why MI6 isn't going the usual route of recruiting someone who is already close to her.

Davis looks down at the fillet on his plate before picking up his knife and fork. "There isn't time. That would mean research to find the best candidate and a lengthy approach before deciding whether that person can be trusted . . . And what if it doesn't work? Then it's back to the drawing board. No, this will be far quicker."

Lyndsey jabs her fork at lettuce. There's a reason why things are done the way they are, why time is built into the process. You go slowly so you don't make a mistake. It's easy to spook a potential asset, and then the whole operation unravels. With a man like Mikhail Rotenberg as the ultimate prize, things could get dangerous. "It's that pressing?"

"He's worth somewhere in the ballpark of ten billion dollars. It's got to be about the money, right? What else could it be? Then the question is, why does Kosygin—assuming he's the one behind the attack—want Rotenberg's money?" Davis lifts a piece of fish from his plate, dripping with buttery sauce. "They're supposedly on friendly terms, yet gunmen shot the French doors on Rotenberg's veranda to pieces. Yes, time is definitely of the essence."

"I'll have to clear it with Langley first."

"No need. Kim Claiborne's already given her blessing."

Lyndsey pauses mid-bite. She doesn't know whether to be annoyed or relieved that Davis has already spoken to the Agency or that Claiborne had not informed her. It brings back the way she felt when she was last sacrificed by Eric Newman. The feeling that she's nothing more than a puppet whose strings are being pulled. A foot soldier with no say in how she's being deployed or how she might die.

"It doesn't appear I can say no," she says, hoping it comes off as breezy and not petulant.

It's funny, too, how the dynamic has shifted since Beirut. There, she felt every one of the years of their difference in ages. Davis was the savvy older man, while Lyndsey was just emerging from what was considered the early stages of a career. Now, they seem more like peers. Something has changed between them, and there is no regretting that it's happened. It just is.

Davis pushes the plate aside, as though he's lost his appetite after a few bites. "There's one more thing I want to talk to you about . . . It's the last thing I said to you at the meeting."

She had almost convinced herself that they weren't going to talk about this again.

He looks up at her now, blinking. "It was unfair of me to drop that on you when we had no time to discuss it. But we can discuss it now."

It was a shock to see him, the first time since Beirut. It reminded her of all those months apart, wondering what had happened to him, what he was thinking. There had been nothing she could do except assume the relationship was dead and that she'd never see him again. She'd had no reason to think it had been anything other than a fling, a way for each of them to assuage the loneliness that comes with being sent to live in a foreign place by yourself. The fact that he hadn't tried to contact her sealed it for her, confirmed exactly that. He'd attached no importance to it, so she shouldn't either.

"What is there to talk about?" She stabs at the lettuce but she, too, has lost her appetite.

"Don't be like that, Lyndsey. Not with me. I'm sorry for what happened. I wouldn't have expected Langley to deal with you that harshly, but thinking back on what you'd told me about the Station"—they'd hated her, a Russian expert, a woman, and a young one at that—"it was stupid of me to assume otherwise." He takes a long drink from his wineglass this time. "Neither of us wanted that, but we both knew we were likely to be found out . . . There was always the possibility it would end like that."

Anger flares up. "I don't know how it ended for you, but they threatened to fire me."

"Why do you think I'm back at headquarters? I got a stern talking to, a black mark on my permanent record. As I said, we both knew where it might lead."

"Well, you're back with your ex-wife, so it appears to have worked out for you."

She doesn't want to come off as angry and petty, but it slips out. He hadn't hidden the fact that he'd been married before, but he made it seem like it was all behind him. That he'd washed his hands of Miranda.

Davis's smile is apologetic. "I can understand how it might seem that way—chastened man runs back to ex-wife at the first sign of trouble—but I can assure you that it wasn't like that at all. We ran into each other at a mutual friend's party one night quite by accident. We ended up talking and, well . . . Miranda had changed. I suppose I'd changed. We got together for lunch a few times and . . ."

"You don't have to explain yourself to me."

"Don't I? Look, I didn't think I'd ever see or hear from you again. I knew you wouldn't be allowed to get in touch with me. So, when Miranda suggested we give it another go, I thought, why not? I'd just moved back in when I was told that you'd been posted to London and your name came up for the Rotenberg case. You can't imagine how I felt . . . The timing just couldn't be worse. It had taken a lot to get to the point where we both wanted to give it a second try. I couldn't throw it away."

Both. Message received. If there had been even a scrap of hope, it is gone now.

"Please don't misunderstand," Davis rushes to add, as though he can read her mind, as though he can feel the door closing firmly against the idea of them. "The time we had together in Beirut was very special to me. If things hadn't gone the way they had, I suspect things would've gone in a different direction with us."

He is so reasonable, so gentle in tone, that any anger she has fizzles out like flat soda. *Of course* she understands. She might even respect him a little more for being willing to address it head-on.

She takes a deep breath. She must get it under control. Bury this feeling right now, for good. It's done. Over. "It's no problem, Davis. Really. I understand. It won't affect our working together on this mission."

Planning for the operation begins the next morning with another meeting at MI6.

The gathering is much smaller than the full task force. Lyndsey's been brought this time to a small conference room. The air is sluggish and too warm. There's a lukewarm tea service waiting on a sideboard and a plate of digestive biscuits, sweet meal cookies slathered with chocolate. Two people sit at a table waiting for her: Parth Arya and another analyst, a young woman probably not long out of university.

The young woman spreads a map of London on the table between them. "You've probably heard a lot about Billionaires Row. It's all over the news. But since you'll be spending a lot of time there while on the mission—Emily Rotenberg appears to leave her home only rarely—we wanted to give you some proper background.

"Its proper name is The Bishops Avenue. The road is only a mile long but accommodates sixty-six mansions. You may find it surprising or ironic, depending on your point of view, that a number of the houses are empty, and have been for years. They've been part of money-laundering schemes. The laws have tightened up now, but for decades Arab princes and Asian businessmen bought the properties in the belief that even during a global economic catastrophe, it was a safe place to stow your money. And if that money was questionable or shady in any way, using it to buy a London mansion was a popular way to wash it clean. These purchases are done through shell companies so that the true owners are extremely difficult to track down."

She flips open a laptop and clicks through pictures of swanky houses. "Walking down The Bishops Avenue, past the high gates and security cameras, you wouldn't know which buildings are vacant and which are simply occasional homes for the owners. For being such an expensive place to live—the average home costing at least twenty million pounds—you'd think they'd be more secure, but as you can see, most sit behind fences and gates that a teenager could navigate without much trouble." Here, she clicks a YouTube video, all queued and ready to go. A young man wearing a headlamp stumbles through an empty, echoey building. This one appears to be long-deserted, and he gawps at crumbling plasterwork and moldy walls.

The young woman pushes the laptop to Parth Arya. He taps and a few photographs of Emily Rotenberg appear. "Here's your target: Emily Rotenberg, née Hughes. Daughter of the eighth Viscount Rampshead. She's been married to Mikhail Rotenberg for a little over five years. During that time, he's jumped from the twentieth richest man in Russia to the second or third; though this year, he tumbled down to fourteen."

Lyndsey studies the pretty face. Emily Rotenberg looks as uncalculating and guileless as a Catholic nun. And she's from an aristocratic family to boot. Surely her marriage couldn't have only been about the money? She knows that's a naïve thought: many women would kill to be in Emily Rotenberg's position.

Arya taps a key and the picture changes. Emily Rotenberg at twelve, in a school uniform. "She attended Queen's Gate, not one of the poshest schools but understandable given her family's diminished standing. The Hugheses weren't going to send Emily to a state school, but neither her position in the family nor her grades indicated she was destined for anything grander. None of her educational records suggests that she has shown more than an average intelligence." *Ouch*. Intelligence is so prized in the spy business that it is a reflex to assess it in others. Cleverness is a kind of currency. To be merely average is seen as a failing.

Arya continues with his scathing assessment. "Her friends and former teachers have indicated that, over the years, she failed to develop a talent in any given field. She managed to get into King's College London, where she studied business and economics though, by all accounts, it was a struggle for her to pass."

He taps the keyboard again. A photo of Emily fresh out of college, most likely, dewy faced and wide-eyed. "A career in business failed to materialize for Emily. She was hired and fired from a succession of positions in the years after university. She was working at a family friend's art gallery when she met Mikhail Rotenberg." Another tap and there materializes a picture of Emily Hughes on the arm of an older man. It looks like they're walking into a gala event, the kind of picture you find in glossy gossip magazines. She looks a bit overwhelmed by the attention, while he is smug, obviously proud of the pretty young woman he has on his arm. Lyndsey tries not to feel sorry for Emily, who, by the hunch of her shoulders and guarded look, seems distinctly uncomfortable with the attention.

"It was, by all accounts, a whirlwind romance. Rotenberg was long divorced from his first wife, a Russian. He was reportedly anxious to start a family. It would make sense that he'd want U.K. citizenship for his children, to give them options. Make it easier for them to stay in the country."

"Not a love match, then?" Lyndsey asks.

"Who knows? Maybe at first. That's not really my area of expertise," Arya replies dryly. He's a quiet, slight young man whose body language says that he takes himself very seriously. "In any case, love match or not, she gave birth to a perfectly healthy set of twins, Christopher and Tatiana, twenty-one months ago. The son is called Kit."

The junior analyst clears her throat before taking up the brief again.

"Mrs. Rotenberg appears to lead a constrained life, but it's not apparent whether that's her own choice or as determined by her husband. She doesn't appear in public much beyond events for her husband's charities. She rarely visits her family or attends the theater or opera or ballet, any of the things the couple did before the birth of their children." Surely that's not so unusual for a new mother, Lyndsey thinks, but doesn't interrupt the briefer.

"Emily Rotenberg also appears to be estranged from her family, and from what we've been able to glean, it's at the instigation of the family," the analyst continues, clicking through a series of family photographs. She stops on one of a young woman with straight dark hair and a somber expression. "This is Emily's younger sister, Jesamine. She was a maths prodigy as a child. She's now the cofounder and chief technology officer of a tech start-up. Very smart, in other words. Despite this difference in their personalities, Emily and Jesamine were very close growing up. Reportedly they had a falling-out around the time of Emily's wedding."

"Do we know what that was about?"

Arya makes a wry face. "The team has scrambled to find what we could on Emily, but I'm afraid we have even less on the Hughes family." Despite what the public tends to think, the intelligence community does not keep dossiers on average citizens. It will be a different story with Mikhail Rotenberg, of course, but Emily's past is not really in MI6's writ.

The junior analyst picks up the brief. "While her husband travels frequently for business, Mrs. Rotenberg does not leave the family home on The Bishops Avenue, aside from seasonal family vacations to Rotenberg's properties on Ibiza and Mykonos. She traveled to Russia only a few times in the courtship period and first year of marriage."

Lyndsey watches a series of photographs flash before her. In them, Emily Rotenberg grows progressively older and sadder, her smile nearly vanishing altogether. Had the young woman any idea of what she was getting into when she accepted his proposal? Or maybe she'd gone into it clear-eyed but underestimated what marriage to an oligarch meant. Maybe she is tougher than she seems, not caring what it took to earn all those billions.

Arya quickly clicks through a few more photos. "This is Igor Volkov, head of Rotenberg's security detail." The picture is of a wiry middle-aged man, bald, chiseled jaw, with a scary scar. He has a thuggish, off-putting vibe. "And this is Arthur Westover, Rotenberg's chief accountant. Used to be with Rheingold Hahns, the Swiss firm, until he was dismissed under mysterious circumstances a few years ago," Arya says, raising his eyebrows. The picture shows a doughy man with stylish blond hair. It's a myth that you can tell someone is a criminal by their face, but one look at Arthur Westover and you can see where the idea comes from. There's a foxiness to the eyes and disdain in the set of his mouth. You know immediately that the man is up to no good.

"Emily Rotenberg is going to pose a challenge. This hermetic life, whether by choice or imposed, won't make it easy to get close to assess her," Lyndsey says, leaning back in her chair with a sigh. They may have to resort to a chance encounter at a store she's known to frequent, or maybe an old tried-and-true trick like an orchestrated minor fender bender. Both seem dicey to Lyndsey. "Have you thought about how we're going to do the meet?"

This solicits a rare smile from Arya. "There's a luncheon for one of the Rotenbergs' charities on Saturday and Emily Rotenberg is scheduled to deliver the keynote. It's as good an opportunity as we're likely to get."

That's scant days away. "And how am I to approach her? You have something in mind?"

The junior analyst nods. Apparently, this is her part of the operation.

"We do. We've set up a false identity for you. You'll be Lynn Prescott, American heiress, spending the summer in the U.K."

"This isn't a throwaway identity," Arya adds. "They've been working on backstopping already. You'll be posing as a real person. The Prescotts are an actual family living outside of Philadelphia. Langley provided the connection; apparently one of its people is related to them. The real Lynn Prescott has been ill from birth and is a recluse. Reportedly, she never leaves the family estate. The family is willing and has agreed to back up your story if contacted."

"That's good, because Mikhail Rotenberg is sure to check if someone pops up out of the blue determined to befriend his wife," Lyndsey says.

"The cover will withstand scrutiny. Not if someone is determined to go to extraordinary lengths, mind," the junior analyst says. "But given the short time frame for the operation, we don't expect to trip their suspicions to that degree."

"We just need you to get close enough to Mrs. Rotenberg to assess whether she would be open to an approach," Arya reminds Lyndsey. "In and out, no fuss. If she takes the bait, we'll get you out and put another officer in, to act as her handler."

Undoubtedly an MI6 officer. The British will want control.

"Langley prefers that we free you up as soon as possible so you can get back to your primary assignment," Arya says. He has no idea that her primary assignment is riding herd on Dmitri Tarasenko, war criminal and double agent placed high in the FSB's counterintelligence unit. Which reminds her: she needs to finalize details of their first meeting. Looks like it'll need to be pushed back so she can attend this charity event.

The junior analyst raises a finger for Lyndsey's attention. "We were thinking you might be able to use Emily's estrangement from Jesamine to your advantage. We have seeded Lynn Prescott's online profile to include that she's also a maths prodigy. Something in common with the favorite sister . . . It might help pique Emily's interest."

Lyndsey blanches. "But I'm not good at math. What if Emily asks me a question?"

Arya grins. "Don't worry—it's not like she's a maths whiz, either. She's hardly going to ask you to solve the Riemann hypothesis." Lyndsey is not happy with his flippant answer, but case officers are expected to be able to handle all kinds of stray, troublesome inquiries. Usually, gentle deflection is all it takes.

Arya starts to collect his papers. "Of course, if—once you've had a chance to observe Emily Rotenberg—you assess that she won't turn on her husband, it's all over. It's your call. Background reading and details for the charity event will be sent shortly. We're here if you have any questions. We've booked the hotel room where Lynn Prescott is supposedly staying. We'll set up a meeting with a tech ops officer to get you fitted up with the trappings of your cover's life, from cell phone down to pocket litter. There's a backstop, as we mentioned, but it extends to your phone, too."

Lyndsey nods as the two analysts gather their papers and laptop. It's moving so fast, faster than most operations. From what they've described, it's not especially dangerous. She'll be in the middle of London. Even if things go wrong, extraction would be easy. If Lyndsey thinks Rotenberg's people are starting to grow suspicious, she can step back. Disappear.

Easy.

Then why can't she shake this feeling of apprehension?

CHAPTER 6

2018

Emily stood in the center of the restaurant and looked out over the crowd.

It felt like she was in the middle of a nightclub. The cavernous room was dim, though everywhere there was the twinkling of light reflecting off decorations, as if someone had hung disco balls from the ceiling. Loud music reverberated off the walls, drowning out most conversation.

And so many people. There had to be at least a hundred, with more arriving by the minute. She didn't know most of them. There were celebrities: movie and TV stars, models and pop singers, people she recognized from telly. (She wouldn't learn until later that some of them were paid to be there, to pose for the photographers and add a little glamour.) Other faces were familiar, too, but she was still having a hard time with Russian names. They ended up being a stream of syllables with no relationship to one another, at least in her mind. Nonsense words that she couldn't make stick. She had no talent for languages, she'd been told in school.

Her family was there, of course. It was the rehearsal dinner, after all. They'd been at the church a few hours earlier, Russian Orthodox, to be told where they were to sit or stand, to practice their parts.

It was the hottest restaurant in London and Mikhail had rented out the whole thing for the night—snap, just like that. It was the entire floor of an old warehouse in Covent Garden, now transformed. The walls were covered in gorgeous tiles that begged to be touched, the walls painted deep jewel-box colors. The twinkling bar soared all the way up to the high ceiling and took up half a wall. Waitstaff swanned by with trays of delicate canapés and fantastical cocktails. "Think of the expense," Emily's mother had murmured in protest, to which Emily could only smile. It just went to show that her parents didn't understand how rich Mikhail was, that he was in another league when it came to power and access. He could literally have or do anything he wanted. To be fair, infinite wealth was a hard concept to grasp; she couldn't claim to have fully internalized it herself. She got giddy thinking about it.

Most of the people here tonight appeared to be Russian expatriates, friends and associates of her soon-to-be husband. Older men in the worst-fitting hand-tailored suits Emily had ever seen, accompanied by their sons wearing fancy designer hoodies and coils of gold chains. With them, beautiful young women in slinky dresses like it was a cocktail party and not part of a wedding event. The biggest wedding of the year, the papers trumpeted. Second only to a royal wedding, if you could imagine.

In the center of the swirl were her parents, looking a bit lost. Which they rarely did, in Emily's memory. They weren't hayseeds, after all. Her father was a viscount and had been to social events of all stripes since he was a child. Plus, he was a senior bank director and her mother a professor. They were not unworldly. But for however much they knew of British society, they were not part of *this* world. Mikhail's world.

She made her way to them. It took some effort. As she crossed the floor, she was constantly intercepted by well-wishers who asked her in heavily accented English if she was ready for the big day tomorrow or where they were going for their honeymoon. She thought she would rescue them, as everyone was ignoring them, perhaps because they were so obviously English. Mikhail's friends felt self-conscious talking to the English, she knew. The two sides tended to regard each other warily, like combatants assessing each other from opposite sides of the battlefield.

She gave them a polite, slightly nervous hug. Her mother leaned in to inspect the huge, glittering necklace circling her throat. "That's lovely," she said, nodding at the constellation of diamonds. "Did Mikhail give it to you?"

"A wedding present."

"Could probably take care of the entire roof and all the windows at Rampshead Hall for what that cost," her father said. The dilapidated family manor house was never far from his mind, as the last of the line. He polished off the rest of the wine in his glass and reached for a second from the tray of a passing server.

"Mummy, where are all our friends? I thought everyone was coming tonight," Emily asked, looking around in dismay. She'd expected to see family friends, or at least a few of the relatives. Maybe an old chum from school or university, though truth to tell, she'd never stayed close with any of them.

Her mother sighed. "There will be more at the ceremony tomorrow, my dear. But this sort of gathering"—she made a face like she'd smelled something bad—"it's not really their thing. You mustn't expect too much of them. It's asking a lot to come tonight and all day tomorrow . . ." She trailed off, flustered.

You'd think they'd be happy for a free meal at the best restaurant in the city. Rubbing elbows with all these people you'd otherwise only see in the papers. Emily was pretty sure there were some movie stars in the crowd, maybe even a minor royal. Camera flashes went off in the center of the room. There were photographers huddled outside the door. The media were covering this. Her mother was being ridiculous.

Feeling anxious, Emily scanned the room for her sisters. Her older sister, Marilyn, was at the bar, working her way through a plate of canapés, her husband, Roger, by her side. Roger was a former Royal Marine, rugged and capable, but he looked slightly comical here, out of place in his tweedy suit and grim countenance. She'd always thought him not only dull but a bit slow. An excellent match for horsy Marilyn, though. They were perfect together.

Would people one day think the same of her and Mikhail?

Then there was Jesamine, her younger sister. She was in the corner, talking to a pair of older Russian men. She seemed uncomfortable in her silky strapless dress, unable to fend off their undisguised leering. She kept tucking her hair behind her ears, trying to shrink behind her glass of sparkling water. Jesamine—maybe the most socially adept of the three sisters—was naturally outgoing and confident, but tonight she was terribly awkward. Not like herself at all.

Jesamine, seeing that her sister was looking at her, bolted upright like a hare caught out in the field. *We need to talk*, she mouthed.

Suddenly, Mikhail was at her elbow, fingers on her back. He was handsome tonight in his fine suit of whisper-soft Italian wool. His hair was styled as well as she'd ever seen it (normally the receding hairline made his forehead a touch too prominent), and he wore a few bejeweled rings, just enough to make the eye follow his glittering hands. Everything about him gave the impression of the happy groom. "There you are, darling—and hello, Cynthia, Evan," he said as he nodded at Emily's parents, who stood clutching their wineglasses in a rictus of formal politesse. "I hope you are enjoying yourselves."

(Jesamine, Emily noted, had turned away from her. Odd.)

"A lovely party," Cynthia said.

"Rather big for a rehearsal dinner, don't you think, old chap?" Evan gestured with his glass at the crowd. "All these people aren't part of the ceremony tomorrow, are they?" Emily cringed. Her father knew but refused to acknowledge the imbalance of power in the family dynamic. That his soon-to-be son-in-law should not be kidded or lectured or subjected to the gentle condescension her father had for all foreigners.

"It is our wedding," Mikhail said with a cheerfulness Emily recognized as forced. "I am not going to be stingy with my friends, not when they want to *celebrate* with us. Generosity—it is the Russian way." When Emily's parents said nothing, Mikhail reached up and hooked the diamond necklace with his index finger. A drop of vodka splashed from the crystal shot glass onto Emily's collarbone. "Did you see what I got for your daughter? What do you think of it?"

Don't mention the roof of Ramsphead Hall, Emily prayed silently.

"See, again—generosity. You don't need to worry. Your daughter is marrying well. *Very* well. I will take care of her. She'll never worry or want for anything ever again." When Mikhail smiled, you could see his canine teeth. They were really quite large.

The better to eat you with. Where did that come from? Emily caught herself.

Hours later, Emily fought her way across the crowded restaurant to a quiet room in the back. Outside, they were dancing, the music screeching, thumping. But here, inside this office, it was quieter. Calmer. The restaurant manager left it at their disposal for the evening, "in case the family members needed a place to escape for a little privacy," the woman who ran the place had said. It was as though she knew what an ordeal the evening was going to be for Emily.

She stood upright (in her tight dress, there was little choice), a hand against the satin stretched taut over her stomach, the other hand fiddling absently with the heavy diamond necklace. She was exhausted. She took a deep breath, let it out slowly. She tried to ignore the throbbing of her feet, tried not to think about what was coming for her tomorrow, a schedule of activities that would put the Queen to shame.

Fitting, perhaps, for tomorrow she would become a queen—of sorts. She would have a monarch's fortune and the property without the burden of ruling, without needing to worry about taking care of other people or fretting about their livelihoods or happiness—or anything, really. It was a life she'd neither imagined nor wished for, but it was about to be hers all the same. What a lucky girl, everyone said to her in awe whenever the subject came up. Funny, she never thought herself particularly lucky.

She was ready to go home, but of course that was not going to happen. The party would go on until the wee hours. That was how the Russians measured whether a party had been a success. People had to be staggering from alcohol poisoning, crawling to get to their cars on their hands and knees. You knew if everyone'd had a good time by the number of people passed out on the floor.

She was about to sink onto the couch (the velvet a little worse for wear) when the door opened behind her, and in walked Jesamine. Her sister looked terrible, her makeup mussed like she'd been running sprints. She'd been dancing, most likely. Even more unlike Jesamine, she looked upset.

"Jes, what's the matter?" Emily took her hands: they were ice-cold.

Jesamine's mascara-streaked eyes searched Emily's face. "You can't do it, Em. Listen to me. You don't want to marry that man."

It was as though someone had punched her in the face. She knew her family were against the marriage, but this was uncalled-for. Even if things had been a bit rushed getting to the altar, they'd had their chance to say their piece; to get all hysterical at the eleventh hour was too much.

Emily dropped her sister's hands. She stood very tall. "I realize this marriage is not what anyone expected for me . . . I certainly didn't expect it for myself, but . . . it's my opportunity and I'm going to take it. I'm not like you, Jes, or even Marilyn. I'm not clever. I'm not going to find a cure for cancer or build a house in the wilderness with my own two hands. This is the best I'm ever going to be able to do—and it's awfully damn good if I say so myself—and I'm not going to let it pass me by."

Jesamine's face twisted with pain. She drew in a ragged, stuttering breath, wet with tears. "Em, Mikhail is a horrible, horrible man. I don't think you know how bad he is."

"You can't judge Mikhail the way you'd judge other men. He's not like the boys you know from Cambridge."

"Emily, he doesn't love you. Not the way you deserve to be loved."

Emily wanted to laugh. Jesamine might've been the smart one, but she was also terribly naïve. "I'm not marrying my childhood sweetheart, Jes. It doesn't work like that with men like Mikhail. This is an arrangement. Like in olden days."

A shadow fell over Jesamine's face. She started crying again. "You know what he's like . . . you *know* . . ." she whispered, and there was something about that whisper that sent a chill down Emily's spine.

"Jes, don't say another word. I don't want to hear if you saw Mikhail snogging some slag in the cloakroom. It doesn't matter." What did it mean, in the end? It was not worth throwing away a lifetime of security.

Jesamine gasped. "That's what he said. He said you'd only get mad at me if I told you and you'd marry him anyway . . ."

Her stomach got cold and heavy, like she'd swallowed a stone. She'd known she'd have to deal with this kind of nonsense with Mikhail, but she hadn't expected it to happen so early. *Let me get through the wedding at least, for god's sake.* "That's right. You don't need to tell me if you caught some slut trying to steal away my husband at the last minute."

Jesamine drew back like she'd been slapped.

Emily strode to the far end of the room and away from her sister, shaking like a leaf in the wind. "This isn't your concern, Jes. I'm a big girl and I can make my own decisions. I'm marrying Mikhail," she said flatly.

Jesamine stood, biting her lower lip. She kept staring at her and breathing hard, her chest rising and falling with quick little breaths. Emily braced herself for a big row, screaming and shouting, but instead, Jesamine bolted for the door. Hand on the knob, she turned back one last time. "Go on: stick your head in the sand and pretend that you're not making a huge mistake. But if you go ahead and marry this man, I will never ever speak to you again. Never." And then she was gone in a blur of ivory silk. It was so unlike her sister, so unlike anything Emily had ever experienced, that for a long time she could only stand there with her mouth open. The last five minutes had been insane, completely insane.

Call off the wedding because her sister demanded it? Unthinkable. This was Mikhail Rotenberg, after all. He wasn't just any man.

She couldn't do that to him. She couldn't.

And so, she didn't.

CHAPTER 7

PRESENT DAY

Sometimes it takes something totally unexpected to make you realize that your life has been a sham. A farce. That you've been totally, miserably unhappy.

That's what happened to Emily. She met a new friend, and it put everything else into stark relief. Suddenly, she feels optimistic again. Sunny. *Almost* ready for anything.

Almost ready to turn around the great disappointment her life has become.

It happened at a charity luncheon in Battersea. It was the usual dreary affair. She's done so many of them for Mikhail that she knew exactly what to expect: a hundred or so women, round tables set with lots of crystal and flowers, a photographer from the *Times*. Emily had been dreading it, especially after the break-in, knowing that it will be in the back of everyone's mind, the only thing anyone would be able to think about when they looked at her. *There she is, that awful Russian mogul's wife. Didn't they just have some sort of home invasion on their vulgar property on Billionaires Row? Serves them right.*

The event is for one of Mikhail's charities, the type of thing that's expected of rich people and which helps to keep him on the good side of British authorities. Emily swears he does more for the British than he does for his own people back in Russia. This fundraiser is for pensioners, meals on wheels, or some such thing. She can't keep track anymore. It helps wipe away the sour taste in Londoners' mouths when they think of what happened with Ukraine, but for the amount it costs to put those designer dresses on the backs of the women in attendance, you could've bought meals for a week for every pensioner in the county, so you have to question who really benefits. Of course, she would never say this to the organizers, the people who work at the charity, the ones who put the luncheon together. They live for this sort of thing. But Emily thinks it, every time she's among them. Even though her dress is undoubtedly the most expensive in the room, she thinks of herself as a stealth socialist.

She's standing in the wings, nervous about the speech she's to give. She hasn't written it: something like that would never be entrusted to her. No, it came from the PR firm Mikhail hires to manage his brand. She's practicing when this woman literally runs into her. "Oh my, I beg your pardon," the woman says as Emily startles at the jolt to her back. She turns to find a blonde wearing some sticky drink all over her pastel suit, a look of tremendous embarrassment on her face.

Emily hands her a handkerchief to mop up. Poor thing seems out of place, doesn't seem to know anyone. Doesn't recognize Emily, doesn't realize she has just knocked into the guest of honor. She apologizes profusely and her American accent gives her away immediately. *An American*:

Emily feels so much more relaxed in her presence. Someone who will know little about her, who will not be silently judging her.

"My name is Linda Prescott but my friends call me Lynn," the woman says as she presses Emily's fine Belgian linen to her dress. "I'm from Villanova. That's outside of Philadelphia."

Should she confess that she's not sure if she could find Philadelphia on a map? "What brings you to London?" Emily is only too happy to talk with her while waiting for the event to get underway, a relief to have someone between her and the milling herd of rich women waiting to take their seats. She always feels like she's on display at these events, like an animal in a zoo, a target for hurtful comments on her weight or the ugliness of her dress. To question what Mikhail ever saw in her, or she in him. Besides the money, that is. Because Lynn is here, however, Emily can pretend that everyone isn't thinking these things. No, she can talk and laugh and smile and pretend all those other women don't exist.

"I'm doing what used to be called the grand tour," Lynn Prescott says in that open, honest way of all Americans, which Emily finds so refreshing.

Lynn explains that she has just recovered from a long illness, one that stole her childhood, to be honest. "The only thing I did for fun was . . . math. I had a tutor who brought me these math puzzles to do in my spare time. He didn't let on that they were famously hard . . . Then one day, he told me he'd been sharing them with the professors in his graduate program and they wanted me to work on one of their research programs. It got written up in the news and everything. Helped me get into college, too." She laughs. "It was the last thing my parents expected."

Lynn goes on to tell her about a childhood spent in and out of hospitals. Such a sad story but she's able to tell it without sounding self-pitying in the least, and Emily appreciates that. Emily has not had that kind of positivity in her life in a long, long while.

She takes Emily out of her head, helping her to forget to be nervous. Emily has been positively dreading giving the speech. It isn't as though anyone wants to hear from *her*. They were expecting Mikhail, but he changed his mind, saying it would be better for Emily to be seen in public. Emily knows it was the home invasion; he doesn't want to go anywhere that gives reporters the opportunity to question him.

Lynn points over Emily's shoulder to the audience. Round white tables glittering with crystal and silver. Huge arrangements of pink and yellow roses—rather treacly, if you ask Emily. At the tables, handfuls of Botoxed and liposuctioned women in expensive clothing and too much makeup. The Russian wives, their husbands expected to contribute to Mikhail's interests. There's also a smattering of British ladies who lunch, the crowd who are expected to support things like this even though they don't particularly care for the oligarchs.

"There's some serious money out there," Lynn says. "Serious faces." In that entire sea of faces, Emily honestly felt like there was no one in her corner—and then Lynn miraculously appeared, backed into her, and spilled a mimosa all over herself, and everything was better.

"This is only the second time I've ever been to the U.K.," Lynn says, stuffing the handkerchief in her pocket, "but my first extended trip. To anywhere. It's a little overwhelming." She says something again about her lonely childhood owing to a long, serious-sounding illness that she is just getting over. Emily doesn't remember the name of it—the speech had been hanging over her head and it slips away from her again. It touches Emily how similar they were, two lonely children grown into lonely adults. They may have had the benefit of money but that doesn't buy everything, does it? Lynn is living proof that it doesn't buy health. Emily is living proof that it doesn't buy happiness.

There is something else about Lynn that makes it easy for Emily to feel at ease with her, more than the shared loneliness. It took a little while for Emily to put her finger on it, but Lynn reminds her of her younger sister, Jesamine. There's the math connection, but there's more to it than that. It's her expression. So serious. Jesamine was such a serious child and yet she always took Emily seriously, too. Even when other people—their parents, for god's sake—dismissed her ideas as silly and called her flighty, Jesamine always listened to her. Asked her opinion.

Jesamine will have nothing to do with Emily now.

The way Lynn looks at her, listening intently to her every word, compels Emily to trust her. To like her. To feel comfortable in her presence.

The main reason Emily feels relaxed around the American is that she doesn't seem to want anything from her—unlike every other single person in Emily's sphere. Emily offered to pay to have her clothing dry-cleaned by her service (the best in London), and even offered to buy a new outfit for her, but Lynn Prescott kept refusing. *No, no, I couldn't.* It could be nothing more than simple manners, but Emily rarely sees such manners at all these days. Most people seem to be waiting to squeeze something out of her: money, a favor from her husband, a connection made with some celebrity.

Users. They're all users.

But Lynn Prescott does not seem like a user. It is such a relief. Someone who doesn't know who Emily is and doesn't care once she finds out, other than to admire Emily for being so civic-minded and responsible. As though Mikhail really cares about hungry shut-ins.

When the speech is over, the American finds Emily again and asks her loads of questions about things she's seen in the U.K. so far, and what she should do next, what she shouldn't miss. There is something so earnest and, frankly, *needy* about Lynn (clearly Lynn *needs* Emily, and when was the last time anybody needed her with no strings attached?) that

Emily feels it is only natural to invite her to tea the next day. Even though Emily can hear in the back of her mind what her husband will say, asking what possessed her to make friends with this American and what does she really know about this Lynn Prescott, anyway?

Honestly, it's just tea. Emily does not see the harm. It's not like she does this sort of thing all the time. It is no exaggeration to say that she has *no* friends. None. The few friends she had from school have fallen away. Her sisters have washed their hands of her. And she doesn't count the Russian wives as friends, more like spies sent by their husbands.

Or—maybe even sent by Mikhail. She wouldn't put it past him.

It doesn't matter. Emily isn't asking for the moon. Everyone needs a friend.

Emily sends Lynn a text that evening to set up their tea. Usually, the only time out of the house that Mikhail approves of are playdates for the twins, and these are always at the home of a Russian expat, one on a carefully curated but ever-changing list of families who are acceptable to Mikhail. These are always fraught affairs, the hostess a bit on edge, seemingly afraid of displeasing Emily—as though she's difficult to please or judgmental in the slightest. And they always treat the Rotenberg children as though they're made of glass, as though Emily *expects* such treatment. They're two years old and that's all children do at that age, run and fall and fling toys at each other indiscriminately.

There was that time when one child poked Kit in the eye and the wound looked serious for a day or two. Mikhail was terribly upset at Emily for letting it happen, but also at the family of the child who'd done the poking. Kit is his little prince. Emily is afraid that Mikhail already has mapped out the boy's whole future for him, expecting Kit to take over whatever empire Mikhail has amassed by then. Mikhail was terribly concerned that the wounding was going to leave a scar or damage his eyesight in some permanent way, and it all passed with neither scar nor damage of any kind, but Mikhail never forgave the family. There were no more playdates at their house, needless to say, and Emily is fairly sure the family moved away shortly after. It was a social gaffe that proved impossible to overcome.

Anyway, Emily is absolutely giddy at the prospect of having a new friend who is not connected to any of that. Lynn Prescott is not Russian, has no children, and is not even part of the British set who might know something about Emily. With Lynn, she can be whoever she wants to be—can even cease to be the oligarch's wife for a brief moment.

If Lynn proves discreet enough, maybe one day . . . if she's really and truly not a user . . . perhaps Emily can even confide her darkest fears in her. It would be lovely to have someone she can speak to on that level. She hasn't had that in ages and ages. Westover pretends to be her friend, pretends to be in love with her—like Emily doesn't know that he's secretly gay. They carry on like they're chummy, the best of friends, but obviously Westie doesn't count. He is an employee, and if there were anyone else even slightly suitable to talk to in the house she would ignore him entirely.

Anyway, it's too soon to know with Lynn. Emily doesn't want to get her hopes up but she has a good feeling.

It was hard to settle on the place to take Lynn for her first afternoon tea in London. If she wanted someplace iconic or classic, the choice would obviously be the Ritz or the Savoy, or even those mile-high scones at Claridge's. But going to any of those places would be making too public a statement. It would be like putting yourself on display for everyone to see, and who knows, they might even end up in the gossip pages of some grasping newspaper. Though if you said this to Emily's ten-year-old self, that one day the London papers would get excited just to see her in public—how they love to run pictures of her, always referring to her in that sniggering way as "the oligarch's aristo wife"—she'd have thought you'd lost your mind. Ultimately, Emily settles on the Berkeley Hotel in Knightsbridge, known for catering to the fashion crowd, but also because it is possible to be sequestered out of the public eye with a nice private table for two.

They take the Bentley, which Lynn gawks at discreetly (not many Bentleys in America, Emily reckons). She seems to enjoy the sheer luxury of being whisked through choking London traffic by chauffeur. Emily points out landmarks along the way and Lynn politely coos at each one. She's not been to the Berkeley so that is an added treat, getting to introduce her to a new place. They are given a wonderful booth before a pretty, young waitress brings out the full kit of finger sandwiches and amusing tiny pastries and steaming pots of tea. The spread is not too lavish so their waistlines won't be in danger of exploding over one afternoon's indiscretion, but decadent enough to feel like they've splurged.

Lynn sweetly indulges Emily's questions and tells Emily all about herself. Emily finds it a relief not to be the center of attention, to be able to lose herself in someone else's story. Lynn tells her that, as a child, she'd been diagnosed with a rare metabolic disorder. The story is quite dramatic. It had meant frequent trips all through her childhood to a famous hospital, and before long her family moved to Villanova to accommodate all the trips. It kept her out of school and confined to the family's estate with only a tutor and a nurse for company. There had been no other siblings or children in Lynn's life. Lynn tells Emily of playing by herself on the expansive grounds, being led around on a very gentle pony but not allowed to have any cats or dogs for fear of being scratched or knocked down. She got to see another child only occasionally, when a visiting cousin was passing through, say, but for the most part, all she knew of the world had come through books and the television and the internet. Emily thinks of how sad and lonely her childhood would've been without her sisters, particularly Jesamine. The way it is now.

Eventually, Lynn says, the doctors came up with a treatment—a miracle of modern science—which has enabled her to leave the birdcage of her existence for the first time and experience the world. This happened only recently, the treatments completed, and London is her first foray into the outside world. "I'd read so many books—I was a huge Dickens fan—that this was the first place I wanted to see," she says almost sheepishly over her teacup. It makes Emily a little sad to think Lynn had based her first trip out into the world of the living on some nearly ancient novels that have nothing to do with the London of today.

"There's so much more to England than Dickens," Emily says, finding her tongue. "The rest of the country is absolutely beautiful. It's too bad you weren't a Thomas Hardy fan—I could whisk you away to Devon and Somerset. Or Robert Burns—we could take a trip up to Scotland."

"I'd like that. Either one!" Lynn blurts out, her cheeks reddening charmingly.

"I'd love for you to meet my children," Emily finds herself saying. It's the most natural thing in the world. What mother doesn't like to show off her children, especially when they are as sweet and adorable as Tatiana and Kit? It would be nice to share them for once with someone whose motives Emily doesn't question, who will see them only as children to be loved and enjoyed and not as pawns to curry favor with their father.

"I would love to." Emily positively beams.

The Berkeley is famous for making witty cookies that look like handbags and cocktail dresses, Jimmy Choo shoes and *Vogue* editor Anna

Wintour, because of the connection to the fashion industry, and Lynn insists on wrapping these up for Emily to take back to the children. As though their chef can't make anything the twins could possibly desire; still, it is a very sweet gesture that makes Emily like Lynn even more.

And then Lynn does something that positively floors Emily: she digs into her purse and pulls out a credit card. "I want to take care of the check. I insist. You've been so kind to me." Emily cannot remember the last time someone wanted to take care of the bill. For one thing, it's the Russian way to pick up the tab: it shows largesse, but it also shows who has the power at the table. She senses no power play from Lynn, however.

They part with a promise to get together soon, this time at the mansion so Lynn can meet the twins. By the time Emily drops Lynn off at her hotel and arrives home, she is giddy with happiness, which Mikhail picks up on right away.

Predictably, he is less than pleased. "You spent the entire afternoon with a woman you just met?" he asks, arching his brows. "An American?"

"I met her at *your* charity event. She's very nice. She has no connections in the city, nobody to talk to. She's very lonely."

Mikhail is like this, suspicious and mean, because he has never known hardship. He'd like you to think that he's a self-made man, made all these billions himself, but that wouldn't be true. For instance, he says he got nothing from his family when he started out, but that's a very Russian thing to say, Emily has since learned. Russians with money or connections never want to admit this. It seems to be deeply suspect, a statement on their character, somehow harkening back to the elitism of the tsars. They avoid anything that smacks of privilege. So, the men with all the money these days—she doesn't say "oligarchs," Mikhail positively hates that word—all say that they came up with their ideas on their own, maybe even while they were still in college. As for the funding to get them started, they all claim to have earned it selling T-shirts outside rock concerts or by starting some other little business where they saw an opening. They like spinning these myths about themselves, telling others that they are hardy pioneers, scrappy go-getters, entrepreneurs, geniuses. The truth, however, is they all came from money to begin with, every single last one of them. Their fathers and mothers had emerged after the fall of the Soviet Union with newfound wealth, mostly by grabbing state-owned companies when everything was being privatized. In some cases, it's university connections that helped them. Not one of these men likes the history he was born with, as though it was too dirty or not good enough. Just being successful wasn't good enough for them: they had to be mythic. They have all created new realities for themselves. New pasts make for unlimited futures.

And the most ambitious of them—or perhaps the most ashamed—leave Russia for other countries. They take their families to a place where the past can't catch up with them. Where they'll be safer. They all keep houses in Russia. Kosygin has continued Putin's edict: he doesn't allow them to cut all ties, and there must be surrogate hostages if nothing else. Still, they all spend the year hopping from one place to another. Monaco or Mykonos in the summer, skiing in Gstaad or Courchevel in the winter. London, New York, and Paris for shopping. Some of the oligarchs rarely stay anywhere for more than a month.

What a lonely life it must be. Emily prefers to live in London. For now, at least, Mikhail likes it, too, being less nomadic in nature than his friends.

As far as Lynn Prescott is concerned, however—maybe he can't bring himself to trust someone who has never left home. "What is her name? I'm going to have Igor check her out."

Emily groans. "Is that really necessary? We've *just* met. She's *just* a friend. It's not like she's marrying into the family." He will use any excuse to take away anything special to her. Her stomach tightens at the thought.

"We need to check out anyone who gets close to you. Especially under such unusual circumstances."

"Unusual? I meet people all the time at these things."

"And how many have you followed up with tea or invited to our house?"

Emily has to give him that, though it's usually because he won't let her make friends and she knows it and has given up trying. But there was something special about Lynn and so she didn't shut her down. Didn't give up before it had started.

So—fine. If doing a little digging will make Mikhail happy, put his mind at ease, she will let him. But he'll find nothing, because Lynn Prescott is a sweet, normal person who has come into Emily's life at exactly the right moment because Emily needs her.

"Do what you must. And I promise not to gloat when you come back with nothing."

CHAPTER 8

TALLINN, ESTONIA

The stewardess passes in the aisle on her last sweep through the cabin as Lyndsey looks out the window of the plane at the city below. Tallinn's old town is unmistakable, with its twisty streets of red-tiled rooftops. The city is so well-preserved that it is like stepping back in time.

The man sitting to Lyndsey's right had tried to engage her in conversation at the beginning of the flight. A grandfatherly sort in a tweedy jacket, perhaps he thought she needed company since she was alone. "Are you going on holiday?" he asked in accented English. She tried to place the accent he was trying to suppress. Was it Russian?

This trip is not for pleasure.

Tallinn is an easy three-hour flight from London. It sits perched, like a crown, at the crossroads of political ideologies. Helsinki waits across the Gulf of Finland. St. Petersburg, the city of spies, sits to the east.

Lyndsey has been to Tallinn before, the Estonian capital being an easy place to meet Russian assets away from the tangle and pressure of Moscow. It's not completely carefree—there's plenty of Russian surveillance—

but even with the Russian presence, it's less dangerous than trying to meet in Russia itself.

Everything about this weekend has Lyndsey on edge. It's because she had to rush to make the flight after the last excursion with Emily. It seems she had barely exited the Bentley before she needed to run to her apartment, throw clothes in a suitcase, and hurry to Heathrow. She planned to use the flight—quality time alone, slipping on noise-canceling headphones to discourage conversation with her seatmate—to pick through what transpired with Emily.

The point of the first meeting is to get a second, and then a third, to open the door to friendship to give Lyndsey the opportunity to understand Emily on a deeper level and decide whether she had it in her to turn on her husband. Lyndsey went over every minute of the encounter with Emily, looking for flaws, a misspoken word, a dropped stitch in her backstory, an instance when she pressed too hard to make a good impression. She can detect none. Emily was evaluating Lynn Prescott, that was evident, but she was genuinely engaged. Emily's body position was, for the most part, open. Only a few times did she fold in on herself—shoulders rounding, chin dropping—and that was when Mikhail's name came up. Lyndsey steered the conversation away from him once she'd noticed the pattern.

Now comes the other half of the equation, the whole reason for Lyndsey's mission: *what do I think of her?*

One thing she knows: if she were to meet Emily in real life, she wouldn't like her. She assumes that Emily gives the impression of being a nice person that in real life she cannot be. Her husband is ruthless, from the background material Parth Arya's team prepared for her. He has crushed competitors with thug-like tactics, stolen or defaulted on pensions, shuttered businesses that kept whole villages employed. The most egregious crimes happened when he was starting out and had partnered with an old gangster from the Gorbachev era. Men like that do not change as time goes on—they just get better at covering their tracks. Emily may not be actively evil, but at the least she's complicit.

In the spy business, however, they're not paid to make friends with nice people. In this line of work, they're interested in bad people. They work on the birds-of-a-feather principle: bad people know other bad people, and they will lead you to the worst people. Emily has compromised herself morally; the question is, will she do it again by spying on her husband?

Perhaps she will find it redemptive.

People who live behind a wall of secrets generally have something to hide. Lyndsey assumes that it says something about Emily's character that she went ahead and married the man, especially since it seems she isn't madly in love with him. Judgmental, but that's the intelligence business: making assessments, sifting through layers of secrets someone wants hidden, coming to judgment.

Lyndsey saw the key to gaining Emily's trust the second she met her: Emily assumes people only make her acquaintance because they want something from her. Maybe it's because her husband is surrounded by sycophants, and she assumes the same is true for her. That could be why she has so few friends: she pushes people away because she always thinks the worst of them.

The funny thing is, for all Emily's distaste for users, she apparently can't see that *she* is one, too. The only people allowed in her sphere are there to do things for her and her family. Her every exchange with another human being is transactional. She married for money and she *hates* this about herself.

Which means the key to winning Emily's trust is to *never* make this an issue. Emily must never, ever feel that Lynn Prescott is using her. That this friendship is about Emily's money.

The sad thing is that Emily probably could've been a happy person if she hadn't married Mikhail Rotenberg.

There's something else, Lyndsey senses. Emily Rotenberg is afraid of her husband. Which means the operation might not go the way MI6 hopes. Some wives who've been bullied and abused may want to get even with their husband. Dish out a little payback. But most of them won't. It's harder to do than it looks. Just ask the police how many domestic abuse victims press charges against their spouses—not that Emily is in the same situation, not exactly. It doesn't appear that Mikhail has physically abused her. Just emotionally—at least as far as Lyndsey has seen so far, which is only a little. And she hasn't observed her in Mikhail's company, which should be telling.

Still . . . she senses Emily's situation is bad. Maybe that's how she needs to think of Emily, as a victim of spousal abuse. That way, she can remain sympathetic, be on the woman's side instead of blaming her. There are unseen reasons why Emily married Rotenberg. Levers that can, perhaps, be worked. It means there's a glimmer of hope that the wife can be turned against the husband.

If she's suffered at her husband's hands, if there's an ounce of pride left, Emily Rotenberg might relish the opportunity for a little revenge. To be the one who takes down her husband's golden empire.

A voice crackles over the speakers, first in Estonian, then in English. "Welcome to Tallinn, where the temperature is . . ." That's Lyndsey's signal to put all thoughts of Emily out of her mind. For the next day, she needs to be completely focused on the mission at hand. Lyndsey won't be able to do justice to the meeting with Tarasenko if she doesn't clear her head. Though it's hard to say which op is more important—Langley and Vauxhall Cross probably have differing opinions—there is no doubt that Tarasenko is the more dangerous of the two. She feels a bit like a snake handler. One lapse in judgment and those poisonous fangs will sink into her forearm and she'll know she made a fatal mistake.

Lyndsey drags her rolling suitcase behind her, hurrying through Tallinn Airport toward passport control and customs. In her pocket is a passport that bears her picture but a different name. It's always a little nerve-wracking to travel undercover, worrying that some new technology will be waiting for her at passport control to trip her up. Surrounded by Scandinavians and Finns, she is standing in line when her cell phone buzzes in her pocket. She pulls it out: there's a message on the secure texting app, the one that Langley uses to reach her. *You'll be met by Station tonight at midnight at your hotel.*

That's it, no details, but of course they wouldn't send any. Messages while she's on a mission will be kept brief to give away as little as possible in case they're intercepted. She has no idea what this is about, but there's no use speculating now.

Once she clears customs, it's a taxi ride to the hotel downtown with nothing to do but wait until Tarasenko makes contact. She's staying at the Three Sisters, a little boutique place in the old part of town, away from the international chains where most of the business travelers stay. One less chance to run into Russian intelligence, who are sure to have those lobbies staked out. Here, it's easier to blend in with the tourists from Sweden and Norway and, yes, Russia, who hop over for a holiday weekend.

After a stroll through the shops—working her way through store after store of handknit sweaters and mittens, Kalev chocolates, keepsake boxes made of juniper—she heads back to the hotel to find a message waiting for her at the front desk. *Nāganaga Bar, tonight, 10 p.m.*

The concierge shows her where the bar is on a map. It's only a few minutes' walk from the hotel, so Lyndsey takes a stroll to check the place out. No case officer likes to walk into an unfamiliar place while on mission, especially at night. Better to check out the potential for ambush, to look for possible escape routes and dead ends in the light of day. She's surprised once she finds it: it seems like a perfectly ordinary café, the kind of place where you meet friends casually for appetizers and a drink after work. She wouldn't think this kind of place would appeal to Tarasenko. She'd thought he'd prefer the dark, smoky bars closer to the international hotels, the places where businessmen like to go where they can pretend to be someone else and do things they can disown in the light of day.

He probably plans to go back to one of those hotels soon, because their meeting tonight will not last long. And that's fine: she needs to be back at the Three Sisters in time to make the rendezvous with Station.

Reconnaissance done, she heads back to her room for a quick nap. She has a few hours to kill and it would be a good idea to be rested, if she's able to fall asleep. She can already feel the anticipation for the meeting tonight with Tarasenko. There's a wisp of dread there, too, threaded through the excitement. Staying two steps ahead of a charging bull is easier if you're not tired.

Lyndsey gets to the bar fifteen minutes before the appointed time. She doesn't really think it's a trap or that Tarasenko will have it staked out by FSB. It's her habit, good tradecraft ingrained in her.

But Dmitri Tarasenko is already there, waiting for her. Naturally. She spots him right off, remembering him clearly from a few months earlier. She remembers how he looked in the FBI interrogation cell, and again later at the safe house in the Virginia woods where he received his operational training. The funny thing is that she remembers him as brutish and hulking, a trapped wolf looking for an opportunity to escape his hunters and to take his revenge on the ones who trapped him. On *her.*

And here she is about to sit down with him, unshackled.

But in the dim light of the bar, she would almost not recognize him. He sits at a high-top table with a beer in front of him and a bowl of crackers at his elbow, watching a soccer match on a television screen suspended over the bar. A thin leather jacket is draped over the back of his stool and he's wearing a linen shirt. He could be on holiday, perhaps out to meet a friend. He's not a ruthless Russian intelligence officer or a former soldier responsible for the deaths of dozens of Georgians. He looks . . . normal.

He's also . . . handsome. That thought surprises her, registering somewhere deep inside her, primal. There are so many stories about handlers and assets having affairs that it's practically a cliché. They're men and women, after all. Only human. Add the thrill of danger and being in together on something, just the two of you, and it can be irresistible to some people.

She never thought of herself as one of those people—but then, there was Davis. There was a rule against what she'd done with Davis Ranford, and she disregarded it, and look where that got her. She wonders fleetingly if she has a psychological need to disregard the rules. A need to *break* them. This is generally a death knell in this line of work. Rules exist for a reason and higher-ups want to see that they're being followed. It's gotten other case officers into trouble, better men (arguably) than her.

She doesn't have time to think about it now, though: Tarasenko has spotted her. He rises from the stool, picks up his jacket and his glass, and heads toward the back of the bar, disappearing around a corner. *Follow me.* She doesn't right away, though. She must maintain the illusion of normalcy. She also doesn't like that he's trying to control the situation. He should be following her lead. Still . . . it's not unexpected, not given who he is. She stops at the bar for a glass of the house wine, a dubious Lithuanian white. Then she heads after him.

The back hall leading to the restrooms is empty. Could Tarasenko have gone into the men's room, expecting her to follow? She's about to push the door back to see if he's waiting for her when a man brushes by, giving her only the slightest backward glance before heading in himself. She can see in the split second the door is open that the restroom is tiny and lit very brightly. Tarasenko isn't in there.

It's then she sees a dark pocket to the side and stairs leading to a basement area. She trots down to find him waiting for her.

"Hello again," he says. His voice is pleasantly deep.

She leaves her wineglass on a cardboard box and nods at the stairs. "Let's go outside." At the end of a hall, she finds a back door, propped open with a piece of wood, perhaps to relieve the heat in the tiny, busy kitchen. It's not that she feels particularly unsafe in the bar, but she'd rather not meet in a place of Tarasenko's choosing. Better to maintain as much control as possible.

He falls a step behind as he lights a cigarette. The smoke is heavy and spicy, more like a cigar's. Some horrible Russian brand. Machismo is part of everything in Russia, built into the fabric of life. How nasty, how rough, how unpleasant—every little thing is a test of endurance, meant to toughen you up for the existential challenge that is life.

"Would you like one?" he asks, waving the cigarette.

"No, thank you."

"You Americans, so obsessed with health. Smoking is a pleasure." He falls into step beside her. "Where are we going? To a safe house? We're safe enough here . . ." He gestures at the velvety landscape surrounding them. "Don't forget, I work in counterintelligence for the FSB. I know their game plan in Tallinn. We're not being followed."

And he's probably right—they're fine—though her first reaction is that he could be lying to her. What he doesn't know is that there's a small team of watchers from Tallinn Station on their tail tonight. She's drawn him outside for exactly this purpose, so they can be on the lookout for a Russian security detail or surveillance team. It's their first meeting since he was arrested in Washington, collateral in the Richard Warner case. Then he made his offer to bring in Morozov, the Prize (*that should be Morozov's code name*, she thinks fleetingly, *a certain poetic justice there*) in exchange for his freedom. With a man as dangerous as Tarasenko, there are precautions that must be taken. There will be no shortcuts. She'll know soon enough whether Tarasenko told the FSB that he's been flipped and has turned triple agent.

"How have things been since you returned?" she asks.

He shrugs. "As you might expect . . . I got a good grilling when I first got back. It is humiliating being caught by your FBI. Morozov was furious. Not only losing our canary, but then being forced to give up Richard Warner. That meant he had to tell Putin everything." His smile is vaguely sinister. "Morozov is in the doghouse now, as you Americans say. He's lucky to still be alive, and he knows it."

Morozov is feeling the pressure, then. Good. "Is he lying low for now? Is that his style?"

Tarasenko draws heavily on the cigarette, then expels a long stream of noxious smoke. Gravel crunches underfoot as they walk down the alley. "He is not happy. He is quiet but, no, it is not his style. He would like to punch back, to change his luck by pulling off some coup, but that would be a risky game and he knows it."

A man who feels he's being treated unfairly can be an opportunity. "What's his relationship like with Kosygin? Do they know each other from the KGB days?"

"Morozov is being cagey about it. The new president is establishing himself: no one wants to make themselves a target by saying the wrong thing."

"Does Kosygin make Morozov nervous? Nervous enough to talk to us?"

Tarasenko chuckles. "You want to flip him?"

"What do you think? Would he do it?"

He sends another long stream of smoke into the night sky. "I don't know. He is a proud man . . . He would need to be out of options. Completely trapped in a corner, and I do not think he is there, yet. Morozov is a wily one. He still has lots of friends he can turn to. Going to the Americans would be among the last things he would do to survive, I think."

We'll have to force his hand, then. "Have you given any thought as to how you're going to lead us to him?"

"I must think about this carefully. I told you: I don't want to leave Russia, I just want to get out from under Morozov's thumb. He takes too many risks for my taste. I'm tired of being his servant. He doesn't care what happens to me, and I'm not so selfless that I'll put up with this kind of treatment forever."

No: he doesn't seem like the kind of man who would put up with this for very long at all.

"Then give us Morozov and we'll both be happy," Lyndsey says.

"It won't be easy." This is already becoming a familiar refrain. His favorite excuse. He's going to need to be nudged out of his comfort zone if they're ever going to pull off this operation.

"That's a given. If it was going to be easy, we wouldn't need you and you'd be sitting in a federal prison."

Lyndsey's barb seems to have stirred something in Tarasenko, makes him understand that she'll tolerate only so much delay. "He manages his life tightly. He is not like you or me. He has trained himself to need no diversion, no variation in his routine. His schedule is the same every day. He gets into the office by eight a.m. by private driver and leaves punctually twelve hours later, unless an emergency keeps him longer. He rarely goes out in the evenings. His wife passed away a few years ago and he has not taken up with anyone since. He never sees his adult children and only speaks to them every couple of months by telephone."

"Friends?"

Tarasenko snickers. "A man like that has no friends, only professional associates. And he only gets in touch with them when he needs a favor. No, wait, that's not strictly true. There are a couple guys he sees occasionally from the KGB days and an old friend from the military. But even that's rare, maybe once a year? He really is a very lonely man." From his tone, it's obvious that Tarasenko doesn't consider himself to be anything like his boss. He's not lonely, not pathetic. No one will ever say this about him.

"Does he have a dacha? Some place he gets away to?" Most Russians of any means have a country home. Morozov should have a nice retreat, a good place to wait things out.

"He does. He has a *gosdacha*"—owned and allotted by the government to elites—"but he hasn't gone there in a long time. Well over a year."

"Where is it?"

"Peredelkino. It was once a great artists' colony. All the famous Russian writers and poets had dachas there during Stalin's time. Why he prefers Peredelkino, I don't know. All Russians are terrible snobs when it comes to literature, you know. Maybe he thinks it makes him look like an intellectual and not a run-of-the-mill apparatchik."

Lyndsey stores both bits of information for future use. She'll need to talk to the experts at Langley about Peredelkino, to see if they might see an opportunity there. In the meantime, Tarasenko needs guidance. "We need you to think of any points of vulnerability the man has. Any leverage we can use against him." That's a given. "Also, if you get any advance warning that he's on the move, we need to know about it."

"Putin forbad him from leaving the country, and Kosygin hasn't lifted that. And Morozov is not an idiot. He's concerned that you'll try to kidnap him, because of what he did in Kiev."

"We also know Morozov's getting antsy. He's been trapped inside the borders of your country for a decade and is itching to get back to all his favorite corners of the world," Lyndsey reminds him. It's been mentioned in numerous intelligence reports.

Tarasenko does the lazy, one-shoulder shrug he seems to favor. "He may be restless but he's also not stupid. He could only cross Kosygin if the odds were in his favor. If he had a plausible excuse. Such an excuse will be hard to come by."

"Your job is to help us find that one thing that would be irresistible to Morozov, and we'll fabricate the excuse. Let us know if he starts talking about it again. If he plans to go somewhere even *slightly* close to the border."

"Is your agency sure it wants to do something so aggressive under the current circumstances?" He's right, and he knows it. The hostility may have gone underground since Putin's removal, but it's still there. Snatching Morozov while on Russian soil would undoubtedly need to be okayed by the POTUS, it's that provocative.

"Don't you worry about that. You just keep us informed of his whereabouts."

"Yes, ma'am." He gives a fake salute. "You'll see that I can follow orders."

"Good."

They are back on the main road not far from the international hotels.

Tarasenko looks up at the huge building across the street, a recent build, modern design, all stone and steel and glass. He arches an eyebrow. "Would you like to get a drink? As I said, I doubt we've been followed tonight. But if you're worried about us being seen together in the bar, we can always go up to my room."

That deep voice has turned inviting. His gaze caresses her cheek.

He must know that the chances of Lyndsey warming to him are slim to none, and yet he seems determined to try. Maybe it's the case officer in him, testing her boundaries, seeing whether she has a flaw he can exploit.

He looks like he would be good in bed, leaving women purring like kittens while he made his escape. It's something that his ego would demand. But she is not that reckless. Besides, after what happened with Davis, her reputation has already been tainted. She cannot risk doing anything that would make it stick.

"No, I think this is where we should part." Then she remembers: Rotenberg. She could see what he knows about the state of things in Moscow, but she knows the dangers of crossing operations. It's generally not a good idea. It's better to keep Tarasenko and Emily Rotenberg completely separate.

He's listening. So attentive, eager to please. It's almost charming, if she didn't suspect he was doing it for the wrong reasons. Her mind is made up in that regard, however. There will be no fraternizing with her asset. She decides it would be better to see what he knows. He's a tool to be used. "Would you have any idea if Kosygin is mad at any of the oligarchs in particular at the moment?"

"I have heard he's talking to all of them, setting expectations. He doesn't care that they suffered from the business with Ukraine: sanctions, losing their yachts, and freezing their assets. They owe Moscow for everything they have. You make a bargain with the devil, you eventually get burned." He frowns. "The oligarchs are scum. We all know it, us commoners. No respect for us peasants. Peasants are the soul of Russia, you know. We *are* Russia. Those oligarchs, pompous peacocks, thinking the country revolves around them, instead of the other way around."

Apparently, she touched a nerve.

"I will see what I can find out for you. It would be a pleasure," he says, flicking the butt of his latest cigarette to the ground and grinding it under his heel for good measure. "Is there one in particular you have in mind?"

She hesitates. It's exactly the thing she would ask, if the roles were reversed and she were trying to work him. But he's right, and letting him in on the secret might loosen some tidbit of knowledge. "I'm posted to London now, as you know, and just the other day there was this incident . . . An attack on the home of an oligarch—"

"Oh yes. Mikhail Rotenberg. The biggest parasite of them all. It's all anyone can talk about in Moscow, how Rotenberg is finally getting his comeuppance."

"Does that mean he's not under Kosygin's protection?" She has a million questions for Tarasenko but decides to play it dumb for now, because that would be playing it safe.

"Nobody knows. There's even a rumor that has to do with one of Kosygin's former mistresses. But it's all gossip at this point."

This seems so petty, like so much tittle-tattle, but it doesn't surprise her that this would be a form of entertainment. "Would that be enough to cause a break between the two men?"

"It wouldn't take much to get on Kosygin's bad side, from what I've heard. He makes Putin look like a kindly old grandfather."

"It sounds like maybe you know more about Kosygin than you're letting on . . ."

He shrugs. "Not really. Nobody knows much, or if they do, they're not saying. It's like he has been living in a deep cavern—or put there, maybe, by Putin back in the KGB days. Kosygin smelled Putin was vulnerable and came crawling out . . . Let me find out more for you when I'm back in Moscow."

"I'd appreciate it. Oh—there's one more thing. Eric Newman. Have your people heard from him? Has he been in touch?"

Tarasenko thinks. "No—why?"

"He's given us the slip, and we think there's a good chance that he might turn to Russia. The FSB would treat him right. And it would appeal to his ego."

Tarasenko grunts. "I'll see what I can find out. For you, *kukla*, anything."

Kukla. Doll. He'd said it the first time he'd seen her, when they'd come face-to-face in the FBI interrogation room.

She will show him one day that she is no *kukla*, no toy to be played with.

She checks her watch. She has a good half hour to get back to the hotel. "Have a good evening, Dmitri. I'll be in touch," she says briskly. His shoulders fall momentarily—not pleased to be rebuffed but he can't have expected it to turn out otherwise—and he pivots in the direction of the hotels. Watchers will remain on his tail for a little longer, and tomorrow at the Station she will get a readout of his evening.

There is a man waiting outside the Three Sisters. From a distance in the dim light of a streetlamp, he appears middle-aged. He wears glasses and a navy-blue sportscoat that's seen better days. He's on his cell phone, jabbing at buttons.

The man puts away his phone as Lyndsey approaches. "Tim Rickard," he says as he offers his hand. They shake, and he sets off briskly toward the tiny parking lot behind the hotel. He steers her toward a battered Volvo station wagon, its color hidden under a layer of last winter's road chemicals and dust. Once they're buckling up, Lyndsey asks, "What's this about? Station told me nothing."

"Station wants you to join me at a meeting with one of my assets." Rickard starts the engine. "Irina Babanina."

"Why is that name familiar?"

"From the 2000 summer Olympics. I assume you used to watch the gymnastic competitions, like most little girls?" Lyndsey thinks back to that time, when she would've been a teenager—not little, but she doesn't bother to correct him. "Irina was expected to win the overall gold medal. She was the number one ranked female gymnast in the world going in." Rickard sounds like a proud father—well, case officers do develop emotional bonds with their assets. Ill-advised, but inevitable. He keeps his eyes forward as he swings the car onto the road, into sparse traffic. "She finished third."

And now, twenty-three years later, she is an asset for CIA. It seems improbable.

"She finished third because something happened to her one night in Sydney. The thing that happened to her was Vladimir Putin." Rickard continues driving, not lifting his eyes from the road, as he tells Irina's story to Lyndsey, one he undoubtedly heard over and over as the asset was quizzed about her motivations during the vetting process. He describes, as dispassionately as possible, how the teenaged gymnast—thrumming with nerves on the eve of her first time performing in the Olympics, her lifelong dream—was brought to the Russian president's hotel suite. She thought it slightly strange, as she expected to meet him the next day with the entire team in what was supposed to be a friendly photo opportunity. But here she was being escorted up to the presidential suite, the escort introducing her to Putin before quickly slipping out and closing the door behind her. Putin offered her a drink, which Irina turned down, telling him that she had a competition the next morning. He congratulated her on coming to Sydney as number one in the world, told her that all of Russia was proud of her. Then he told her that she was a very pretty girl, and she should be proud of that, too.

Prettiness, he said, was fleeting. As fleeting as an Olympic career. She needed to make the most of it.

She ended up on her back in his bed, as she knew she would, shaking the entire time as she stared up at the ceiling and wondered what would happen next. There were no questions when she returned late that evening to the competitors' village, no sharp reprimand from her coaches, and the next day in the balance beam event she stumbled badly on a landing and twisted her ankle. It dogged her throughout the competition, allowing Yulia Orlova, who had been her closest competitor all year, nipping at her heels in the international standings, to steal the gold medal.

Lyndsey twists inside. You tend to hear ugly stories in this business.

"She was Putin's mistress for a decade," Rickard says as he swings into a deserted industrial park. He parks, cutting the headlights. "She's a smart one, though. She's never forgotten what he did to her, what it cost her. Maybe he should've picked Yulia to be his mistress, all things considered."

Rickard leads the way to a door. Kask Saatmine, a shipping company. A woman waits for them in an inner office. She is tall and slender and wrapped in a cashmere shawl. When she turns to face them, she starts back in surprise, perhaps not expecting her handler to bring another person with him. Irina Babanina may no longer be a teenager but she is beautiful, with a triangular cat's face and huge dark eyes and long silky locks the color of espresso. She moves with an uncommon grace.

"This is a colleague of mine," Rickard says. Not apologetically. There's no negotiation in the world of handlers and assets. You trust your handler and learn to accept things. "You said you had something important for me."

Lyndsey knows she's not to question why she's here. Rickard or the Station have a reason why they think she needs to hear what Irina has to say.

They sit on a trio of cheap upholstered chairs. The office is threadbare and dumpy: totally plausible as a cover, identical to many cheap family businesses in countless industrial parks. In that way, it's flawless. Rickard turns up the radio and Irina slips off the cashmere. She sits majestically, shoulders back, head held regally on her slim stalk of a neck. Not like most assets in Lyndsey's experience: hunched, shaking, fallen in on themselves, the assessment part of what Lyndsey does automatically. It's Irina's athletic training, yes, but there's something else there. She is not ashamed of what she is doing.

"I was with Sven last week," she begins. Lyndsey trusts Rickard will fill her in on the details later; whoever Sven is, his name is not a surprise to Rickard. "He told me that he had to fly to Beijing on a special mission. This is the third time in a month."

"Has he told you what this mission is about?"

She scowls slightly. "He's still being cagey. He says it's for Kosygin, though. Sven's mentor in the SVR"—the Russian Foreign Intelligence Service—"is an old friend of Kosygin's. Sven speaks Mandarin well. Kosygin doesn't want this operation—whatever it is—to go through the Foreign Ministry. He doesn't trust them. The most Sven would tell me is that Kosygin is trying to set up some kind of secret agreement with the Chinese. But that's as much as he would say."

Rickard leans forward. "Irina, we need you to really press him on this. It sounds like it could be important. You need to find out what's going on."

Lyndsey doesn't feel like she's able to take a breath again until she is back in the Volvo with Rickard, heading back to downtown Tallinn. Rickard is both animated and deadly serious at the same time. His knuckles are white on the steering wheel. "Sven is a middle-level officer in the SVR. Not particularly important. This backdoor connection to Kosygin just sort of fell in our lap."

"This secret dialogue with the Chinese—think there's something there?"

Rickard tilts his head. "The analysts in Russia Division say official Russian outreach to China since Kosygin took power has been nil. Zilch. Things hadn't been exactly rosy in Putin's day, either, you may recall. He was disappointed that they didn't support him more forcefully on Ukraine. They could've made it harder for the U.S. to act, but they didn't."

"How so?" Lyndsey asks. Ukraine and all that drama seems like a million years ago, instead of months.

"The U.S. would've had to listen if China was serious, wouldn't we? China could hurt us a lot more economically. Could complicate our lives in other ways, too. Russia has zero leverage over the U.S. except for nukes—of course."

"But China never steps in."

"Right. China has yet to voluntarily take a role on the world stage except when acting in its own interests. It never speaks up in the UN Security Council, for example, unless it's something in their backyard. It abstains during the vote more than any other member of the council. So, this has the potential to be big, depending on what's actually going on. Irina has to get Sven to tell her."

Lyndsey thinks for a minute. "Do you think she can?"

"She's been working for us for a long time and her track record is excellent. I'd be surprised if she's not able to bring us the goods." It's nice to see such confidence in an asset.

Lyndsey resists asking the question that keeps coming back to her, until she cannot. "And Sven—is that why she came to CIA?"

Rickard looks at her now. He knows what Lyndsey wants to know. "You mean, did we direct her to go after Sven? Yes, Lyndsey, we did. She'd been working for us for a while by then. She saw Sven was interested in her and she asked if we wanted her to follow up. We're not pimps—it was her initiative, her choice. She's brought us a lot of information over the years from men in important positions."

"Putin, too?"

He turns back to the road. "No, he'd moved her out of his life by then. But it's not what you think, a woman scorned and all that. She's doing this to get back for the way she was treated by the system, that part is true. But it's because she had a child with Putin—allegedly—whom he refused to acknowledge. They got in a huge fight over it, and he dumped her. She did this to take control back of her life, and you know what? I respect her for it."

The lobby of the Three Sisters is dark by the time Lyndsey returns. She has a couple hours before her flight back to London. "Thanks for bringing me along," she says to Rickard as she gets out of the car. She's not sure what connection it may have to Rotenberg but it's part of the process. You gather piece after piece of the puzzle until the bigger picture starts to become clear.

"I imagine it's going to raise some alarm bells back in Washington. I have the feeling this is going to make some people sit up and take notice," Rickard says as he drives away.

CHAPTER 9

The first thing Emily does when she opens her eyes in the morning is reach for her cell phone to check her text messages. She doesn't bother to open the curtains first or check on the children—that's what the nanny is for, for heaven's sake—but she thumbs open the text app and scrolls down, down, down.

Mostly it's automated reminders for appointments (hair, nails, the concierge pediatrician, blah, blah, blah). Emily sinks lower into the pillows. Not one friendly voice, no one to ask how she is doing, if she's recovered from the other night . . . What did she expect? She slinks lower when she realizes she had been holding out hope that she might hear from Jesamine. As she hopes every day and is disappointed every day.

But all is not bad news. There, buried among the chatbot-generated messages, is one from Lynn. *Finally.* It has only been a few days since their afternoon at the Berkeley, but when Emily had next invited her to lunch at The Bishops Avenue and there was no response, she'd just about given up. It was quite the rude awakening. Emily is not ignored or snubbed very often.

Emily holds her breath as she reads through Lynn's texts. There was a reasonable explanation, as it turns out: she had been in the hospital, suffering a minor relapse of some kind. She wishes Lynn had contacted her; she'd have been happy to visit, hold her hand, bring her chicken soup or a potted plant or whatever she needed to feel better.

Fortified, Emily rises from bed and goes into her closet. As she dresses, she thinks about Lynn. She was afraid it meant her new friend had cooled to her. That maybe she'd found out more about *the husband* and decided these were not the sort of people she wished to be friends with. Lynn seems to have integrity, unlike most people Emily deals with. Emily realizes this makes her sound like a moody schoolgirl but honestly, that's how she feels sometimes, like she's back at Queen's Gate, worrying whether the cool kids will ever like her. If—even after snagging a husband like Mikhail—she's still seen as a perennial outsider.

Maybe that's why Lynn's silence hit her so hard. As for the girls at Queen's Gate, well, *if those girls could see me now, married to practically the richest man in the world . . .* She supposes they *can* see her—and yet not one of them has reached out and tried to connect, to tell her how surprised they are to see how far she's risen.

They just ignore her. Like her family.

She goes through to the bathroom. She stands in front of the mirror, brushing her teeth, staring at her own sad face. *Why so sad, girl, when you are so lucky?*

Sometimes Emily is at a loss to explain how she ended up in her present situation or why she is so miserable. She came from a good family. An old and respected family. Not that there's much to the title besides a moldering family estate in Cumberland that she hasn't seen in thirty years. The family home, the place where she grew up, is a smallish house in South London. She and her two sisters were raised to be genteel, but the family hadn't the means to keep up with their more-well-heeled relations and friends. It was fine for her parents—her father, a senior director in a bank; her mother, Cynthia, a professor of medieval literature—who were low-key by nature, but Emily found their shabby existence mortifying. There was never enough money to keep up with schoolmates at Queen's Gate, where she was a day student. She was always quiet, trying not to stand out and draw the attention of the queen bees, who could be quite cutting. Being a viscount's daughter meant nothing at Queen's Gate, where there were daughters of pop stars and movie people, millionaires, and foreign dignitaries, as well as actual royalty. Emily Hughes was the daughter of a banker and a professor, nothing more, and she could never forget it.

Emily spits in the sink and reaches for the facial scrub. She pulls her hair back into a ponytail and turns on the hot-water tap.

Whereas her sisters had been able to distinguish themselves with their superior athletic skill and intellect, Emily had been maddeningly mediocre. The older and athletic one, Marilyn, takes rich people out for pony treks and shooting weekends. She always was more comfortable with people who were richer than they, Emily muses as she rubs microbeads into her cheeks. Her thoughts about her younger sister, Jesamine, come more tenderly, like she is prodding a bruise. Jesamine is so unlike anyone else in the family that the sisters frequently teased their mother that she must be the product of an interdepartmental affair she had at St. Robarth's. Emily remembers the very last time she saw Jesamine, the terrible row and the look on her face that said their relationship was ruined. That's how Emily knew things had changed between them forever.

Of course, Emily doesn't see much of any of them. Mikhail says it's because they're snobs and they look down their noses at foreigners, but Emily knows it's not that. They don't understand why she did what she did, and people typically avoid what they don't understand. They think they know exactly what kind of man Mikhail is, but she doesn't believe they do, not when she doesn't understand him herself. She knew when she met him that he's not a good man, not entirely, but she worked through that in her mind because she understood this was her opportunity and she'd never get another like it. And once she'd accepted this, she let it all happen, succumbing to the whirlwind force that is Mikhail Rotenberg: the courtship, the proposal, the wedding.

But her family . . . They think something must've happened to have her marry a man like Mikhail, that Emily can't possibly be the same person they knew.

But she is. She is exactly as her parents raised her and she's aware that this is a slightly damning thing to say. They don't want to acknowledge their role. They don't like what Emily's marriage to Mikhail says about *them*.

Face tingling, Emily heads back into the dressing room to find her favorite driving moccasins. She kicked them off somewhere last night. Maybe they're under the bed.

She's about to get down on the floor when Westie appears at the door. "Hullo!" he calls in pure forced cheerfulness. Westie the moneyman, short and chubby, well scrubbed in his carefully controlled way. He wears a sweater tied around his shoulders and a polo shirt: he thinks he's chic but he's a hopeless dresser. "Are you going down to breakfast, my love? Shall we head down together?"

My love. He likes to pretend they are the married couple, he and Emily. He makes out as though he is in love with her in a gentlemanly, restrained—that's to say nonsexual—way. *If only Mikhail weren't in the way*, he likes to say dreamily when they are having tea together, making eyes at her over the rim of his cup.

He does it because he's another user. His intentions are so obvious, he practically *glows*.

As though she would've married a man like him, even before Mikhail came along. It's fun to pretend, to let him play, but she hopes he doesn't believe that she's so easily fooled. So easily manipulated.

"Go on down. I'll join you in a minute." She's not in the mood for his company at the moment. It's almost like he's paid to be her friend.

Like everyone in her life since marrying Mikhail. All users. She supposes that makes her one as well. Birds of a feather and all that.

Still, she has a new friend. Lynn, she's pretty sure, is not a user.

Westie shrugs and trundles off.

On her hands and knees, searching. Her mind drifts again to her family... Why does she have the same punishing thoughts every morning? Going over the same old ground, the unpleasantness and disappointment... it's as though she's cursed. As though she finds comfort in the pain, as crazy as that seems. As though she just can't let these wounds heal.

And these daydreams seem to happen more frequently as things have worsened between her and Mikhail.

She's not sure when her parents became disappointed in her. Maybe it was when it became apparent that she would not be as athletic as Marilyn or as brilliant as Jesamine. Both her mother and father are sedate and bookish, and so it couldn't have been a surprise that she'd turn out the same way. It's all right to be bookish if you're smart, but Emily supposes it's the lack of blazing intellect that makes it difficult for them to accept that they had a daughter whose only attribute is being pretty.

What they ended up pinning their hopes on was that she'd make a good marriage. For this, she was ideally suited: from a good family, well schooled, with nothing scandalous in her past. She was naturally shy, however. She didn't meet men on her own and her social circle was almost nonexistent, so she wasn't meeting former classmates' eligible brothers or the like. Here, her parents did the requisite spadework, finding potential husband material by working their network of friends and associates. She went on dates, and it was all pleasant enough, but the boys her parents preferred—the ones with better prospects—found her lacking. It was her mother, of all people, who explained this one evening in the kitchen when Emily had returned from yet another failed date. She would undoubtedly produce pretty children, her mother explained, but that was not enough. *You have to try harder, my dear.* If she didn't, she would never find a suitable husband. She'd end up one of those sad women who hovered in the middle of things, the color being drained out of her little by little, until she became completely invisible, even to her husband and children.

She never said, *We just want you to be happy.*

In addition to struggling to find a spouse, Emily struggled to find employment. She would've been happiest behind the counter at a flower shop, waiting on customers all day, or working day care like Lady Diana Spencer. But that wouldn't do, and so Emily's parents gently nudged her into a variety of positions, one after the other as each, invariably, proved not to be an ideal fit.

She was working in an art gallery when she met Mikhail. Her parents considered it the low point in her struggle to find a calling, one step away from working in that flower shop. Emily didn't know anything about art and so embarrassed herself on a daily basis, but the owner was a friend of her mother and had just lost his last helper. He needed someone attractive and pleasant to greet visitors and pour champagne and Emily could certainly do those things. It was meant to be temporary, only until he found someone more suitable who could also run the office and had the right temperament for selling ridiculously overpriced art to skeptical people.

It was just Emily's luck that Mikhail walked into the gallery one day. He'd come to see the work of a rising star by special appointment before the show was to open that weekend. Emily wasn't even meant to be the one to show Mikhail around; the owner, smelling a big sale, had planned to handle it, but his car broke down on his way to the gallery. That left Emily to handle the notoriously prickly, rich Russian billionaire who was coming in to find something to decorate a loo in one of his many properties.

He liked that Emily had nothing to say about the art that she was meant to be showing him. She remembers blushing a lot as he spent the entire time asking questions about her. How long had she worked there? Did she like working in an art gallery? And then, more personal things: Did she live nearby? Did she have a boyfriend? Was she free this weekend? Could he take her out to dinner?

When things between them turned serious, Emily thought—naïvely, or maybe hopefully—that her parents would be pleased. Mikhail was not an ogre, like many Brits had been led to believe about the oligarchs. He was smart. He came from a good family. And he was rich, not just comfortably well off. But, of course, that didn't please them. They didn't come right out and say it, but they abhorred Mikhail. They had their ideas of what his world was like, and they wanted no part of it.

They weren't wrong, as it turned out. Not completely.

The extent of his wealth was unfathomable to Emily then—and still is, if she is honest. She had no idea that people could be so wealthy, that you could have so much money that absolutely nothing was out of bounds. After a lifetime of denial—not being able to go away on fancy school trips to the Alps or getting a new car for her birthday, as all her parents' money went into propping up the family estate, trying to keep it from falling completely into ruin—Emily could suddenly have anything she wanted. It has been so overwhelming, frankly, that it's a superpower she rarely uses. She leaves it up to Mikhail to decide where they go on vacation, how they decorate the beach house at Mykonos, even when she gets a new gown. She thinks he's starting to get annoyed with her indecision. "My little mouse," he's called her on more than one occasion. Only his tone has gone from endearing to exasperated.

If I'm a mouse, it's because you made me one.

Circling back round to Lynn, that's one reason why Emily likes her so much. They're a lot alike, particularly their childhoods, but she's got one main difference. For everything Lynn has suffered, Emily can tell that she is really quite strong. It's a quiet strength; it's not like she's pushy or demanding attention or anything like that. She reminds Emily of Jesamine. Maybe it's that determination that Emily is drawn to. She knows she could count on Lynn if she had to, even though they've just met.

Emily doesn't have many friends, let alone ones like Lynn Prescott who want nothing from her. Most of the women she comes in contact with are wives of other Russian expats, all of them businessmen and oligarchs who need to make nice with Mikhail. Her interactions with these women have dwindled to almost nothing. Sometimes she feels like a princess in the fairy tale, trapped behind a forest of thorns and brambles, only she's not waiting for her prince to rescue her because it's the prince who put her there. Her social life now is almost exclusively playdates for the twins, as Mikhail wants them to grow up around Russians as much as possible, to absorb the culture and language. To prepare them for later in life. He really wants them to be more Russian than English, even though the family lives here in London.

Just thinking that she will see Lynn later that day, Emily is happy all over again. She's going to be with someone who is interested in her for being *herself*. As pathetic as it sounds, she has needed this so desperately. She cannot be just Mikhail Rotenberg's wife for the rest of her life. A purse to dispense money, a portal to favors and benefits.

Even her parents. She'd offered them the money to repair Rampshead Hall to its former glory. She'd even sell that flashy diamond necklace to do it, if that would make them happy. Her father almost took her up on the offer, she could see it in his eyes, but her mother had snapped at her as though she had offered them poison. *Have you forgotten about Ukraine? We'll not take that man's blood money*, she'd shouted dramatically before ordering Emily out of the house.

Come to think of it, that might've been the last time she'd spoken to them.

Kneeling on the floor next to her bed, still hunting for the moccasins, Emily notices something sparkly in the thick carpeting. She reaches for it and pulls it out. Funny, it's a piece of jewelry—well, hardly what she would consider jewelry these days, considering the vault of diamonds and pearls and emeralds in her dressing room. It's a little pin made of polymer, a parrot in bright, tropical colors. Something a little girl would wear. She hasn't seen it in years, though she knows where it has been kept: the top drawer of her nightstand, in a small box filled with trinkets from her childhood, all the funny little odds and ends that don't fit elsewhere but that she can't bear to get rid of. She vaguely remembers sifting through the box last night, after an excess of wine had finally turned her maudlin.

She remembers the day she got it: a family outing at the zoo. At the end of the day the Hugheses, like families everywhere, went into the gift shop. Jesamine picked out this pin for Emily, because she had been quite taken with the parrots in the aviary. She'd used her own little stash of coins to buy it for Emily because she knew it would make her happy. Emily had worn it nearly every day for a year as a reminder of how much her sister cared for her.

This silly pin.

Emily bursts into tears.

Call Jesamine, for god's sake.

But she knows it's too late.

CHAPTER 10

In the next week, Lyndsey is with Emily constantly, so much that there are times she feels like she's been swallowed whole. They see each other every day, shopping or playing tennis or going for facials at a place that Emily adores. When they're not together, Emily is texting. Sending photos of something cute one of the children has done, distracting herself during a playdate with the Russian Stepford wives, asking what Lynn wants to do that weekend.

Lyndsey sits at the desk in her cover office, dutifully reading reports from Langley while nibbling a yogurt. This whole thing with Emily is a new experience. Even her relationship with Theresa Warner, which continued after their brush with catastrophe, was never like this. She has never had such an intense friendship with another woman, not even in high school or college. Being fatherless, Lyndsey was never popular. Kids are wary of you when you're different, as though your bad fortune could rub off on them. In college, desperate not to mess up, she'd been a tireless grind with little time for socializing, intent on not blowing her one chance at getting out of her small town.

Patterns were set by the time she joined CIA. Not being able to carry cell phones inside secure facilities probably has something to do with it, she figures, since it makes it hard for her to stay in touch during the day the way people expect. She can't text during work hours, not even with a doctor's office or her mother. As Lynn Prescott, she has a cell phone with her 24/7 so she can be at the beck and call of an oligarch's lonely wife. It feels unusual and maybe borderline creepy; there's also something oddly nice about being wanted and missed *so much*. She's never had this kind of closeness, not even with a lover. Is this what relationships are supposed to be? It's like a marriage. She's expected to be another person's entire world.

It is exhausting, though. She must continually check her phone. And then—as the texts pile up—she must also curb the impulse to become grouchy. Heaven forbid she snaps at Emily. She must be patient. Even though she is expected to answer promptly, she must always take that extra second to weigh her words, to assess what she's going to say from all angles. There is no room for a slipup.

Lyndsey scrapes the bottom of the yogurt up. Emily's obsession will wear off. Lyndsey is a new toy and once Emily gets used to her, she'll slow down. Or Lyndsey will be gone by then, depending on what MI6 ultimately decides. Or if Tarasenko suddenly sees a way to deliver Morozov.

An email appears in Lyndsey's queue from a reports officer back in Russia Division. *Kim asked me to forward this to you*, it reads, strangely terse. Kim Claiborne, the boss, would not have told the reports officer why Lyndsey needs to see this report, *need to know* being held strictly on Lyndsey's mission.

It's an email from Nikki Park to Claiborne. Nikki is one of the diplomatic analysts in Russia Division. Lyndsey doesn't know her personally, only that she had been at the State Department before joining the Agency. Lyndsey skims the email: it looks like Claiborne tasked her with checking out Irina Babanina's intel. *From information we've gleaned so far, the Russian Foreign Ministry's China Division is still in the process of formulating a new China policy for President Kosygin. Given that there is no official policy, the prospect of a secret initiative to Beijing initiated by Kosygin would be of high interest to Russia watchers.*

The cell phone on Lyndsey's desk buzzes angrily. She picks it up.

It's Emily. *Tea at four??? After chasing the twins around, I need to get out of the house. Cream puff?*

Lyndsey half smiles at the text. Emily is always trying to convince her to indulge in one little luxury or another: a sweet, a cocktail, a pair of ridiculous shoes, a new spa treatment. Emily seems to feel it's her duty to get the poor little rich girl to enjoy life now that she's free of her medical malady, but these indulgences are really for Emily. These little outings are the only freedom Emily has known in the last few years. She is the Emily Hughes she was before she was sucked into Mikhail Rotenberg's orbit. When she is with Lyndsey, she is free of everyone else's expectations.

It is at these moments that Lyndsey feels sorriest for Emily. She understands how profoundly unhappy the woman is. This is when she starts to *like* her.

Lyndsey's been surprised by what slips out of Emily's mouth sometimes, that Mikhail would never approve of this or that. It's the sort of thing that all wives say now and then, but with Emily it's constant and over the most trivial matters. Why would a man as rich as Rotenberg care if his wife bought another ostrich-skin tote? Then, once or twice, Emily has pointed to another woman—usually a young blonde with the lanky physique of a model—and said, "She's exactly Mikhail's type." Lyndsey winces every time and can barely keep from telling her to stop. Every comment is relatively harmless on its own, but when taken all together it paints a sad picture of what is going on inside the Rotenberg marriage.

Lyndsey texts back: *Absolutely. Sounds delish. Cream puffs it is.*

They sit at a small booth at a fancy little patisserie in West London. On the plate in front of them is an assortment of bijou-perfect clouds of pastry and cream. The store advertises that their choux is in the French style, which is to say the thinnest, most delicate shells of pastry filled with an ungodly amount of flavored whipped cream.

Emily pops one whole into her mouth, chewing slowly and with obvious relish. When she catches Lyndsey watching her, her cheeks turn pink. "You must ignore me when I'm being such a pig."

Inwardly, Lyndsey winces but . . . it's an opening. She picks up one of the tiny choux. "You're not a pig. I think you're entitled to a few of these after what you've been through. You know—what happened out at your place."

Emily freezes. She knows exactly what Lyndsey is referring to.

Lyndsey toys with the pastry on her plate. "You know, I'd be happy to listen, if you want to talk about it. You've never brought it up, never mentioned it in any way. It must've been terrifying . . ."

Emily's still quiet, but you can tell she's mulling it over. Undoubtedly, she's had little to no opportunity to talk about such a traumatic experience. She should welcome this.

Her eyes flit left and right to see if anyone might be listening, if the couple in the next booth seem to be paying *too* much attention. "The home invasion, you mean?" she asks sotto voce.

"Is that what it was? Burglars?" Emily gives a half shrug. *There is something she doesn't think she should talk about, something she's suppressing.*

Lyndsey continues. "The frightening part is that whoever did it must've known you had private security. They were armed to the teeth. That seems pretty ballsy for a burglar." When Emily says nothing, Lyndsey presses a step further. "And what did the police say? Have they found out who did it?"

"We haven't heard from the police since the day it happened."

"It must've been scary . . . all the shooting, and there you were with your children. It must've made you angry, to be so helpless to protect them . . ."

Emily's eyes get that faraway look in them. Her shoulders hunch and her breathing shallows. *She's remembering and she's frightened*—but she says nothing.

She's shutting down. It could be because Lyndsey is a new acquaintance, and Emily doesn't know if she can trust her yet. Or maybe she's so used to Mikhail's controlling nature that she doesn't dare tell anyone what she really thinks.

Lyndsey decides to be more direct. "You don't think it's because of who your husband is?" After a big step forward, she takes one small step in retreat. "Oh, I'm sorry, I didn't mean to be rude. It's not like I know anything about him, only what I've heard on television. I mean, what *is* an oligarch, anyway?"

Emily's eyes go slightly unfocused. *She's deciding what to tell me.* "I know what you're thinking but my husband barely knows Viktor Kosygin. A man in Mikhail's position *has* to be on friendly terms with the government. From what Mikhail tells me, you can't do business without the authorities reaching out to you from time to time."

That much is true, Lyndsey knows. But Rotenberg was more than a mere business associate to Putin. Omni Bank floated millions and millions of dollars in low- and no-interest loans to the government during Ukraine, according to Arya. Who knows what Kosygin expects from him?

Lyndsey decides to make one last push. She holds Emily's nervous gaze. "And how would you feel if you found out Mikhail was more culpable than you think? If he had been involved in Russian government business? Would it bother you?"

Emily's stare is frightened, then hot, then shrouded. She morphs before Lyndsey's eyes, wanting to be seen but at the same time, afraid to let anyone know what she really thinks. *She probably hasn't shared her true feelings with anyone in years.*

And she isn't going to today. "I don't understand what you mean. Mikhail has nothing to do with the government, no more than I, a British citizen, could be held responsible for what Whitehall does. It's just that we're conditioned by the media to be suspicious of anything that comes out of Russia."

She doesn't really mean that. Lyndsey can tell by the tone of Emily's voice and the wavering distrust in her eyes. It's what she's been coached to say.

Still: she doesn't say unequivocally that Mikhail is *not* a criminal. There may be hope. Not all is lost. She might open up to Lyndsey eventually, when they've had time to build trust.

Lyndsey decides to give her a break; Emily can take only so much pressure. She leans back in the chair and reaches for her espresso. "I'm sure you're right."

They finish their coffees and have the remaining choux boxed up for the children. As they wait for the check, Emily tilts her head. "You sound just like my sisters . . . They've asked the same questions, you know. They're very clever, those two, and they're rather suspicious of him."

Lyndsey fixes Emily with a firm look, so there is no mistaking her meaning. "But *you* wouldn't be involved in anything illegal, would you? No matter what your husband may have done, it's not like *you're* part of it. Because otherwise, I don't think you'd be able to sleep at night. You'd want to do something about it, because you're a good person, right, Emily?"

But Emily has no answer for her, except a nervous laugh before she gets up and exits the patisserie.

CHAPTER 11

Another playdate for the twins. You'd think Emily would be able to send them off with Miss Wilkinson (who has stayed on despite her tremendous fright, thanks to the nice bonus they've given her) but no: Mikhail insists that Emily go. He says it's because Emily needs to get out of the house so people won't gossip that she's become agoraphobic after the break-in or that there's something wrong with her, but she knows there's another reason.

"The car is waiting out front," Mikhail growls as she runs by, looking for a shoe that Tatiana has shed somewhere along the way from the playroom.

"I'm going as fast as I can," Emily replies, letting a hint of anger creep into her tone. She's doing *him* a favor, after all. The least he can do is act like he knows it.

While it is lovely to see the twins enjoying themselves, these little outings are no fun for Emily. She feels judged every minute by the Russian trophy wives: what she wears, how she looks, how she acts. She's bombarded with little suggestions, all in imperfect, heavily accented English. Lose weight, take up barre and Pilates, dye her hair even blonder than it already is. Obviously, they see some deficiency that Emily does not. The Russian wives view their marriages as their jobs and they'll be damned if they're going to be ousted for a younger model—the way *they* replaced the wives before them. Have any of them asked the first wives how they feel after being deposed? Emily suspects they're happier.

Unlike the first wives, the trophy wives signed prenups, so if they get dumped, they take next to nothing with them. They'll get their clothes and the cheaper jewelry and furs, maybe one of the smaller properties if they're lucky. For most of them it's back to Russia and on the hunt for a new husband, some sad man a rung or two down the ladder from the one they just lost. Emily wonders if the same fate is waiting for her . . . only, would any self-respecting Englishman take her for a wife? He'd have to love her *a lot* to take on all the questions that would hang over her for the rest of her life. Or as long as her story lingers on the internet, which is to say *forever.*

The Bentley deposits them at Oksana Agapova's lovely place. It's also in north London, but not as exclusive an address as The Bishops Avenue. Mikhail insisted that Emily go today because Oksana's husband is quite prominent in their circle, the president of a Russian oil interest with his fingers in several other pies. While he is not one of Kosygin's cronies—and miraculously managed to remain in London despite being tight with Putin—you can't be in the oil business in Russia and not be connected to the Apparatus. What happens today will get back to Kosygin's people. Mikhail wants Emily to send a message.

Oksana's children are older than Kit and Tatiana, so the Agapovs also invited a bunch of other Russians to finesse the situation, make the ulterior motives less obvious. There is a lively mix, with the twins being the youngest of the bunch, all the way up to teenagers. Loud shrieks and exclamations in Russian drift in from these rooms, along with the clattering of shoes on polished floors. The nannies take turns riding herd, two or three at a time remaining with the children while the rest slink out of view for a smoke and a gripe session.

That leaves Emily with the mothers. They sit in a circle on precious antique chairs in a perfectly curated room, thankfully tasteful by Russian expat standards (but still eye-rolling by English ones). Oksana's husband aspires to be accepted by the English gentry—poor fool, to aspire to such an impossible task—and so he hired an English interior decorator for his home and office and an English tutor for the children and his wife, trying to flatten her flamboyant Muscovite accent.

The wives eye Emily over their wineglasses like they're vultures and she's the rabbit carcass in the middle of the road. She's food, basically, but who's to know if she's been poisoned? Anxiety makes her suck down the chardonnay more quickly than is prudent.

Oksana, ever the gracious hostess, is the first one to pounce. "So, my dear Emily, we hear there was excitement at your house recently. You must tell us." This sets off a round of murmurs, more ghoulish than sympathetic.

Emily feigns ignorance. "Not much to tell, really. It was all in the papers."

Glittering eyes fall on her. "You never tell the papers the truth, this we know."

"We want the *inside* information."

"Two of your security guards killed, yes?"

"I heard they got inside your house . . . ?"

The questions flap around her. Emily ignores the chardonnay this time and takes a deep breath to steady herself. While it is difficult to remain calm, she knows she must. *Stay on message*, Mikhail had stressed. *What we say and how we act in the wake of the break-in is very, very important. We are being judged. We mustn't appear guilty.*

Time for Mikhail's precisely if strangely worded message. She takes a deep breath. "We don't understand how this could've happened. But if we gave the impression that we were deserving of some sort of corrective measure, then we are ready to make whatever amends are necessary. If we've erred." It might seem like an admission of guilt, but Mikhail insisted that it's not. *We're not guilty of wrongdoing, but if we are, we're sorry.* Emily feels like she's reciting an apology from a teleprompter.

Nervous sideways glances are exchanged, or maybe the wives are just disappointed that there's no denial, that she and Mikhail were not going to flail about like stunned birds inviting further attack.

There's disappointment—but relief, too. Not from all of them; some undoubtedly want Mikhail to go down. But a few of them seem almost grateful that Mikhail is capitulating, that he isn't going to dig in his heels or turn traitor by doing something regrettable. That would only make it harder on all the oligarchs, both with their British hosts or the new dictator in Moscow who holds their lives in his hands. They all know how precarious their lives are: Mikhail could have done, well, anything . . . or he could have done nothing at all. Actions are misinterpreted all the time but it hardly matters.

Sometimes, there only needs to be a pretext so that punitive action can be taken.

Emily is outside the playroom, hiding in the corner and counting the minutes until she can leave without scandalizing everyone, when she is approached by Nadija Sidorova. She is a third wife and a little younger than Emily. Emily's not sure she even has a child, or, as the wives sometimes joke, an insurance policy.

Nadija, with her storkishly long legs, eyes Emily like she's an exotic creature she's only heard of but never seen outside of Animal Planet.

"Have we met?" Emily's voice is halfway between civil and pointed. She's tired and wants to be anywhere but here. An Englishman would understand her tone but it's wasted on Nadija, bouncing off the broad space between her eyes.

"I'm Boris Sidorov's wife." She extends a hand that is capped off with neon-orange dragon lady nails. Emily shakes it once reluctantly. Nadija's look is all pity and curiosity but at least it seems sincere. "Are you okay? You seem upset."

Emily doesn't want to be engaged. She wants this woman to go away. "Never better."

Nadija looks left and right, almost comically, but the two are alone. Emily was trying to find a maid to fetch her wrap without raising alarm bells. There is no one within earshot, though it's just a matter of time. "You don't know, do you? I told Boris that you didn't know."

"Know *what*?" Now Emily is getting cross.

"The reason behind . . ." She nods vaguely north, in the direction of Hampstead Heath and Billionaires Row. Emily's home. "It was Kosygin. He gave the order."

It's funny: Emily has suspected this, of course, but hearing it said aloud is ridiculously disconcerting, like she's just been told she has cancer. It's like gravity has suddenly been turned off and her insides are floating. The contents of her stomach—two cups of tea, a mimosa, no food for what seems like days—pushes up her throat.

Emily has suspected this was the case because who else would dare go after her husband? To hear Mikhail tell it, he has been able to manage

Russia's new strongman. He's agreed to lend Kosygin money. He's advised Kosygin on problems both personal and national—though he has not given Emily any details.

Nadija grasps Emily's forearm and pulls her deeper into the alcove, farther away from the rest of the expats. Now they are cut off from view and it's just the two of them. Up close, Emily sees Nadija is really very pretty, in a milk-fed way. That won't last long, of course. Being married to an oligarch takes its toll. No matter how well Nadija takes care of herself, she will be looking over her shoulder for the rest of her married life, for Boris is known as a ladies' man. In the Russian expat community, it's impossible *not* to stray: there's a constant stream of beautiful young women flowing through. The divorced men bring in a rotating cast of Russian starlets and Eastern European models. Not to mention the daughters of these titans of Russian industry—though most of them have English and Continental swains, to be sure, but it's not unheard of for the odd girl with a daddy issue to fall for her father's best friend.

When it comes to women, there is no shame among this lot. Machismo is coin of the realm to Russian males.

But Emily doesn't think Nadija Sidorova has the grim determination of, say, their hostess. She knows she's an endangered species and is counting her days. Hopefully she has stockpiled a little cash on the side or has been hoarding her jewels.

Emily feels sorry for her, but she also has the nagging feeling that Nadija feels sorry for *her*.

Emily pulls her arm back. "Kosygin wouldn't have ordered the attack. That's impossible. He and my husband are close." She realizes that sounds ridiculous, even as the words leave her lips. *Keep your friends close and your enemies closer.* Machiavelli probably has nothing on Viktor Kosygin.

Nadija's hazel eyes widen. "You haven't heard," she gasps. For a moment, she looks torn, like she might walk away from Emily and leave her to her fate.

And in that second, Emily *knows*. Mikhail has done something terrible, something grossly arrogant and stupid. Whatever it is, he's signed a death warrant for them both.

No one would tell her because why should they risk their own necks? It's not like they have friends, only friendly competitors. No one likes Emily very much because she's British. They tolerate her because she's Mikhail's wife and because she can be useful in her own right: an introduction to an important British person, a recommendation to the posh day school. But they don't forget that she's part of the tribe that looks down on them. Who reminds them every day through hundreds of little slights that, though they may be rich, they're also *Russian trash*.

Now it's Emily's turn to grip Nadija's arm. "Tell me. What have you heard?" Emily won't let her go until she speaks.

Nadija is frightened. Maybe she's realizing what her little bout of pity is going to cost her. She's going to be the one to tell Emily the awful secret. Boris might divorce her over this. But it's her fault; she's the one who opened her mouth.

"Your husband slept with one of Kosygin's mistresses," she blurts out.

For an awful moment, the words just hang in the air. Emily doesn't think, *That's impossible*. She's not that naïve. She figures Mikhail has cheated on her, though for the sake of her health she hopes it's not been more than once or twice. It would take a superhuman effort not to, not with all this prize flesh paraded before him every day. But to take up with one of Kosygin's mistresses? Has Mikhail believed his own propaganda, started to believe that he was untouchable? Or was he merely suicidal?

Seeing that Emily is struck speechless, Nadija fills her in. One of Mikhail's special tasks, it appears, is to handle Kosygin's mistresses. Now that Kosygin is the big man in Russia, they may be thinking of embarrassing him.

"Someone told Kosygin that your husband has slept with one of these women."

Emily's stomach roils. "What's her name?"

Nadija shrugs, but Emily isn't sure about the sincerity of that shrug. She might not know who the slut is—or she just doesn't want to tell.

Emily wants to tell her to take her stories to someone else. The wives, they all know the game plan under such circumstances: deny, denounce. Stand by your husband.

But Emily doesn't protest. She feels in her gut that what Nadija says is true. There have been strange phone calls and texts lately. Times when Emily knew he was thinking of someone else, when he'd get that faraway look in his eyes. But she figured these were old flames, her husband thinking back on some slag he'd dated during the times between Anya, his first wife, and her. Stupidly, Emily never pressed. She agreed to live in a universe in which her husband was not to be questioned or doubted.

"I'm sorry," Nadija says before prying Emily's hand from her arm and darting away.

Emily goes to the powder room and locks the door. She pulls out her phone and types "Kosygin's mistress" into Google. A few images pop up, thumbnails of leggy, pretty, young women. They look so similar that they could be churned out of a factory: thin, cat-eyed, sleek haired. There is something predatory in their expressions, the way they stand.

She remembers one terrible time when she suspected Mikhail was having an affair. Emily never met the other woman, never knew what she looked like; she was determined to keep the high ground. She was the mother of his children, after all, and that came with a measure of dignity. She couldn't start whining and clinging or he would lose all respect for her. She knew that much. If there had been others, she told herself, they must have meant very little because Mikhail never let her catch even a glimpse of them. But this one had been different. She began texting him often, signaling that she was on the decline. He would pull out his phone, look at it with disgust, then put it away unanswered. It was plain what was happening. Even Westie was fed up. He'd wanted to tell Emily something at the time, she could tell.

Now Emily thinks: maybe it wasn't any old mistress. Maybe it was one of *Kosygin's* mistresses, either begging him for more money or, perhaps, threatening Mikhail for whatever indiscretion they'd committed together.

Yes, she feels it down to her marrow: Nadija is telling her the truth.

Emily is sick all the way to The Bishops Avenue. She can't even respond properly to her children as they head home in the car; she leaves it up to Miss Wilkinson to answer their questions and wipe sticky hands. "I have a headache," Emily tells the nanny as an excuse. Well, it's true; the news has made her positively ill. She wants to crawl into bed and pull the covers over her head and never, ever come out.

Luckily, Mikhail isn't there when they return. There's no telling what she might've done if she'd seen his lying face. She wants to rail, to scream, to shake her fists at him. To have him feel her pain and know how badly he's betrayed her. It's not just the sleeping around—as bad as that is—but to put them all in a bad position with his boss, the omnipotent beast master.

Now she must cool down and figure out the right course of action. Confronting him would be a mistake. All Russians seem to have bad tempers—something in their DNA—but Mikhail is among the worst. Though, she supposes, he wouldn't have gotten to where he is without being feared. However, that was not the way Emily was raised. In her family, there's no excuse to be beastly to your spouse, especially when you're in the wrong. But he is the billionaire, not Emily.

She's not in a horrible position, as oligarchs' wives go. For one thing, they don't have a prenuptial agreement. Surprising, isn't it? She thinks Mikhail didn't insist because that way it would look like he had proposed because he really loved her. Maybe he'd thought Emily needed to be convinced of his sincerity, or her parents. Maybe the lack of a prenup indicated he expected it would last more than five or ten years.

That sincerity, if it ever existed, has been absent for a while.

And now he's wronged her. He's put himself in a very bad position. In a divorce, she could get quite a bit of his fortune. If she had proof.

She wants to confront him, but she needs to be smart. She needs to play the long game and not go for a quick bloodletting. To forego the satisfaction of telling him that she knows what he did.

But first: she must find proof.

The sad thing—as she wipes her browser history and dabs her tears—is that she really loved him once. When they were first dating, he tried so hard to sweep her off her feet. That was probably what made her fall for him: no one had ever cared that much what she thought of them. They were very happy at first, even Mikhail: Emily truly believes that. He loves to explain things to people but especially women, to show them how to do things properly, tell them which books to read, how to dress. She was an innocent thing then, over a decade younger than him, inexperienced, his perfect type. That changed after a few years, of course. Inevitable in any marriage, not just theirs. You disappoint each other in countless tiny ways. Reality sets in. Nothing is perfect forever, even for people with endless supplies of money. If anything, having money makes it more difficult.

This afternoon, as she paces and tries to calm herself before Mikhail returns, she feels all the love she ever had for him drain away like blood from a corpse.

She shall be bloodless by the time he returns.

She can no longer be the fairy princess living behind a wall of thorns—living in a bubble, if she is honest with herself. The time of indulgence and self-pity is over.

She shall be a completely different woman. She has to be.

CHAPTER 12

This afternoon, Lyndsey is with Emily at The Bishops Avenue. It's an overcast day that threatens rain, so they are in the conservatory with the children for an afternoon of play. Set inside the giant, glass-walled space is an enormous dollhouse, elaborately detailed and seven stories tall. A ridiculously expensive folly, it's the kind of thing you might expect to find in Buckingham Palace or the residence of the last tsar and something Lyndsey could only have dreamed about as a child, but it is obviously wasted on the twins. Too young, perhaps, or—though Lyndsey doesn't want to believe it—too spoiled.

Tatiana throws piece after piece of its delicate miniature furniture at her brother. It sets Lyndsey's nerves on edge and yet she can't let it show. After all, a rich person wouldn't care what someone else's child does with her toys. She could crush a doll to a pulp underfoot and Mommy would only buy you a replacement.

She drops to the floor next to Tatiana. "How about if we set the baby in that chair?" she says as she rights the tumbled chair, then sets the tiny doll that has been made to look like Tatiana on it. For a moment, there is calm. Then, Tatiana knocks it aside a second time, sending the doll tumbling ass over teakettle while squealing with delight.

"Tatiana, behave yourself or Mummy's friend will think you have no manners," Emily says, but Lyndsey can tell she isn't truly upset. It's the sort of thing she says when there is another person in the room.

Emily sighs exaggeratedly. "I swear she has gotten so much worse in the past year. And yet Kit is such a darling. Never any backtalk, always so good." She smiles at her son, who is picking up his sister's scattered toys with delicate precision, brows furrowed in concentration. "Maybe it's because he understands his father expects a lot from him. Boys being so important in Russian culture and all."

"But what about Tatiana? Does your husband act the same way toward her?"

Emily laughs. "Hardly. He tells her that she's a princess. My parents are appalled."

Emily's parents are never around, Lyndsey has noticed. The same is true for Emily's sisters. Though Emily mentions her sisters and parents not infrequently, as she has just done, acting as if they talk constantly, though the evidence suggests otherwise.

Lyndsey's time with Emily is usually in the middle of the day. Emily has yet to ask her to go out in the evening. No drinks or dinners or dancing, no openings at art galleries or fetes at mansions. To Lyndsey, Emily seems to be a homebody, preferring the company of her children and trusted friends to being surrounded by strangers. All the more reason those little asides about her parents and sisters are so telling. *Emily misses them.*

Emily sits up suddenly, bright-eyed and grinning. "I have the most fun idea. Why don't you stay here with me while you're in London?"

The offer strikes Lyndsey as strange, though maybe this is the kind of thing rich people do: invite complete strangers to move into their homes. The unexpectedness of it momentarily knocks Lyndsey for a loop. And she is instantly wary. It could be a trap. But, of course, she must smother any reaction.

Emily beams. "That way we can spend as much time together as possible while you're in the city, see? You won't be in London long—didn't you say you were leaving at the end of summer?"

Maybe it's a throwback to boarding school. You end up pining for those childhood days when you were surrounded by your friends all the time and want to relive the relatively easier times of childhood.

Or maybe she needs someone to fill up her lonely evenings. Emily occasionally mentions going out to an event for Mikhail but these are rarer than Lyndsey would've expected. It seems Mikhail isn't home every night: Emily has let that drop, each time with a hint of resentment in her voice.

"I don't know what to say. That's extraordinarily generous of you . . ."

Emily waves a hand airily. "We have empty guest rooms and it's not like you'd be intruding on our privacy. As you've already seen, there are plenty of people living here. Mikhail likes to be surrounded by his entourage at all times. It's like a perpetual slumber party." She drops her voice. "You'd be doing me a favor, really. The house is always full, yes, but they're all Mikhail's cronies. There's no one here for me. It can be quite lonely. I thought it would be fun to have someone on my side for a change." She gives an exaggerated pout, but it's not really pretend.

Lyndsey's mind races to work out the pros and cons. Living inside would make it much easier to continue her assessment. She'd have an excuse if she's found snooping. On the other hand, it would be extremely stressful and dangerous. She'd be living in the enemy camp. There'd be no downtime; she'd have to live her cover 24/7, an exhausting proposition.

Would Langley let her do it? she wonders.

Or Davis? How would he feel about her doing something so dangerous?

She needs to buy time. "It sounds like a lot of fun. And it would be so much nicer staying here than in that hotel . . . but I can't help but think you'd get awfully sick of me."

Emily's laugh is genuine. "I doubt that would happen. The past week has been the most fun I've had in a long time."

"Well . . . let me sit down with my calendar and see if it would work. Give me a day to think about it, okay?"

A slight, quizzical look flits over Emily's eyes—*What's there to think about?*—but she just pats Lyndsey's hand. "Of course. No pressure, as you Yanks say. Have you ever thought what an incredibly American expression that is? 'No pressure'! That's what you Americans are all about, aren't you? Pressure!"

Lyndsey smiles at her as cheerily as possible. *You don't know the half of it.*

Once she's back in her office in the nondescript building, the first call she makes is to Davis.

"It's a windfall, Lyndsey," he says without missing a beat. "An absolute windfall."

She feels slightly put off by his enthusiasm. "You don't think it's too risky?"

"I trust you will know if they suspect something. You can handle yourself." This is a vote of confidence, though a more cynical person might say he was shifting the burden onto her shoulders. She doesn't like that there's a question in the back of her mind with Davis that there isn't with Claiborne, because of their shared past. It's made her job that much stickier.

"There's something else you should know," Davis adds. "Whitehall is absolutely livid. They say CIA wants to make Kosygin out to be a bad guy because he's ex-KGB. Whitehall wants us to just give him a chance."

"They're sticking their heads in the sand."

"Typical diplomatic corps cowardice," Davis says without flinching. "I don't need to tell you that a stronger relationship between Russia and China could be disastrous for the West. Given China's worldwide economic influence, it could be catastrophic for the Western order."

He's right, but it's difficult to admit. And given China's historic reluctance to interfere in world events, it will be hard for experts to admit as a possibility.

She hangs up and then calls Claiborne's office back at Langley. Once her boss is on the line, Lyndsey tells her about the opportunity to move into the Rotenberg household.

"Is it necessary for the mission?" her boss asks.

"It sounds like it might be."

But Claiborne is circumspect. "If you want to risk it, that's your call. But ask yourself if it's worth getting in so deep. If something happens, there'd be no backup in the immediate vicinity. We might not be able get in to help you in a reasonable amount of time. Do we know what communications are like inside? It might be hard to get in touch with us. They probably monitor their Wi-Fi, but do they monitor phones connecting to cellular? You'd think someone like Rotenberg would be paranoid enough to have that kind of precaution in place."

She considers asking Claiborne about Davis's response. It's a very long shot, but you could argue that it's a counterintelligence issue. He might be trying to control her. It's just a seed, but she's starting to wonder if Davis is playing mind games with her, if something else is going on. He could be counting on their history, knowing that she might subconsciously do this solely to please him. Every case officer does this instinctively to a small degree, but you shouldn't do it to colleagues. The trick is to realize what you're doing and to stop yourself. The bad ones enjoy it too much and try to control everyone in their life.

Is he wrong to ask? But she lets the moment pass.

"I don't want you to take any unnecessary risks," Claiborne says again. "Rotenberg is getting more important by the minute, yes, but we didn't send you to London to work for MI6 . . ." She trails off, leaving the rest implied. *Don't let Davis lead you around*, she means. Maybe Claiborne understands more than she is letting on. "The longer we leave Tarasenko to his own devices in Moscow, the more likely he is to renege on our deal. You need to stay on top of him. Rotenberg is not your priority, not yet at least."

Lyndsey has barely ended the call when her personal cell phone buzzes. She picks it up: *Theresa Warner* flashes on the screen. A wave of embarrassment passes over her. She forgot to get back to her the other day.

She presses the button. "Theresa! It's good to hear from you. I'm sorry I didn't answer your text. It's been so busy here . . ."

"No doubt." Theresa's slightly patrician voice is familiar. She sounds tired—and irritated, not pleased that she had to track Lyndsey down. Or maybe it's something else.

"Is everything okay? Brian?" Theresa's son has always been her first priority.

"Brian's fine."

"And Richard?" Lyndsey almost wishes she didn't have to bring up Theresa's husband. It's got to be a strain: the man's only been home for a few months. Theresa needs someone to talk to, but she lost most of her friends in the years after Richard's supposed death. Lyndsey winces to think what a bad friend she has been, leaving Theresa to go through this on her own.

The things women endure for their husbands. It's inevitable that she thinks of Emily and Mikhail.

Theresa laughs but it's unnaturally brittle. "Richard? He's going back to work, if you can believe it."

"At Langley?" Lyndsey *can't* believe it. You'd think there'd be a prohibition against it. At the least, a series of visits with an Agency shrink. No one in their right mind would let him back in the building so soon. He's too much of a security risk.

Not to mention that she was just talking to Claiborne—certainly she'd know if Richard was cleared to go back into the building. But she hadn't said a thing.

"When will you be back in Washington?" Theresa asks, interrupting Lyndsey's thoughts.

"I don't have any trips planned, sorry. Is something wrong? Is there something—"

"Wait a minute." She sounds wobbly, and now she hesitates. In the background, there are footsteps.

"Who are you talking to?" It's a man's voice, muffled. Richard.

"It's Lyndsey," Theresa says.

"Let me talk to her."

There's a pause as she hands over the cell phone, Lyndsey wondering all the while what is going on. It's not like she's been chummy with Richard—ever.

"Hello, Lyndsey. How are you?" It's Richard's voice but it doesn't sound like him at all. He's tense and guarded and distant. There's a heavy note, like a shoe waiting to drop.

But Lyndsey doesn't want to believe the worst. *It's nothing. So, he's acting strangely . . . It's normal after what he's been through.* "Hi, Richard. How are you?"

"I can't complain. I hear you're in London."

"Yes. There are worse places to be stationed in Europe, I suppose. They could've sent me to Siberia."

"Yes." A stiff, awkward silence stretches between them. Has she made a gaff bringing up Siberia? Is it too much like a Russian gulag? Has it brought back unpleasant memories? All she hears is Richard's breathing on the other end, until Theresa mercifully takes the phone from him.

"Brian needs your help with his homework," Theresa says to Richard as she ushers him away. Then, she says into the phone in a near whisper, "I need to talk to someone, and no one will take my calls at Langley. No one."

Lyndsey doesn't like the sound of this.

"I need your help, Lyndsey, but I obviously can't really talk right now." Meaning her husband is nearby, listening. "I'll call you later, when I'm alone. Okay? Answer the phone this time." The last part is strained.

Lyndsey is filled with remorse for not texting her back before. Something is wrong and she's thousands of miles and several time zones away. What can she possibly do to help Theresa? "I will. I promise."

She feels a twinge as she puts her phone away. Theresa is not the only one to whom Lyndsey has been a bad friend.

The next day, after Claiborne's questions about security inside, Lyndsey decides to stop by the Rotenberg mansion unexpectedly. It will be a good test; she's never been by when they haven't been expecting her. She brings a device with her that makes technical measurements from signals it grabs out of the air. It will help her better understand how communications are being monitored, what safeguards might be in place. There are other things she can check out, too, such as procedures at the gatehouse, how long it takes when you're not expected, who on the security team gets alerted. If she's lucky, she'll have a few minutes alone inside without the usual housekeeper escort.

She spent the evening considering Emily's offer. Lyndsey wishes she could say that her decision is based on a thorough review of the pluses and minuses, but that would be a lie.

Objectively, there's no contest. She shouldn't do it. Too risky.

However . . . there's not a case officer alive who wouldn't jump at the chance. And the spy business is a profession for risk-takers. For show-offs, to be brutally honest, for people with perhaps too much confidence in their own abilities. For people who want to flirt with disaster to confirm just how exceptional they are.

She *knows* this, has seen this flaw in far too many of her peers, and yet . . .

She's eager to let Emily know before she changes her mind. She tells herself that from what she's seen so far, it's not especially dangerous. There are only a handful of guards on duty at any time and a perimeter wall that's scalable in an emergency. She doesn't know Volkov, the head of security, has only nodded at him once or twice, but he seems professional. He doesn't seem like the kind of man who'd shoot at one of his employer's wife's friends in a moment of confusion. She's fairly certain that she could get out of there if she really needed to. If her life depended on it.

Sure, there could be something brewing with Kosygin that she's not aware of. He seems to need to get his hands on Rotenberg's money, if the reason is murky. Everyone's antsy after Ukraine. Kosygin could have needs that CIA and MI6 aren't aware of—yet. After one failed attempt, who knows what he might try next: kidnapping a family member, poisoning, another attack on the house?

And yet . . . Lyndsey still wants to do this. Her mind, it would seem, is made up.

Before she heads out, she makes an appointment with London Station to visit the Station's technical operations lead. He's a former navy technical specialist. Very serious-minded, like a lot of the technical staff she's worked with. It's a profession that requires and values expertise and efficiency: there's not a lot of time for fooling around when you're planting bugs in enemy territory. Lyndsey finds him in a storeroom surrounded by racks of equipment and go bags. There's a sagging couch pushed against one wall—there's a lot of waiting in this profession—and a mini-fridge undoubtedly stocked with energy drinks. Tech ops officers seem to live on them.

"From what you tell me about this guy"—Rotenberg, he means—"I'd be surprised if they're not checking every packet that goes over their network." The tech ops officer has neatly kept facial hair and he runs his fingers over the part circling his mouth as he thinks. "If you use a VPN"—virtual private network—"or something else to protect your communications when you're inside, it might make them suspicious. I mean, your average Joe doesn't do that sort of thing. Considering your cover, it would be better if you use a wiped phone and laptop when you're inside, and keep your secure phone powered down so they don't detect it. Even better: don't even bring it in with you, so a nosy housekeeper doesn't come across it hidden in your things."

She bristles at the idea of carrying a second phone on her person inside the mansion. It seems like the kind of thing that's only done by people with secrets and Lynn Prescott is not the kind of person who would have secrets. She listens as the tech ops officer shows her how to use the secure cell phone and operate the VPN they've installed on her personal laptop. "You can always say it's something your family makes you do, to protect yourself," he says of the VPN, shrugging. "Rich people are quirky. But it's your choice." She nods mutely.

These precautions don't bother her much. It's all part of her training, drilled into her head since the days at the Farm. *Do this, don't do that.* Tradecraft has become second nature to her. She'll be okay living under Rotenberg's roof. The part that makes her nervous is the actual attempt to turn a member of the household, whether it's Emily or someone else. Westover is a possibility; he's the one who has access to the data. Lyndsey feels in her gut that her greater chance of success, however, is not with the sly accountant but with the wife. The British aristocrat may agree to turn on her husband, but then the question is whether she will be able to get her hands on the information they need. There's something inherently dangerous: Emily is not part of the secret world. She lives with danger—real, palpable danger—every day she's been with Mikhail Rotenberg. She's been a hair's breadth from saying something indiscreet or doing something foolish and incurring her husband's wrath. That makes Emily Rotenberg like an unexploded bomb.

Lyndsey's reconnaissance operation that afternoon pays a few dividends. The guard who screens visitors at the gate recognizes her name and buzzes her through quickly, so that was not as helpful as it might have been. She had a feeling that the security hub is in the gatehouse, where video from security cameras both inside and outside the mansion would be monitored, since she's seen nothing like this in her travels around the house so far. That's not to say there might be a hidden room somewhere, but Volkov seems to keep that business outside the house. It's a hunch.

Once inside the house, Lyndsey has her first experience walking around without Emily. Anya, the housekeeper who meets her at the door, explains that Mrs. Rotenberg is in the garden, and agrees to let Lyndsey find her way by herself. She seems happy to get on with her duties.

Lyndsey decides to use the opportunity to scout out the office wing, which Emily seems to avoid. If caught, Lyndsey can always say that she got mixed up and turned around: everyone complains that the house is a poorly laid out maze. They'd be apt to give her the benefit of the doubt—the first time. As she walks toward the hall that leads to Mikhail Rotenberg's home office, however, she hears voices. She recognizes Rotenberg's baritone, even if she can't make out what he is saying. He's speaking in Russian and, while her Russian is good, she can only make out every fourth or fifth word. He's too far away. The other voice she's pretty sure is Arthur Westover's. He's also speaking Russian but without a strong Muscovite accent. He learned his Russian in school, not on the ground.

She pauses. As much as she'd like to know what they're talking about, she doesn't want to be caught. She could probably explain her actions to a servant, but at this stage in the relationship with the Rotenberg family, she doesn't want to make the patriarch suspicious. She follows her trail back, then onto the sweeping terrace and down the path to Emily's favorite outdoor spot.

Lyndsey rounds an overgrown clump of maiden grass to see Emily sitting with another woman. They're still a distance away so Lyndsey can't make out who the other woman is, but she feels a slight twinge of concern: that's where she and Emily had their first tête-à-tête. It feels funny to see her there with someone else.

She quickens her step, as though there is some disaster to be averted. "I hope it's not too much of a bother, dropping in unannounced like this . . . I wanted to tell you I've made my decision," she calls out cheerfully as she approaches. She's not worried in the least; Emily is so naturally easygoing that Lyndsey can't imagine her ever being cross with her.

Emily is smiling at her, as expected. Happy, as always, to see her.

So unsuspecting. So trusting.

Lyndsey turns, expecting to be introduced to the other woman, expecting a stranger . . .

Only it's not a stranger. Lyndsey recognizes the woman immediately.

It's someone she used to know. Someone she used to work with at Langley.

The woman sitting with Emily Rotenberg is a spy.

CHAPTER 13

Somehow—as the three women sit together in the garden, sipping champagne—Lyndsey manages to keep her curiosity in check.

"I was driving to a charity committee meeting when—wham! My car was broadsided by a delivery van." Emily tells the story with a grin on her face and a champagne flute in her hand. "There I was on the side of the road, trying to figure out what to do—call the charity and cancel? Call Westie to swing by to take me to the meeting? Go to hospital to see if I'm suffering whiplash?—when this angel pulls up and offers me a ride."

"She looked like she was in shock," the Good Samaritan says quietly.

"Mikhail wouldn't have wanted me to accept a ride from a stranger," Emily continues. "And considering the recent home invasion, it might seem like an unwise choice, but what could I do? And look at her!" Emily gestures at her guest. "She's hardly a homicidal maniac or serial killer. And it turned out that she knows one of the women on the committee, Nigella Cumberland, so I knew right then and there that Dani had to be a good person."

Emily thinks the whole thing was an accident, a coincidence for which she is grateful to have met a good person. A new friend.

Lyndsey, silent throughout, knows it was anything but.

Lyndsey checks her watch: she has two hours to dry-clean herself before meeting up with Dani Childs. She sent a message to Langley asking for everything they had on Dani but knows there's not enough time to go through headquarters to set up a meeting. Plus, she doesn't want to risk a proposed meeting getting nixed: it was a bad shock, seeing a former friend from CIA turn up at a meeting with her target. She needs to get to the bottom of this.

So, Lyndsey reaches out to Dani via a risky message through LinkedIn, where Dani has an account touting her skills as a researcher and investigator. Yup, this is the same woman Lyndsey knows from Langley. *We must talk.*

Lyndsey first met Dani Childs at the Farm, the two of them assigned to a firearms refresher course. Dani was just out of the clandestine service trainees' program that Lyndsey had graduated from two years earlier. Those two years normally were significant, the difference between someone being introduced to the world of espionage and someone who was out there living it. The two women fell in together, sensing they had more in common than they did with the others in the class. One night in the sprawling cafeteria, killing time before lights out, she and Dani swapped stories over beer and pretzels. She learned that Dani had joined the Agency right after graduation from Boston College. She'd never considered working at the Agency—she thought she might go into police work, plus she wasn't sure how well the Agency treated Black employees—and was surprised to have been given this opportunity. Lyndsey gave an abbreviated version of her story, skipping the part about her work with postdocs on a lie-detecting computer program, and focused on growing up fatherless in a small Pennsylvania town. How she, too, was still surprised to find herself at CIA—though perhaps not for the same reasons as Dani.

Their friendship took the most likely course, working at a place that sent you on frequent overseas assignments: it was spotty. Lyndsey had been sorry to learn that, as the years ticked by, Dani's career foundered. It happened; the washout rate among case officers was not insignificant. They drifted apart further, and Lyndsey was not surprised to hear a year ago that Dani had left the Agency.

All the more reason for her surprise at seeing Dani Childs with Emily Rotenberg.

Maybe you couldn't rule out some incredible coincidence, such as family friends, but Lyndsey didn't think so. It would be too outlandish: a former intel officer just happens to make the acquaintance of MI6's hottest target? No, Lyndsey would bet a week's wages that Dani is here on a job.

The only question is, if not for CIA, then for whom?

Hence, the request—no, demand—that they meet.

Lyndsey had done her homework last night. After leaving Emily, she went back to the office to use secure communications. Her first email was to Claiborne, and Lyndsey is grateful to see a reply in her queue this morning, a little help before she heads out to meet with Dani.

CHILDS RESIGNED IN 2019. RECORDS SHOW THAT SHE HAS BEEN SELF-EMPLOYED IN PRIVATE INTELLIGENCE, THOUGH WE HAVE HEARD THAT SHE MAY BE WORKING WITH INTENT, ED MARTIN'S PRIVATE INVESTIGATIONS AND RISK ASSESSMENT FIRM.

ED MARTIN IS FORMER AGENCY. HE WAS A CASE OFFICER IN EUROPEAN AND SOUTH AMERICA DIVISIONS FOR TWELVE YEARS BEFORE LEAVING TO START INTENT WITH TREVOR CONWAY, FORMER MI6. INTENT HAS A GOOD REPUTATION PUBLICLY, THOUGH BOTH CIA AND MI6 HAVE HAD ISSUES WITH THEIR HANDLING OF SPECIFIC CASES.

WE DEEM IT IMPERATIVE THAT YOU DETERMINE IF CHILDS IS WORKING FOR INTENT ON THIS CASE OR IN HER OWN CAPACITY, AS WELL AS WHO IS HER CLIENT. IT COULD CHANGE LANGLEY'S VIEW ON YOUR PARTICIPATION IN THIS MISSION.

Lyndsey can understand Langley's hesitation if it turns out there are others interested in Emily Rotenberg. As Claiborne has pointed out, while CIA would like to see Rotenberg brought to heel, MI6 has the lead in this case. Lyndsey is there to manage a tricky asset, and since there are Russians involved in the MI6 case, too, CIA won't want to risk getting Lyndsey's cover blown in London. The chance of leakage goes through the roof if a commercial company, a pay-for-play outfit, gets put into the mix. MI6 would be hard-pressed to control the situation. And the fact that both agencies have had issues with the way Intent has handled cases in the past ensures that there can be no coordination now. Intent would not be considered trustworthy, and in the intelligence business, trust is everything.

Everything rides on this meeting with Dani.

In the tote bag at Lyndsey's feet are a few props to help along the way, since she has no team to help divert any potential followers. She casts a wary eye about as she takes a circuitous route through London: first, a stolid black taxi, then an Uber, then a double-decker bus. As she ducks into vehicles or around corners, she does the quick change that's part of her tradecraft: donning a baseball cap, tossing her jacket into the tote bag and throwing on a pashmina, pulling her hair into a ponytail, slipping on a different pair of sunglasses.

She's pretty sure she's not being followed anyway, which is a good thing because her mind is roiling, still, from the sight of Dani Childs sitting next to Emily at the mansion. Did she imagine that Dani's eyebrows had shot up at the sight of her? Dani might've known to expect her if she'd done the same level of fastidious preparation on which the Agency insists. And there's no chance that it isn't related to an intelligence op: there isn't a snowball's chance in hell that Dani just happened to make the acquaintance of Emily Hughes Rotenberg, not when it entailed knowing Emily's schedule that day, her likely route, and the names of the women on the charity committee.

As Lyndsey approaches the rendezvous point, she feels a growing sense of frustration. It would be a colossal waste of time if she were to be called off the case. She'll have to walk away from Emily, but that doesn't mean she'll stop worrying about her. She is surprised to find that she might miss her, too, just a little bit. And if she is honest with herself, she also feels a flicker of disappointment because it means she'll no longer see Davis, even in passing. Her memories of their time together in Beirut are good. He was unlike anyone else she'd known—sophisticated, dry witted, charming. It's disappointing to realize that she needs to let go of him, even vague hope. There is no future there and he has given her no reason to think that could change.

The agreed-upon location for the meeting is a few storefronts ahead, a bookstore. It's a grand place with large arched windows up front that look onto the high street. Inside, it's like something out of a movie, with a vaulted reading room and an endless hall of books. On a Tuesday afternoon, there are few customers, only a couple pensioners padding softly through the aisles, the hushed tones making it feel more like a library than a place of commerce. Lyndsey heads for the travel section, as prearranged. The section is emaciated—who buys travel books when everything you could need is online—and, as expected, devoid of customers.

Only there, perusing a volume about Morocco, is Dani.

Dani Childs hasn't changed much since the last time Lyndsey saw her at Langley. She has a very identifiable hairstyle that makes her easy to spot if she's not wearing a wig or hat, the tools of their profession. It's still cut short, flattering and chic and easy to care for, a plus in their line of work, one that makes it easy to pull wigs on and off. Lyndsey usually has to fuss with bobby pins or hairnets to manage her shoulder-length hair. Otherwise, Dani looks a bit tired, as though she hasn't slept much. Or maybe it means she is training harder. She'd always been on the athletic side, but maybe her new life demands that she be even stronger, tougher, nimbler.

There is no hug, not even a handshake, nothing to call attention to them. Lyndsey plucks a book from the shelf—*Epic Travel Adventures*—and sidles next to Dani. "Nice to see you again—if a surprise."

"I was thinking the same thing," Dani replies. "How long has it been? I take it you're here on business."

"You, too?"

Dani smirks. "A girl's gotta eat."

"How you met Emily . . . the accident with the delivery van." Lyndsey frowns. "Tell me that wasn't your idea."

Dani doesn't respond; she knows Lyndsey might disapprove. Causing a car accident isn't outside the normal bag of tricks, but that's for a state intelligence agency. These things are weighed, the risks assessed. Maybe it would be condoned for the takedown of a wanted criminal or terrorist.

For the wife of a corrupt businessman? Is it even legal for a private company or a private operator? Suddenly, Lyndsey can see why MI6 and CIA might have issues with Intent.

She's not here to deliver a lecture, however. She might as well get to the point. "I assume we're here for the same reason."

"To find out where Rotenberg has hidden his money."

"I heard you're no longer working at the Agency—and you might be working for Intent on this case."

Dani flips a page lazily in case anyone is watching. "I made a mistake striking out on my own after leaving Langley. I hadn't been with the Agency long enough and didn't have enough contacts to start my own business. A mutual friend introduced me to Ed Martin. This is my first case with Intent. If I do well, there'll be more work."

"Who hired Intent?"

Dani gives her a sly smile. "Like I said, this is my first gig with them. They haven't told me who the client is. But even if I knew, I couldn't tell you. It's not my decision to make."

"Not even for old times' sake?" Lyndsey might as well play that card, even though—late nights at the Farm notwithstanding—they were never close.

"Have the Agency speak to Ed Martin." Dani closes the book and puts it back on the shelf. "I doubt he'll do it, but they can ask." Lyndsey can tell from Dani's posture and her precise degree of tenseness that she's being careful but so far, she's telling the truth.

"MI6 and CIA are deciding whether to work with Intent on this. My guess is that it would depend on the degree of cooperation Intent would ask for. MI6 isn't going to want to hand a copy of Rotenberg's financials over to Intent, if that's what they're after. MI6 isn't going to share prosecutorial material with a private company. Intent will have to readjust its sights. Is there something else you'd be happy with?"

"Again, it's not my call. I'll have to ask." Dani sighs, obviously irritated. "As usual, Langley expects to get everything it wants. That's the problem with intelligence agencies: they don't really know the meaning of the word 'cooperation.' They don't do two-way streets. A word of warning: if the top dogs can't come to an agreement, you shouldn't assume Intent is going to step aside."

"I think Langley would expect Intent to step aside because it's the right thing to do. Langley and MI6 are trying to avert war."

"Intent is trying to avoid a war, too, just from a different angle." Dani's smile can either be interpreted as serene or smug. "Don't get me wrong—I used to think the same way. The Agency is always right because, well, it's the Agency. The federal government always gets its way in the end. But Intent has a right to conduct its business—"

"Dani, I can't share what I have with you because it's classified, but it's getting serious. The quickest way to defuse the situation is to take Rotenberg's money off the table. Don't let Intent screw this up. Whoever the client is, whatever their claim to Rotenberg's billions, it's not important right now."

"If it's *that* important—and how can you be so sure that you're right?—then all the more reason for Langley to compromise."

"I don't think Langley is the problem here. It's MI6. Maybe you can ask Trevor Conway about that . . ."

"I'll talk to Ed, but you know as well as I that it'll be better if we work together. It doesn't have to be adversarial." She starts to walk out of the travel section, heading down one of the wide aisles, and Lyndsey has no choice but to follow.

Dani looks over her shoulder at Lyndsey. "You know, this is the reason why I left the Agency. It's all about control. There's never any discussion. The attitude, the tone . . . it's very parental. You can't tell me you haven't experienced it. I know you did—I heard about Beirut."

She's bothered now. Lyndsey can tell by her voice. Lyndsey takes a deep breath. She doesn't want it to get prickly, to shut Dani down. With what's at stake, it's better to have Dani operating in plain sight. An argument could send her underground. Time to slow this conversation. "Why did you leave the Agency, anyway? I don't think I ever heard."

Dani's face hardens a little. "I thought about it a lot after I left. I remember one incident that happened right at the beginning. I guess it set the tone. It was in my first office, part of the training program, you know. The team chief favored this one guy. He was handsome, white. The rest of us—women, men, old, fat, people of color: you know, everybody else—we did the work but any gold nuggets that turned up, they went straight to him. The team chief's pet. She didn't even try to hide the favoritism. And when I told her once that I didn't want to give up my gold nugget, the one I'd worked hard to find, she said I didn't get it. I had to wait my turn. I was the one who'd done the digging and I should've been rewarded for it, but anyone who doesn't fit the ideal is put on a different timeline. Eventually I came to see that it was always going to be that way. My turn would never come. They'd just keep telling me to wait. That was just how it was.

"Then, I had an 'attitude.' It started to feel like things were stacked against me and the job is hard enough without feeling that way, so I decided to quit."

Lyndsey knows what she's talking about. She knows she hasn't felt the full brunt of it, but she's had her own experiences being a woman in a field in which men are favored. But Lyndsey senses there's something more there. Possibly a secret Dani is hiding or that she's trying to run away from. There's a hunch to her shoulder. The way she ducks her head to avoid Lyndsey's gaze.

Or maybe she's tired of having to explain herself.

"There is life outside the Agency, you know," Dani says with another of those sly smiles. "Private intelligence is booming. I chalk it up to the current environment. Politicians, companies—they want every advantage they can get, and they've woken up to the fact that they need people like you and me. We have specialized training and experience. Ed says his business has tripled every year since they opened."

"I've heard that, too." Of course, who knows if it's true? It's not like anyone can see Intent's books. People can say anything they want about themselves, their successes—it's rare they're ever called on it. This is something you learn in the intelligence business, where you see the truth behind what the public is told and what the newspapers have been able to unearth. Inconvenient truths get buried underground, hidden from the light of day. You learn that everyone has their secrets. "Do you like working for Martin and Conway?"

"It's not a huge company, so I get to deal with both directly. I'm more comfortable with Ed, of course; we speak the same language being ex-CIA. He's not chintzy with career advice, not like some people at Langley. He wants me to be successful."

"And the work?"

Dani shrugs. "Lives might not depend on what I do, like at Langley, but the work is still interesting. It mostly has to do with business, from what Ed told me when I interviewed. Helping a company to decide if a potential acquisition is hiding something, or if a competitor is doing something illegal." Again, Lyndsey senses Dani might be saying less than she knows. She's heard that private intelligence are sometimes asked to do things that border on the illegal. Depending on the country, laws vary on how private investigators can represent themselves, if they can lie about who they are, whether they can do stuff that's usually the preserve of law enforcement or intelligence, such as recording conversations. She imagines private intelligence firms hire former spooks because they can handle themselves, but these ex-officers know they can't use the same spy tradecraft at a private company.

"I'm not here to change the world, not anymore. I'm just here to do a job. And that's a bit of a relief, you know? Not feeling like there's a weight on my shoulders." Dani fusses with her bag as she turns to leave. She steals a sideways glance at Lyndsey. "You know . . . it's not so bad on the outside. There's none of the bureaucracy, no hand-wringing managers breathing down your neck and second-guessing your every move. I work when I want, take a break when I want."

In the back of her mind, Lyndsey wonders if Dani is telling her to consider leaving the Agency because she's heard something. She wouldn't know the specifics of what happened with Theresa Warner and Eric Newman—because there's no way the Agency is going to let that awful story outside its walls—but maybe there is gossip circulating about her. Maybe people heard she had been placed on administrative leave over her affair with Davis or that she was responsible for Eric Newman's abrupt downfall. Rumors—especially in the absence of information—are pernicious in the intelligence business.

Or maybe Dani is deliberately trying to rattle her.

"You're a smart woman. Why work for the government when it doesn't appreciate you?" Dani quakes slightly, holding something inside. "I work for myself. Period. You can't say that with the Agency. I'd be happy to tell you more, if you're interested in checking out your options."

One of Lyndsey's favorite possessions when she was a child was a big picture book of fables, a beautiful book that her mother probably bought at a library fundraiser, as they had little money for luxuries. Lyndsey remembers reading it to tatters. There was something about the addition of an important lesson with all that make-believe that spoke to her, that she couldn't get enough of. A particular fable comes to mind from that collection, the story of the fox who lost his tail in a hunter's trap. Tired of the other foxes' teasing, he told them that life was much better without a tail and eventually tried to talk them into giving up theirs.

Is life really better without a tail? Maybe this is her ignorance talking, her predisposition to play it safe, to have the security she didn't have as a kid. The longer folks stay with the government, the more they become acclimated. The more it seems silly, even frightening, to think about leaving. They stay years past retirement age, sometimes too tired or jaded to do the job properly, to keep up with the demands of operations. While she is years away from retirement, she wonders if she will become like this: too wedded to the security of her position to ever leave?

Dani's laugh breaks Lyndsey's reverie. "I know what you're thinking . . . 'I'm staying with the Agency until I retire. They'll never force me out.' That's what we all think, until one day it's too late and it's all over, and we never had a say. Or, in my case, my pride wouldn't let me stay any longer. Don't wait that long. It's your life, not theirs. Call me if you want to talk." With a wink and a wistful smile, Dani throws the straps of her tote over her arm and heads for the door. The little brass bell over the door rings cheerfully as she leaves.

CHAPTER 14

Lyndsey waits with Emily in the big, marble-lined cavern that is the entrance hall. They are about to go have a private shopping session for Tatiana and Kit at Harvey Nichols, one of the strange things that filthy rich people do, Lyndsey assumes, as opposed to ordering onesies online or packing them into the car for a quick trip to the nearest H&M.

She is finding her stride after living in the Rotenberg mansion for a few days. Her first priority has been to check out the security situation, of course. She feels like she's being watched, even though she's probably not. Paranoia is good; paranoia keeps you safe. She's seen cameras but they tend to be aimed at entry doors and dead-end corners. She hasn't seen any inside rooms—the rooms she's allowed in, anyway. She'd be surprised if there aren't cameras covering entry to sensitive areas like Mikhail's or Westie's offices. She has yet to find out where the feeds from all the cameras are monitored. She hasn't seen anything like that in the house, but there are plenty of places she hasn't seen, and she's betting that the video feeds go to the gatehouse, which seems to be empty a lot of the time. She'd made a mental note to find a chatty maid who might know more.

Emily walks over to the stairwell and cranes her neck to look up in the direction of the nursery, as though she can telepathically will Miss Wilkinson to get the children dressed more quickly. She gives Lyndsey a strained smile. "Thank you so much for coming with me . . . I despise shopping for the children's clothing, but they grow so fast at this age. It's almost impossible to keep them respectably clothed."

Billionaires' children don't wear hand-me-downs.

"Do you want to wait in the car?" Lyndsey has her reasons for wanting to get Emily alone with her in the Bentley. The driver stands at a distance, smoking and chatting with someone in the gatehouse. He pitches the cigarette and starts to come over when he sees the ladies emerge through the front door, but Emily waves him off.

The back seat of the Bentley Mulliner is a cocoon of luxury. Velvety curtains you can draw over the windows, even with the heavily tinted glass, sparkling chrome accoutrements. "It's the same model as the Queen's," Emily says as she runs a hand over the cushy leather seats.

Lyndsey hasn't had much time alone with Emily since she's moved in, and she plans to make the most of however many minutes they have before Miss Wilkinson shows up. Lyndsey turns to Emily and gives her a sympathetic smile. "You haven't seemed like yourself lately. Is there something you want to talk about?"

Emily turns bright pink. Bingo. There is something she wants to talk about, Lyndsey can tell by the position of her head, the glance back in Lyndsey's direction. "Something between you and Mikhail? It wouldn't surprise me—if you don't mind my saying so."

"I suppose it's obvious." Emily sighs heavily. Full of genuine regret. "It's always been tempestuous."

It's an opening. A tiny crack in Emily's façade but Lyndsey can work with it. "It does seem like you're unhappy an awful lot. Again, if you don't mind my saying so . . . I don't mean to be nosy."

"Unhappy? Yes, sometimes. But then, all marriages—"

"Yours seems more tempestuous than most," Lyndsey rushes to add. "Not that I'm an expert. All I have to go by is what I've seen of my parents' marriage and my parents' friends . . . But I have to say, Emily, what you have, well, it doesn't seem like others."

That last word finds its mark. *Girl, what you have, it's not normal.* Emily's face crumples.

This is when Lyndsey lays down her trap. It's like a snare you might use in the woods, meant to catch an animal in the wild: spooling out the line, knotting it into a loop, covering it with a few leaves. Dropping the crumbs that (with luck) Emily Rotenberg will follow to step her dainty foot right in the lasso . . . And then Lyndsey will give it a gentle tug, so gentle that Emily never feels the cord tighten around her ankle.

Only at that exact moment, the front doors open and the twins come tumbling out, all shrieks and giggles, with Miss Wilkinson bringing up the rear, struggling with her kit bag of juice boxes and healthy snacks.

Lyndsey has seconds before they reach the car, and then all chance of speaking confidentially to Emily will be over for the afternoon.

She takes Emily's hand and squeezes it hard, to get her to stop looking at the twins and to look instead at her face, to look into Lyndsey's eyes as she tries to convey a deeper message to Emily. "If you ever want to talk about it—ever—I'm here for you, Emily. You know that, don't you? You can tell me *anything*."

Today, they are in the same salon where millionaires' wives are given private couture showings, so it's a little incongruous to see a tiny table set up near the cluster of velvet lounge chairs, the table stocked with crayons and paper instead of champagne and canapés, and small plastic toys strewn across the plush silver carpet.

Lyndsey wanders over to a tall window at the back of the room to discreetly check the bars on her cell phone. Reception is excellent. She checks her messages—technically, she's still at work and you never know when some emergency might pop up, something more pressing than day-drinking in an atelier. There's an email from her mother reminding her to call but no coded message from the office.

Dani has joined them at the store. She hands Lyndsey a svelte champagne flute. "Maybe it's because I'm not a mom but there are only so many onesies you can look at, am I right?"

Emily is a safe distance away. She's talking to one of the saleswomen and isn't paying them any attention. She won't overhear them. "Have you gotten the go-ahead?" Dani asks. To bring in Intent, she means.

Lyndsey gives a curt shake of her head. "No official decision yet."

Dani nods in Emily's direction. "What about Emily? Make any headway with her?"

Lyndsey's not sure how much to share. Undoubtedly, they each want to be the one to get Emily to share her secrets with them. They are in competition.

"I'm being careful. She's emotionally fragile."

Dani snorts. "No kidding. I'd be, too, if I were married to an ogre."

"She retreats into her shell if I ask about him too much. I've got to be careful so she doesn't throw up walls."

Dani swallows the last of her champagne. “Speaking of ogres—what’s Rotenberg like?”

Lyndsey’s not sure what to say here, either. “He’s gone a lot, and when he is home, he keeps to his private rooms. He and Emily don’t seem to interact beyond the perfunctory.”

“What a sad marriage,” Dani says.

An odd episode from last night pops into Lyndsey’s head. Perhaps not something to share. She was waiting downstairs in the media room for Emily; they were going to watch a movie together, a mindless rom-com. She had been checking out the room—in innocent fashion, luckily, nothing too furtive, not tearing it apart looking for a microphone or cameras—when she realized Mikhail Rotenberg was standing in the doorway, watching her. How long had he been there? He moved on after a brief exchange, but there had been something about the way he looked at her that she had yet to parse. Was he suspicious? Or curious? It was not a friendly stare, not exactly.

“I’ve got something to tell you . . .” Dani’s eyes are on Emily and the children. She waves sweetly when Emily looks over at them. *Nothing to see here.* “The day before yesterday, Emily told me that Westover keeps a spare key to his office in her room.” She makes a wry face. “Something about losing the key once when he was drunk and getting locked out . . . The housekeeper let him back in, but he didn’t hear the end of it for weeks. They can be brutal on the non-Russians in the house apparently.”

This is good news, wrapped in bad news. Bad news because it means Dani is doing better than Lyndsey in rooting out secrets. She’s managed to wheedle a piece of important information from Emily first.

“Ah. Well, I’ll see if I can slip in there and find the key—”

Dani clears her throat. Held between thumb and index finger is a small brass key. "I pinched it. Had a copy made. I was planning to sneak the original back today."

This is a plum get, and Dani managed to do it right under Lyndsey's nose. The girl is good. She's obviously more open to taking risks, though if Emily noticed the key missing, it could blow up in Dani's face. After all, Emily had just told her about the key. It wouldn't seem like a coincidence.

Lyndsey doesn't ask first. She plucks the key from Dani's hand. "Let me return it. I'm in and out of Emily's room all the time."

Dani frowns. She's obviously controlling her breath. *Angry.* She's worried that Lyndsey will do something with the key, steal her thunder. "But if she catches you?"

"I'll say I found it on the floor, like maybe a maid dropped it while cleaning. Whereas if she sees you with it, she'll assume you took it."

Dani nods. "That'll work. It was in a teacup on the shelf... You can't miss it."

Happy that it's settled, Lyndsey tucks the key in her pocket.

When they get to the house, they fill the empty halls with noise: the children's excited talk, the nanny ushering them along, Emily talking to them in her bright, high voice. The picture of a happy family.

"I'm going to change out of these shoes. My feet are killing me," Lyndsey says as she darts up the stairs before anyone can question her. At the top of the stairs, however, she goes left instead of right, toward Emily's room.

A quick look around. Listening, too, attuned for the slightest sound. No housekeepers, thankfully. She tiptoes in and does a scan around the large, airy room. It's dominated by a sitting area that's mostly free of clutter, thank goodness. There's only one teacup that she can see, a delicate cup and saucer on a bookshelf, as Dani reported. It's rose pink with gilt trim. An antique that belonged to a favorite great-aunt, probably. She dashes across the room and digs the brass key out of her pocket.

But, at the last moment, she can't seem to let it go. Maybe she should hold on to it one more day and—if she can get away without arousing too much suspicion—run into town to have a duplicate made. Just like Dani. What are the chances Emily will go looking for it today or tomorrow?

Still . . . The odds are not inconsequential. Emily had just mentioned the key to Dani. Emily might want to check on it for reassurance. It's human nature.

Maybe not.

But—maybe.

And that is the difference between Lyndsey and Dani. Boldness—some might say recklessness—and caution.

Lyndsey drops the key into the cup. She knows where it is if she needs it. It rings brightly, the sound quickly dying away as Lyndsey retreats from the room.

CHAPTER 15

Emily sits in the media room, hiding from her husband and the housekeepers and everyone else in her life. She needs a few minutes to think. In this house, where things move so fast, there is never enough time to think.

Behind her, the giant television set prattles noisily. When she notices it's on CNN, she feels a twinge of guilt. One of the areas Emily is forbidden to talk about is politics. Few things are as guaranteed to make her husband fly into a rage as bringing up something she heard on the news.

Though he talks politics in his wing of the house, naturally, *especially* with Westie. They engage in endless speculation about the latest political disturbances. (What was it Westie said the other night? "*Russia is still broke from the Ukraine fiasco and if Kosygin can't raise revenue soon, he'll have no option but to turn to the oligarchs.*") And then there is talk with dinner guests—the Middle East, the endless war on terror, the latest strongman's rise of power, the popularity of nationalism across Europe. Emily never expresses interest in any of this in front of

Mikhail. She even will run over to turn off the TV if he walks into the room.

She thinks about switching off the television but likes the white noise. She can hide in it. Still, she doesn't want to upset him and there is *a lot* to upset him lately. The television, radio, newspapers—it seems all they can talk about lately is the anniversary of Russia's withdrawal from Ukraine. "Putin's Waterloo" is how the BBC and CNN described it. Russian media sees it differently, of course. If you watched both Western and Russian television, you would scarcely think they were talking about the same thing.

She doesn't listen to Russia-1 or Channel One news because she doesn't speak Russian, and so she opts for programs designed for English speakers on Russia Today, or RT.

RT is in a tizzy over the continuing sanctions against Russia. How hypocritical, it says. Were there sanctions against the U.S. for its aggression against Iraq or Afghanistan? Do we need any more proof that the American president and British prime minister are keeping their boots on Kosygin's neck, damning his tenure before it's really started? They hate him because he is strong and manly. Then they throw up a picture of Kosygin in a village meeting a group of milkmaids in costume. See how normal and peaceful things are in Russia! How loved Kosygin is.

They don't show Kosygin relaxing in the billion-dollar dacha in Sochi that he took away from Putin, just as they didn't show Putin there, either. Western television has compared the house in Sochi to Saddam Hussein's palace, both grotesque follies dedicated to ego. Emily wonders what Russians really think of the Sochi palace, not that you can find anyone who dares speak his mind. Look what happened to Russian opposition leader Alexei Navalny for trying to stand up to Putin. Arrested and sentenced to nine years in prison. Will Kosygin be the same way, dangerously vindictive?

Her house on The Bishops Avenue is positively tiny compared to the Sochi folly. Is it wrong of her parents and sisters to refuse to step foot into it? "Enabler" is the word they hurled at her. *He's a murderer and you're enabling him, making it easier for him to appear normal. Oh, Em, dear, why can't you see that?*

Is her husband a murderer? What a thing to ask of one's own husband. She has no doubt that he's never killed anyone himself, not with his own hands, just as she has no doubt that some people, a few, may have gotten hurt as a result of one of his business ventures. But it was hardly Mikhail's doing. He can't be held responsible if someone decides to be stubborn or doesn't feel he got a big enough slice of the pie.

These are words she's overheard from his conversations with business associates or that have fallen from Westie's lips, and that it's been suggested she say whenever she's asked.

If the West doesn't lift sanctions, though . . . This could be dangerous. Westie told her recently that Kosygin stopped asking Mikhail for money recently. "Look at it from his perspective: why ask for dribs and drabs like a teenager put on allowance when, by all rights, it's his anyway?" Westie said in a rare moment of honesty last night, after one too many cocktails. "The Russian coffers are pretty empty after Ukraine. The problem for Kosygin is that Mikhail is no fool, and he's spent the last ten years hiding all his glorious loot. You can't take what you can't find."

That is Westie's job in a nutshell: he manages the complex web of shell companies and fake businesses that constitute the Potemkin village that hides Mikhail's fortune. He let her see the files on his computer once, eager to show her how powerful and important he really is. So many companies! It numbered over ten thousand, surprising even her. Westie was testy when she asked why there were so many companies. "You have to hide it in increments. A few million here, a few million there. That way you fly under the radar. A company valued at a quarter of a billion dollars—the regulators will find that. You've heard the expression 'Don't put all your eggs in one basket'? That applies here, too."

As Westie scrolled through his spreadsheets, showing her a dizzying array of names and figures, he'd said to her, "Don't forget: all this belongs to you, too. You didn't sign a prenup."

He'd said that rather sadly, which she didn't understand. You'd think he would've been *happy* for her. It meant she had nothing to worry about, should she ever decide to leave Mikhail. There would be enough money to take care of them—enough money to take care of a small nation. She and the twins would be more than secure for the rest of their lives.

The CNN reporter is standing in front of some white stone building with the word "sanctions" coming out of her mouth every third or fourth word, like drumbeats. Emily squints: she recognizes that building. It's the UN's headquarters in New York. They're going to meet to talk about sanctions. Emily doesn't need to hear any more evidence that greedy Kosygin will soon be coming for her husband's money. Whether Mikhail has done something ill-advised to draw Kosygin's ire hardly seems the point: when a dictator needs your wealth, he needs it.

Though Emily can't help but feel a twinge of anger at her husband and the stupid, stupid thing he has done. She thought she'd stamped out those coals of jealousy the day after talking to Nadija. Why should Kosygin be upset if a man slept with his *former* mistress? After all, he was done with her. Does he expect them to remain celibate for the rest of their lives? Maybe it's a sign that he is as insane as Putin. Let these women get on with their lives, what should he care? Maybe he should establish a convent where his mistresses could go once he'd finished with them, shut them away like little nuns.

She thinks of Anya, Mikhail's first wife. What happened to her? She had been long gone by the time Emily came into the picture. They had met when Mikhail was in college, he an undergrad and Anya in the last year of her master's program. He'd described her as very intelligent and completely dedicated to her work. She was a petroleum engineer. The only picture of her showed a short, sturdy woman in a hard hat and sensible shoes. She seemed completely out of character for the man Emily knew. "It was my first romance." Mikhail had shrugged before putting the photo away. "I got swept up." When it was over, Anya had completely and conveniently disappeared, leaving Mikhail to pursue his life.

Had Anya signed a prenup? Even though he'd come from a well-off family, Mikhail couldn't have been worth very much then, not like he is now.

Will Mikhail expect the same of her? She has no illusions that they will stay together forever. She'd thought when they'd married that they were in love—enough in love to wed, anyway. Maybe she thought that because she *had* to, because it was the only reason to marry a man like Mikhail, but she no longer believes that. It isn't what she expected, not from their courtship. He's come to see it as a marriage of convenience, something they'd *both* gone into in exchange for something else. It wasn't until the twins were born that she fully understood what it was Mikhail had bought: a pedigree for his children. U.K. citizenship.

She'll tough it out for as long as she can for the sake of the children, but when the time comes, she will have no problem letting him go.

It will be an amicable parting for the sake of the children. Mikhail is not the kind of father who will cut his children out of his life. He will go to war rather than let them get away from him, she has no doubt. Even though he isn't able to spend a lot of time with them, it is clear that he loves them very much and that they are important to him. Another Russian trait: he isn't afraid to gush all over his children. If she isn't careful, he will completely spoil them.

She looks up: Mikhail stands in the doorway, his mouth fallen open. His face grows redder by the second. Oh dear, she's spaced out and here he is and the television is on and that dreadful CNN reporter is going on and on about sanctions. She crosses the room for the remote and clicks off the set, but it seems like this takes minutes and not seconds. She didn't mean to upset Mikhail but here he is, his chest heaving, looking like he is about to explode.

"What did I tell you about the news?" he roars. "You did that on purpose, to upset me."

"I'm sorry. I wasn't paying attention."

But even that tiny glimpse sends him into a tailspin. "You empty-headed girl, you have no idea the danger we're in, do you? Weren't you even listening? If the UN Security Council doesn't drop sanctions against Russia, Kosygin will come for us . . ." He trails off, his face growing ashy. "He wants it all. Everything I have. Don't you understand?" He flails his arms as a dam of anxiety bursts open inside.

"Perhaps I don't, Mikhail. I *think* I do, but I probably don't know the extent of it." She knows better than to raise her voice or argue with him. There's only appeasement. *It's my life, too,* she thinks but is wise enough not to say. *My life is lashed to yours, so whatever fate befalls you befalls me, too.*

Get out now, a little voice screeches at her. But that's impossible. He's not going to let her get off this boat until he's good and ready. For all her innocent dreams, there's no packing up the children and decamping for her family's estate near the border. If she tried to run, in the state he's in now, he'll only come after her. An enraged bull with someone to direct his fury at.

"You should not underestimate the seriousness of the situation we're in." Why is he so upset? It can't just be the TV. There's always idle TV talk. It's just so much blah, blah, blah. He's just gotten more bad news, something else he's keeping from her. That's their entire relationship: one reality for Mikhail and another for her. Her reality may be more pleasant—children, family, charity luncheons—but even though he tries to hide it, even though she doesn't understand the exact perimeters of it, she knows which one counts.

"Whatever it is he wants"—she doesn't need to say the name aloud, they both know who is at the heart of this conversation—"just give it to him."

He goggles at her as though frogs and snakes have slithered out of her mouth. "You must be joking. This is *my* empire, *my* prize. I built it out of nothing, with my own two hands. I'm not like the others, Agapov and Sidorov. The KGB gave nothing to me. Why should I let Kosygin take it away from me?"

He can't really believe those words, can he? She wants to shout at him, *I know the real reason he's coming after you. Admit it, you foolish, foolish man. You lying weasel.* She longs for it to be all out in the open but, of course, it can never be. There are rules to this relationship, and they must stick to them until the floor is crumbling beneath them and the roof is falling on their heads.

They're very close to that point. Granules of plaster are dropping from the sky like the first harbingers of a deluge. But they haven't come to the bitter end. Not yet. And there is no panic room to save her.

"Do you think there's a way out of this?" she asks. She wants him to acknowledge the truth. Then she'll gauge how delusional he is.

"There's always a way out." Is there a way to reverse having slept with someone's mistress? Is it a wound time can heal, or will that pain only go away if you apply big infusions of cash?

I hope whoever you slept with, she was worth it. She presses her lips together tightly, so the words don't accidentally slip out.

"You just need to keep your wits about you and do as I say. You can manage that, can't you?" He runs a hand over his hair, taming stray, unruly locks.

What role could she possibly have to play in this charade? Maybe Mikhail can successfully deny he had anything to do with one of those women if it appears his marriage is still intact. *See, my wife hasn't deserted me—how can you believe there's anything to those rumors?* Why would anyone believe she wouldn't accept such behavior from Mikhail when every other oligarch's wife has? And Kosygin wouldn't give a fig for Emily's feelings. If she were to desert Mikhail, however . . . The jig would well and truly be up. There would be no way Mikhail would be able to keep up the lie, not to mention that he would lose face in the macho culture of Russian oligarchs.

Her husband turns to glare at her. Has her last thought—that she might actually hold the key to whether Mikhail survives or falls, lives or dies—shown on her face? Does he know what she's thinking? That she's had one traitorous, mutinous thought?

He is on her in a flash, pinning her against the wall, his forearm pressed against her throat.

She can't breathe.

His face is close, even redder, though it seems impossible, as though he is the one whose airway has been cut off. He leans his entire weight into her, crushing her chest.

And her throat.

"What is going on in that empty head of yours?" he hisses. "What are you thinking? Are you planning some way to get rid of me? If I thought you were even considering such a foolish thing . . . if I believed you were even *thinking* of betraying me . . ."

She struggles for enough breath to speak. "Of course not, Mikhail—"

He presses harder. "That's good, because I'd never let you get away with it. I won't stand for being betrayed, especially by someone close to me."

He doesn't say, *especially by someone I love.* Love is the furthest thing from his mind.

This is it. He's going to kill me.

Could he get away with it? There's not a doubt in her mind.

She sees Kit's and Tatiana's faces in a flash and starts to cry. *I'll never see my babies grow up. I won't be able to protect them from their father.*

Suddenly, the pressure lifts from her throat. He releases her and she drops to the floor, spluttering and gasping for breath. Her skull seems swollen and outsized, her face about to burst into flames at the touch.

Mikhail is kneeling beside her, his hands pulling her face to his chest. Hugging her. "My darling, I'm so sorry, I don't know what came over me . . ." His voice shakes. "I was drinking tonight and it got away from me. I'm not normally like this, you know that. Please tell me that you forgive me . . ."

She tries to stop crying. He's got her head tucked under his arm like she's a baby bird and he's protecting her. Except he isn't, of course: he's warning her. *I could snap your neck like a twig. Don't cross me.*

She says the words he wants to hear: "Of course I forgive you. This wasn't you, you're nothing like this. I believe you, I trust you, I love you, my darling."

There will be bruises on her throat tomorrow. She needs to think what she will tell everyone, what her excuse will be for how they got there. She's already planning to wear a turtleneck.

And there are other things she needs to think about, too.

Important things.

His words come back to her, ring in her ears. *This is* my *empire,* my *prize.*

He will never let anyone else have it, not even a little piece of it.

No matter what the divorce court says.

He'd rather see her dead first.

CHAPTER 16

Davis Ranford paces the floor of the conference room. On the big screen on the wall is Kim Claiborne, calling in via secure link from Washington. Her near platinum hair is pulled back in a bun, her makeup is applied lightly. Tight-lipped, she watches him pace.

Lyndsey sits at the table, also watching Davis. He did not take the news well when she told him the bombshell about Dani Childs and insisted on this teleconference as soon as he heard. Claiborne had the benefit of Lyndsey's email a few hours earlier to prepare, at least.

"This makes a major mess of things," Davis says in not quite a roar but definitely louder than normal. He buries a hand in his hair.

"Does MI6 want to pull out?" Claiborne asks reasonably.

"That seems premature . . . Given recent developments, I don't need to remind you how important this operation is."

"Dani says Intent wants to cooperate," Lyndsey reminds him. "Would it be possible?"

"Yes," Claiborne says at the same instant Davis says, "No."

Lyndsey turns to Davis. "Why not?"

Davis halts his pacing and looks at her, his brow furrowed. "Conway's burned a lot of bridges here. He was a real head turner early in his career. He proved to be very clever and eventually became one of the top men called when they got stuck in a jam. He should've learned to play it cool, but he let the success get to his head. He started thinking that he deserved more than he was given, and when the disappointments came, as they inevitably do in this line of work—assignments not given, an expected promotion fallen through—he decided to take his ball and go home by starting his own 'private intelligence' firm."

"It's getting to be a trend here, too," Claiborne adds.

"Conway's made people here a bit nervous, particularly in the legal department. He went around giving the impression that he was still with MI6, that Intent was a ruse, a front company. It probably impressed some of his more gullible clients, but it made them very upset in the director's suite, I can tell you that."

How well connected is Davis? Lyndsey wonders. This assignment implies that Davis might know what goes on inside the director's inner sanctum, at least more than he let on in Beirut. From what Davis had told Lyndsey when they first met, he was an outcast, a rebel who had made too many enemies and was just waiting out his time. She wonders now if that was a story he'd spun so she would underestimate him, or because he wanted to try it on for size—or wanted to believe it. It seems unlikely that they would put an untrustworthy rebel in charge of the Rotenberg task force.

"It's been more than that," Davis continues. "Conway was caught last year in Brazil trying to bribe government officials on behalf of a client. Very nasty business. Then another case in which it appears Intent used hackers to break into a rival's computer system and stole information on clients. You know how difficult those cyber cases can be, and they're still fighting over that one in the courts but . . . It gives the impression of a company that's willing to play very dirty and doesn't mind breaking the law."

"I have to say I'm surprised. That doesn't sound like the Eddie Martin I know."

Davis raises an eyebrow. "You know Martin personally?"

"It's not like we ever worked together, but he had a good reputation. He was always ambitious, but he's not reckless. Hopefully Conway's acquaintance hasn't changed him for the worse."

Davis resumes pacing. "I can't say I'm optimistic, not after the things I've been told. When you've got a fox in the director's chair, the rest of the company tends to follow his example."

That felt pointed, Davis's tone particularly barbed. Was this a veiled reference to someone at CIA? Maybe even the new director, Chesterfield?

Claiborne isn't cowed. "We'll need to come to a *mutual* decision on this, Davis. For the record, CIA is not opposed to talking to Intent. We could make the approach to Martin, if that makes things easier for your director. We could deal exclusively with Martin—that would send a message to Conway."

It sounds reasonable to Lyndsey, but Davis only grunts.

"The real issue here is that we don't know who Intent is working for. Dani wouldn't give me a clue and claimed she didn't know," Lyndsey says. "Who else would be interested in finding where Mikhail Rotenberg's money is hidden?"

There's a short silence. Eventually Claiborne says, "We can't necessarily assume they're working for the Russians. There are perfectly legitimate reasons why another entity might've hired Intent. It could be an international agency rooting out corruption, say some group at the

UN or a nongovernmental organization. I've heard the World Bank's corruption unit has been targeting oligarchs for involvement in Crimea. It could very well be one of them."

"Could they be working for your side? What about the FBI? Would it hire contractors?" Davis asks.

"Possibly, though unlikely. Still, I'll put out feelers," Claiborne says. "Let's get this question answered before we make a decision."

After the videoconference, Davis brings Lyndsey back to his office. It's always interesting to see the office of someone you only know personally. It's telling, of status and one's opinion of oneself, what we want the rest of the world to believe. Davis's office strikes Lyndsey as careful. It's sedate, not too big but not too small. It's not splashed out with memorabilia, like you see sometimes with someone who's insecure. It doesn't prop up a shaky ego or try to bully visitors into obsequiousness. As a matter of fact, if anything it looks like temporary digs, a stop between overseas assignments. There's a cardboard box in the corner and almost no personal items laid out. No photographs, especially not of a woman, on his desk.

They take two chairs in the corner. It's an interior room and so there are no windows. Not a power location. A young man follows them in with two cups of tea, then Davis waves him away.

"A nasty shock seeing this Childs woman?" Davis asks.

"It was disorienting suddenly seeing someone I know from Langley."

"There's no danger that she would out you to Emily Rotenberg? To earn her trust?" Davis doesn't wait for an answer. "It's dangerous having her in the mix. She could slip, call you by the wrong name . . . Is her tradecraft good, do you think?"

"From what I recall, yes."

Davis pours a thin trail of sugar into his tea. "If the agencies decide not to cooperate with them . . . what then? Trevor Conway is not the kind to tuck his tail between his legs and scamper off. It will definitely make him angry."

"I'll talk to Claiborne. We'll make it clear to Martin that he has to keep his partner from doing anything stupid."

"Good luck with that."

"The company seems to be getting a lot of work. That means they have something to lose. They can't afford to get crossways with us."

"Maybe." Davis taps drops of tea from a spoon and lays it on a napkin. "How can you know for sure that they're playing by the rules, eh? These companies tend to not be transparent. They're not really legislated, so there's no oversight unless they fuck up. Still, we'll get the legal office to take a good look at them, see if we've got leverage anywhere. The best thing would be if they pulled off the case, really. Less chance of tripping over each other—at the least."

At the least. This case was supposed to be a quick in and out, an evaluation of Emily's willingness and suitability, and now there's the chance of being outed in front of all the Russians in London, a considerable audience. It's a safe bet that Londongrad is crawling with SVR and GRU—General Staff of the Russian Armed Forces, shorthand for military intelligence—and MI6 and MI5 can't keep track of them all. This could have ramifications for the Tarasenko case. If her name floated up to SVR, it could mean more surveillance. A closer look. She can't afford to lead a trail back to her asset.

Davis eyes her over the rim of the cup. "It's good to see you, Lyndsey. Apart from the case," he says, now calm.

She smiles at him but it's rueful. "We agreed to keep it strictly business, didn't we?"

"Does that mean we can't be friends? It was meant harmlessly."

"If you say so."

One thing she knows: she can't afford to get tangled up with someone who isn't sure of what he wants. Not that she's looking for a serious relationship. She's not counting the years she has left to make babies. She's not on dating apps or pestering friends for introductions. Though maybe she should. All her friends are in serious relationships and it seems they've all come from dating apps. Dating apps are tricky when you're in the intelligence business, however. It makes you suspicious; how do you know the handsome stranger who clicked on your profile and just happens to live fifteen miles away isn't a foreign agent? Yet if you say this to anyone outside the profession, they'll think you're paranoid. There can be no doubt that foreign intelligence services are scouring places like Tinder (and LinkedIn, too) for people who work at CIA.

Davis lowers his cup. "I'm sorry about what happened in Beirut, you know. After you were sent back to Washington, I was warned not to contact you, of course, standard operating procedure. So, it's my fault as much as it's anyone's. But if I'd known they were sending you to London, well . . . I probably wouldn't have taken this last step with Miranda. But that was months ago. It's too late, I'm afraid."

"Not that I'm trying to resurrect anything, but if that's the way you feel, is it fair to continue with Miranda?"

He fumbles as he puts down his cup. "What do you mean?"

"If *my* husband wanted to be with another woman and was only staying with me out of—I don't know—loyalty or obligation, I'd want to know. I wouldn't want him to stay out of pity."

He sighs. "It's not that simple, I'm afraid." Marriages are invariably complicated; she gets that. You can get stuck on thorns you didn't know were there. Maybe they're drawn to replay old dramas, reopen old wounds. She's pretty sure there's something tricky here. A man like Davis—handsome, smart, witty—wouldn't be available otherwise. There are unseen complications, an invisible force field that keeps him untouchable. Perhaps they're both fucked-up and deserve each other.

She picks up her purse and rises from the chair. "I need to get back to work."

"Now you're mad."

"Not at all. But given the circumstances, it would be best if we agree to put the past behind us. We can work together, but we shouldn't talk about what we had or what could've been. Let's leave the past in the past. I've accepted that it's over." She's telling him that he should, too.

Lyndsey is in an Uber heading to her office when she receives an encrypted text from Tarasenko. *I have information for you, kukla. I promised I would find something for you and I have.*

The New Boss has been sending one of his spies to meet with the Chinese.

She thinks immediately of Babanina. The former gymnast had given them the same information. Lyndsey's stomach drops: it seems like too much of a coincidence. Could Tarasenko have found out about Babanina? Maybe he had Lyndsey followed after their meeting in Tallinn. If that were the case, however, the last thing he'd do is bring it up to her. He'd want to avoid giving himself away.

Names? Who's the Russian agent? Who is he meeting with? And what is this about?

Patience, kukla. I just found out about it through Morozov. He heard that one of his old nemeses is running this special operation for Kosygin. Everyone is vying to be Kosygin's new special friend. The old goat is not happy one of his friends is in the lead. As soon as I know more, I'll be in touch. But it is always interesting when Russia and China talk, no? America's worst nightmare.

America's worst nightmare indeed.

Lyndsey sighs. This could be important, but it's also the first bit of intelligence from Tarasenko, which means his credibility hasn't been evaluated yet. It appears to corroborate Babanina's information, but it still needs to be vetted. She makes a mental note to cable Langley to have someone look into it and try to find out what these secret meetings are all about.

She bites her thumbnail and stares out the car window. Should she pass this along to Davis? He could get MI6 working on it, too. But the fact that Tarasenko is working for CIA is compartmentalized. It hasn't been shared with MI6 yet. If she gives it to Davis, he'll want to know where it came from. And . . . it could be nothing more than a bit of misdirection from Tarasenko meant to waste her time. Passing bad information would only complicate her position on the task force.

All signs point to no.

She'll follow the rules this time. Langley will attempt to verify Tarasenko's tip first.

CHAPTER 17

The strangest thing happens to Emily today. She runs into Oliver Wainwright.

It is one of the rare times when she is outside of the house but alone. She has no children with her, no bodyguard. She is returning from her parents' lawyer's office and, considering the circumstances, the randomness, she can almost convince herself it was fated to happen. She dropped by to sign papers dealing with the family estate and decided to nip into the chemist's to pick up something she'd run out of, some perfectly ordinary thing she'd normally put on the list for the housekeeper.

She sees the sign for a Boots through the rain-streaked windshield of her Aston and decides on the spur of the moment to pop in. When was the last time she'd been in a Boots? The idea excites her, to have a tiny taste of what her life had been like before, when she was a normal person who did normal things like buy magazines and sticking plasters and a bag of her favorite candy.

It is an even bigger surprise, then, to find Oliver standing in the first aid aisle. He is looking over razor blades or some such, looking as dazed and overwhelmed as she feels at that moment. Emily had dated Oliver in college. He was probably her longest romance and, what's more, it had happened at that time in her life when she was just starting to be an adult, to feel free to make her own choices. A vivid time, an important time, which made the bonds you forge then all the deeper and more important.

Or at least that's the way it feels when she sees Oliver in the aisle, water dripping from his raincoat to the checkered lino floor.

He looks so good. He looks like he had in college but now as a proper adult. His hair is trimmed correctly, not the shaggy mess it had been. His clothes are serious adult's clothes, a bespoke charcoal suit and shoes that are clearly well cared for. He is handsome now, not just cute.

Emily introduces herself, even though part of her doesn't want to. *We were friends once; it's what a normal person would do*, she tells herself. *It's not weird or suspicious in the least.* He tells her that he's not long out of medical school and a fully certified doctor now. A gerontologist ("Britain's population is aging . . . Old people are our future").

"Do you have time for coffee? We should catch up," he says, and even though Emily knows she shouldn't—she's a married woman with children—she finds herself saying yes.

They go to a café around the corner, the rain stopped by then, and find a quiet little table. She shows him pictures of Kit and Tatiana on her phone and he tells her how beautiful they are, how he always knew she would have beautiful children.

She bursts into tears.

"Oh, Emily, what have I done? I'm so sorry," he says, reaching for her hand. As she tries to stifle her sobs and dabs her nose, she realizes it is the first time a man had been kind to her in a long time and that she is responding to this as much (more!) than his dark eyes or breathtaking smile. Kindness is not the instinctive response of a Russian husband.

It turns out he knows she is married and to whom, and while he doesn't say anything aloud it is clear from the look on his face that he thinks he knows what her marriage is like, what it is about. She knows he probably isn't wrong.

She tells him too much, in too public a place. It all comes spilling out of her, her frustration, anger, and fear. Speaking to Oliver is like coming upon an oasis in the desert. For so long, she's had no one else to talk to. It's a mite soon to share personal information this dark with Lynn. Some day she will, but for now their relationship is Emily's safe place, unsullied by Mikhail's dirty business and her bad choices. She doesn't want her new friend to look at her the way her parents do. Not yet. It's too soon to disappoint her.

But Oliver, someone to whom she'd once been so close . . . It is an omen, like it is predestined. The universe knew she needed someone to talk to and put him in her path. The exactly right person at exactly the right moment. Perhaps it is selfish but once she starts speaking, she can't stop. Even as his eyes grow wider, even as his kind expression warps into a rictus of horror, she cannot stop herself.

"Em, oh, Em, what have you gotten yourself into?" He holds both her hands across the table. He wants to do more, she can tell. He would cuddle her, wrap her up in his strong arms if they weren't in a public place.

She wants to eat his kindness up with a spoon. "You have to get away from him. You see that, don't you? You need time to think straight, if nothing else. Stay a few weeks with your parents—"

She cuts him off. "I can't go to my parents. They've cut me out of their lives. It would be impossible."

He tilts his head like a confused Labrador.

"There's no one, Oliver," she says bitterly. "I left my whole world behind when I married. That's the way it works with men like Mikhail."

He lets out a slow breath. "I've known men like that. A surprising number of doctors. They cut you off from everyone you know because it's easier to control you. It's a classic abuser scenario."

He doesn't know the half of it.

Then he says the magic words. "I have a place you can stay, you and the children. A country place in Cornwall. It's been in the family for ages, nobody ever goes there. He'll never find you. You can stay as long as you like. It'll give you time to think."

They sit closer now, chairs nudged toward each other. His hands hold hers tightly.

"I don't know, Oliver—"

He fishes a hospital calling card from his pocket and scribbles a few lines on it, a cell phone number and his personal email. "If you change your mind, you can call me anytime, night or day."

She slips the card into a pocket. It feels like security. For the first time in ages, the heavy burden she's carried on her shoulders feels lightened. Slightly.

She keeps Oliver's business card hidden away in a jewelry box. Even though she doesn't look at it again, it calls to her like radar, *ping, ping, ping.* It's like she's got Batman's Bat-Signal and can send up the call for her own personal hero at any time. Her secret salvation.

It makes her alternately calmer and more agitated. Calmer, because she has a lifeline. More agitated because now all she can think about is using it. Every little worry, every brusque aside from Mikhail, and she thinks about pulling the rip cord. What a surprise it would be for

Mikhail to come home and find her and the twins gone. Drawers left open after suitcases are packed hastily. A scribbled note left on the table, *Don't bother to try to find us, I've gone away so I can think about the proper thing to do . . .*

It's a fantasy, and it makes her complacent. Stupid girl.

For days afterward, she notices Mikhail is acting more strangely than usual. She is attuned to his moods the way a mouse would be attuned to the resident house cat. He's slightly more abusive, his temper shorter. They bicker constantly. By turns, he avoids her and hovers in the corners observing her. *Don't assume that he knows about Oliver.* She's seen this behavior before when there was something else going on in his life—a difficult business deal or brief estrangement from Putin. Or so she would've thought before: Nadija has changed all that. Perhaps she was wrong before. Perhaps it was mistresses calling, demanding, wheedling. She reminds herself that doesn't know her husband at all.

While she stays calm outwardly, inside she's a seething cauldron of anger. There's no reason to endure this abusive behavior, not anymore. Not when she's got a means of escape. *I'll show you*, she thinks. *I'll disappear.* For once, she's got the upper hand.

Still . . . She doesn't call Oliver. The thought frightens her, like jumping out of an airplane. Sure, you've got a parachute strapped to your back but that doesn't make it any less terrifying. It's the last resort and she's not sure she's there yet.

Then one day, she comes in from the garden to find the house strangely quiet. The children are gone. Her heart seizes with a cold, white fright. When she realizes Miss Wilkinson is gone, too, she is marginally less afraid—maybe they've gone to the park—but when she asks the housekeepers, they act as though they've suddenly forgotten how to speak English.

It's not until she tracks down Igor Volkov that Emily learns Mikhail has taken the children. "He's just taking them on a little excursion," he says, trying to pretend this is normal. "For candy, I think. A father should spend time with his children."

Which is ridiculous. He's never taken the twins anywhere on his own. Mikhail is up to something. He is sending her a message.

She calls Oliver that night. His personal number. It's nine in the evening. He should be home by now . . . She forced herself to wait as long as possible before calling so that she would get through to him. She wouldn't be able to bear waiting for him to return her message.

"Hello?" The sound of his voice makes her feel better immediately, like clutching onto a life buoy in the middle of the ocean.

"Oliver? It's me, Emily. I—I'd like to take you up on your offer."

CHAPTER 18

Lyndsey waits outside at a café in Pimlico. It's a nice place, but small. Tiny tables and chairs are set out in clusters on the sidewalk with weekday foot traffic passing on the other side of flimsy metal fencing. Her latte is noticeably good. There are so many cafés in the city—multiplied by all the cities in the world—and it strikes her as odd that so many are good. Another of the many quotidian wonders that give her pause from time to time.

A man walking by stops and does a double take. His face lights up, his smile is broad. "Fancy seeing you here! In London of all places. Do you remember me?" He is careful not to say her name and it's not by accident.

Even though the chances are slim that someone is following either one of them or listening at a nearby table, she responds to the pantomime. Pimlico is far from any of her usual haunts, and far from his hotel, too. "Would you like to join me?" She pushes back the chair opposite her as he winds his way around the metal partition. There is no air-kiss or hug; they're not those kind of friends.

Lyndsey hasn't seen Ed Martin in a few years. He's short and trim, in his late thirties. He dresses slightly idiosyncratically: a tattersall pocket square, modish sunglasses, a rakish haircut. He will stick in your memory for an extra beat—an indication, if you are in the know, of why he probably left the Agency. He has a stubborn need to be noticed, the instinct to display himself, which is not helpful in the spying business. Ed Martin will never be one of William Colby's "gray men" who can blend into the background and go unnoticed right under a watcher's nose.

Lyndsey and Ed started at CIA at roughly the same time. They took the same fieldwork classes at the Farm. Maybe they were in a firearms refresher course together. But everyone in the clandestine service knew Ed Martin, or knew of him. There was his tendency to flash, for one thing, but also because he had a stellar reputation. Not to mention he was known for being a good guy, a trait as rare as it was appreciated. In this business, having a good head on your shoulders and being easy to work with counted for a lot, and for this reason he was brought into all kinds of projects. There was a rumor that he was going to be pulled into the director's suite as an executive assistant, which was considered training for greater things to come. Nonetheless, he left to start Intent. Lyndsey hadn't worked with him much, but they knew each other. Well enough for that day's conversation, anyway.

"Kim mentioned I might run into you while I was in town," he says after ordering a cup of tea. This roadside meeting is no coincidence: Claiborne's office arranged the whole thing.

"You're in town to see Dani," Lyndsey says.

"To see how she's getting on. This is her first time working for us. We need to evaluate how it's going. Funny the way you two ran into each other the way you did. We figured headquarters might be snooping around Rotenberg but we didn't expect it to be—firsthand."

"I don't mind telling you that it makes me uncomfortable. How well do you know her?"

He arches a brow. "Why are you asking me? I'd been led to believe that you two had a history."

"We were friends once, but it's been a while. Did she tell you why she left the Agency?"

Ed Martin's frown is twisted. He doesn't want to speak. "I don't know about this, Lyndsey. I don't want to betray a colleague's confidence . . ."

"Ed, I need to know I can trust her."

He drums his fingers against the table before deciding to dish. "I can tell you that she left under a cloud. It had to do with an operation in Kazakhstan. It went south—no one killed, thank god—but it got pinned on her. You know how it is . . . It's often hard to get to the truth of things. It comes down to he said, she said. I tried to check it out with people I know who are still on the inside, but no one was familiar with the case. So there you have it. Intent decided to take a chance on her, if that helps you feel better."

If Lyndsey had asked Langley to set up a meeting with Dani, they probably would've refused. The only reason Claiborne hasn't stopped cooperation with Intent is because she doesn't know.

Martin clears his throat. "I don't think that's the whole story with Dani, Lyndsey. I think it's hard for some people to get a fair shake at the Agency. And so, they move around a little more than most, knock on different doors, trying to find someone who will recognize and reward their hard work. But they never find that person and it makes them look aimless, and it's easier to pin the blame on them when something goes south."

He's not wrong. In Lyndsey's experience, you don't even need to appear aimless to get blame pinned on you. You just need to have made one or two wrong steps.

"Look, this will be a quick one. In, out, and it's over. And you're both professionals. I'm sure it won't be a problem."

His breezy attitude covers a multitude of shared concerns. What happens if they come to cross-purposes? They can't both win. And the agencies are used to winning. They take it for granted. They have the legal mandate, after all, have privileges and capabilities that a private company doesn't. Companies like Intent are meant to be supporting players, handling small jobs and dirty tasks. You might even question if what Dani Childs is doing is legal, let alone ethical. How has she presented herself to Emily? What pretend persona is she hiding behind?

"Ed—what's this all about? You didn't get into business to compete with national agencies."

The waitress comes with his tea: a cute teapot, cup, and saucer, all of it like something from a dollhouse. He gives the waitress, a young woman in a long navy apron, his complete attention while she is there. He is ever the gentleman. Then he turns back to Lyndsey. "Well, you can't afford to turn away business. It's not like our customers *have* to come to us." It's the old argument why the intelligence agencies aren't like private industry: the customer base is built-in. CIA and MI6 don't need to compete for business, but not everyone sees that as a good thing. Critics argue that makes the agencies complacent. There are some who think a private intelligence firm like Intent is better at delivering results. That they can be more nimble, more resourceful.

He pauses before taking a sip of tea. "But if it's any condolence—no, this line of work is not quite what I'd expected. Customers expect to call the shots more than I'd imagined. I thought they would have more respect for our experience, our judgment. The way it is in government. Instead, we're treated like a handyman, brought in to fix a sticky door. Still . . . It pays the bills."

"And in this particular case"—she's careful not to name names—"what is it you've been hired to do?"

He pours more tea into his cup. "The same thing you're after, I imagine: find out where the money is hidden. We've split the tasks among the team: Dani is seeing what she can find out here in London. I'm about to head down to Panama to talk to Rotenberg's, ahem, money managers."

"The ones who handle his offshore accounts?"

Ed smiles politely. "Maybe I can find someone willing to help us out. Yes, that's the sort of thing a spy agency might do, but I'm learning that it can be more efficient to go through a firm like ours. We can cut to the chase. No one's going to run to the newspapers if we offer to pay for information. No long-winded vetting process, no national embarrassment if the thing goes south. We take the political drama out of it, make it a purely cash transaction."

Or a purely criminal transaction, depending on the point of view. "Is that legal?"

Ed Martin shrugs. "It depends on the national laws and whether the individual signed an NDA. Then there's the moral issue . . ." He shrugs again. "Let your conscience be your guide, as Jiminy Cricket would say."

The whole world is turning into a dark web—or maybe it always has been.

"Doesn't that sound much simpler, Lyndsey? You and Vauxhall Cross don't have to tie yourself up in knots. Let us help you out."

"I'm afraid our requirement hasn't changed: we'd need to know who you're working for before we could even consider it."

"If it were up to me, I'd tell you. But Trevor is adamant."

"You can see how this makes it look like you've got something to hide."

"Doesn't everyone have something to hide?"

"If you're working for the Russians, we can't help you. Not if it's going to lead to something criminal or could result in Rotenberg's death."

"What if it's money *owed* to the Russian government? Would that make a difference?"

"Are you trying to tell me that this has to do with unpaid taxes? If that's the case, they can make an official request for assistance to Her Majesty's Government."

"We both know that's not going to happen." Ed takes a long swallow of tea while he thinks. "As I said: if it were up to me, I'd tell you everything. But Trevor . . . He tends to make things complicated. I didn't know what I was getting into when I agreed to go into business with him. He's melodramatic. It's good for the business: he's good at pitching clients, he knows how to sell it. He can make you believe he knows exactly what you need and that he absolutely, positively can deliver it. I know what you're thinking, but that's not always a bad thing. We bring peace of mind to a lot of people."

"You're regular Good Samaritans."

"There's a place for a business like ours," he counters. "Not everyone can afford—or needs—their own intelligence service."

"It sounds like you run a private detective agency."

"With a difference. We're more *strategic.* We don't go after cheating spouses and embezzling business partners—well, not usually." He chuckles. "Since going into business with Trevor, I've learned there's very little he won't say no to if the price is right." He finishes with a grimace.

Lyndsey picks up every twitch. *Why is he telling me this? Does he feel an urge to confess?* "How well did you know Conway before you decided to go into partnership?"

Ed's shoulders relax. *Happy to no longer be talking about Dani and the*

Rotenberg case. "We'd worked together on a mission and somehow—miraculously, you know how it is, busy, busy—kept in touch afterward. When he decided to leave MI6, he proposed that we go into business together. His mind was already made up; he saw the opportunity. He told me he was getting offers all the time from the established companies like Kroll and Black Cube. But he wanted to try for the brass ring. Start his own business. Why should he make someone else rich, was what he said.

"He thought we'd be the perfect partners. We complemented each other. And two heads were better than one, from an optics point of view. The business would look more impressive with principals from two major intelligence agencies. He had mentors, retired seniors who were ready to be on his board of directors and steer clients his way. I'd told him repeatedly how jealous I was that he was able to leave government and, with that silver tongue of his, he talked me into making the leap . . ."

Lyndsey remembers what Davis had said. "What do you know about the circumstances of his departure? I heard there was bad blood."

He sets his cup onto the saucer carefully. "Isn't there always grousing when you leave? Unless you're such a fuckup that they're happy to see you go . . . I know there are qualms over Trevor, and it's nothing I haven't seen for myself. Trevor is great with ideas. He could sell ice to the Eskimos. But with that comes all the things that give management fits: moving too fast and not being careful enough, overpromising, missing some of the details. He's great at making the sale, then it's my job to make sure we can deliver."

She pushes her coffee cup aside. "I don't know exactly what Conway did to make Vauxhall Cross unhappy with him, but they've described a couple of his moves, like his insinuating that Intent is actually an MI6 cover operation. MI6 will not agree to cooperate on this case."

Ed flushes, his fair cheeks going bright. "Well, yes . . . He's made an enemy or two at his previous employer."

"You must trust him if you went into business with him." The question is whether Ed Martin is deliberately fooling himself. The charm of a good case officer—like a world-class grifter—is hard to resist.

"He's passionate but he's not self-destructive," Ed assures her. "And I'm too practical to have gotten involved with him otherwise. I'll admit, the company has done a few questionable things . . . I should say *we've* done a few questionable things. There are times when you get caught up in the moment and you forget that it's not the same as when you worked for Uncle Sam. You must constantly remind yourself that there are lines you can't cross. But you *do* have to remind yourself."

Ed finishes his tea. He fishes a few pound coins from his pocket and lays them on the table but not before leaving her with one last word. "Dani is *good*, Lyndsey. You can trust her."

But Lyndsey is not one to let others make judgments for her.

She starts to gather her things. She's made an appointment to meet Emily for lunch and needs to make the trek across the city. She pauses. There's a question that's been nagging her since talking to Dani, when a bug was put in her ear. She knows Ed better, trusts him to give her a straight answer. "I was surprised to learn you'd left the Agency. You were respected there, really respected. Why did you decide to leave?"

A knowing smile. "I saw that it was now or never. I'd started to question whether I had it in me to be a lifer."

A lifer. Lyndsey thinks of the grim-faced salt-and-pepper-haired men (and it's usually men) she sees bustling up and down the halls on the seventh floor. The men who sit in the chairs that matter, who seem to be there every minute of every day, who never go home. For whom doing anything else with their lives is unimaginable.

Is she destined to be a lifer? She has never pictured herself sitting in one of those chairs. Can't imagine them letting her.

"Is it better?" she asks. "Being on the outside?"

He cocks his head and the wind catches a few strands of hair, lifting them on the breeze. "It's a trade-off, isn't it? If you like calling your own shots—like Trevor—then it's heaven. Not something you'd be able to do with the Agency, obviously. Not having twelve layers of bureaucracy stacked overhead. That part is great. But . . . you won't be briefing the president, either. You won't be speaking to Congress or at the Pentagon. You won't be smuggling an asset out of denied territory or be part of some daring midnight raid. But I've got a couple years on you and believe me when I tell you that for most of us, those opportunities slow down and the appeal of risking your life over and over diminishes with time. Especially once you marry and have children."

"Are you married, Ed? I didn't know—"

"Yes. Married with two little boys." He smiles and pulls his phone from a pocket, then flips through to a photo. The two little boys mugging for the camera give an idea of what Ed must've looked like when he was young with their sweet faces. Dark eyes twinkle with love and mischief. "I don't see as much of them as I thought I would when I left the Agency. I discovered that it takes a lot of energy and time to run your own company. I'm home less than when I was with Langley. But, on balance, I don't regret it. A certain vitality came back to me, something I hadn't felt in a long time. Of course, maybe you should check in again in a couple years when all that vitality has been spent." He reaches out and touches her arm. "All I can tell you is that I wouldn't have hassled you for dating Davis Ranford. I wouldn't have gone all paternalistic on you. I would've trusted your judgment."

That mention of her personal life is so surprising that she does a double take. When was the last time she didn't feel like someone was looking over her shoulder?

He winks as he flips her his business card. Thick white stock with *Intent* placed discreetly in the center on one side. On the other, *Answers, Not Questions.*

"Call me anytime. Hopefully, we'll talk again soon."

CHAPTER 19

Emily is dressing to meet Lynn for lunch in town. Shedding the casual clothing she wears around the house for something that she can be seen wearing in public. How funny it feels to dress up. It means a few minutes of blessed escape. A fancy ahi tuna salad with poppy seeds at that new restaurant that everyone is talking about. Will they be able to get a table without a reservation? Will it be a problem for the wife of one of the richest men in the country?

As she scoops up her earrings, she notices Westie hovering in the doorway.

She takes in the look on his face: so, so very concerned.

They haven't spoken much lately and for this she feels a twinge of guilt. It's because of Emily's new friends, Lynn and now Dani. They take up her free time. She doesn't need old reliable Westie anymore. She supposes he's not happy about it and has come to make her feel guilty for abandoning him. His expression says something else, however. That is not the face of a man with hurt feelings.

Does he know about Oliver? Maybe he went snooping in her room—she's caught him at it before—and found Oliver's card. Her heart rate picks up. *Pit-a-pat-a-pit-a . . .* Trapped little bird.

"You look like you're going out." Westie leans in the doorway like a vampire waiting to be invited in.

She nods while slipping on earrings. "Lunch with Lynn at the Savoy."

He makes a face at the name, then rushes in, closing the door behind him. "That's exactly why I've come to talk to you. It's about Lynn."

"Oh?" Emily says, employing the tone of voice she uses with the twins to imply caution. She's going to nip this in the bud. She doesn't need Westie to pour any of his usual poison into her ear. He's always trying to control her. She doesn't want to hear anything negative about her friend.

He slides onto a tufted stool. "Emily, how much do you know about her? I mean, *really* know about her."

She stops fussing with her earrings and gives him a look meant to stop him in his tracks. "What are you talking about? Do you mean have I put a private detective on to her? I should think that Mikhail would have done that before he agreed to let her move in."

"He did, of course. But it was just a cursory look. I don't think he dug very deep." Westie runs a hand over his cheeks like he's distraught. Like this bothers him as much as it bothers her. "It's just, well . . . There's something funny about her. Something doesn't add up. Don't you think she comes and goes a lot? I mean, she doesn't know anyone in London. Who is she going to see? Does she tell you where she's going?"

"For god's sake, Westie, she just moved in. She probably doesn't feel very comfortable. You know how it is here, like a strange little adult sleepover party. I'm sure this is all new to her. I told her to come and go as she pleases." Well, Emily didn't tell her this, not exactly. She told Lynn she should make herself at home. No one in their right mind would believe you're supposed to make yourself at home in someone's thirty-million-pound mansion.

Westie shifts on the stool, restless. "There's more to it than that . . . I've been thinking. Hear me out, Emily. She says she's from the Philadelphia area—and, well, I'm familiar with Philadelphia. We had family living there, and when I was young we'd go and visit them. They'd take us all over. So I'm familiar with that region of the United States. It's quite a busy little area, let me tell you and, funny, your friend Lynn doesn't seem to know all that much about it. She doesn't have any stories about places she likes to frequent or sights she's seen."

He's right and for a split second, Emily feels a stab of panic. But there's a reason for that, isn't there? "She's been sick her whole life. Practically a shut-in, she told me. She probably just hasn't been able to do very much, not like most people." Westie doesn't know this, of course, and he pales satisfyingly. She hopes he feels bad now for doubting Lynn.

He thinks for a moment. "Sick her whole life? She doesn't seem sick now."

"Apparently there was some breakthrough recently on her disease, one of those miracle gene therapies we keep hearing about."

He tilts his head to one side. "And what disease was that, again?"

"I didn't say. She told me but I don't remember."

"Do you think you can find out?"

Emily twitters nervously, turned back to the mirror. "Goodness, Westie, it sounds like you think she's up to no good."

"We need to be careful about who we let into the inner circle. You understand that." He's so solemn. "Your husband is in a precarious position, Emily, now more than ever . . ."

"Mikhail can just give him the money, like he always does."

"Emily, you're not paying attention. It's different this time. The New Boss doesn't want a loan. He needs a lot of money—fast."

"It's up to Mikhail to get us out of this mess. It's not like I can do anything about it, can I?" She whirls around from the dressing table, cutting him off. "You're always worried about Mikhail. What Mikhail thinks, how he feels, whether he's happy." Westie would be a fool not to worry about the whims and moods of his mercurial boss—but these are rhetorical questions. They both know why. "Aren't I allowed to be happy, too? Don't come to me complaining about Lynn. Lynn makes me happy. It makes me happy to have a friend. Someone I can talk to—finally." *Someone who doesn't just want to use me, like you*, she wants to say. She knows she sounds whiny and petulant, but she can't help herself. She's so damned sick and tired of tiptoeing around her husband that she almost can't take it anymore.

For a moment, he's silent. It's very serious, that silence. He takes a deep breath before saying, "I understand how you feel, Emily, I really do. But it's all our necks on the line if things go pear-shaped. All I'm saying is that it's a very dangerous time and we have to be careful. Look, where's the harm in having someone look at Lynn again? If she's who she says she is. If there's no ulterior motive, then there's no foul. And if she's not . . ."

He lets the rest hang in the air. They both know what happens then.

A spike of adrenaline shoots through her. This all seems wrong, so—untrusting. And something inside her wilts, as though she's failed Lynn, a woman who's only offered her friendship. Who volunteered to step into this terrible maelstrom to give her this gift.

But that is Emily's life. "Promise me you won't bring this up to Mikhail and I'll take care of it. I'll look into it, and if there's any merit to your suspicions, I'll tell him myself." He's looking at her doubtfully, but at last he nods.

She holds her breath until Westie leaves, afraid to think lest he is able to pull her thoughts from the air. He's only doing his job, protecting his boss (not to mention his neck), but she sees now where his allegiance lies. He's just confirmed what he truly is: weak. If he *really* wanted her, this would be the moment when he showed his true colors. The moment when he stood up to fight for her. But instead, he's folded like a wet paper napkin.

All the better, then, that she is counting on Oliver to save her. That's right: in a few days, she won't have to worry about Westie's suspicions. She and the children will be gone, starting a new life.

She *almost* decides to do nothing. After all, she doesn't want to doubt Lynn . . . but damn if Westie's poisonous idea isn't already burrowing into her head. Even though Westie promised he wouldn't go to Mikhail, he might be lying. He might be marching his cowardly ass to Mikhail right now to rat out Lynn. Westie could still screw things up for Emily: she's not out the door yet. And what if Westie is right? Mikhail would be even madder at her if it looked like she didn't follow up on Westie's suspicions.

Oh Lynn . . . And to think Emily has been feeling bad for deciding not to let her know she is leaving with Oliver. She wants to tell Lynn, but it is too big a risk, really. It's the kind of secret you have to keep close to the vest. And, look, it's just as well: what if Lynn isn't who she says she is? What if she has an ulterior motive? Granted, Emily can't guess what that might be—Westie's suspicions fell apart at this point—but it just goes to show that you can't be too careful.

Emily knows she can't just go to *any* private investigator. Imagine the scandal if she picked the wrong one, if her trust was betrayed and the story sold to the newspapers. She needs someone to vet them for her, to find one who is competent and whom she can trust.

And then it comes to her. Her parents have had their solicitor Jermyn

Tholthorpe for a long, long time. They like him, but more importantly, they trust him. She looks up his information on the computer, then calls and asks to be put through.

There is a longer wait than expected—don't they recognize her name?—but eventually a man comes on the line. Tholthorpe is cheerful. "Dear Emily, what a pleasant surprise. It was so nice to see you drop by the office the other day." By the tone of his voice, you'd think he had been close but of course, that's not the case. He wasn't even invited to the wedding—but then again, her parents hadn't wanted any family friends to attend.

But he's also a smart man, a canny man. It may've been that he wanted nothing to do with what Emily was involved in now. Maybe he disdained the whole Londongrad crowd like so many of her parents' circle.

"I need the service of someone I can really trust," she says in her best mistress-of-the-castle voice, to let him know she is grown-up and capable of making adult decisions on her own. "It can't get back to my parents and it especially can't get back to my husband.

"I need someone investigated."

CHAPTER 20

Lyndsey is running late by the time she arrives at the Savoy Grill. It's tucked inside the plush Savoy Hotel on the Strand, not the kind of place Lyndsey Duncan would go for lunch but the kind of place Lynn Prescott, dependent for so long on television to keep her company, would jump at. It's the flagship restaurant of that famous television chef, the one who's known for screaming and throwing things at his staff, and Emily picked it especially, thinking it would be a big treat for Lynn.

Unusually, Emily is not there already. Emily tends to be prompt. They don't want to seat her until the entire party is there but when Lyndsey mentions that she's dining with the wife of Mikhail Rotenberg, well, an exception is made. They escort her to the best table in the place, centrally placed. Lyndsey wishes she could disappear as she sips wine and waits: there are too many diners taking selfies, commemorating their once-in-a-lifetime trip to this place. Fans of the TV show, no doubt. When they see the fuss made over Lyndsey, they start to eyeball her and whisper. Is she someone famous? Should they take her picture, too? *Please, don't.*

Twenty minutes later, Emily sweeps in. Oh, something is definitely off. This is not the usual neurotic Emily, manically, determinedly cheerful. She gives Lyndsey a distracted kiss on the cheek before sinking into her seat and pours herself a big glass of white burgundy before the waiter can rush over.

"What's wrong?" Lyndsey asks but Emily ignores her, sucking down wine instead. She eyes Lyndsey over the rim of her glass as though weighing a question.

"How are things in Philadelphia? Spoken to the family recently?" Her voice has a high, interrogative edge to it.

Where is this coming from? Emily has never asked about Lyndsey's family before. "Everything's fine. I spoke to my mother last night and told her we'd be lunching at the grill today. She was so excited. She said I should get a picture of the chef if we see him."

"Hmm." Emily is thinking, finding what Lyndsey said unsatisfactory, apparently. "You know, maybe we should visit them sometime, you and me—what do you say to that? You must be getting homesick."

"Yes, that would be fun," Lyndsey says, drawing the words out to stall for time. "But, Emily—what is this all about? You're not yourself at all."

It's not just this sudden interest in Lyndsey's backstory. She's witnessed a definite decline in Emily's mental state lately. The woman is falling apart under the stress, no doubt. She seems to be hiding something, too, judging from her behavior the past few days. Then there's the drinking: normally healthy by anyone's standards, it's kicked up a notch lately. "Emily, you can't go on like this. You're going to have a nervous breakdown."

Emily refills her glass sloppily. "I don't know what you mean."

"Something is going on. If you don't want to talk to me, that's fine, but you should see someone. Talk to a professional. I'm worried about you."

"I can see why you feel that way, but everything is going to be okay." She reaches between the china and pats Lyndsey's hand. "Shall we order?"

They nibble, of course: caviar and oysters and a cheese plate. And more wine, lots of it. Lyndsey paces herself, switching between wine and water, but Emily downs glass after glass in rapid succession. She probably doesn't even notice that Lyndsey is not keeping up with her.

This is worrisome. Lyndsey doesn't know if something specific has pushed Emily to the edge, but given what's happening in the outside world, the real world, she thinks it might be time to move up Emily's recruitment, to feel Emily out without revealing her connection to MI6 and CIA. It's too soon to tell Emily the complete truth; there has to be a fall-back, a way to get to the data if Emily doesn't take the bait.

Lyndsey's heart rate picks up as she scoots closer to Emily. She's aware of all those cell phones and cameras around them: this is the last thing she wants to see posted on social media. She pries the wineglass from Emily's hand. "We need to talk about something serious."

Emily looks from the glass to Lyndsey in surprise but says nothing.

"I have to ask . . . You know what's going on in the world right now. Russian troops are still on the border with Ukraine. We've narrowly missed World War Three . . . Everyone is wondering what this new Russian president is going to do."

Emily tosses her head petulantly. "That has nothing to do with me."

"Doesn't it, though? Your husband—"

"My husband is a businessman. He's not involved with Russian politics."

Lyndsey squeezes Emily's hand. "You know that's not true. You know that he has a tremendous amount of power. Emily, it's *me*. You can tell me how you really feel. I can tell that something's been bothering you lately . . ."

Emily drops her habitual smile for one moment, but then she laughs. "You think I'm upset because of Viktor Kosygin?"

"Surely you're aware that what happened in Ukraine could happen again. Think of the people who were killed, or who lost their homes and their families. A lot of people think it's going to happen again, only this time NATO is going to be pulled into it."

Emily's face hardens. She shrugs but Lyndsey has clearly upset her. "What about it? There's nothing I can do about it."

"What if there was something you could do? Would you?"

Emily sits, frozen. Calculations are going on inside her head, Lyndsey can tell. She's confused and trying to figure out why her normally cheerful, breezy friend is bringing up difficult topics and asking her uncomfortable questions. This wasn't what she'd bargained for. Emily pulls her hand back from Lyndsey's, a smile fluttering apologetically as she escapes.

Emily snatches up the wineglass, sloshing expensive white burgundy over the edge. "I—I don't know what's gotten into you today, Lynn. Naturally, I feel bad for what happened, but it's all in the past. And, as I've said, it's got nothing to do with me. You're right—I haven't been myself lately but all that's going to change. I can't tell you any more at the moment, but you have to trust me. Soon—very soon—everything is going to be different."

There is something about the wild gleam in Emily's eyes and the tremor in the hand that lifts the wineglass that makes Lyndsey believe her. Which is bad news; if there's something afoot, the entire operation could be in jeopardy. Her stomach tightens. "What are you talking about?"

But Emily stands firm. She will not budge, she will not allow herself to be trapped. Instead, she gives Lyndsey an enigmatic Mona Lisa smile. "I'm not at liberty to say. But you'll see. It will all be for the good. You'll be happy for me."

Once they are home from the Savoy Grill, Emily disappears for the day. Was it something Lyndsey said? She fears she's spooked her hostess. One thing she knows for sure: despite all the worrying signs, the tics in Emily's behavior, the suddenly exaggerated mannerisms, it could cause more harm than good if Lyndsey tries to follow up too soon with Emily. Better to pretend that nothing's amiss for now and reassess in the morning.

She goes downstairs for a nightcap before turning in for the evening. The house is quieter than usual tonight. She hasn't seen Mikhail all day, which means most of the security detail has been absent, too. The children were given dinner in the playroom and, still full after that late lunch, Lyndsey told the housekeeping staff that she wouldn't be dining. The rest of her afternoon at The Bishops Avenue was spent in solitude. She felt a little like a child in a fairy tale, wandering the halls of an abandoned castle. Alone, and yet aware every minute that the walls might be watching.

Whiskey and wine stand in decanters on the sideboard in the media room, and Lyndsey is pouring a generous helping for herself when Westie stumbles in. He looks to have been drinking for some time. He's normally neat and tidy, but tonight his clothes are mussed, like he's been napping. He reeks of alcohol. When he sees Lyndsey, he pulls up short and gives her an insincere smile.

He snatches the faceted decanter and splashes more whiskey in his tumbler. "All alone tonight? Why aren't you with Emily? That's why you're here, isn't it, to keep her company?"

Westie's dislike of her is obvious enough: it practically emanates off him like a bad odor. But she knows not to burn this bridge. If Emily proves to be a dead end, Lyndsey might need his help to complete the mission.

"I assume she's not feeling well. Besides, we spent the afternoon together—maybe she's tired of my company," Lyndsey says with a self-deprecating smile.

"Lots going on right now with the business and such," he says as he lifts the glass to his mouth. Not that he needs any more to drink: he's already slurring his words. "Never a dull moment in the Rotenberg household."

"I suppose not." She motions to the seating area, big comfy chairs meant for watching movies in the big theater room. "I don't think we've had a chance to get to know each other yet. Why don't we have a drink together?"

He balks.

"Come on, one drink. A nightcap." She smiles so warmly that he'd have to be a jerk to turn her down. He follows her and drops onto one of the chairs, somehow managing not to spill a drop.

She focuses all her attention on him, capped off with that warm, attentive smile. "You're Mr. Rotenberg's chief financial officer?"

Westie's chest swells a little at that. "I help him manage his financial affairs, that's true."

"From what Emily's told me, Mr. Rotenberg owns a lot of companies. That's got to be a lot of work."

He makes an obscure gesture with his hands, like he's shuffling papers. "I don't have to *run* anything, thank god. I just keep track of the numbers."

"And you work from here?"

"Mr. Rotenberg does quite a bit of traveling, visiting the various companies, making new acquisitions, and I'm expected to accompany him when that happens. But we take our meeting by video, like most people. I can't say that I miss the travel. So damned exhausting."

They chat for a little longer. Lyndsey gets him to tell her his favorite places to visit (he loves warm and sunny climates, Australian beaches, the Maldives) and then to talk about his background (Eton boy, degree from Cambridge in economics before heading off to a big investment firm). He mentions summers spent with cousins in Philadelphia and quizzes her about the sights, and luckily the background reading she's done keeps her from being caught out. They talk cheesesteaks. Dalessandro's or Chubby's? Did he have his picture taken in front of the famous *Love* statue in John F. Kennedy Plaza? Did his cousins take him to the Philadelphia Museum of Art so he could run up the stairs and throw his arms in the air like Rocky? She confesses how she wasn't able to do all of these things herself, due to bad health, but she lived vicariously through her family's stories. Westie's suspicions don't seem completely assuaged by their little chat, but after an hour he seems less hostile, at least.

And the man does love his gossip. The quantities of alcohol he's consumed probably helps. "Milady has something on her mind lately, that's for sure," Westie says, tilting his glass in the general direction of Emily's bedroom. It only took the slightest nudge to get him to return to Emily; apparently the lady of the house is one of Westie's favorite topics. "She's been especially moody the past few weeks."

"Ever since the break-in?"

He shrugs. "We've all been on edge since then."

"You'd think in a neighborhood with all this money, it wouldn't be such a rare occurrence. I mean, I've heard that the high-end jewelry shops downtown get robbed all the time . . ."

He makes a face. *Pish tosh.* "Not out here where it's residential. Not recently, anyway. Too much private security in these houses." He brings a wobbly finger to his nose with a confidential wink. "The Arabs, they're the worse. Bring whole private armies with them—you can't miss when they're in town. Thank god they come rarely, just for the big sales at Harrods." He smirks at his own poor joke and takes another big gulp of his drink. "You needn't worry, though—Igor has hired a few new boys. Put in more cameras on the perimeter, that sort of thing."

Good to know.

Lyndsey is ready to wrap things up for the night with Westie. He's too wary for her to get much further with him; it's not like he's going to invite her up to his office and show her the spreadsheets. The door's been opened, though. She'll nudge it open further over the next couple days and before long, he'll give her something of value.

They meander down the hall and start up the stairs together, Westie leaning heavily on the railing. He lists toward her more closely than he would normally, undoubtedly due to his unsteadiness. Without her support, he would fall to his knees or tumble backward down the steps. She can feel his face close to hers, and inhales his thick, liquored breath.

They are at the entrance to the office wing, where Westie's rooms are. Lyndsey weighs whether to offer to escort him the rest of the way in order to get a better look inside, but he breaks away from her suddenly. He turns, but before he can lurch down the hall on his unsteady feet he says to her suddenly, "One last thing: if you have any influence over Emily, you should convince her to stay married to Mikhail."

This strikes Lyndsey as a strange piece of advice. "Are you saying they're on the brink of divorce?" It doesn't surprise her: the tension in the house is nearly unbearable. Maybe that was what Emily referred to cryptically at lunch. If she's that disgruntled, she might be more open to a pitch than Lyndsey had supposed. The entire operation could be sped up. Lyndsey feels a tingle of anticipation, the way she always does before something is about to go down.

Westie makes a horrible face at her. *Can't you tell?* he seems to imply. "The last four months have been a living hell," Westie says. "Emily has to be careful, though. There was no prenup, and that's a very bad thing. Mikhail is not free with his money. If Emily leaves him, he won't want her to get anything. You understand what I'm saying, don't you? Emily should never sue for divorce from Mikhail because he'll never give her one. Never."

CHAPTER 21

Emily has hidden two of the children's suitcases in her dressing room and she's there on the floor now, with the tiny clothing she's just bought at Harvey Nichols. Her hands shake a little as she folds the clothes and adds them to the things she's already packed away.

She's been getting ready for their escape. Withdrawing cash from every ATM she's passed. Buying a burner phone (you can get them at the corner chemist, utterly brilliant). She's copied her family's phone numbers from her cell phone, which will soon be useless to her, into an old-fashioned address book. She's pictured herself phoning them, teary but relieved, from Oliver's family home, telling them that she's escaped from her husband. How happy they'll be for her. What a grand reunion they'll have—soon.

She pulls out her phone again. The screen is quiet. No text messages.

Where is Oliver? D-day is tomorrow, the day they agreed upon to put their plan into action. They finalized their plans over texts and one hurried, whispered phone call: in the wee hours, she is to put the kids in a car and drive to a truck stop north of London, where Oliver will meet her with a rental car. They will drive north together, in the direction of the Rampshead family estate to fool Mikhail, to throw him off their track (no danger there, as it stands empty). But once in Cumberland, they'll get a second rental car and head to Oliver's estate far, far to the south. It seems a bit James Bondish to her, but Oliver insisted on the extra steps and of course, she knows he's right.

She draws in a big breath and lets it out slowly. *Oliver is a doctor, he's busy. He'd have contacted me if there's a problem. I have to stick to the plan.*

Still . . . It's been three days and not a word. Her teeth start to chatter and she feels sick to her stomach.

She pulls Oliver's card from its hiding place in her wallet and—looking at the card to make sure she gets the number right, as though that was the problem—punches in his private cell phone number, then holds her breath. She worries and frets while listening to the pips, an endless row of pips until the line goes to voicemail. "Hello, this is Oliver. I'm not available right now so if you could leave a message at the tone . . ."

She leaves a jumbled, barely coherent message and hangs up. She has a bad feeling, but she knows it's irrational, just the residue of unmet expectations.

All evening, Mikhail has left her alone. There have been no check-ins, no sending Westie or one of the housekeepers to keep discreet tabs on her whereabouts. As a matter of fact, he's been out of the house all day—which is not unusual, but there's definitely been something in the air. She tells herself that she's imagining it because of the circumstances. But something feels off.

The rest of the evening passes without a return call from Oliver. Meanwhile, Emily has texted him and sent an email message. With every hour that passes, she knows something has happened to change his mind.

She set the alarm to wake her at three a.m., but she needn't have bothered. She hasn't slept a wink all evening. She made excuses with Lynn and took to her bedroom early but spent the whole time packing and repacking her and the children's suitcases. Making sure she had medicines for the twins in case they got sick; she'll not have Miss Wilkinson and her magic bag of lozenges and juice boxes.

She slings the two children's bags over her shoulder and hefts her own suitcase. She wants to make one trip down to the garage to ready the car, then she'll come back for the children. The bags are heavier than she imagined, staggering her back a step, but she manages to make it out the door and into the hall. As she approaches the staircase, she glances out the window, one that overlooks the back of the property and the garage.

And there is Igor Volkov standing in front of the garage doors. He looks like he's been waiting for some time but he is his ever-patient self, casually smoking. Like anyone smokes outside a garage at three in the morning.

He looks up at that exact moment and sees Emily. Not a flinch or any sign of surprise. It's like he expected to see her. He nods.

And then she knows. Mikhail has found out about her plan, Oliver, the whole works.

She turns and heads back to her room, dropping the suitcases to the floor just inside the door.

When she wakes the next morning—only able to fall asleep with the help of a couple pills—one of the housekeepers brings in a breakfast tray. That is a red flag and a confirmation. It's not Emily's custom. She takes breakfast downstairs with the children in the conservatory whenever weather allows. She didn't ask for a tray.

The housekeeper has left it on a side table. Coffee, chocolate croissants. A single red rose in a crystal vase. Very pretty. Very unusual.

And a newspaper, folded in a way so that a specific story faces out.

She picks up the newspaper. *St. Albans eldercare doctor in critical condition.*

The story is crisp but caring. A well-loved physician is attacked outside his Knightsbridge apartment by unknown assailants. It's written off by police as a robbery, as his watch and a few other trinkets were taken from him. There's surveillance footage—this is modern London, after all, you can't go five feet without being captured on a security camera—but the assailants wore black ski masks. *The doctor, Oliver Wainwright, of Egerton Gardens, has been transferred to St. Albans, where he is currently in the intensive care ward . . .*

Intensive care. Emily's heart thumps wildly. Mikhail is responsible; there's no doubt in her mind. She feels the certainty as surely as the blood runs in her veins. This was no random assault. Of course, that's what the police would think: they don't know what happened, the dangerous plans she made with Oliver just a few days earlier.

She starts to dress, frantic to get to the hospital. To *see* him. It's her fault that he's there and she wants to see the damage she has wrought. It's not until she's half-dressed that she realizes that she can't go. Seeing him would only confirm what Mikhail suspects, maybe even make it worse, make it seem like there's more to it. It'll be best for Oliver if she pretends that he doesn't exist.

What has she done? *I'm so stupid. Selfish and unthinking.* She gave into weakness and now this innocent man is suffering for it. She knew that her life wasn't her own anymore, but she's been in denial. Pretending that she hadn't made a deal with the red devil.

She dresses for a day at home, abandoning all plans to see Oliver.

Downstairs, Mikhail is in the breakfast room, dining by himself. He's got a plate full of eggs and sausages and he's eating with gusto, which he never does, rivulets of grease from the sausages trickling from the corners of his mouth. He waves for Emily to join him, pats the chair next to him.

She sits across from him instead, silent and still as a maid places a plate in front of her and fetches tea from the sideboard. He is jolly, asking about her plans for the day. But there is a shadow behind his smile, a wolfish glimmer of cunning. He is enjoying her misery. He likes inflicting pain on his wife. He says nothing about the tray, the newspaper story. He says nothing about Oliver. He doesn't have to.

It is clearer to her than it will ever be: she married a monster.

She is nibbling on a cold piece of toast when he decides to pounce. "Oh, Emily, I don't know if you saw the news this morning. Your old boyfriend, the doctor, was the victim of a mugging last night. It was in the newspapers."

She puts down the toast. He actually smiles as he delivers the news. There is not a trace of regret in his voice. He waits for her reaction, eager like a hawk waiting to drop from the sky.

It is inevitable that she breaks. She's still in shock over the news, weakened to the point of exhaustion by the strain of the past few days. This is what he wants but she can't stop. He may be a monster, but she has to fight back.

"You did it. I know you did it, don't deny it," she says much louder than she intended.

The smile dissolves, replaced by a deep scowl. Here are the emotions he's been repressing, freed at last. "I don't know what you're talking about. Why would I want to harm Oliver? He's probably brought it on himself. You haven't seen Oliver for—what? Years. You never know what secrets someone might be hiding. Who knows what trouble he's gotten into. Gambling debts, maybe. He always struck me as having poor judgment."

She trembles with rage. "Oh? And how do you know of him, that we were an item? I don't recall ever telling you about him."

His smile wavers. He doesn't like being caught out. "You've mentioned the name, of course. Forgive me if I checked up on him from time to time: I'm not immune to jealousy, what can I say?"

"You were watching him?"

He snaps his napkin as he removes it from his lap. "What? Nothing like that. It was nothing more than idle curiosity. It's not like I was obsessed with the man."

He can deny it all he wants—she knows he's the one who put Oliver in the hospital. Emily doesn't recognize Mikhail anymore. He's not the suave, worldly, educated man she fell in love with: he's a cold-blooded, bald-faced monster. What's more—what's worse, she sees it now—is that the longer the children are with him, the more they'll become like him. Kit and Tatiana are sweet and unspoiled right now, but how much longer until they are poisoned with his diseased mindset? Until they are entitled and demanding, their sense of morality distorted beyond redemption?

She almost breaks down in tears at the table. Not for Oliver, certainly not for herself, but for her children and the frightening, abnormal life she's condemned them to.

CHAPTER 22

Later that day, Mikhail informs her that another playdate has been arranged for the twins. Emily doesn't want to leave the house, especially not to go to the home of one of the other oligarchs, but this is his way of reestablishing control over her. He snaps his fingers and she obeys. After what happened to Oliver, she is still shaky. It seems nearly every other moment that she's going to be ill. The world spins and dips around her.

Even though she knows logically that they're not in danger from the oligarchs, still it *feels* like she is walking into a trap. Would whoever ordered the assault on their house dare to kidnap the children? It's a melodramatic turn of mind—isn't that her life now, given what's happened to Oliver, high melodrama?—but she knows you can't put anything past these people. That's why the rest of London hates them so: they don't trust the Russians. They're the antithesis of everything British, full of untrustworthy, messily violent passions. There's no telling what they're capable of.

Sadly, she realizes: they think she's one of them.

Lynn is out at an appointment—Westie is right; she does seem to be away at the most inopportune times—and Emily doesn't feel she can ask Dani to play handmaid again and so she has only the nanny to accompany her. Today's playdate is at the home of Kirill Khorkov. He controls a lot of media in Russia and Eastern Europe, which makes him important to Kosygin. He and his wife, Svetlana, a former TV personality, have teenage sons who are a bit old to play with the twins, but these visits are never about the children.

The dynamic at these get-togethers has changed dramatically. Emily can tell by the way the adults distance themselves from her, clustered at the far end of the room, glancing back at her. It's as though she has the plague, whereas before, it was like she was the queen visiting a lesser royal's home. Even Miss Wilkinson gets the cold shoulder. At least they're kind to the children. The Russian way. They adore children, even if they send them into coal mines and potato fields and factories to work.

The talk over vodka shots and caviar is all about Kosygin. He is pressuring all the oligarchs for money, not just Rotenberg. No one else's home has been shot up, though. Everyone is careful not to criticize him openly, but they are bewildered: why is he demanding so much? They were all nearly ruined over Ukraine. They only managed to remain in London by the skin of their teeth. He is ruthless, as bad as Putin. Russia is cursed with bad rulers.

Emily is swilling white wine in a corner when Svetlana comes over. Her hostess looks like she doesn't want to be within ten feet of the infamous Emily Rotenberg but it's her responsibility. Or so Emily assumes.

Svetlana towers over Emily, and Emily is not short. Emily recalls that Svetlana was on the Russian Olympic volleyball team in her youth. Or maybe it was the basketball team. Emily can't remember. Either way, this is over six feet of brassy-haired woman stuffed into a leopard-print dress and six-inch Louboutins teetering nervously at her side.

She peers at Emily through the heavy makeup and overpuffed lips, her face a mask of pity. *This over-Botoxed woman feels sorry for me*, Emily realizes. *Me!* At least Emily has managed to keep the physical features she was born with. Mikhail hasn't sent her to be plumped up with dermal fillers and silicone implants.

"Thank you for inviting us over today," Emily says. She clears her throat, preparing to deliver Mikhail's latest back-channel message to Kosygin, which she has dutifully memorized. Mikhail is sure this is why the Khorkovs set up the playdate. There could be no other reason.

But Svetlana raises her hands and waves her off. *Stop.*

"I am sorry for your troubles," she says in painfully accented English. She's been living in London for more than ten years and her English is still terrible. Then again, she rarely speaks it. The Russians are strict about only using Russian in the home for the children's sake.

"My troubles?" *Keep up a brave front*, Mikhail told her.

Svetlana again does the dismissive wave. "No need to pretend. We all know. Everybody knows."

Emily's shoulders slump. She fights the urge to cry. She looks at her children, playing alone. The rest of the horde have run off. The Khorkovs' teenage boys are probably showing the others the media room or taking them swimming in the indoor pool. The juvenile voices speaking Russian echo down an empty hall, trailing the fiendish laughter of adolescents.

Svetlana appraises her with a shrewd eye. "You look like a smart lady . . . You come from a good English family, yes? Let me tell you something, for good of the children. We all agree: Mikhail has crossed a line. There is no saving him. But you . . ." Her heavily powdered eyes crackle as they settle on Emily. "Why don't you leave him? Save yourself."

Svetlana looks over her shoulder—left, then right—before continuing. As though she is sharing a deep secret, doing her a special favor. "You are not like the rest of the wives. We are alone in this country. There is nothing for us in Russia, either." Emily can see that. In their culture, these women have achieved the best that most can hope for: marriage to a rich man. The society is so misogynistic that the odds are stacked ridiculously high against them attaining anything on their own. Even Svetlana, who has been a world-class athlete and TV personality.

Like them, Emily had been raised to think that marriage would be her occupation. And her salvation. She always thought she needed a man to take care of her.

But . . . maybe she doesn't. Svetlana might be right: Emily shouldn't need Mikhail to survive. If she were to leave him, surely her family would step up. She could live with her parents until she got on her feet, until some arrangement for support could be worked out with Mikhail. He wouldn't abandon them completely. He doesn't want his children to live in squalor.

But—no. She can't sustain this fairy tale for more than a few seconds, especially after what has happened to Oliver. Mikhail would not let her leave with the children. He'd hustle them onto a plane and head off to Moscow, right into Kosygin's arms, before he'd let her take them away. As she tries to come up with a plausible story—going to Whitehall, begging the police for protection—she starts to sweat. None of them would work. It's impossible. There's no scenario in which he doesn't have her tracked down and the children forcibly taken away, or that doesn't put her parents in mortal danger if they try to stand up for her.

Svetlana touches her shoulder, bringing her out of her frightened reverie. "What I said—think about it, yes? I can help you, if that is what you want."

Emily tries to push her conversation with Svetlana out of her head as they head home. She keeps up a running dialogue with the twins in the car, then takes them by their damp little hands to the nursery with Miss Wilkinson, where the two women tuck them in for a nap. Only when she is back in her rooms, door locked and curtains drawn—as though that will keep her husband from reading her traitorous mind—does she allow her thoughts to drift back to the talk with Svetlana.

It *should* be possible to get away from Mikhail. She just has to figure out *how*. It's not something she could do all on her own; she'd like to think it is possible, but she's afraid she's too weak. It would be easier if she had someone to help her, someone she could trust.

The first person she thinks of is Westie. He's made jokes about the two of them running away together. Does his little fantasy include children? Probably not. And she knows Westie isn't strong enough. If it came to a showdown with Mikhail, the kind where he's being asked to take a bullet for her, maybe even die for her—well, she knows what his answer would be. Arthur Westover doesn't have it in him.

That doesn't mean he can't be helpful along the way, however.

She would like to hurt Mikhail. She's not too noble to admit that, to herself at least. He has caused her so much pain and suffering, doesn't he deserve to get a little in return? The only thing Mikhail cares about—besides his children, whom Emily would never hurt, it goes without saying—is his money.

Westie is the only one who can help her with that.

Her thoughts rush to Lynn, like it's the most natural thing in the world. She was trying to help yesterday at lunch, trying to get Emily to admit that she's bothered by what Mikhail does, the bad deeds he's been involved in. Lynn Prescott is a possibility, then, but does she have it in her? You'd think a woman who grew up behind the walls of her parents' castle, like Rapunzel with some kind of fatal disease, wouldn't be very strong, but Emily senses that's not the case. There's a steely core to this woman. She's a walking paradox. Maybe that's why Westie doesn't like her. Maybe he senses that she's something he'll never be.

With Lynn's help, she *might* be able to do it. But Lynn is still too great an unknown. And as much as she admires Lynn, Emily doesn't feel she can put all her eggs in that one basket.

Still . . . she knows she's made the right decision—and not a moment too soon. She must figure out a way to save her children—and herself, otherwise who will look after the twins?—and she must do it soon, before it's too late.

CHAPTER 23

It's a quiet morning in the Rotenberg mansion. Emily has left for the concierge doctor's office, complaining of a pounding headache. Miss Wilkinson has the children in the upstairs playroom. The men have melted away, as usual, although Lyndsey hears the occasional male voice rise in the background, muffled and indistinct.

The perfect time to do a little snooping.

Now that Lyndsey has spent a few days here, she sees that she's not going to be joined at the hip with Emily every minute of the day, as she feared. There are moments when Emily has an outside appointment or is wrapped up with the children. There are even times when she disappears, even if it's only to slip off to make a call, only to reappear with a slightly guilty look on her face.

Lyndsey has used these moments to poke around the house, to test for weaknesses and get to a better picture of the household's routines. When the housekeepers wrap up their daily duties and go to the kitchen for a long coffee break. When Volkov slinks off to the gym over the garage for his daily Krav Maga workout. When Westie has his daily videoconference with Stern De Leon, their money launderers in Panama. Very private, of course. No one is allowed in that wing during that time, not even Volkov, not according to what Emily told her once, innocently, at breakfast.

This morning, Lyndsey has a mind to try Westie's room, to drop off the device the tech ops officer gave her. See what it can pick up. It would mean paying a visit to Emily's room for that key. The men's voices sound farther away than Westie's room . . . It's a risk, but it's time to take risks. If Emily is thinking of leaving Mikhail, there's no telling how much longer Lyndsey has.

She's passing the entrance to the children's wing when she hears voices. The conservatory is out of sight but the rooms that lead to it are open, the layout a maze back there. She recognizes the voices: Dani and Westie. Her skin prickles. Was Dani expected today?

She and Dani are on the same team now, she reminds herself. The urge to listen in, to *be sure*, is strong. It's not knee-jerk competitiveness, she tells herself. She's undercover. If there's a slipup, it's her life on the line.

It sounds as though they are alone. Lyndsey creeps toward the sound, careful to remain out of sight. They are joking, teasing. Lyndsey feels a fleeting pang of jealousy: hadn't she bonded with Westie last night, and here he is being cozy with Dani. Sure enough, Dani has been able to breech Westie's prickly shell, cleverly playing the good-time girl. She and Westie gossip about the household like schoolchildren. What a mousy twit Miss Wilkinson is, how happy Westie will be to see her get the sack. Dani makes fun of Volkov's accent. She admits that one of the newer security guards, Lev, is a hottie.

"So, tell me what you know about Lynn." Westie sounds peevish. Maybe he wasn't so drunk last night, after all. He could've been trying to trick her. "You all seem to get along like gangbusters, but you didn't know each other before, did you?"

A pause. "I didn't know her, not really, but we'd met once through a mutual acquaintance. At some function at Villanova. I have family there, an uncle who's a professor."

Another pause. "Then can you be sure it's her? When was the last time you saw her?"

"It was years ago but . . . why are you asking me this?"

"We put a private investigator on to her—don't give me that face. We vet anyone who gets close to the family. We put one on you, for god's sake! Anyway, the report on her came back kind of fishy."

His last few words are barbed. Lyndsey's insides go squishy. Even though the entire house of cards is bound to come tumbling down soon, one way or another, she can't help but feel fear. A reflex, a knee-jerk reaction. There is no vulnerability like being undercover.

"You think this is someone *impersonating* Lynn Prescott? Why would anyone do that—to pass bad checks?" The tone is incredulous, almost mocking. Relief surges through Lyndsey: Dani is being a trooper. She could've played along with Westie to get in better with him and fueled his suspicions, but she didn't. "Do you think this woman is some kind of con artist?"

Westie snorts. "Now you're making fun of me."

"I think you're batshit bonkers, but if you're serious, maybe there's something I can do to help. I told you, I have relatives in Villanova. I can ask them to check up on her."

Westie makes an agreeable noise and Dani swiftly steers the conversation off in another direction—*Yes, Lev is a hottie but have you taken a good look at Max's ass?* Lyndsey is tempted to stay but she's pressing her luck remaining in one spot too long, and there are more important things she could be looking for. Dani has Westie covered.

She continues toward the office wing. If Westie's taking a break in the conservatory, there's a chance—remote, perhaps—that he left the door to his office open. It might be her opportunity to snoop around in there, get the lay of the land. She heads in that direction as quickly but quietly as she possibly can. Up the stairway like a ninja, listening carefully for any indication that someone might be heading in her direction. She's just outside the office wing when she hears someone coming. She slips around the corner and into the first room she comes across. It's supposed to be a library, though there are too few books to be anything but decoration. It's meant to give the impression of a library without the frightful waste of shelf space. She pretends to peruse the meager shelves as the footsteps grow closer.

It's Mikhail Rotenberg. His strong Roman nose proceeds him, but even if not for that nose, she would recognize the tread. Heavy, fast. Lyndsey holds her breath, expecting him to pass by without so much as a nod of acknowledgment. That's what he normally does. At least when others are watching.

This time, however, he stops and—though he's behind her and she can't really see him—seems to take stock of her.

He walks toward her. Tread heavy on the carpet, too.

Her heart rate jumps. This is new.

He stands beside her, though a comfortable distance away. This close, she sees he is taller than she thought. What's more, there is a gravity to him. Maybe it's the way he stands, so upright, his shoulders thrown back. Like a Russian officer. Or maybe he is posing for her, trying to impress. He usually is dour and distracted, so it's disorienting to have his full attention. He regards her with curiosity, as though he hadn't really looked at her, really *seen* her before. Like he's just noticing the pleasing lines of a teacup he's already used a dozen times.

He's not really an attractive man. In addition to that large nose, he has a broad mouth and small eyes. His brow is heavy. He would look crude if he didn't adorn himself with fine things: expensive clothing, delicate gold cuff links, a fancy watch. He smells faintly of men's lotions, spicy and warm.

He nods at the shelves. "Looking for something in particular? I would be happy to make a recommendation."

She smiles at him. "I'd be surprised if we had similar taste in reading material. I like to keep a book on the nightstand in case I'm having a hard time falling asleep."

He runs a finger over the spines, then settles on one. He pulls it out. "A good book is a good book. Here's one I enjoyed." It's the biography of a mogul in the tech business, one that was on the bestseller list last year. It's not a surprising pick; safe, even.

"I'll give it a try." He brushes her hand as she takes the book from him, his fingers lightly caressing the back of her hand. His skin is dry and cool, and slightly weathered. Did he do that on purpose? It seems like an excuse for them to touch.

She tucks the book under her arm.

He doesn't continue on his way. Instead, he turns back to the bookcase, taking a leisurely look at the books, making a show of reading the spines. He is not in any hurry, clearly the master of all he surveys. "So . . . I'm embarrassed to say I don't know all that much about you, Lynn. Emily has told me a little, of course. That you grew up in Philadelphia. You were sick, as a child . . ."

"Yes."

"And—if it is not too intrusive to ask—what was the disease? I don't believe I was told . . ." He holds her gaze, his eyes sharp like a hawk's. He's not flirting.

She takes a half step back from him. "It's pretty rare. I doubt you've heard of it—"

"Still. I'd like to know." His smile is wry, but serious. He's not going to give up.

"The common term is Fabry disease. It generally starts in childhood, when you're an infant, but sometimes onset is later, even in adulthood. Up until around the time my case was diagnosed, it was thought that females could only be carriers." She's been given a brief on the disease and has only to pick through the details to weave her story. "I was lucky . . . even though my symptoms were severe for a woman, it still was tolerable. Then, five years ago there was a trial for a new type of medicine. My doctor got me in a round of the trial, and it's done wonders."

"It sounds like a miracle." He studies her face, picking over her features as carefully as though sifting through sand. He thinks he will be able to tell if she's making it up but he never will; she's well schooled in concealing her feelings. Like an actress. "And what is this miracle-working doctor's name?"

He's going to track this down: she can tell by the set of his face.

"Reginald Hopper. He's in the research department, though, not the hospital." He exists, he's a real medical researcher. The Agency reached out to him as they constructed the backstory, asked him to verify their story if someone called. He will say he's not at liberty to speak about specific cases, that HIPAA is pretty clear on this. Even a billionaire should understand that a doctor won't risk his license to satisfy a stranger's curiosity.

So, Mikhail Rotenberg doesn't trust her. Lyndsey would've been disappointed if he wasn't a little curious, at least. And no one wants all this meticulous legwork to go to waste.

He steps closer. "What a shame. I understand you've been pretty isolated for most of your life." His voice is low and calm, almost a caress.

She doesn't take another backward step, curious to see where Rotenberg is going. "My parents were overprotective, perhaps, but they were afraid that if something happened, I wouldn't be able to get the care I needed in time."

"What a lonely way to grow up." He is standing so close to her that they're practically touching. It's daring; anyone could walk by and see them. Emily could come home at any moment. It's as though he's deliberately pressing his luck.

"It was."

"I don't imagine you had a boyfriend, then, if you were kept at home alone."

Is he wondering if she's a virgin? This thought repulses her, but Lyndsey manages to smile for him. "That's right. I didn't get to interact with many people at all. Almost none my own age."

He laughs with a slight raucous edge. "You must be delighted to be out in the world. Eager to make up for lost time. Lost opportunities." It's obvious, what he's insinuating.

He's practically standing on top of her now. Lyndsey is not short, but Mikhail uses every inch to his advantage. She can feel the heat from his body, the warmth of his breath. He's not subtle with his intentions. He wants her to make a move, to touch him. What she can't figure out is whether it's a test. He can't truly be interested in her. Well . . . he would be interested in a conquest, and Lyndsey is pretty sure that's all he wants. He's not drawn to her as a person. In the least flattering scenario, he's only interested in her as a probable virgin upon whom he can bestow that first sexual experience.

A wave of nausea washes through her that she can't show. She can use this—though she doesn't want to.

Her sympathy for Emily is amplified a hundredfold. To think that this poor woman is shackled to this man. Though . . . she must know that this sort of thing happens. It must be part of the package when the power imbalance between partners is so great. He gets to have whatever he wants, and she can't complain. It might even be part of the dynamic, Mikhail's demands becoming increasingly outrageous, testing the limits of their damnable deal, perhaps, wondering what it would take to get her to stand up to him.

Sad, sad, sad.

His face is close to hers now. He's inhaling her scent, taking in what he can of her. He's not even being subtle. Her stomach roils; it's happening too suddenly. She hadn't considered that before she left this house, Rotenberg would make a move on her, though now she wonders why it hadn't occurred to her. Maybe because Emily is so beautiful, it's hard to imagine any man wouldn't be happy with her alone.

Noise echoes down the hall from the front of the mansion. A door opens and there's the sound of heels on stone and the bright metal clatter of keys. Mikhail steps away from Lyndsey quickly and in that split second, his whole attitude changes. He's back to his normal aloof self, giving her a cool look of superiority. Then, he is gone.

Just as Emily steps around the corner. She has the windblown appearance of someone who has been driving a convertible with the top down. She smooths her hair. "I'm back! I hope you weren't too lonely. That doctor is a miracle worker, I tell you. I feel one hundred percent better. Let me show you something marvelous that I picked up on the way home . . . A little treat for myself. If I don't deserve it, who does?"

That night before dinner, Lyndsey goes for a walk, heading for the green fields on the Heath. Once she is a good distance from the Rotenberg property, she takes out her phone and uses the encrypted app to leave a message for Davis. *Call me.*

He returns her call in less than five minutes. She assumes there's a team monitoring it for him, as cell phones aren't allowed inside Vauxhall Cross, any more than they're tolerated in Langley. "I called as soon as I got this message. Are you all right?"

She's touched by his concern. "Something happened that you need to be aware of: Rotenberg made a pass at me."

What happens next is a complete surprise. The normally cagey Davis Ranford roars over the phone, a sound like an explosion, an unchecked emotional burst. He's mad. After what he'd told her just days earlier, she thought he had no feelings for her anymore, that he's packed them all away in a box and put it on a shelf.

"He did *what*?"

"We were alone together for just a moment. We were interrupted. I'm not sure what would've happened next if we hadn't been . . ."

"Do you feel safe?"

"In the mansion? Yes. Normally, there's always someone around. This was an anomaly." She's being sensible. She doesn't get a threatening vibe from Rotenberg. Lyndsey feels confident that nothing would get out of control.

On the other end, Davis is quiet, trying to gather his emotions again. If he has any residual feelings for her, however, now it's time to set them aside. They must get practical. Rotenberg has given them this opportunity. They mustn't waste it. It would be wrong not to take advantage of it.

She must admit—if to no one but herself—that there's another reason the idea appeals to her. Right now, in the scorecard that keeps track of how well she and Dani are doing, you might consider Dani to be ahead. Dani wrangled a copy of the key to Westie's room, a plum. If Lyndsey could get close to Mikhail, there's no telling what she might learn. What she might be able to do. And quickly.

This is the kind of thinking that Lyndsey needs. Staff officers play by the rules, but contractors don't have time for niceties: they need to get the job done. Lyndsey must move out of her comfort zone if she is to compete and she must admit that the prospect is appealing.

Davis hems. "By your silence, am I to assume that you'd consider it?"

Leading a target on romantically . . . It's been done, of course. It's practically a staple of the tradecraft, though not encouraged for professional officers. It's better to play on other weaknesses or insecurities. Flirting is often part of the mix—who doesn't like to have their ego stroked?—but case officers are discouraged from sleeping with assets.

There's that comfort zone again. Inside, she squirms.

But Rotenberg wouldn't be her asset. And she wouldn't sleep with him. Letting him think she's interested would be a way to get closer to him, to slip into his personal space and coax more information out of him. This scenario wouldn't normally appeal to her. It seems cheap and tawdry, the kind of thing that would get talked about back at Langley, and there's already enough talk about her. More importantly, there are Emily's feelings to consider. It seems like a personal betrayal. Though this shouldn't matter—this is a matter of national security. Emily is not her friend, strictly speaking. Even though, in a roundabout way, Lyndsey would be doing it *for* Emily. To help *save* Emily.

It seems like she's trying to convince herself it's the right thing to do.

But the truth is that Emily is a target. Like her husband, though not as important as her husband. Lyndsey has grown to like the woman more than she should. She doesn't want to hurt her or put her in a bad position if she can help it. She needs to keep her own emotions out of the equation. There is a job to do.

"Are you still there, Lyndsey? Is it worth trying?"

"Possibly. Probably." Who is she kidding? "Yes. Definitely."

It isn't until she's ended the call and is making her way back to the mansion that an unpleasant thought occurs to her: was she nothing more than an opportunity to Davis? She stops dead on the sidewalk, traffic on Hampstead Lane whizzing by without taking notice of her. Suddenly, the lights and noise and cars are all very dizzying and surreal. Everything is turned upside down.

Because—maybe—the man she had trusted with her secrets has been playing her from the start.

She remembers when they met at that diplomatic cocktail party in Beirut, the tall, elegant Englishman giving her a weary smile from across the room. Had he known from the moment she walked into the party that she worked for CIA, that her line about working in the U.S. consular office was a lie? Had he decided here was an opportunity walking into his life, a young CIA agent who wasn't looking too hard? He'd be a fool not to take it.

And when they were separated, he hadn't gotten upset or tried to get in touch with her because it was never real to him. It was only an opportunity, run its course.

Only here she is back in his sphere of orbit, and he thinks maybe the opportunity has *not* run its course as he'd thought. As MI6 thought. She's here on a special assignment, which could mean her once-promising career is back on target. Maybe this relationship could be useful again, if he could get back into her life.

She chokes on air. Desperately needs water. Her cheeks flush, the streetlights become brighter like there's a sudden surge of electricity.

From shock. Shock and recognition.

He wouldn't be so calculating, would he? Had Davis Ranford turned her into an asset without her realizing it?

CHAPTER 24

Oh dear, oh dear, oh dear.

Emily had driven herself today to her doctor's appointment, a rare occasion. She's felt this way more and more since the incident with Oliver, that it would be better for everyone if she had less interaction with other people. Drivers, housekeepers, even the security guards: the less they know of her whereabouts, the better. Better for her, too. Probably.

Because she has driven herself, she brought the car around the back. It's closer to the garage, which she likes because she is tidy. She also prefers to enter the house from the back, through the patios and closer to her wing of the house, which is how she thinks of the children's wing. That way she's farther from Mikhail's wing—the offices, Westie's room—with much less chance of running into him. Emily takes pains to be quiet as she enters the house and trots silently up the stairs. She doesn't want to disturb her husband.

Only once she's inside, she sees what's going on in the library. Sees her husband standing next to Lynn. Sees how they stand so still, so unnaturally still.

She knows what those postures mean. What it means when neither of them look at each other but don't separate. The long, pregnant silence.

She manages to suppress a yelp. She was driving the Tesla and it's practically silent, that's why they didn't hear her come up. She tiptoes downstairs, as quiet as a mouse, slipping out the way she came. She doesn't exhale until she is outside again.

Shaking, Emily gets back into the car and, not knowing what else to do, drives around to the front of the house. She stays in the car for a moment, collecting her wits. It's hot inside the black sedan, but she doesn't move. She almost relishes the punishment of heat, the tight confines. She wants to cry. She wants to bang her fists against the steering wheel and curse and thrown a temper tantrum.

It's not because of her husband. She's past caring—much—what he does anymore. He's capable of awful things, terrible betrayals, much worse than this, she's sure.

No, what's torn her guts out, what's turned her world upside down, is *Lynn*. How could Lynn do this to her? Emily trusted her, brought the girl into her life, let Lynn near her children. Made her part of the family.

Lynn doesn't seem capable of such betrayal. She is the *opposite* of scheming. But Emily saw it with her own eyes, Lynn with her husband. It was an *intimate* scene. Maybe Lynn is naïve . . . It would be understandable, having been shut up for so long, raised cloistered like a nun. Unfamiliar with the ways of men. She would have no idea how tricky they can be, how selfish and scheming . . . No, it's not Lynn's fault, Emily decides. She hasn't misjudged her. The poor woman is being manipulated. Mikhail can be persuasive, clever as a fox. Emily's experienced this herself.

She gets out of the low-slung car. Her clothes are twisted and sticky.

She's been sweating in that hotbox of an automobile. She wants to take a cold shower and change into something fresh. She needs to get away and lie down in a dark, cool room. She needs to replay in her head what she saw, to analyze every nuance. To make sure she's not misinterpreting. To collect her thoughts before she runs into Mikhail.

Because . . . Here's the thing, the part Emily doesn't want to be true but that she can't ignore: what if she's wrong? What if Lynn isn't the naïve little thing Emily wants her to be? What if she's flattered by Mikhail's attentions? Or curious? Did Emily invite a serpent into her home? She was so ready to trust this woman with her safety and the safety of her children . . .

Is she wrong? Has she been wrong all along?

CHAPTER 25

The next day, the house is bristling with activity—and tension. It would've been hard for Lyndsey to miss.

First in the children's rooms, Miss Wilkinson going to and fro from a set of suitcases lying on the beds to a closet, stacks of tiny folded things in her hands. When Lyndsey asks if the family is going on vacation, the nanny's face goes ghostly and glum. "It's not my place to say," she murmurs as she turns back to her work.

Emily hasn't mentioned anything about a trip. Something's up.

There's an uptick in activity in the other wing, too, where Mikhail's and Emily's rooms are located. One of the housekeepers appears to be busy in Mikhail's room but Lyndsey can't get close enough to see exactly what's going on. The heavy oak door is nearly completely shut, and she can hardly press her eye to the crack. The logical thing would be to ask Emily about it, but Lyndsey senses this would be disastrous, though perhaps what she's feeling is just residual guilt for what happened in the library. She should ask one of the staff, she decides, but as she turns, she nearly runs into the last person she wants to see.

Mikhail.

He smiles down at her, pleased that she's almost run right into his chest. He doesn't step back but enjoys her embarrassment.

Has he caught her spying? Thank god she isn't any closer to his room. "I heard something going on . . ." she begins, gesturing in the direction of the sounds.

"And you were curious," he finishes for her. "Understandable. Yes, I'm going on a trip. I'll be going away for a while. A few months, in all likelihood."

Lyndsey's pulse quickens. It was always a possibility that Rotenberg would cut and run. The MI6 team had discussed it, but there had been no signs. It was all business as usual. Why hadn't the team developed a contingency plan? Her first thought is that she'll need to get a message to Vauxhall Cross.

"Another business trip?"

He tilts his head, deciding how much to tell her. By the amused smile on his face, it would appear he wants to tell her everything. "Not for business, no. I'm relocating for a little while, until things settle down in London. We're going to Ibiza. I have a villa there. It's comfortable and very private."

Something drops in the pit of her stomach. Is he about to slip through her fingers? It means the operation will be out of her hands. She should be relieved, but she is surprisingly disappointed. Her competitive streak, she figures. "Oh. Well, I'm sorry that you're leaving London, but Ibiza sounds lovely. I've never been there of course, only read about it in books. Well . . . I guess I should figure out where to go next. See if I can get my room back at that hotel . . ."

He smiles more broadly, amused by her confusion. "My dear Lynn, we're not running out on you. What bad hosts that would make us! It's not

Emily's fault . . . She didn't know. I only came to this decision recently, and, well . . . Emily's not coming, you see. I'm taking the children, yes, but not Emily." His eyes beg her to ask for more. He wants to explain, to air his side of the story, to gain her sympathy.

She gives him what he wants. She tilts her head coyly. "I don't understand."

He affects a pose that says *ah me*. "I don't want to appear insensitive toward my wife, Lynn, but . . . I assume Emily has shared that our marriage has been, well, *troubled* for some time now. It's not Emily's fault, you understand, not at all . . . It's just, well, these things happen, don't they? I won't pretend that my life isn't complicated. The stress is, frankly, monumental. And with what's been happening lately—well, it's no secret . . . You know we had a home invasion just a few weeks ago. That's enough to rupture even a solid marriage."

"I'm sorry to hear this. No, Emily hasn't said anything to me. I guess she's been keeping it all to herself."

"It doesn't surprise me that she's been making new friends," he continues. "You and that other woman . . . what's her name? Danielle? Emily was looking for a diversion, you see. For someone else with whom she could busy herself and ignore what was going on in our marriage." There is a touch of bitterness in his tone. "Though I suppose she needs her own support group—that's what she accuses *me* of, you know, buttressing myself with an entourage like some kind of pop star. It's ludicrous, of course. In my case they're not friends, they're business associates. With business affairs of this size and complexity, I need to keep my team close . . ." He trails off. Maybe he realizes how apologetic he sounds, like he's making excuses.

"Oh dear. If I'd known my presence here was going to be a problem,

I never would've accepted Emily's invitation." It seems what the fictional Lynn Prescott would say.

Mikhail rubs the bridge of his nose. "That wasn't what I meant at all. My wife is entitled to surround herself with friends. It's understandable, under the circumstances. But it's just as understandable that, if we're making each other unhappy, that I should go." Does he mean it? He sounds sincere. He's doing a good job appearing evenhanded and considerate.

But then again, he's taking the children away from their mother.

He's quiet for a moment, looking her over. He's trying to read her, to judge how she's going to react to what he says next. Lyndsey can tell he's got something more to say, something he's been turning over in the back of his mind since they were alone together in the library.

He steps closer so that their bodies are almost touching and bows his head over hers. "You've never been in Ibiza . . . A shame, really, since it's so close. And it is lovely, simply lovely. Why don't you come with me? There's plenty of room. The house is on its own peninsula. The views of the Mediterranean are spectacular. It's very private. You don't have to see another living soul if you don't want to. It will be—very safe."

Lyndsey sucks in a breath. In the back of her mind, she'd expected something like this but that doesn't make it any easier when the moment comes.

He studies her hesitancy. "I know how this looks, and I wouldn't blame you for thinking the worst of me." Clearly, however, he doesn't believe that. He can't believe for a second that anyone would think badly of him, to be anything but delighted by the offer he's just made. "But let me explain. Emily and I drifted apart a long time ago and have stayed together for the sake of the children. The usual story, so common it's almost laughable, We practically have separate lives—you must see this, living under our roof. We've had separate bedrooms for a while now. She has her life, her friends, her activities, and I have mine. Only it's gotten to the point where, frankly, I have to question whether it's worth it. Whether it's doing the children more harm than good. They're young; if we were to separate, the damage would be minimal. They probably wouldn't remember what it was like when the whole family was together." He puts it all in a way that makes him sound reasonable.

The wood-paneled hall is hushed, the only noise being the muffled sound of a housekeeper inside Mikhail's warren of rooms, packing. The purr of a heavy-duty zipper as a suitcase is closed, the sound of something heavy being deposited on the hardwood floor.

"I'm so sorry to hear this."

"These things happen in a marriage, don't they? I suppose it was inevitable in one as unusual as ours. I understand that, of course: you realize early on that this kind of wealth is going to skew every relationship in your life. My parents, my siblings. Friends from university. It's almost impossible to stay married. One look at my peers and you can see that's the case. The only ones I truly worry about are my children. Is it possible to raise children who can have anything they want, truly anything, without messing them up? I've seen what it's done to my peers' children . . . So many sad stories. Drug abuse, estrangement . . ." He shakes his head. He seems to have thought about this, to have taken it to heart, that it's not merely an act for her benefit.

"I can see that you're shocked by my invitation to come to Ibiza. I didn't mean to insult you. I'm not assuming that you would be interested in your friends' husbands. You don't seem like that kind of woman—and maybe that's why I'm attracted to you. You're a decent person." He sighs, tilting his head, weighted by heavy thoughts. "I'm surrounded by these opportuning Russian women, you know . . . I don't mean to sound immodest, but I'm propositioned by them all the time. It's the money, I know that, not for my scintillating personality"—self-deprecating chuckle—"but I find their constant conniving and scheming to be exhausting." He smiles at her, more warmly this time. "Well . . . you haven't said no, or stormed off, so can I hope that you might be considering the invitation?

"But I have one additional suggestion: before you come to a decision, why don't we spend some time together, get to know each other better? Come out to my apartment in town. Emily won't need to know. We can have dinner there. It's wonderfully private. How does that sound?"

It sounds exactly like what Davis would want to hear. But Lyndsey isn't sure how she wants to play this. Going to an apartment alone with him doesn't sound like a great idea. There's no telling what Mikhail's true intentions are, and she's inclined to think they're not as gentlemanly as he claims. It seems the perfect scenario to force himself on her, and if he meets with any hesitancy or resistance, later claim that she consented, that she knew what to expect when a gentleman invites a lady to his pied-à-terre.

How far is she willing to go for this mission?

She can't see herself sleeping with Mikhail Rotenberg. Officers have been known to sleep with assets, and maybe even targets. She can't speak to why they did it, what was going through their minds, if it was the only way to accomplish the mission, but for her it's a nonstarter. She would not be able to hide her dislike for him at close quarters. The best-case scenario would be to get close enough to find the information she needs without compromising her integrity.

But the clock is ticking now: Mikhail won't go to Ibiza alone, after all: the entourage will go with him, including Westie and all access to the financial data. This could be her last chance.

She feels cold with uncertainty. Every nerve in her body is telling her it's a bad idea. She thinks of the key in Emily's room. Maybe Davis and the brains at Vauxhall Cross will come up with a way to get to that data before Rotenberg decamps.

But in the meantime, he's waiting for an answer.

There's really no other answer she can give, not at the moment. Her job is to keep her options open. Her personal feelings can't enter into it. It's all pure cold, hard judgment.

"I don't want you to think the wrong thing about me, either . . . I'm not the kind of woman who steals her friends' husbands. I wouldn't even know how to do something like that." She forces a blush. "But . . . having said that . . . I see that the situation between you and Emily isn't what I thought it was. And I'd be lying if I said I didn't find you—intriguing." Another blush. "Dinner would be lovely." She whispers it, not believing that she's saying it.

He takes her hand in his great meaty paw and squeezes it. It takes every ounce of willpower not to pull away. "I'm so happy to hear that, my dear. Don't give it another thought—I'll take care of all the arrangements."

CHAPTER 26

Emily cocks an ear to the noises down the hall. Mikhail is in the house.

Emily hates it when Mikhail spends the night at home. Even though these nights are few and far between lately, they are invariably uncomfortable. They spend no time together anymore, not even for dinner with the children. And now that Emily has Lynn for company, it's been easier to ignore her husband, to ignore the big, gaping hole torn into the middle of her life where her marriage should be.

Mikhail will undoubtedly make an appearance before the night is over. She hears him in the background: a bump here, a raised voice there. He's on the phone or talking to Westie or bellowing at Igor. He never has guests over at The Bishops Avenue, not like Emily; he saves that for the Knightsbridge apartment, away from her prying eyes.

Nevertheless, at some point tonight, Mikhail will make an appearance. He'll be at her door to ask a question, an excuse to make a snide remark or to criticize her for something she'd done. He's not dropping by for sex: that stopped months ago. (Thank goodness, judging from these reports of his sleeping with another woman, or who knows what disease he might've picked up.) Still, her stomach knots at every one of these appearances. She has no idea what he wants, aside from torturing her.

She is rubbing moisturizer into her hands, her nightly ritual, when the door swings open. Her husband is not quite drunk but not sober, either. It makes her think of that scene in *Gone With the Wind*. Does that make her Scarlett O'Hara? She loved that movie as a child but never cared for that character very much, appalled to see a woman be that calculating, that grasping. Her mother hadn't cared much for the character either, wrinkling her nose whenever Vivien Leigh was on camera. Emily wants to think it was only what women were forced to do in the old days. Funny how such a beautiful woman could, in reality, be so ugly.

Mikhail's dark eyes skim over her, up and down. When they were dating, there was desire in those eyes, but she hasn't seen that warmth in a long time. For the children, yes: Mikhail loves his children, but they are still small. They are harmless, pliable, unquestioning. They still run toward him with their arms outstretched. *Daddy, daddy. Papochka*, he corrects them.

"I have something to tell you," he says. "You have probably noticed some activity today. I am having things packed up for me . . . and the children."

The children. She feels a sharp stab in her heart. "What do you mean? What's going on, Mikhail?"

"I'm going away for a while. After what happened"—the oblique way he refers to the home invasion—"it would be best." His smile is smug. He's not going to tell her what's going on. He's going to make her draw it out of him, one painful piece at a time. When did things get so bad between them? Was it because of Oliver? No, it had started before that. If she were truthful, she'd have to say it was like this from the very start. With

Mikhail, there is always something being held in reserve. He is always hiding something from her like a sadistic little boy.

"Why is it best? Have things changed? Are we in danger?"

He pretends to be considering her questions, as though he hasn't worked all this out in advance. "You didn't hear me, Emily. I'm not taking *you*. This is only for me and my loved ones." *Loved ones*. He casually studies his hands, as though they have suddenly become fascinating, or that they are to blame for these cruel machinations. The faint smile is still planted on his lips: *he's enjoying this*. "Yes, you could say that the situation has gotten complicated. It would be prudent for me to go away for a while, some place private. I am taking the children with me because it is in their best interest."

"It's not in the children's best interest to be separated from me."

"It will only be for a short while, until things calm down."

"Why can't I come with you?"

He makes an unpleasant expression, like he's bitten something sour. "Whom would that serve? Neither of us would be happy, Emily. You know that's true."

"It would serve the children, and that's what's important. They'll want to be with their mother."

"You can't expect me to leave them with you after what almost happened." He glowers at her. This is probably the closest he will come to talking about Oliver. He certainly won't mention him by name. He came too close to being surprised.

His mood changes. He smiles and waves a hand airily. "They'll be perfectly fine with me. They'll have Miss Wilkinson. And Miss Prescott. They seem to have grown quite attached to her."

Zing. In goes the figurative knife blade. "What are you talking about? Why would Lynn go with you?"

He shrugs. "It hasn't been quite decided yet but . . . She is a charming woman, Emily. So fresh, so—unjaded. I am so glad that you made her acquaintance, truly. You will not be surprised to hear that we have gotten quite attached to each other."

Emily struggles to breathe. The betrayal is staggering. Her husband is going to run off with her new best friend. She's not sure *whose* betrayal is worse.

But it's also hard to believe. Mikhail is acting too crafty, tiptoeing around like a fox circling the chicken coop. He's hedging his bets. "She hasn't agreed to it, has she?"

He purses his lips, a tell Emily figured out years ago. "Not yet, no." He cannot picture a scenario where she turns him down, that is clear. And why should he? Has any woman said no to him? A man with his money and power, a man who can buy you anything, take you anywhere, make anything possible. Who would say no?

That's why I fell for him. Emily's cheeks flame at the self-confession.

Tears well up. Emotion builds like water throwing itself against a seawall. A thought forms in her head. *What a relief it would be to let it loose, to let the ocean rage and let the chips fall where they may.*

"Why must you take everything, Mikhail? First my children and now my friend, too. You can have anything, anyone . . . Why deliberately hurt me like this?"

He stands back, studying her, but she sees that her outburst has shaken him. He didn't expect her to lose control like that. To say the words, speak the truth.

She's done more damage with Oliver than she'd thought possible. Finding out that she was going to leave him, that she had found the strength to pursue her independence, that was the ultimate betrayal.

But Mikhail had persevered. And now he's going to crush her like a bug. To utterly destroy her.

She takes a deep breath, forcing herself to calm down. "You're a bastard, do you know that? Why not just give me a divorce, Mikhail? Why must you torture me like this?"

This gets his attention. He does a double take, as though she's wounded him. "I'm not torturing you, Emily, no more than *you* are torturing *me*."

Then: "Divorce?" He says the word as though it had never crossed his mind. How could it not, when it's all Emily can think about? "We can consider divorce, if that is what you want. We'll need to come to terms that are acceptable to *both* of us."

He can't be serious. It would be a disastrously bad time for a divorce. Mikhail wouldn't want to risk exposing his financial Potemkin village in court. It would be like putting chum out for sharks, as far as Kosygin is concerned.

If he would grant her a divorce, though . . . It's not like she would have demands, not for herself. She never thought she'd be rewarded for this train wreck of a marriage, to walk away from it outrageously rich. What's really at stake would be the children. "What terms do you have in mind?"

He shrugs again. "I don't know. I haven't been thinking about it. That you want a divorce is a surprise to me." This is a lie, of course. "I will need to talk to the lawyers." He is perfectly controlled, not heartbroken in the least, while Emily is afraid a fresh flood of tears will start again.

Having sunk all his arrows into her vulnerable body, he turns and walks away.

After closing the door, Emily has a good cry. She buries her face in her hands and lets herself sob. Big, wracking sobs. Not because Mikhail doesn't love her anymore—did he ever love her? There is no sense of loss there, only relief.

She cries now because she doesn't know what will happen to her. She has isolated herself from the rest of the world for Mikhail. If she loses him now, what does that mean? She can't go back to her family, not after seeing what he did to Oliver . . . and he hates her parents, would be happy for the slightest excuse to wipe them off the face of the earth . . .

Even if they divorce, it doesn't mean Mikhail will let her go. He might toy with her for years, not allow her to have a life of her own, to get close to another man. Look at what happened to Oliver.

For the thousandth time, she curses her shortsightedness. How did she get in this mess?

She's not so naïve that she thinks he'd let her continue to raise the children. He'll try to take them away from her. He wants them raised Russian. She's nothing more than an impediment. She doesn't speak the language or know the customs. She hates to travel to Russia, even the huge compound in Sochi, and can't stand any of his associates. At best, he'd let her visit Tatiana and Kit, but the thought of not living with her children nearly drives her mad. It is worse than having a dozen white-hot knives plunged into her chest.

Without question, losing her children is the worst thing that could happen to her. Staying with Mikhail is the more favorable option, by far. As horrible as that is.

But he has made it clear that he no longer wants her.

There has to be a solution. She must hang on day by day. She must drag it out. Keep Mikhail from disappearing with her children until a long-term solution presents itself.

She can't think long-term right now. Survival is all she can handle at the moment.

The next morning finds Emily in bed, staring at the creamy plaster ceiling. She made it through the night with a few pills, but now she can't make herself throw back the covers and put her feet on the floor. Even with the pills, she's barely slept a wink. She spent the night picking over the exact words Mikhail used to describe Lynn.

Of all the troubles pressing down on her, Lynn should be the least of Emily's worries. Emily no longer wants Mikhail—if a sudden gust of wind were to drop a house on him like the Wicked Witch of the East in *The Wizard of Oz*, she'd be relieved—so why would she care if another woman took him off her hands? And yet, the thought gnaws at her. That a woman she trusted and brought into her life had the nerve to go after her husband.

Lynn is too smart to want Mikhail. Surely she must realize he is a snake, a dangerous, dangerous snake. Doesn't she have any sense of self-preservation?

Oh, right—the money.

Maybe Westie was right and Lynn Prescott has been planning this all along. Maybe this was the reason she'd sought Emily out at the luncheon and pursued a friendship. It must be hard to meet men when you spend your life in hospitals and doctors' offices. Maybe she'd seen *Forbes* in some doctor's waiting room and decided to use its article on the richest men in the world as a shopping list.

Emily wants to throw up. Heat spreads over her face, sweat breaks out on the back of her neck at the thought of being duped by Lynn, her sweet friend. She doesn't *want* to believe it. She *doesn't* believe it, no, not really . . . though there's something strangely comforting in thinking it's Lynn's fault.

That this has happened to Emily is fitting, too, in a *Mikado* let-the-punishment-fit-the-crime kind of way. After all, Mikhail hadn't been sitting home alone when Emily came along. Anya, his first wife, may have been out of the picture but Mikhail had had a mistress when Emily met him. Granted, Emily hadn't been aware of the woman's presence until after the mistress had been eased out the door. Emily now realizes guiltily that she'd thought little of it at the time, perhaps because Mikhail had described the woman as a mistress, not a girlfriend, implying that the relationship had been merely one of convenience, without emotional attachment. But Mikhail had thrown over a woman to be with Emily, and so it is karmic justice that the same thing happens to her.

Emily rises from bed, puts on a robe, and goes to the windows that face toward The Bishops Avenue. You can't see the road but the house is quiet enough for her to hear faint rustlings of the morning traffic. She jams her hands in the pockets and remains planted at the window, reluctant to start her day.

How blithely she's gone through life, Emily realizes. How little regard she's had for others. If she'd been paying attention more, been more attuned to others, maybe she wouldn't be in this situation. She'd have seen the warning signs. Known not to get involved with a womanizing, opportunistic ass like Mikhail Rotenberg.

That last fight with Jesamine comes back to her. Her sister had said similar things, thrown it all in Emily's face. *Fooling yourself . . . He'll hurt you, you'll see . . . He cares for no one but himself.*

How did Jesamine know? Well, she'd be pleased to know that she was right. Maybe one day Emily will get to tell her. Maybe one day her sister will return her phone calls and texts.

Emily can't put off starting her day any longer. She picks up her cell phone and scans through email messages. There aren't many. Only there, buried among the junk, is an email from Tholthorpe, her parents' solicitor. How did she miss that?

She clicks it open. *Dear Emily, I hope this email finds you well. I did as you asked and had a man see what he could find on this woman of interest to you. He's a good man, former DCI with the police, now retired. Thorough but discreet. I've attached his report. Do let me know if I can be of further assistance.* Emily thumbs down a little further: yes, there's an attachment, no two. An invoice from Tholthorpe's firm, of course, can't forget that. Another bill to be paid. Oh well; it's Mikhail's money and spending it this way feels fitting.

She opens the investigator's report. Her eyes fly over the words: family in Pennsylvania and New York State . . . Generational wealth, so Lynn's comfortably well off, but that wouldn't rule out being a gold digger. There's something about the sudden proximity of gobs of wealth that can turn some people—men as well as women, in Emily's experience—dotty.

There's only one photo, and it's terrible. Grainy. Obviously cut out of another photo, zoomed in on the presumed Lynn Prescott, a thin woman with yellow hair and huge sunglasses taking up most of her face. It bears a passing resemblance to the woman Emily knows but honestly, it could be anyone. Useless.

But this is interesting . . . Emily scrolls up and down, checking and rechecking . . . There's no mention that Lynn's been cured of her wretched childhood disease. This report makes it sound as though she's still a recluse living in her parents' home in Villanova.

Surely, it's an oversight. She doesn't know how these private investigators work, but she assumes it's mostly off databases, not that Tholthorpe has sent someone to Pennsylvania with a pair of binoculars to spy on the house.

What else in the report might be wrong?

The question pecks away at the back of her mind. Tholthorpe has made the situation worse, not better.

She decides to complain to the lawyer about the thinness of the work and to demand another pass. Put boots on the ground, as the newspapers like to say about military endeavors. This is a kind of war, isn't it? Emily is fighting for her life. Given the circumstances, it's more important than ever that she know exactly the kind of woman that Lynn Prescott really is.

CHAPTER 27

Is this a mistake?

Sometimes you don't know if you're making a mistake until it's done. Stepping off a diving board. Leaping out of an airplane. Squeezing the trigger.

Lyndsey fumbles with her earrings. It's normal to be nervous, she acknowledges. Even though, compared to other things she's done, dinner with Mikhail Rotenberg is comparatively low risk. She's snuck out for an assignation with someone many times. Meeting assets, that's her bread and butter. Well, Rotenberg is a target, not an asset. A foe, not a friend. Operations officers rarely get to go on a date with their targets. But she is cozying up to him like an asset, so in her mind he exists in a weird space between the two.

She feels bad for what she's doing to Emily. The whole thing is an elaborate little charade, starting with the lie that got her into Emily's sphere in the first place. Now, lying again, telling Emily that she is meeting a family friend for dinner in town when in fact she will be getting a taxi to whisk her away to Mikhail's Knightsbridge apartment.

She stands before the closet, trying to decide what to wear. She needs to pick her clothes carefully, walking a fine line on the signal she wants to give Mikhail. She can't look too eager. She should appear to not have made up her mind. She flips by a low-cut blouse. Definitely nothing seductive. Besides, it would make Emily wonder about whether the story about the family friend was true. She settles on a charmeuse blouse, shortish skirt, reasonable heels. She pins up her hair and dabs on dark lipstick.

Emily meets her downstairs. There's an air of restlessness about her but Lyndsey attributes it to her impending spell of loneliness, knowing she will be without her human crutch. "You look so nice," Emily says with forced cheerfulness. "Mikhail is staying in town tonight, so it's just me. The lady of the manor, rattling around her empty castle." Her smile is saccharine. "Enjoy your night with friends. I'll probably be asleep by the time you get back. I'll just watch a little telly and make it an early night." Emily plants a dry kiss on Lyndsey's cheek as she sees her off at the door, her eyes on Lyndsey's back as she gets into the taxi.

Stop thinking about Emily. Think about the night ahead.

"Posh address," the taxi driver murmurs as he pulls up in front of the building that houses Mikhail's apartment, not far from Brompton Square. Lyndsey pays conspicuously in cash. She's aware of the doorman studying her as she crosses the threshold. She's not as flashy as the women who usually are headed to Mikhail Rotenberg's apartment, no doubt.

Turns out that Rotenberg has the penthouse. Naturally. He opens the door himself to welcome her. He gives an abbreviated tour, starting with the wall of windows that look over the city. "It's just a little pied-à-terre," he says, and true, it's more modest than she expected, smaller and more private. Yet over-the-top in its man cave way, stuffed with leather furniture and conspicuous art objects, the walls painted in shades of charcoal and dark gray green. She imagines there's a famous designer in London known for this sort of thing: interior designer to dot-com billionaires.

They appear to be alone. The servants have either been dismissed for the evening or there is a suite downstairs or tucked in a corner where they are hiding. The table has been set and the plates are covered by silver domes. "I ordered dinner from my favorite restaurant," he says. "I hope you approve of my choices." The customary arrogance appears to have been bled from his voice for the evening, but she can't rule out that it's a well-practiced act.

He hands her a glass of wine and they sit near that huge bank of windows, the velvety sky punctuated by a dusting of twinkling white lights.

"Why don't you tell me about yourself?" Lyndsey says. "I've heard a few things"—she is careful to leave out from whom she's been told—"but I feel as though I hardly know you."

Mikhail smiles broadly. He does love to talk about himself. It's interesting to get the story from his side, how Mikhail Rotenberg views himself. "You might say that I'm a self-made man," he begins, starting with his time in university, a young man with vital interests and his own view of the world, already independent from his family. His view is slightly more flattering than what Emily has told her or that Lyndsey's read in MI6's file. Upper-class Russians downplay their family connections, preferring to be seen as self-made. "My parents were intellectuals, not well-connected Communist Party people," he says, though the MI6 report says they are both. "I had a little money when I graduated from university and was able to use that to buy a couple fledgling businesses. The Wild West days after the fall of Communism were over but there were still opportunities if you knew where to look." He partnered with an older businessman who got him into a few good deals in oil and shipyards. "From there, it was a matter of buying promising businesses when the opportunity presented itself and making them successful." He takes a drink, as though toasting himself.

"You make it sound easy," Lyndsey murmurs. What he's not admitting, however, is the machinations that took place behind the scenes to make things go his way. The bribes, the threats. To get anything done in Russia in those days took a series of agreements or confrontations with everyone who had a say or levied some bit of authority. Where administration was still unsettled, whether at the neighborhood level or all the way up to the Duma, everyone was out to grab as much as he could for himself.

They are sitting close now. She's practically tucked under his arm. So far, he has been gentlemanly. He hasn't so much as laid a finger on her, but being this close to him revolts her. She wants to shimmy away—and she will as soon as the opportunity presents itself—but she doesn't want to shut him down. She's been trained to control her feelings. It was all part of the training at the Farm. Learning to keep your emotions in check, to detach from a situation, to think two or three steps ahead.

"Easy? No." He chuckles. "And I wouldn't deny that maybe I've made some bad choices. I put my business before my personal life, especially in the beginning. The pressure to succeed in Russia is high. Muscovites aren't apologetic about their ambitions: money and success are all they think about. It's how you are judged. I couldn't resist in the early days. But now . . . let's just say that as I've gotten older, I'm learning the value of pleasing myself."

It's all a self-serving lie, of course. Perhaps not *entirely* a lie: Mikhail Rotenberg has probably always sought to please himself.

They work their way through most of the bottle. When he asks her to tell him about herself, Lyndsey does a careful retelling of what she's given

Emily already; it's not hard, having committed her persona's backstory to memory. *The best cover is the truth*, they told her during training at the Farm. *Keep your story as close to the truth as possible, that way you'll have less to remember.*

"It was tough, I'll admit," she says. She uses the opportunity to draw away from him and settle into the sofa. "Growing up almost entirely by myself, no friends my own age." To make Lynn Prescott more believable, Lyndsey draws on the pain she suffered during childhood when she lost her father at just eight years of age. She pulls from the years feeling apart from other children. She was a lonely child, just like Lynn Prescott. They are not so different.

Mikhail pours more wine into her glass. He appears to hang on her every word, soaking up her little stories as though every facet of her life is fascinating, but Lyndsey wonders what is going on in his head. For once, her powers of observation falter. It's like playing chess with someone who is just good enough to hide how hard he might be working.

Her sense is that—where they are tonight, what they are doing together notwithstanding—Mikhail Rotenberg is still not sure what to make of her. Whether to believe her. Which means he either enjoys flirting with disaster or has decided he must have her (for whatever reason) and logic be damned.

They are almost through appetizers when Emily comes up in conversation. Lyndsey was wondering when that would happen—*when*, not *if*; it seems impossible that they would be able to navigate this evening without her. Her presence is like a ghost in the room, hovering between them, looking down on them in disbelief.

"I never meant to hurt Emily," Mikhail says as he toys with a piece of prosciutto wrapped around a crisp straw of bread. "I knew as soon as I met her that she would be the perfect mother for my children. And it was time for me to have children, to have heirs. To have people with whom to share the fruits of my labors."

"She is a wonderful mother."

He smiles wistfully. "I was so enamored with my idea of her as a mother that I completely forgot that she had to be a wife, too. *My* wife. I tried, I did—as did she, Lynn, don't misunderstand me. But shortly after the twins were born, it became clear that I'd made a mistake." He sees that he's made an error and quickly covers. "We *both* saw at that point, I think, that we had chosen wrongly. And now we are at this crossroads. We have made these two beautiful little people. Our children, so perfect. But we should no longer be married. So, what do we do? Should we part, to make ourselves happy? Or do we stay together for the children's sake?"

She thinks back to her own childhood. The most important thing to children is for their family—the root of their security—to remain intact. And that is, undoubtedly, what the twins would tell their father if they were of an age where they understood things like divorce.

But adults are the ones who make the decisions, adults who are supposed to understand that everyone has a right to happiness. People should be allowed to part ways and start again—even if there is a lot of pain.

He tilts his head. "There is one other thing . . . about Emily. Perhaps you've noticed."

Lyndsey's ears prick up. "What do you mean?"

He sighs. "She has changed. She is not the woman I married. This is inevitable, of course, especially after one has children. But in the past year I've noticed . . . she's an unhappy woman. Her unhappiness has twisted her. I've tried to get her to see a therapist. She refuses. Instead, she drinks. What is it people call alcoholism these days? Self-medicating?"

Lyndsey thinks about their time together. There's always wine. She has a hangover most mornings after a night with Emily. Maybe there's a grain of truth there.

And Emily has seemed frazzled, but who in her position wouldn't? They'd had armed thieves—or worse—break into their home. Her husband is a corrupt oligarch at the beck and call of a vicious autocrat.

Or Mikhail Rotenberg could be laying the groundwork for a defense in divorce court. *She's unstable, she drinks too much. Even her friends think so.*

They go to the dining table, laid out and waiting for them like something in a fairy tale. The food is delicious, clearly intended as a prelude to seduction. Buttery and bright pink tenderloin, so rich it melts on the tongue, accompanied by caramelized green beans. The vinaigrette on the salad is both fruity and tart, brightening the palate. The Château Lafite he brought out from his cellar is easily the best wine she's ever had or ever will have in her entire life. She's afraid to think how much it probably cost.

He's been careful to avoid any talk about money. Most of the women he wines and dines are probably only interested in his wealth. They would be excited by lists of businesses he owns and how they've appreciated in value. He would entertain these women with stories of flying around the world to tend to his businesses; parties with celebrities; of waking up in the most expensive, luxurious hotels and private estates on the planet. He sends his Bentley to pick them up and maybe jets them to Paris or Vienna for dinner. The opposite of everything he's done tonight for Lyndsey, in other words.

With those women, it's a given that the evening will culminate with sex in that private jet, twenty thousand feet above the ground. There could be no other ending, and both parties would know this. What about tonight, however? His modest approach might mean that he has modest expectations. He may want something different from Lynn Prescott than he does from the Russian models and starlets that are his usual conquests—though she doubts it.

Or he's figured out that the path to a yes from Lynn is very, very different.

"Let's go out on the balcony for dessert," he says as he heads to the kitchen, where their dessert has been hidden from view.

She opens the door to the outdoor space. It's almost a misnomer to call it a balcony, it's so big. She stands at the railing and lets the glow from the city wash over her.

Mikhail comes out with a tray. On it is another bottle of wine, two small etched glasses, and two dishes filled with some confectionary concoction. The wine he pours into the glasses is an amber tone and has a sweet bouquet. "Hungarian Tokay, a weakness of mine," he confesses. "Cheers." They clink glasses.

As they sip and look over the cityscape, Lyndsey thinks about what to do next. What to say next—and where anything she says might lead her. The only reason she is here is that she needs information from Mikhail Rotenberg, specific information. Not the kind of things you discuss while on an evening of seduction.

But what she does tonight might lead her to that information one day.

They dip tiny silver spoons into dessert: meringues and cream, brandied cherries and chocolate sauce, toasted hazelnuts. As they eat slowly, he points out famous spots on the horizon, although they are mostly invisible in the inky darkness. Westminster Abbey, Hyde Park, the Royal Albert Hall. Tate Modern, across the Thames. They're all just twinkling lights in a pool of black. He promises to take her to these places, if she wishes. He will show her all of London, arrange tours for her at museums and backstage at theaters, parts that the public never gets to see, guided tours by artists and museum directors or other dignitaries who don't have the time to indulge such favors—unless the favors are for Mikhail Rotenberg.

He tells her that this dessert calls to mind one that his mother used to make for him on special occasions when he was a boy. The brandied cherries were her favorite.

The oligarch is showing his weaknesses to her. That is how he plans to seduce her, to manipulate her: by showing her his soft, melting core.

They go inside. He pours brandies and sits close to her on the sofa. The lights are low, the air warm, the brandy plying its charms. Mikhail sits casually next to her, arm along the back of the sofa behind her, and tells her stories from his childhood. Of being a young boy watching the fall of the Berlin Wall on a news program, not grasping why his father rushed home from his office that day or why his mother was crying with joy.

"All my life, it's been work, work, work. Strive to get ahead, to be better, to be the best, the biggest. To make my father proud, to keep my mother secure. Not so unusual," he says with a sigh. His voice is quieter and gentler than she's ever heard it. "None of it has turned out the way I thought it would. It's all"—he runs a hand over his face roughly—"more complicated than I thought it would be. And always, always to someone else's benefit. It's always take, take, more and more." He doesn't have to say who that person is.

At one point, he leans in for a kiss. It is more gentlemanly than she'd imagined. Tentative, testing. He is going slowly and deliberately, wants to be sure this is what she wants. That she's comfortable.

His hands on her back, in her hair, on her forearm make her skin crawl.

She holds herself in check. She can't flinch, not even the littlest bit, or he will feel it.

They talk a bit longer. They lean into the velvet pillows and sable throws. He wants to know more about her, what she thinks. How is she finding it, this foray into the big wide world after a lifetime of sequestration? Is she eager to see more, to travel to the corners of the globe? He can give that to her, he says. "I'd like to do that for you. Take you to my favorite places. Show you how glorious the world can be." His smile is broad and knowing. He thinks he has caught her. That she's almost eating out of his hand.

Lyndsey gives herself over entirely to her persona; it's like being in a play, slipping entirely into a character. "Well . . . I'd like to go to the Greek islands, to the Maldives, to Bondi Beach in Australia. All those places I've only seen in movies."

"You're a beach girl, then. Fitting, because I'm sure you look dynamite in a bikini." He promises week-long cruises on three-masted schooners, full crews to attend to their every need.

And then it comes, the moment she has been dreading. The moment that can make or break everything.

He leans over her, trying to force her backward onto the couch. He presses his weight into her, against her, his chest flattened against hers, his hips shifting so that he is climbing over her. On top of her.

In a minute, she will be pressed underneath him and Mikhail Rotenberg does not seem like the kind of man to stop once he has gotten started. A wave of panic rises inside her—in this position, she could quickly lose control—but she forces it down. There's still time to get out of it, but she hasn't got much longer.

She presses her hands against Mikhail's chest as she forces her way upright again. She pulls back from his reaching lips. "This is going too fast," she says, pushing him away. "I'm sorry, Mikhail, but . . . I'm not used to this."

He smooths an errant lock of hair. "I thought this was what you wanted."

"I do—at least, I think I do. But I need you to go slowly. You understand, don't you?"

What can he say—he'll look like a cad if he continues. It's a test of how badly he wants this prize: a thirtysomething-year-old virgin, his wife's best friend, whatever the temptation is that has drawn him to her.

Has she spoiled it? she wonders. Ruined her chances?

Shortly after midnight, he sees her down to the private garage. He holds her hands and kisses her again, more aggressively. A promise of what he wants to do if she would let him. He says he will not press her tonight; he knows she is not that kind of woman. He is *happy* she is not that kind of woman. He's ordered a private car to take her back to The Bishops Avenue. It cannot be one of his cars, for obvious reasons.

They will need to be careful, he reminds her. He knows he can trust her. "You're smart," he says with a laugh. Implying that his wife is not. "That's another thing that drew me to you. You have an innate cleverness and quickness that you don't find in most people."

If he only knew.

He kisses her again before finally letting her slip into the back seat.

Once the car has pulled away from the curb, she lets out a sigh of relief. Never has she been so glad to see an evening over.

She looks out the rear window, watching him get smaller.

She has finessed this first test, but what will she do the next time they're together?

CHAPTER 28

When Lyndsey wakes up the next morning, the taste of brandied cherries and Mikhail Rotenberg's kiss still on her lips, she finds a message waiting for her on the secure messaging app.

We need you to come in 2 p.m. today, followed by an address. *Utmost urgency. Obey all protocols.*

Duty calls.

Lyndsey endures a full two-hour dry cleaning—buses, the Underground, Ubers, and taxis—to get to the address MI6 provided. To a safe house, a nondescript building on an ordinary, unassuming backstreet. She walks by cars and occasionally sees the outline of a figure behind the wheel and, once in a great while, feels a tingling sensation that makes her assume it's a watcher. She could be right or wrong: there is no acknowledgment as she passes. That's part of the business, too, and you get used to it. She has the feeling that MI6 wouldn't normally bring a CIA agent into the debriefing of an asset, but then there's no denying that things have reached an extraordinary point in this operation.

The crew at the safe house puts her in a room the size of a closet to observe the interrogation behind one-way glass. "The asset is a Russian expat," Davis had explained over the secure line. "He's on the fringes of Rotenberg's circle. Obviously, we don't want to run the risk of him seeing you." Davis sits beside her now, the two of them crammed together in the tiny space. Their shoulders and upper arms press together like old times, like when they lay in bed together in her Beirut apartment.

Lyndsey doesn't recognize the man on the other side of the window. He's in his forties, thickset, with graying wiry hair and a slight ethnic look, as though he might be from one of the Central Asian republics. A Kazakh or Kyrgyz, perhaps.

He is understandably uncomfortable. He keeps his gaze down and his fingers fidget, as though he wishes he were cradling a cigarette. He's sweating, but that could be because he's run a surveillance detection route, too, a more arduous one than Lyndsey because his life and the lives of his loved ones depend on it. He dabs at his damp forehead with the back of his hand. The British officer sitting across from him offers a serviette.

There are three people in the room with the asset. His handler, an MI5 officer, sits across from the asset. He's in his fifties, maybe, thin and severe looking, wearing an out-of-fashion tweed suit. A middle-aged woman in a skirt and eyeglasses sits at a table toward the back of the room, a notebook open in front of her. It's her responsibility to take notes while the other handles questioning.

The last is Parth Arya. Lyndsey hasn't seen him since he briefed her for the operation, sent her to ensnare Emily. The asset keeps glancing nervously over at him, so presumably they've not met before. This interview is significant enough to bring in the head of the oligarch team.

"In an earlier meeting, you'd given us some information on the

Rotenberg attack," the MI6 officer says gently, like a teacher prompting a schoolboy to a playground confession. "Would you mind repeating what you'd said?"

The asset's eyes flick to his handler's face. He clears his throat. "Yes. I heard this a couple nights ago from a man who works for Boris Sidorov. He is Sidorov's chauffeur. He overheard it while his boss was talking on the phone in the back seat. Sidorov knows everything that happens in the Russian community, so it must be true."

"Could this man, the chauffeur, have been lying? How well do you know him?" the handler asks patiently. Even this gentle probing is too much, however, and the asset must reach for his cigarettes, pausing to look to the handler for permission. The handler nods.

After the first drag on the cigarette, the asset is visibly more relaxed. His shoulders lower, his face muscles unclench. He takes a second drag, then clears his phlegmy throat. "I don't know him, no. But he seemed to be telling the truth. There was no reason for him to lie. It was just a few of us playing cards. He was upset, like he had just learned this and was shaken up and had to tell somebody. We do it all the time, you know. Talk among ourselves about the bosses."

So, the asset was not one of the rich expats. He worked for one of them, part of the sea of Russians who surrounded the oligarchs, the bookkeepers and bodyguards, drivers and housekeepers and nannies. The army of nameless, faceless people, underpaid and often threatened with the loss of their crummy jobs and cushy overseas positions for the slightest infraction, real or perceived. Little people who—with the right motivation—made good spies.

The handler pushes the saucer of his teacup toward the asset so he can use it for an ashtray. A veil of smoke begins to collect in the air between them. "So—what did this man overhear?"

The asset taps ash into the saucer. "That Oleg Galchev was behind the hit on Rotenberg."

Davis leans forward. In the room, Parth jerks, then catches himself before the asset notices. It's the first time he's moved.

"Galchev?" the handler says. "The big media guy?"

"Yeah, the same. Sidorov said Putin never liked Galchev, but now that he's gone, Galchev sees his opportunity to become one of the big players. He's been getting close to Kosygin. Sidorov said it was well-known in Moscow that Galchev had it in for Rotenberg for a long time. Sidorov said Kosygin must've decided to take Galchev up on the offer, or else it would not have happened."

"And you believe him?" the handler asks.

The asset shrugs. "He's never said crazy shit before. The things he's got from Sidorov have come true . . ." He seems to be searching his memory. Again, this will be a question for the handler and the reports officer. They will be keeping track of the veracity of the claims made by the asset, the usefulness of his sources.

Things are winding up. It's almost a throwaway, but the handler asks one last question. "Is there anything else Sidorov said that you can remember?"

The asset scowls and scratches his head. At length, he says, "Yes. He said something about making Rotenberg pay for China. But he didn't explain what he meant." The man shrugs.

China. She'd deliberately withheld what Tarasenko had told her in that alley in Tallinn. Because Tarasenko, as a source, is compartmented, as is Babanina. Because she had no authorization to give it to the Brits.

Davis and Arya look unimpressed but Lyndsey wants to shout, *He's telling the truth*. There's something important here. Something they don't know yet. *Make Rotenberg pay for what?*

Neither the handler nor the woman taking notes react in any way in front of the asset. They're very controlled. It's maddening for the asset, who must be dying for reassurance of some kind, but they don't want to interfere with him, to subconsciously nudge him in one direction or another. What he's brought to them is very important. It must be as pure and untainted as possible.

Arya, nothing more than a sylph at the back of the room, quietly exits. Lyndsey would've missed it if not for Davis nudging her before exiting the closet himself. She follows.

Davis leads her down a narrow hallway and through a heavy, soundproof door. The room he's taken her to appears to be a kitchen. What should've been a normal kitchen in a normal apartment has been made drab and institutional. It's practically bare, with only a few assorted mugs on the counter and a glass container half-filled with sugar. There's no decoration on the walls. The hand towel draped over the edge of the metal sink is gray and shapeless from endless wringing. The only window in the room has a heavy curtain drawn over it. If she were to check the refrigerator and cupboards, Lyndsey is sure she would find the bare minimum, which is the case in safe houses everywhere. A jar of instant coffee and powdered creamer, a bit of a stick of margarine still in the wrapper and a few packets of ketchup from a fast-food place.

True to form, Arya stands at the stove tending a kettle, a random mug with a tea bag at the ready on the counter. Davis slides into one of the chairs at the kitchen table. "You can speak freely. He won't hear us. The room is soundproofed," he says to Lyndsey. Or as soundproofed as possible.

Davis leans against the wall. "Obviously this is big news, but I need someone to fill me in." To Arya, he asks, "Who is Oleg Galchev?"

Arya lifts the kettle just before it begins to scream—no sense alerting the asset to activity down the hall—and fills the teacup. "An arriviste oligarch. Made his money ostensibly in media but we suspect he's behind a couple of the internet troll farms that have been plaguing us lately. Making himself helpful, you know. We'd heard he was desperate to get closer to Kosygin but we didn't know how seriously to take this."

"Very seriously, I would think," Davis says. "And what better way to climb a few rungs up the ladder than by taking out one of the guys in front of you?"

"But why is it possible now?" Lyndsey asks. "What did Rotenberg do that made Kosygin change his mind?"

Arya dunks the tea bag. "We've heard rumors that Rotenberg pissed off the boss . . . *Really* pissed him off. It's something personal."

Davis lifts his head. "Such as?"

Arya's cheeks color a little. "It's of a salacious nature. I'd rather not say until I know for sure that it's true. Besides, it might just be a fig leaf for Kosygin. An excuse to move on an oligarch without frightening the rest."

Lyndsey pictures the oligarchs like a herd of deer at the watering hole. Not caring which member of the pack is brought down by the approaching lion, as long as it isn't *them*.

Davis turns to the analyst. "Well, get to the bottom of it. Find out what's really going on here. Let's see if we can corroborate the chauffeur's information. Task other assets. Make it a priority. If Galchev is trying to take out Rotenberg, someone will know something. Do we have anyone close to Galchev?"

Arya snorts. "It shouldn't be hard to find someone. He's a bit of a loudmouth. Those types tend to surround themselves with more of the same."

"Good. Needless to say, time is of the essence."

Lyndsey rubs her temple. Her every instinct is to mention China. She wants to tell them she has another source with this same information . . . But she doesn't have the authority to do that. Tarasenko's status is compartmentalized NOFORN—not to be shared with any foreigners. That includes Brits.

The answer is not to name her source, no matter how hard they push to get it out of her.

"Look," she says, abruptly interrupting them. "I have something to tell you. I think there might be something to this China angle."

"China?" Arya raises his head. "I thought he was talking about dishes . . . plates . . ."

"We got some information—I can't share the source—that Kosygin has approached China through back channels. We don't know what it's about yet. I should've told you earlier, but the information is still being corroborated. One of the sources is being vetted."

Davis exchanges a look with Arya before turning to Lyndsey.

"Do you trust this source?" Arya asks. "Do you *believe* him?"

Your first reaction is usually the truthful one, and Lyndsey is surprised to find that she does. Tarasenko doesn't want to end their relationship by giving her obviously false information. He's given her the truth, but whether it's only to lull her into a false sense of security in order to pull off a bigger betrayal down the road . . . that, she can't tell yet.

"Yes, I do," she says softly.

"All right then," Davis says with a hint of sarcasm. "We'll see if MI6 can turn up anything on this China angle."

Davis waits until Arya has left the room to turn to Lyndsey. "By the way, we haven't told the rest of the task force about this latest development with Rotenberg. About *you* and Rotenberg."

"Oh."

Davis began to trace his finger along the tabletop. "I've been giving it more thought and . . . I don't know how I feel about this. It's the kind of tactic that can hurt you down the road, you know?"

Didn't she. A woman in the business had to be careful with her reputation. It could be used against you. A complaint circulating among peers ("You heard how she managed her big success . . . ?") about taking shortcuts and the like. It had been used against her in Beirut by jealous peers who'd wanted to see her taken down a peg. Her mistake was in giving them the means.

She gestures in the direction of the room where the MI6 officers are with the asset. "If Galchev is as pushy and impulsive as Arya makes him sound . . . Could he be the one who hired Intent?"

Davis thinks for a moment. "It's possible. It would be smart of him to send someone who isn't Russian . . . A flanking maneuver of sorts. It makes me wonder what else Intent is up to. I think it's time to call Trevor Conway in for a talk, as little as Vauxhall Cross will want to do that. We'll see what else they've been up to. Now that we know Galchev is part of the equation, we've got to figure out what it means."

CHAPTER 29

Emily tiptoes to the door of her bedroom and double-checks the lock. She doesn't want to be interrupted, not by Lynn, not by her children, not by any of the staff. She especially doesn't want to be discovered by her husband, though the odds of that happening are slim. It is afternoon and he is working—whatever it is that he does that he calls work.

She lies on the bed with a box of tissues, pulling them out as the one in her hand quickly becomes sodden with her tears. Is she crying over Mikhail? No, not really . . . She is crying for herself. How did things get this bad? Why is her life going to shit so suddenly? No one would've predicted this when she was a little girl. No one told her, *Enjoy it while you can because one day you'll be living at the bottom of a deep, dark hole that you can't get out of.* No one warned her that she was going to take her promising life, her easy life, and screw things up completely.

Should she admit defeat? If she does, Mikhail will get the children, but she will be free. There is no question that the children will be worse off, even with nannies and money, so for Emily, this is a nonstarter. And she *knows* that she's not just being self-serving here. The children are young. They're still at the age where they want a parent's attention. Where the mother is more important to them than the father. The day will come when they prefer the comfort of things—cars, ski trips, famous celebrities singing at their birthday parties—and the magical ability to do or have anything. And then Mikhail will be the one they turn to. Daddy, with his deep pockets.

But at two years old, that day is a long way away.

Then there is Lynn, the woman she thought she could trust. That lovely friendship has gotten all turned around. She finally broke down and told Dani—who else does she have to talk to?—but Dani seemed to think it off base. "Lynn? I don't see it," she said, even after Emily told her how she'd caught the two of them with their heads bowed together intimately. Then the two of them just happening to have appointments elsewhere the same evening. *A wife knows*, she'd insisted to Dani, who nonetheless gave her a dubious look. "Let me see what I can find out," Dani had said, and then two seconds later Lynn burst in on them with a bottle of wine and glasses. She *had* to have overheard them—how else to explain the look that passed between Lynn and Dani? Like Emily had lost her mind. Like she's adrift in the seething tangle of her emotions, so lost and unable to see it.

Well, she is adrift. She has never, ever felt so helpless. So *lost*.

That was when she ran upstairs to her room.

She dabs at her nose. Maybe she is being hasty. Mikhail may be gone before he's able to steal the children away. The way things are headed, he will be dead or inside a Russian jail. It feels wrong to think these things about her husband—if she's being honest, to *wish* for these things—and a shiver runs down her spine as though an ice cube is being pressed on her vertebrae. But it's quite possible. If the rumors are true and if the worst person in the universe is gunning for her husband, then the *best* Mikhail can hope for is to lose all his money. And "all his money" still means he'll probably be left with a couple million dollars. It just means he won't have unlimited wealth. That he'll need to be careful how he spends it, though it's not like he'll be living in a cold-water flat or cutting coupons.

But Mikhail is stingy and stubborn. He wouldn't give in to anyone, not even the grudge-holding Russian president. He wouldn't give him the satisfaction. Mikhail feels entitled to everything he has, that he earned every tainted dollar the same way a ditchdigger or construction worker has earned his pay. The idea is so ludicrous that it makes her want to laugh. He's so wounded that Viktor Kosygin would be putting the squeeze on him, a man who apparently believes *everything* belongs to him.

And that's the problem, isn't it? Mikhail doesn't want to admit that his empire is conditional, that he only gets to have it if someone else *lets* him.

He picked the wrong man to count on.

Much like Emily herself.

As she dries her tears, she remembers what Svetlana Khorkova said to her the other day. *Have you thought about saving yourself?*

She couldn't understand how a woman as accomplished and determined as Svetlana Khorkova could be shackled to a man like Kirill. He is not half the person his wife is in terms of character, and yet she wasn't able to get a tenth as far in life as he has.

The unfairness of life. The least deserving, it seems, get to be the winners.

Does Svetlana resent it, question it, cry herself to sleep over it? Maybe. But then she picks herself up and dusts herself off and does what she has to.

And then there is the other thing Svetlana said, when she gripped

Emily's arm and drew her close so she could whisper directly in Emily's ear, so there wasn't a chance of being overheard by either a passing party-goer or an FSB microphone hidden somewhere in the walls.

There is someone who would like to talk to you. Someone who can help you.

Then she pressed a piece of paper with a phone number into her hands.

Emily, at the complete end of her tether, abandoned and alone at the bottom of a deep dark well, could use some help right about now.

She picks up her phone.

CHAPTER 30

Lyndsey walks Dani to her car. She'd overheard Emily confess to Dani that she thinks Lynn is having an affair with her husband, hence the awkward round of drinks. After that, Emily broke away abruptly, running up the stairs and slamming her bedroom door behind her.

Dani stands by her car, dangling the keys. She gets to retreat to the quiet luxury of a hotel room and Lyndsey wishes she could leave with her. "Thank you for heading off Emily."

"She thinks you're fooling around with her husband," Dani says, incredulous. "All that drink has finally gone to her head."

Lyndsey lets out a heavy sigh. "No, it hasn't. It's true."

They end up driving to a quiet corner on the far side of Hampstead Heath. Any onlookers will think the two dark figures in the car are only two teenagers snogging. Lyndsey hasn't figured out what she will say to Emily about her disappearance when she returns, but she has to talk to someone. It is a rare occurrence at Langley when you feel you can be completely honest with one of your colleagues—you only make that mistake once—but in that moment, she feels as close to Dani Childs as she's been to anyone.

They sit in the dark. Dani cracks a window and lights up a cigarette. Insect trills and chirps and far-off, muted laughter of the inebriated wandering through the park provide background noise.

"I feel I can trust you," Lyndsey says, as much an admission as a prelude to what she is about to say. She doesn't bother to explain why she is opening up to Dani. There is no one else. She feels comfortable with Dani because of their shared experiences, their shared outlook. She will understand why Lyndsey is even considering this little exploit involving Mikhail Rotenberg in a way that no one else will. "What Emily told you is true: Mikhail Rotenberg made a pass at me and MI6 wants to use this."

Dani bobbles her cigarette, nearly dropping it in her lap. "You're kidding."

"I wish I were. We had dinner last night at his apartment. I managed to control the situation and nothing happened, but I guess Emily found out about it."

Dani sends a stream of smoke out the window. "How d'you think *that* happened? Did Mikhail tell her?"

"Maybe Emily pays the servants to keep tabs on her husband. He's not universally liked in this household."

"Do you think he's that much of an asshole?"

"Probably."

They switch gears, talking for another half hour about funny incidents in training at the Farm and mutual acquaintances. It feels good to forget about Emily and Mikhail for a while, to escape from the claustrophobic confines of the mansion. Dani chain-smokes, shedding ash through the cracked window with a flick to the filter with one of her beautifully manicured nails.

Eventually the laughs and small talk dwindle to silence, and Lyndsey cannot avoid what's waiting for her.

"So, what are you going to do about Mikhail?" Dani asks.

Lyndsey rubs hard at her eyes. "Time is running out. He's about to leave for Ibiza and you know what that means for the financial data. I may have no choice but to go with him."

They sit in silence, cigarette smoke wrapping around them, filling the car. They both understand what this will do to Emily, and also that it will make the mission that much more dangerous, in a private villa at an isolated location.

"Not what you signed up for, is it?" Dani says at last, flicking the last cigarette butt out the window.

She drops Lyndsey at the end of the avenue. There's a quick wave before she pulls away in a cloud of exhaust fumes and red taillights, and then Lyndsey heads toward the mansion, walking quickly and rubbing her arms to ward off the cooling night air. Confession feels good in the moment and she's glad she's done it, but now that she's alone again, she worries that she's made a mistake. Telling someone your secrets gives them power over you. She really, really hopes this lapse of judgment won't come back to bite her before the operation is over.

It's amazing how much of Lyndsey's time is spent running all over London.

It's eleven a.m. and she's already out the door, heading for the Tube stop at Highgate. Last night, the excuse she gave Emily for her disappearance was a phone call from home, an emergency involving her parents for which she required privacy. Emily hadn't seemed to believe it, but she didn't hassle her over it. Today, her reason for leaving is a doctor's appointment with a specialist on the other side of town. *No telling how long this is going to take, sorry.* She is afraid for a minute that Emily will insist on coming with her for moral support and is relieved when Emily says nothing.

She's spent the requisite amount of time cleaning her trail in order to feel confident visiting her office, the strange empty little place near her apartment, another spot she hasn't seen for an unseemly amount of time. How funny it feels to be back, even though it's barely been two weeks. The air seems stale, like the room has been holding its breath waiting for her. The couple of officers who share the space must have come and gone in her absence, but the furniture looks untouched. There's no food in the shared refrigerator, no restaurant takeout boxes. The place feels dusty and lonely.

Lyndsey hops on the secure computer and spins up the VPN. She wants to reach out to Claiborne and bring her up to speed but also to find out what she knows. She contacts Claiborne's secretary via text—*Any chance Kim can take a call?*—and she's surprised when the answer is yes. The call is quickly established via a secure video channel.

"Good to hear from you. I'm glad you called. There's a couple things we need to talk about." Even though the hour is early in the U.S., Claiborne looks a bit tired already. There are surely a number of other emergencies on Claiborne's plate: missing assets, the prelude to an operation gone sideways, some internal dispute. Lyndsey is surprised she has time to talk to her. "A solicitor's office contacted your backstop about your story, wanting to know if you are who you say. Jermyn Tholthorpe's office. Does that name sound familiar to you?"

Lyndsey scribbles it on a scrap of paper. "No, but I'll see what I can find."

"His list of clients, the ones we can find, looks to be older, solidly middle-class families. He doesn't appear to have a connection to Rotenberg, but obviously he's working on behalf of someone in their camp. So, you've made them nervous enough to check you out."

"Hopefully that cover story holds," Lyndsey says between slightly gritted teeth. "Now I have something for you: it looks like I may have to go with Mikhail Rotenberg to Ibiza." Lyndsey brings her up to speed on the situation with Rotenberg. "I don't think I'm going to be able to get the information on my own before he flies the coop. I've been scouting Rotenberg's wing every chance I get, but they practice good opsec." Operational security. "They clam up whenever I come around, don't leave notes or laptops lying out in the open. The accountant, Westover, is no slouch, and it probably helps that he's extra paranoid. He never lets his laptops out of his sight. I think he takes them with him whenever he leaves the mansion."

"There's one more thing we need to discuss," Claiborne says unexpectedly. "I reached out again to Ed Martin to see where they are with their investigation, but he's out of the country. Department of Homeland Security was able to tell us that he's in Panama. He flew out a couple days ago, straight from London."

"Doesn't Rotenberg do business with a fund manager in Panama?"

"He certainly does. Only the best: Stern De Leon. We think that Intent's strategy is divide and conquer: Martin in Panama and Dani in London, trying to crack the wife. Martin might be targeting Dom De Leon, we think. *Go to the top* is Conway's motto, apparently. If he can't get De Leon to talk, he might try to get one of their account managers to flip. They use local people to sign the documents and be the make-believe heads of their shell corporations but generally don't pay them enough to make them immune to temptation. This is definitely an area where a private company like Intent can move faster than we could."

"If he is able to get something . . . would it be worth cooperating with Intent in some way?"

"We're not the impediment here: MI6 is. Whatever Trevor Conway did to burn his bridges with Vauxhall Cross, he appears to have done it in spectacular fashion."

Lyndsey rubs her face. So tired. "Oh, I almost forgot: have you found anything on Kosygin's secret mission to China?" It's come up three times now. That's plenty of smoke: there's got to be fire.

Claiborne rifles through some papers on her desk. "China Division found something. One of their assets reported that someone close to Zhao Ming, the foreign minister, has been meeting regularly with an emissary from Russia. No particulars were given, but the meeting was reportedly on the down low. Needless to say, the asset has been tasked with finding out more."

No smoking gun, but it tracks with what Babanina and Tarasenko said.

Claiborne continues. "There's a PDB"—Presidential Daily Brief—"going out later this week. Once this gets out, we'll be under constant pressure to find out more." Claiborne groans as she checks her watch. It's a reflex. Their time is winding down. "Look, I have to run. To close the loop on Rotenberg, do what feels comfortable. Don't let Davis push you into anything just to serve his ambitions. We'll have your back, whatever your decision is." Maybe Claiborne thinks Davis is being overly ambitious here, willing to take a chance with Lyndsey's neck on the line. In any case, it's nice to know that Claiborne will back her up.

"Watch out for yourself. Things could get ugly fast," Claiborne says before signing off.

CHAPTER 31

Lyndsey has just returned to The Bishops Avenue and is about to join Emily and the twins in the conservatory when her phone buzzes. There's a text message on a secure app.

Pimlico Station, white Ford van "Whitney's Florists," in 30 mins.

It's coming from the messaging relay for Vauxhall Cross. It must be important, whatever this is about, for the quick turnaround. No time to do a proper dry-clean, which means she could be risking exposing herself. Plus there's the problem of explaining it to Emily. She's been gone far too much lately; Emily is surely going to call her out. In the end, Lyndsey leaves without saying a word to anyone like a sneaky teenager, deciding she'll deal with it when she gets back.

There's not much Lyndsey can do to clean her trail in thirty minutes, but she does her best. She finds the van in the crush of traffic and climbs in. The driver gives her a curt nod before hitting the gas. She crouches in the back among random bits of surveillance equipment, alone. No explanation is offered as the driver, a middle-aged man with a neon-orange knit cap, concentrates on traffic. She can't see where they're going, but fifteen minutes later, the van's cargo door slides open and she's in the underground garage at MI6.

She's taken to a conference room where Davis and Parth Arya are waiting. Grim faced, Davis hands her a tablet. Video footage, obviously taken on someone's cell phone, shows the charred remains of an office building. It's a black hole in the ground with thick smoke rising overhead. The camera pans back and forth over the skeletonized building, one side simply burned away so it stands open to the sky. Water drips from exposed beams, while off to the side, firemen are rolling up long hoses. The background is strafed by the steady strobe of lights from a police car, just off camera.

In the background, the sun is just starting to make pink streaks on a dark sky. Palm trees, silhouetted, sway in the breeze.

"This is Stern De Leon's headquarters in Panama City," Davis says. "The footage was taken by one of our people. Apparently, there was quite the dustup there late last night. From what the people on the ground have been able to pull together, a team of shooters tried to gain access to the building after closing. They met with little resistance; no one there but a couple elderly security guards and Dom De Leon, one of the principals. They shot their way past the security guards quickly—that's what you get for doing security on the cheap. This is when our watchers arrived." Davis taps the screen a couple times and the video switches to a twilight scene. Flashes of light are seen through large, blackened windows, accompanied by muffled pops of gunfire. "The Panamanian police were already on their way—the neighbors must've called—or the watchers would've gone inside to see what they could find." Indeed, in the background of the video, you can hear sirens wailing, quickly getting closer. Windows shatter and a huge lick of orange flame suddenly flares up from inside.

"It looks like the assailants decided to torch the place once they heard the sirens. Whether Dom De Leon was killed by the people who broke in or in the fire isn't clear at the moment," Davis says as he closes up the tablet. He nods at Arya. "Arya's team is pulling together its assessment, but given the swiftness and the level of violence, it has the look and feel of the same people who raided Rotenberg's place."

It was clumsy, he means. A ham-fisted assault that preferred brute force over finesse, perhaps meant to scare the intended victim into a quick capitulation. Only in the case of the Rotenberg home, they were routed because Igor Volkov was a competent professional. Here, they were found out because they were too impatient to wait until the neighbors had gone to bed.

Arya speaks. "Unfortunately, it's impossible to know at this point why the assailants chose to torch the building. It may be because they were being forced to leave before they got what they came for and were burning it down so no one would get the data. Or maybe they got what they wanted and were burning the place in order to muddy their tracks. The upshot is: we have no idea if the assailants got what they came for. The analyst on the money laundering team who's been following Stern De Leon says the firm deliberately kept an antiquated bookkeeping system. They relied on paper—ledgers—for a lot of their recordkeeping. There might be a spare set of books off-site for safekeeping . . . but it wouldn't have the most up-to-date information."

"I think at this point we'd be happy to get in the ballpark," Davis says.

"But it sounds like you're pretty sure it has something to do with the

Rotenberg case. Let's face it: we don't know that. It could be coincidental—" Lyndsey starts.

Davis holds up a hand, silencing her. "There's one other casualty. The police found Ed Martin on the scene, severely wounded. He's in hospital now, in a coma."

She feels, for a moment, like she's in free fall. She thinks back to meeting Ed just a few days ago, how they'd fallen in so naturally at the café—probably for having both come from Langley. There was a natural camaraderie. He was so easy to talk to. They were both part of a small world, the Central Intelligence Agency, both citizens of a place that was a world unto itself.

Arya sets the tablet on the table. "There's another development. After the UN Security Council voted to uphold sanctions on Russia, Kosygin's office issued a terse statement about how it was an unfair condemnation of the Russian people, et cetera, et cetera. Some of the team are seeing this as a sign that Kosygin is through pretending to be a nice guy. They feel something is on the horizon."

Davis pushes back from the table and rubs his face. He's as frustrated as Lyndsey.

On one hand, Kosygin is trying to say and do all the right things, to make Russia look like a good international neighbor. On the other hand, he's attacked Rotenberg, shot up his house, and gone after the team that hides the oligarch's money. There may be a good reason why, but from what she can see, the pieces don't add up.

It feels like they—Lyndsey, Davis—are running out of time.

The three sit in silence for a moment.

Lyndsey thinks of Ed Martin. His situation is grave. She thinks of the photograph he'd shown her, the faces of his little boys. If Ed had stayed at

CIA, chances are he'd be perfectly fine right now. Going home to his family instead of fighting for his life in a hospital bed.

Davis is staring at her as though he's asked her a question. "What?" she asks.

"I said, given what Arya just told us, being part of the Rotenberg household right now is very, very dangerous. Galchev is likely to do something drastic."

She expects him to say that she won't be going back to The Bishops Avenue, that they're pulling the plug, that she needs to leave *right now.*

But—he doesn't. Instead, he cocks an eyebrow and says, "Do you think you can hang in there a little longer, Lyndsey? Because after this"—he points at the tablet, the footage of last night's fire still flickering—"Rotenberg is sure to react. If no one in Panama will talk, or if they don't back up their records . . . then Arthur Westover's records might be the only key to where all of Rotenberg's money is hidden. You may be our last chance to get our hands on that information, Lyndsey. Our only chance."

Ah. Mission, of course. Mission always comes first.

Davis is up and pacing now. "I wouldn't be surprised if he bolts . . . He was planning to leave anyway. He might change the destination, to be on the safe side, and I'm sure he's playing this very close to the vest . . . Which means we have two choices, Lyndsey. We can either snatch the laptop now, or"—he rubs at his mouth, *it's something he doesn't want to say*—"you have to go with him. Those are our only options."

"The preferable one would be to get Westie's laptop now," Lyndsey says. "Do you think you can do it?"

The key. The teacup in Emily's room. Hopefully, there will be enough chaos at The Bishops Avenue, enough pandemonium, so she can slip in without being challenged.

"We'll see, won't we?"

CHAPTER 32

Lyndsey's mind is still reeling as she arrives at The Bishops Avenue, the video of the fire still vivid in her memory. Inside, the house reverberates with noise. Voices are raised, housekeepers shouting instructions to one another, feet clattering on the marble floors. There are more people in the house than Lyndsey has ever seen before, certainly more than she thought were in the Rotenbergs' employ. Outside, too, the security guards have made themselves more visible, with two young Russians outside the gate, watching the street.

Between the confusion and the fact that she's been living in the house for a while now, no one pays attention to Lyndsey as she trots up the stairs. She thinks briefly of checking Westie's room first, to see if the door might be open but she decides not to waste the time. Get the key first. Getting away will be easy; MI6 is watching the house. If Lyndsey steps outside, a car will pull up to whisk her away. All she has to do is get the laptop and get to the street. Then she's home free.

She passes housekeepers on the way to Emily's room. One of them nods at her (she's been noticed) but Lyndsey continues on calmly (*it'll all be over soon*). It almost seems like someone is looking out for her when Lyndsey finds the door to Emily's bedroom standing open, even though there's no packing going on here, even though everyone knows Emily is not going away with the family.

The smell of cleaners emanates weakly from the direction of the bathroom. The room is neat as a pin, the curtains pulled back to flood the space with light.

Someone could come by at any moment and ask why Lyndsey is in here by herself. She must hurry.

She crosses to the bookcase. The teacup is there but appears to have been moved slightly. The housekeeper, surely.

Lyndsey reaches inside the cup. It's almost an afterthought now as her mind races ahead to the next step, breaking into Westie's room. What if he's there?

But the key is missing.

Sweat breaks out on her brow. Now what?

She thinks of Dani: she has a backup, clever girl. And she remembers Emily saying that Dani is going to visit today, which is fortuitous, though she can't remember what time she's expected. She must find Emily, to ask. It's a bit tricky because Emily is still mad at her, and then there's the matter of needing an excuse for her unexplained departure, but she trusts a workable fabrication will come to mind.

She follows the sound of children's voices and laughter coming from the conservatory, accompanied by high, female voices. Her luck continues to hold: Dani's here, sitting cross-legged on the floor as she plays with the children. Faces turn up toward Lyndsey as she walks in, and Dani's looks slightly puffed as though she's been crying. Maybe she's heard the news about Ed Martin already.

Emily is cool, sitting by the table littered with cups of brightly colored punch, presumably for the children. "Where were you? You just disappeared on me—again."

It seems stupid to have to play this game when everything is about to blow sky-high. "I had to run to the pharmacy. I went to take my medicine and the bottle was empty. Such a stupid mistake . . . I can't imagine how that happened." Lyndsey drops her purse and jacket on an empty chair.

Emily asks no further questions, but Lyndsey can see she's far from satisfied by her answer. Still mad at her and suspecting every time she steps out of the house that she's having a rendezvous with Mikhail. Hoping to let it die, Lyndsey sidles over to where Dani plays with the children at the huge dollhouse. Tatiana is moving a horse figurine inside an oval paddock, complete with striped jumps and flags, while Kit occupies himself to the side with a toy truck. Lyndsey catches Dani's eye over the children's heads. *We need to talk. Alone.*

A few minutes later, the nanny interrupts to say she needs to get the children ready for their tea. The twins obediently get up from the floor and reach for Miss Wilkinson's hands and, perhaps because they look so sweet, or maybe because she's disgusted with Lyndsey and can't bear to be in her presence another moment, Emily decides she's going to help. "I'll be back down shortly, so don't leave again while I'm gone," she says to Lyndsey somewhat pointedly. But at least the two women find themselves alone together.

Lyndsey stretches her hand out. "Do you have the key to Westie's room on you? I need it."

Dani's face clouds immediately.

"You heard what happened in Panama . . ."

Dani brushes under her eyes with the back of her hand. "The office didn't have much information, just that there was an attack and the facility torched."

"The decision's been made to move to the endgame. I need to get that laptop now."

Still, Dani doesn't make a move to give her the key. She frowns. "But—the key is mine. That's my prize. I'm not going to just hand it over to you."

Lyndsey does a double take. "You're joking. At a time like this—"

"I'm not going to let you steal my thunder. I watched that happen too much at Langley, people who claimed to be your friend waltz off and take all the credit."

There's an undercurrent of menace in Dani's tone. What was it Dani told her when they met? This assignment was her trial; if she messes up, there won't be any more work with Intent. She was having a hard time making her own way after she left the Agency. She can't afford to lose this gig. And this girl doesn't like to lose.

"Dani, don't be stupid." The word tumbles out in the heat of the moment. "Haven't you figured it out? The client you're working for is Oleg Galchev. He knew Ed Martin was going to talk to Dom De Leon, and yet he sent in a team of commandoes and set the place on fire in a fit of Russian machismo. He put Ed in the hospital. You can't hand Rotenberg's data over to the enemy. You *can't*."

Dani takes in a breath sharply. She narrows her eyes at Lyndsey as she tries to tell if the other agent is telling the truth or not . . . But it makes sense. Galchev has been using Intent as an advance guard, but—perhaps unhappy with results, or wanting to do something more satisfying and visceral—following up with his own clumsy, violent strikes. It only takes Dani a few seconds to come to the same conclusion, that there's nothing more Intent can do, and indeed it may only make matters worse, and so Dani digs into her purse and pulls out the brass key.

She presses it in Lyndsey's palm.

Lyndsey sprints up the stairs, past housekeepers, not caring if she runs into Emily. The end is almost near. She'll get the laptop and any hard drives she sees lying around, any notebooks or anything else that looks like it might be of use. She'll find a bag to dump it all in so she can smuggle it past the guards and get to the gates . . . And then this nightmare will be over. Mission accomplished.

Westie's room is right ahead. The hall is mercifully clear. No need to make excuses as to why she's in the forbidden wing. She tries the knob first, but it's locked. She drops to her knees so she can see what she's doing in the dim overhead light and pulls the key out of her pocket. But . . . there's a problem. The key isn't going in. She tries a second, third, fourth time. It's not working.

Either Dani deliberately gave her the wrong key, or Arthur Westover changed the lock.

She takes a deep breath. She doesn't want to believe Dani would sabotage her like that or that, under the circumstances—Lyndsey standing in front of her, hand out—she would've had the presence of mind to do that. Chances are greater that it was Westover, made nervous by the recent developments and houseguests he didn't trust, spooked by his own drunken disclosures.

Under normal circumstances, she would pick the lock. She had training at the Farm but that was years ago and she's undoubtedly rusty. However, she didn't bring her set of picks with her. They would've been too hard to explain away if Volkov or a housekeeper went snooping through her things and found them. She'll need to get a set.

Stealing around the corner into the hall's dead end, she pulls out her cell phone and calls the waiting MI6 driver. "Don't ask questions: get me a set of lockpicks as fast as you can. Toss them over the fence, at the jog in the road with the streetlamp. You see the spot? Call me back when you've done that. Hurry."

She goes back to her room to wait. She doesn't want to run into Emily and get dragged into an emotional conversation. No, this close to the finish line, she just wants it to be over. Afterward, maybe, she'll get permission to get in touch with Emily and tell her everything, explain that she didn't mean to hurt her. That what was done was done on behalf of both their nations, and surely she'll understand. Maybe, one day, even be grateful.

The phone, in her pocket, buzzes at her. Could the driver have gotten the lockpicks so soon? Her heart sinks when she sees it's the private messaging app she uses for communicating with Tarasenko. Is it a risk to answer? Yes, but . . . She has a bad feeling about this.

She presses the button. "Yes?"

"It's been announced on television." It's Tarasenko, and he's breathless. "Orders have been issued for Mikhail Rotenberg's arrest. It's allegedly because he has been hiding his assets using offshore companies to avoid paying taxes. What a joke! None of the oligarchs have been paying their share of taxes—they must be shitting themselves in fear right now.

"Rotenberg is officially an enemy of the people. Russia-One has been showing nothing since the announcement but pictures of Rotenberg's Sochi mansion. It's overrun with police. They're taking possession of it."

Lyndsey almost drops her phone. She saw Mikhail leave the house this morning. Wherever he is at this moment, there's a chance he doesn't know. Or perhaps someone is alerting him right now. He could be at his Knightsbridge apartment in a panic. Surely, he has a plan for this, has worked out a protocol with his lawyers and his entourage. There must be bags packed and waiting, money and passports, funds diverted . . . Oh, wait. That one important piece was taken away from under him just last night when his funds manager was killed.

It's been a chess game all along. The pieces are falling into place.

Tarasenko continues. "This proves I was right, doesn't it? You see—I told you the truth."

She almost laughs. "Do you want me to say I trust you now? You know it's not going to be that easy."

"*Kukla*, what is it going to take?" he purrs. From his tone of voice, she can tell he's playing with her.

She's got to get off the phone. "Thanks, Dmitri, for this information. Is there anything else? Because if not—"

He chuckles. "There is something else . . . It came out on one of those gossip shows on television. They confirmed that one of Kosygin's mistresses had an affair with him. She says he told her about the shell companies. Trying to impress her."

Oh no. She has a suspicion, though it pains her to give it voice. "Was it Irina Babanina?"

"The gymnast?" He's clearly confused. "Why would you think of her? No, it was Anna Sokolova. She said she slept with Rotenberg for the money. She explained how Rotenberg had taken over the job of paying off Kosygin's mistresses, making sure they kept their mouths shut now that he is top dog. So, now the press is hounding all of them to see who else he slept with."

Lyndsey breathes a sigh of relief. She was afraid that Babanina had been caught, but no. It was some other unfortunate woman.

"It's an embarrassment, for sure. To be disrespected like that by the man who would be your consigliere. It makes you look weak. So, what choice does Kosygin have? Now they're saying Rotenberg has been cheating the Russian state out of millions and millions in taxes, and he needs to come in to answer for 'bookkeeping irregularities.'" Tarasenko snorts.

"Thank you, Dmitri. I owe you." The last part comes out reflexively, because her mind is always racing steps ahead.

Tarasenko laughs. "Yes, you do. Oh, and don't think I won't hold you to it. The next time we see each other, I'll remind you. And do not worry: I will not make it hurt too much." He is too pleased with himself. "One last thing: did you find out anything more on the angle with China?"

"No. You?"

He grunts. "No. But I have heard Morozov mention it, too, so it seems the senior people know something is up. This is bigger than it looks."

"Well, if you hear anything—"

"Let you know. Yes, yes." He hangs up.

Lyndsey drops back onto the edge of the bed. This will undoubtedly change everything. When Mikhail finds out, his plans will change. He will want to go into deep hiding. Tech billionaires have built secret hideaways on uncharted Pacific islands. She can't imagine anything less for Mikhail Rotenberg.

The window of opportunity to get that financial data is closing rapidly.

Westie. There's no other way. There isn't time to check in with Vauxhall Cross: they'll still be drawing up plans. She needs to decide on her own. If she can't get those lockpicks or, more likely, she can't get the door open, she'll track down Westie and convince him to hand over the data. Dangle an offer of immunity, though she's not sure if that's a promise she should be making.

She has run out of options.

CHAPTER 33

Ten minutes pass, fifteen. Still no call from the MI6 driver.

Lyndsey must find Westie. She must ask Emily.

It's by no means certain that Emily will tell her anything. By now, Emily's coolness has gone to frost, as though she can read the guilt on Lyndsey's face no matter how hard she tries to hide it. She wishes she could tell Emily not to worry, to explain to her that it's better if she isn't with Mikhail. That they've entered an extremely dangerous period. There's Kosygin's own people, of course: they'll be hard at work trying to get Rotenberg, petitioning Whitehall to turn him over. Maybe even dispatching their own people to kidnap him. And now that Rotenberg is a public enemy, Galchev—who sounds a bit psychopathic—may be itching to finish the job. Once they're on the move, they'll be scurrying down back roads to airports, filing aboard private jets, hoping the pilots and stewardesses and whoever is involved can keep their mouths shut . . . Rotenberg and his entourage will be terribly exposed.

That includes her. Lynn Prescott is supposed to be going with him.

Shooting a private jet out of the sky is a neat and easy way to get rid of somebody.

Her heart clutches when she remembers the children. If only there was a way to convince Mikhail to leave the children with their mother. Without Emily, she feels it will be her job to protect them. Her objective is Westie's laptop and hard drives, but if she must choose between two children and the equipment, well . . . This isn't an action hero movie. It may be well nigh impossible to save both.

She pounds her fists against the wall in frustration. Then she slips her phone into her pocket and rushes toward the children's nursery, where they'll be having their tea. And that's where she finds them, the children sitting at a table by the window, Miss Wilkinson trying to convince Tatiana to have another bite of her sandwich. Emily sits next to Kit, drinking what looks like fruit juice in a child-size glass and staring out the window.

Emily jerks her head up when Lyndsey steps into the room, her expression sharp. She's too good a mother to start screaming at her husband's new whore in front of the children, Lyndsey knows. She'll be civil. She won't set a bad example.

"Oh, you're still here," Emily says. "I would've thought you'd decamped by now with the rest of Mikhail's people. Since you're not one of my people, not anymore."

Lyndsey decides not to take the bait. "I'm looking for Westie. Do you know where he's gone?"

"He went off with Volkov. They've gone looking for Mikhail. I don't know where anyone is lately. I'm not part of the in crowd." She smiles ironically. "But I'd have thought you were."

Lyndsey wants to tell her so badly. There's no reason for this animosity when they're on the same side. She is about to speak, to try another tack, when the phone in her pocket starts to vibrate, alerting her to a text.

When it rains, it pours. It's from MI6's secret number. *Flash sale at Kate's Closet! Kicks off at 5 PM! Don't miss it*, the text reads, accompanied by an address: Pond Street in Hampstead. It's not a sale, of course. It's an alert to a secret meeting they want her to attend, disguised so anyone who might see it wouldn't think twice.

Davis wouldn't send a message like this unless it was of paramount importance: *flash* is a term they use for official messages of the highest priority. Alerts that need to get to the president or prime minister, surprise attacks, acts of aggression. She checks her watch: five p.m. is less than an hour away. Whatever the reason for the meeting, it must be urgent for them to scramble like this. It will be hard to make an excuse and get away, especially in this precise moment, when there's so much to learn. Emily has been peevish lately whenever Lyndsey has to slip out at the last minute.

The look on Emily's face clearly asks *What's going on*, but she's not going to ask.

Think quick. "I'm afraid I'm going to have to step out for a bit," she says, looking away so she won't see the sour look that passes over Emily's face. "I put in a special order at a shop for a p-r-e-s-e-n-t for someone"—the twins' birthday is a few weeks away—"and that was the shop telling me it was in. I'm going to need to pop out to pick it up."

Emily's frown isn't her usual delicate, pensive one. This one is dark like a storm cloud. Clearly, she doesn't think Lyndsey is being honest with her. "Send one of the housekeepers to get it. Or the driver. It's no bother. Half of them have nothing to do all day, anyway." It's not like her to complain about the help. Emily catches Miss Wilkinson out of the corner of her eye, wincing.

"Oh . . . I'd rather go myself. Make sure it's exactly what I ordered. And I wouldn't mind poking around to see what else they might have . . . It's a charming little shop."

"Oh? Well, in that case I'd like to go with you. It sounds delightful." Only there's no delight in her tone of voice. *Emily doesn't trust me.* Or maybe she's trying to get out of the house? Maybe she knows the noose is tightening around her husband's throat. Maybe she's seen the news.

Lyndsey does a little scrunch of her nose, like a rabbit. "Oh, maybe some other time? I want to surprise you, you know?"

They are at a standoff. Emily can't push again without it seeming strange, but if she does, Lyndsey has run out of excuses. The children, even though they don't know what's going on between the adults, are starting to get anxious, and therefore restless. Kit slides off his chair and starts to amble out of the room. Emily gives Lynn a pointed look before turning to the nanny, who runs after Kit without a word needing to be said.

Emily scowls at her. "You're lying and I know you're lying. The question is, where are you really going? No, the *real* question is, do I really want to know? I suppose I already know so . . . fine, run along and I'll see you later. Say hello to my husband for me, will you?"

Lyndsey hesitates. It's a risk saying anything but . . . She steps close to Emily. "I can't tell you what's going on now, but I will someday. Please trust me."

Emily jerks back from her as though Lyndsey is a snake dropped suddenly from a tree. She glances at her children. "What are you talking about? Why should I trust you? What aren't you telling me?"

She's still one of them, Lyndsey reminds herself. It's not safe to say anything until she knows what's going on, what this emergency meeting with MI6 is about. It stabs at her heart to do this, but—it'll be over soon.

That's the only consolation.

"Stay inside. Don't go anywhere. For god's sake, don't go on a playdate. Don't even answer the phone. I'll be back as soon as I can." Emily gives her a look of fear and confusion but doesn't ask anything more. Maybe she understands that the day they've been dreading has finally come.

Lyndsey was going to wait until she was well clear of the mansion before sending for an Uber, but in a near-miracle, she manages to hail a taxi at the end of The Bishops Avenue. As the cab shoots through the traffic, Lyndsey keeps an eye out in case anyone is following. She has the cab drop her a few blocks from the destination and uses the last fifteen minutes to wend her way in and out of shops, hoping to throw off anyone who might be clinging to her trail.

She stands in front of the address that appeared in the text: it's a black-painted door, obviously leading up to offices. There's a short run of doorbells, maybe seven, with harmless sounding names like "Wellesley-Jones Importing" and "Advantage Services." There is no label for Kate's Closet. Which one is she supposed to ring?

She tries the door: it's open. It leads to a wide staircase, a little down-at-the-heels, filthy with dust and debris in the cracks and corners. She doesn't see an elevator, although there might be a service one at the back. She starts up the stairs, listening to the echo of her footfall. The air is stale.

There's a man on the second landing, young and clean-cut looking. He doesn't seem tough, but he looks capable of handling himself. He's meant to be here as a lookout and first line of defense, in other words. He was busy with his cell phone, but now that she's arrived, he gives her the once-over and then nods at the staircase. "One more floor, first door on the right."

So, this is another MI6 safe house. The other offices in the building might be MI6, too, to reduce the possibility of being overheard by nosy neighbors. It's all very quiet and feels empty.

The space she steps into is not the main attraction; she sees that right away. It's just a small room with folding chairs arranged in front of a big one-way glass window that looks into the next apartment. It's meant for observation. There's another room behind them, probably used to house recording equipment and the like. There's absolutely nothing finished about the room. It's all sawdust and drywall and bare bulbs.

Davis steps out from the back room carrying two takeout cups of coffee. He hands one to her. "Sorry for the last-minute notice, but you needed to be here. We're bringing Rotenberg in."

"I heard that an arrest warrant's been issued in Russia for Rotenberg. Have they formally asked the U.K. to hand him over?"

He nods. "An hour ago, as it was breaking on the news. There's probably a team of FSB operatives on their way now, looking to take Rotenberg in, in case Her Majesty's Government doesn't comply with their request. So—the equation has been changed: Rotenberg's running out of options, which means he might be open to cooperating with us. We're going to make him an offer: his freedom in exchange for information."

After spending weeks focused on Emily and thinking of Rotenberg as the target, it's a huge mental leap. Lyndsey tries to process it quickly. "Do you think he's really going to walk away from all his billions?"

"It's as good as gone already, and he must know it. There's not a chance in hell that Kosygin is going to let him keep any of it. If he doesn't accept our offer, he's going to a Russian jail and we know what happens to people there. He's got to see that they're playing hardball."

Lyndsey turns to look through the glass. The safe house is all dressed and ready for the curtain to go up. On the other side, it looks like a British drawing room. Tall oak bookcases, heavy curtains. High-backed wing chairs upholstered in leather. There are four or five men in the room already—our side, Lyndsey imagines. They are thinking ahead to what they will say, even as they fuss with a tea set or reposition chairs. Lost in their thoughts. One says, "Check one two, check one two," for the sound technician running the equipment in the next room. The oldest one, a very distinguished-looking man in a tweedy suit and thick-rimmed glasses, seems to be running over a conversation in his head. Silently practicing what he is going to say, like a lawyer about to speak before the jury.

"He's not MI6," Lyndsey says, nodding at the tweedy man.

"He's with the Foreign Office. They're the only ones who can make this sort of offer on behalf of Her Majesty's Government," Davis says. "Though of course Vauxhall Cross weighed in."

The rest of them are with MI6. Lyndsey catches a glimpse of Parth Arya as he glances out from one of the back rooms. His pay grade is too low to be at the table—all the big dogs in MI6's equivalent of Russia Division want to be there when they make the offer—but they were kind enough to bring him in to witness the culmination of the operation. It's not every day you get to be in the same room as your target. The feeling, Lyndsey knows from experience, is rather surreal: to suddenly hear his voice live, the cadence and inflections you know so well. To see what the face looks like in the flesh. To see how he walks, all his gestures. And, of course, Arya knows Rotenberg better than anyone else in the safe house, will know whether he's lying or bluffing, will know how best to counter any counteroffer or refusal. Lyndsey feels a little better, actually, knowing that Arya is nearby.

Just as she feels better knowing Rotenberg won't be able to see her. She cannot imagine what his reaction would be if he were told that he'd been harboring a spy in his household. Or that he had almost brought a spy into his life. He might say that he suspected her, if he were to be told. He'd say something like that to save face. But she knows that he hasn't had an inkling. He wouldn't have acted the way he did with her that night if that were the case. She fooled Mikhail Rotenberg—well, his ego had a big part in it—and for this she is proud.

She fooled Emily, too, but she is less proud of that.

A half hour later, there is a commotion in the hall. Though muffled, Lyndsey hears the door to the street open, then the tread of several people on the stairs. Men, by the sound of them; the tread is heavier, with no click-click-click of heels. There are snatches of speech, the words undecipherable, just a casual exchange. She recognizes the timbre of Mikhail's voice, however, and to hear it now makes her tense.

When the door to the flat opens, she takes an unconscious step back even though she knows that she cannot be seen. Mikhail Rotenberg and another man, one she doesn't recognize, step into the room. Who is the man with Rotenberg, and where are the others she heard enter the building? One of them is sure to be Volkov, the head of security. She's pretty sure she recognized his voice in the mix. She cannot imagine Mikhail would move about the city without him now that there is a figurative price on his head. But, noticeably, no trace of Westie.

She knows from Mikhail's expression that he's aware of the warrant for his arrest. He is pale, shaken, a man around whom the walls are closing.

There are murmured introductions all around. Everyone is nervous, though they take pains to hide the extent. The man from the Foreign Office—he introduces himself as Sir Anthony Lambsdale—steers the group with the quiet authority of an archbishop in his chambers. The chairs have been arranged so that when everyone sits, he is opposite Mikhail. The man with Mikhail turns out to be his London lawyer and sits to Mikhail's left. The MI6 officers flank Lambsdale on either side, like a typical team of negotiators. A young man in an ill-fitting suit brings in a tea service on a tray and makes sure everyone has a cup before he glides out silently.

You would almost feel sorry for Lambsdale, to be in his delicate situation, if you didn't know he'd been in this position many times, the go-to man in the Foreign Office for such offers of refuge made to men who deserve no such kindness. But the times make for strange bedfellows—it's a familiar refrain in the intelligence business, so what goes on today is not shocking to Lyndsey. Depressing, perhaps, that in the end you make a deal with the devil; but as the Brits like to say, *needs must*. Better to bring in a rogue and thwart your adversary. Better to have the rogue where you can keep an eye on him than to let him run free. This way, you take him off the street (ostensibly), keeping him from committing other crimes. You benefit from his knowledge, milk it and pore over it and decide how to best use it to pursue other bad guys, badder bad guys than the one you have just put in your pocket. That's the plan anyway—or the excuse.

While it all makes sense, it's not really satisfying. Because you know there are victims who are not going to be vindicated. These victims will never know that their tragedies have been deemed less important, that their pain has been sacrificed to serve the greater good. On one hand, you could argue that they'll never know, so where's the harm? It's these unpleasant twists of the mind, twists of ethics, that bother Lyndsey. There are people in the intelligence business for whom this is nothing. Who take it all in stride. Some even revel in it, as though these kinds of moral gymnastics are, somehow, proof of their superiority in some sense. Like the cliché assassin who seeks justice for victims, that because it's the ends and not the means, it's okay to hunt and kill others. It's a twisted sort of logic that has never sat right with Lyndsey.

"We should get right down to it, so as not to waste your time, Mr.

Rotenberg," Lambsdale says in his plummy accent. They are two men of the world facing each other, two men who—in their own ways—have enjoyed all the benefits and luxuries that the world has to offer. That is not to say that they've enjoyed the same pleasures, but for now they will pretend that they are the same sort of men. That they are equals.

Lambsdale steeples his fingers like a professor or perhaps a judge and peers at Rotenberg through them. "It has come to Her Majesty's Government's attention that you appear to have run afoul of someone in a very high place. Your government has asked us to arrest you and extradite you to Moscow."

Rotenberg recoils, as though someone has placed a snake before him.

"Have no fear, Mr. Rotenberg. Her Majesty is not inclined to respond favorably to their demands. Not at the moment, anyway. But that's what we're here to discuss. You are in a dangerous position. Our people have assessed that the attack on your property on The Bishops Avenue is a result of this falling-out between you and the Russian president. Please don't bother to deny this, Mr. Rotenberg," Lambsdale adds as Mikhail opens his mouth to speak. "Your protest will be duly noted, but our experts have made their assessment and we have faith in their capabilities. Viktor Kosygin has seized your homes in Russia and is moving now to put several of your companies into receivership. The managers of a number of them are already under arrest. You must assume their cooperation with Russian authorities.

"And then there is the matter of the assault on the office of your funds managers in Panama. Dom De Leon was killed. The firm's offices were burned to the ground. Several of their local employees have gone missing. We do not know if the assailants were able to seize the company's records and accounting of your businesses—"

"It wouldn't do them any good," Mikhail growls. "The records for all my businesses are divided among four systems. You can't understand the full picture without getting your hands on all four sets of books. Dom De Leon didn't have a full record. The only full set is at my office at The Bishops Avenue."

The MI6 officers nod. Arya peeks around the corner; even he looks impressed.

"Please, Mr. Rotenberg, it would do no good to protest. Your government's actions against you have erased any possibility for maneuver."

All eyes swivel to Rotenberg. He's gone ashen. None of what Lambsdale has said is news, but it's hard to have the facts thrown in your face, one after the other. Does he grasp that his back is against the wall?

"But I've done nothing wrong," he croaks.

"We sense that the charges against you are—well, if not actually bogus then surely inflated—and that's why Her Majesty's Government is prepared to make you an offer. We all know how this disagreement with Viktor Kosygin is likely to turn out. They never end well, do they?"

Another man takes up the banter now, a middle-aged man with a decidedly more sinister demeanor than Lambsdale's. He's beefy and has a very unpleasant look on his face. He's a human nettle bush or puffer fish, the kind of creature you know instinctively to stay away from. A man who knows how to make threats, whether they're shrouded in velvet or delivered with the heft of an iron mallet. "No matter how well protected a man is, they always seem to find a way in, don't they? If they don't manage to poison you, then it's prison. And no one ever gets out of one of their prisons, do they? Oh, maybe as a ghost, ready to wither and die within a few years. A man like yourself, a man who's only ever done what's been asked of him—well, it doesn't seem fair that this should be your fate, does it?"

Mikhail lifts a cynical eyebrow. "What do you *think* you know of me?" he growls before the lawyer puts a hand on his forearm, cautioning him. He shakes the hand off. "This is a nightmare. It's a misunderstanding. We'll work it out."

Undoubtedly, he's been coached. When the request to meet with the Foreign Office came in, the lawyer must've figured on the worst. Deportation, questions regarding financial matters, tax problems.

"Maybe. That would be the best outcome, wouldn't it?" Lambsdale continues. They're playing good lawyer, bad lawyer. "You're not the first Russian citizen to find himself facing the sudden ire of his government. But I don't think you can count on a happy ending, Mr. Rotenberg. That's why we've asked you to meet with us today. It can't have escaped your attention that we're not meeting at Whitehall. This is not an official function of Her Majesty's Government. This is more of an informal testing of the waters."

"We wanted to see how you are feeling, Mr. Rotenberg. After all this unfortunate activity," the second man says. They are like a pair of foxes worrying a sheep in the field, taking turns nipping at its hocks, slowly but surely driving it into a corner. "We wanted to see where you were at intellectually. Emotionally."

Mikhail lifts his head. "How do you think I would be? I'm miserable."

"Which is perfectly understandable"—Lambsdale is practically purring now—"when you find yourself in the crosshairs of someone as volatile; powerful; and, frankly, as dangerous as Viktor Kosygin. You have to be concerned, at this point. Wondering how you are going to protect yourself and your family. When you have powerful enemies, you need powerful friends."

There is no Russian in the room to overhear him. Rotenberg is alone among the Brits. Pale as ivory, he closes his eyes, like he's enduring great internal pain. "What do you wish to tell me?" Mikhail asks. The lawyer again tries to get his attention, but the oligarch waves him away.

"We're prepared to make you an offer." Lambsdale puckers slightly. "In exchange for your cooperation, we can provide you safety. We can keep you and your family out of their reach."

Mikhail laughs mirthlessly. "Do you really think you can keep someone safe if Kosygin truly wants you dead?"

The MI6 officers all shift restlessly in their chairs at the affront. "*Of course* we do. We have many, many times over. Protected our assets. Helped them to escape and put them someplace far outside of Russia's grasp."

"They weren't one of the richest men in the world," Rotenberg's lawyer snaps. "Do you think a man like that can simply disappear?"

"I can't walk away from my responsibilities," Mikhail adds. By responsibilities, he doesn't mean the companies he owns. He's not thinking of the men and women whose livelihoods are tied to him, shareholders or regular citizens who have accounts at his bank. He means his fortune.

"We're prepared to help you to retain at least some of your assets—depending on their nature," the MI6 officer says. It's a discreet way of saying depending on which were ill-gotten. The British government can hardly be seen as protecting a Russia kleptocrat from relinquishing his illegal spoils or to escape his responsibilities as a Russian citizen. "We won't be able to come to a judgment until we've had a chance to go through your finances, but our intention is not to leave you penniless." It's not British money, after all. He's mostly only fleeced his own countrymen.

Mikhail sits back imperiously, a deep frown on his face. His lawyer leans over, whispering in his ear. He's probably telling him there're not going to be any good outcomes. It's a matter of choosing the one that's least bad—and the least bad is keeping him out of prison. Life expectancy drops very quickly in a Russian prison. He would be lucky to live five years, a miracle to see age sixty.

Davis, sitting next to Lyndsey, sighs carefully. Even though the wall between them has been soundproofed, they don't want to chance being overheard. If Rotenberg agrees, it means all that work—the past few weeks, the running around, the manipulating, the gentle turning—will be for naught. *Do you ever feel bad about it?* she wonders of her former lover. *Are we doing the right thing?*

Rotenberg suddenly leans away from his lawyer. "Would you put me in a house somewhere like this, cooped up like a prison? That would be impossible." After the life he's gotten used to. Jet-setting around the world. Rubbing shoulders with powerful people and celebrities.

"We'd provide security, of course. But in the beginning . . . yes, you'd have to reconcile yourself to the fact that your activity will be constrained. It'll be for your protection. You understand that." Everyone knows of the trail of corpses of men Putin left behind. Will Kosygin be any different?

Lyndsey almost feels bad for him. Mikhail sits like a man who believes he has just been condemned instead of one who has just been saved. He should think of the night that armed gunmen broke into his home, the dead bodies of his security guards on the lawn, rather than the loss of all his fine things. If he doesn't take this offer, he is a dead man. It may take a month or a year, but before long he will have come to the end of the line.

He appears to chew the inside of his cheek as he thinks. Maybe it's not as big a shock as she imagines. Maybe he's known for ages that this day would come, seen others in his position who have ended up in prison for years or died mysteriously. He's stood at the graveside at friends' funerals, an eye on the crying widow, the orphaned children.

"He wants everything," Mikhail blurts suddenly. "It's not just a matter of need. It is personal. He wants to ruin me." His voice drops to a whisper. "There is something you need to know." Mikhail's expression turns dark, and he casts a distrustful look around the room. Obviously, he's not going to talk around so many people.

"Let's clear the room, shall we, gentlemen?" Lambsdale says, ever cheerful. The extra Brits rise like chastised schoolboys and shuffle to the hall. A few jealous looks as they leave the room, wondering if they will be filled in later. It's not until the last man has closed the door that Mikhail relaxes the tiniest bit. He releases the breath he's been holding. Color starts to return to his face.

It's just Mikhail, Lambsdale, and the MI6 officer.

And a few microphones and cameras placed around the room.

"So . . . what is it, Mr. Rotenberg?" Lambsdale finally betrays a hint of impatience. "If there's something that might be deemed sensitive, we need to know before we proceed. We can't have any nasty surprises once we put your deal in motion."

Mikhail sucks in his breath and holds it. He knows he needs to confess but he still doesn't want to. He has lost and he hates it. "Sensitive . . . Yes, this is indeed very sensitive." He shakes his head again ruefully. "Everyone has been wondering how Viktor Kosygin was able to overthrow Vladimir Putin so quickly."

Davis leans forward hungrily. It has indeed been the million-dollar question in intelligence circles, all the world's agencies trying to piece together what happened to the former Russian president. It's like the earth simply opened up and swallowed him whole.

Rotenberg looks down at his hands resting in his lap. "It was me. I gave Vladimir to him."

For a moment, there is silence in the room. All eyes are on Rotenberg. For once, Lambsdale seems to be at a loss for words.

Rotenberg lets out a long sigh. "Vladimir was destroying the country. The war with Ukraine was sheer lunacy. It was leading us to civil war.

Something had to be done." He shivers at a recollection, then continues. "Kosygin reached out to me. He told me he needed me to lure Vladimir out of his office in Novo-Ogaryovo, away from his entourage. Someplace where he would let his guard down, if only for a minute."

"And you did this for him." Lambsdale sounds both astounded and impressed.

Rotenberg bows his head. *Judas.* "Vladimir had been pressing me to use Omni Bank to give him a loan. The war with Ukraine and the economic pressures from sanctions had emptied the national treasury. He needed a huge amount of money to give him time to work out what to do next. I asked him to come to my home in Moscow to talk about it—in private. He trusted me. And he was confident that if it were just the two of us, he would be able to close the deal." Rotenberg smirked uneasily, remembering the night. "He left his guards with the car when he came in—and Viktor Kosygin was waiting for him."

Again, there is silence as everyone pictures the scene. The betrayal is breathtaking.

The MI6 officer clears his throat. There is one last thing they need to know. "And . . . where is Putin now? What happened to him?"

Rotenberg looks up, miserable. "I expect only Kosygin can tell you that."

A few more moments tick by as the two negotiators regroup. Finally, the MI6 officer raises a hand in Rotenberg's direction. "There is one thing we don't understand . . . Why is Kosygin going after you, if you helped him out? Isn't he in your debt?"

A wistful smile slips over Rotenberg's face. "You'd think that would be the case, wouldn't you, and I suppose it only goes to show how untrustworthy Viktor Kosygin truly is . . . He does owe me, though I suppose he knows my secret, too. It is a blood bond between us, but it is also a horrible thing I have done, something no one else should know . . ."

"Could he be trying to silence you, because of what you know?"

Rotenberg sits back suddenly, like a puppet jerked by his strings. "After I did him this *favor*, Viktor seemed to believe he could trust me, that maybe I was the only one he *could* trust. He asked me to take on a very *personal* task. He had a few indiscretions in his past and he needed someone to take care of them. To pay off these women and make them understand that they were not to talk about him." Mikhail almost blushes. "That is how I met Anna Sokolova."

"And you had a tryst?" the MI6 officer asks, dubious.

Lambsdale asks the obvious question. "Weren't you worried about what would happen if word got back to Kosygin?"

"Considering the position I am in now, it may seem foolish that I was not more cautious, but—no, I did not. You must remember, I did not know Viktor well. I didn't expect him to care. Their affair was in the past. And to be honest, I don't believe it's the reason he's trying to destroy me now. It is an excuse he can tell the public. He needs everything I have, and he cannot just take it without upsetting the other oligarchs. You see, Viktor Kosygin has a plan—a grand plan. Allow me to explain."

Mikhail takes a deep breath. He seems worried, but also relieved, as though he will finally be able to lay down a huge burden that he has been carrying. "You see Viktor on the television, on CNN and the BBC, and he assures the West that Putin is gone and Russia wants to be a good international citizen. You think, 'This is a miracle', and everyone is happy with Viktor Kosygin because he stepped in and saved the day. Thank god for Viktor Kosygin. But it is all a lie. Viktor Kosygin is just as ambitious as Vladimir Putin—maybe more so. He has the same outsized ego. He wants to be remembered as the greatest ruler Russia has ever known. He hasn't renounced Putin's war on Europe—he's only hit the pause button.

"Putin didn't expect pushback from the United States on Ukraine. He knew he could threaten Europe, make them think twice before going to Ukraine's defense. But he did not expect the United States to step up—he thought the U.S. was isolationist enough, and believed Russia's propaganda, and would stay out of it. He found out the hard way that Russia has no real leverage against the U.S.—except nuclear weapons, and even Putin realized he would face a hailstorm of opposition if he went for nukes. Viktor, on the other hand, knows he needs an ally and there's only one country that can take on the United States: China."

In the observation room, Davis and Lyndsey exchange a look. China.

Mikhail leans forward. "Viktor intends to reacquire the former Soviet states and build his buffer zone against the West. But he can only do this if he can keep the U.S. from getting involved. That's where China comes in.

"When Europe withheld technology from Russia under sanctions, that hurt us. Oh, we bought some parts for weapons systems on the black market, but it was too expensive to be sustainable. So much was simply unobtainable. Kosygin saw the problem: Russia had no way to hurt the U.S., to make it back off. But China does. The threat of China withholding goods, particularly semiconductors, would make the U.S. stop and think. The technology sector especially needs China. It would make the Googles and Apples and Amazons of the world less cavalier about shutting Russia out, like they did during the war with Ukraine.

"But China would hardly do this out of the goodness of its heart. Look at what it did for Putin: almost nothing. China only acts in its own political interest, everyone knows that. To get China to take on the U.S., it would need to be compensated, and compensated *well*. Kosygin needed a lot of money for a bribe this big. That is where the oligarchs come in. That is where *my* money comes in."

The room is silent for a minute. You can tell Lambsdale and the other negotiator are turning the pieces over in their heads. "And after he secures China's cooperation?"

Mikhail smiles like a teacher who has explained a difficult problem to a struggling student. "Then he can proceed with his plans for conquest."

"Without your billions, would Viktor Kosygin be able to proceed with his plans?"

Mikhail shrugs modestly. "I could not say for certain, but I think it would be difficult. Ten billion dollars is a lot of money, even for a sovereign nation. And, I think, if I were to break with Kosygin and turn to the West, the other oligarchs might follow suit."

It seems Mikhail Rotenberg will have a measure of revenge.

After the tumultuous confession, when the earth seemed to spin very fast, everything goes still. The two negotiators blink at each other like they've just awakened from a dream. They've just been told a terrible, nefarious plot that could send the world order as we know it crashing—and in the next breath, learn that there could be a solution right at hand.

Lambsdale and his colleague bow their heads together and murmur to each other before continuing. After a moment, Lambsdale turns back to Mikhail.

"Very well then. It's important that we bring you under Her Majesty's Government's protection, wouldn't you say?"

They tell Rotenberg what is going to happen next. Time is of the essence, they have determined, so he will be moved today. *Now.* A security team will escort him back to The Bishops Avenue, where he will be given two hours to pull together necessities. His family will be brought with him.

"But you must bring all four sets of data," Lambsdale says in the sternest tone, like a schoolmaster. "Without the complete set of records, there can be no deal."

Mikhail says he wants to go to America. The U.K. is too dangerous. Too many Russian expats. London is Little Moscow. No matter where they try to hide him, he will be dead within a month. Look at Sergei Skripal, Alexander Litvinenko. Lambsdale doesn't bat an eyelash. "It won't be a problem," he says smoothly. "On this, the Americans see things the same way we do." *Has it been prearranged with Washington?* Lyndsey wonders. It might not be as easy as Lambsdale says. A man like Rotenberg could be a huge complication for U.S. policy toward Russia—of course, that's all about to go to hell because of this backroom deal with China. There will need to be discussions in the National Security Council and the Oval Office; but in the end, having Rotenberg in hand will be beneficial. Kosygin will know the U.S. and U.K. know about the China plan. China will take this into consideration, even with a big box of money on the table.

They file out the front door, a phalanx of men in gray coats. Normal workday crowds fill the sidewalks, the streets clogged with buses and automobiles. It's an ordinary day, but everything has changed.

Lyndsey turns to Davis. "I've got to go. Emily is going to need me."

Davis furrows his brow. "What do you mean? Your assignment is over. We don't need Emily anymore. We have Mikhail. Let her go."

She turns to him. She grasps his forearm, digging her fingers in like punishment. "He's taking the children, but he's not going to bring her with them. He's going to leave her behind. You've got to do something about this. You can't let the government *help* him do this. We can't be responsible for taking her kids away."

He gives her a quizzical look. "What do you mean? The Crown isn't responsible for the end of her marriage. That was in motion long before we got involved. Besides, I'm sure it'll all be worked out in court when they file for divorce."

That will take months. Emily will be unhinged by then, to think of her sweet children in the care of their father. He may love them in his way but he's still going to raise them to be ogres. Just like him.

"Davis, this is wrong. We can't be complicit."

"It's not our concern. I don't understand why you're being like this," he says, but he means he doesn't understand why she is complicating a straightforward intelligence operation with emotion.

There's no time to argue. She heads for the door, leaving behind a different man from the one she thought she knew.

CHAPTER 34

The summer sun has disappeared below the horizon by the time Emily hears noise coming from her husband's bedroom. It can mean only one thing: Mikhail is back from his mysterious meeting. She'd expected he would be gone for the rest of the evening and spend the night at Knightsbridge for another tête-à-tête with Lynn. She chooses to believe this deliberately, wanting to think the worst of him, and revels in the sour taste that washes up in her mouth.

He's making quite a racket in there. Slamming things, throwing back closet doors, rushing about. That's rare for Mikhail. He doesn't like to show his anger. He likes to be in control. He's trying to tempt her to seek him out, to see what he's up to, ask why he's upset. Like a little boy pitching his toys around the room, it's always a play for attention. Suddenly, Emily is very tired. Tired of his games. She wishes she had a different life.

But . . . she's made a promise, hasn't she? Accepted a new position, as it were. She's not just the oligarch's wife, not anymore. So, she puts down her magazine and goes to the dresser drawer for the thing she picked up earlier, the reason she kept the door locked all day (there are children in the house, after all), slips it into the pocket of her dressing gown, and pads silently to her husband's suite.

She catches Mikhail coming out of his dressing room. There's a suitcase open on his bed—which is strange, considering he has a special station in his dressing room just for packing. He has clothing in each hand, snatched hastily from shelves, and he's frowning at them, like he's not pleased with any of his choices. His face is flushed and he's been breathing hard.

He stops when he sees her in the doorway. That smile she has come to hate, the one of infinite coldness, creeps over his face.

"What are you doing? I thought you'd finished packing for your trip," she says.

"A change of plans," he says.

"But you're still going away . . . ?"

"Astute as always," he sneers. He throws one item of clothing into the suitcase and throws the other to the floor. "I am going away for a while, but not to Ibiza. The children are still coming with me," he adds, lest she get her hopes up. Yes, she can hear muffled sounds coming from the children's wing. Miss Wilkinson will be tearing those packed cases open, rearranging things. Will she know what is going on? Otherwise, how will she know the right things to pack? The thought of her children crying for a missing toy or—or their mother—suddenly fills her with fear.

Mikhail snaps his fingers for her attention. "Gone again, Emily, in one of your little daydreams? You really should see a doctor. Now, you asked, so pay attention when I answer. My plans have changed but not in one important regard: you are still not coming with us, Emily. You are staying here . . . or go to live with your parents, or to live wherever you want. But you are not coming with us."

Her hand slips into the pocket and touches *the thing* for comfort. It does what it's supposed to: it makes her feel instantly better. And instantly worse. "Where are you going?"

"It's none of your concern. You should know that everything is going to change. I've made a deal with the British government." His voice does a funny thing here. It breaks in a sign of weakness and regret. It's a lovely human moment but it doesn't last, he won't let it. He shakes his head, pushing the thought away. "Things have progressed beyond my control, I'm afraid. Kosygin has become—unreasonable. I'm taking the only recourse left to me. I'm going into a witness protection program. I'll be going into hiding with the children. You'll never see your children again, and all the lawyers in the world won't be able to help you. The British government will make sure of it."

The first thing she feels is the sensation of falling, like she's in an elevator and the cable's just been cut and she's falling dozens of stories a second, thundering toward the unforgiving ground. So much pressure bearing down on her, too much pressure to endure. Her body is going to fly apart from the force of it, her head come flying off, her arms, her heart explode into hundreds of bits. Everything is about to shatter and it's all out of her control.

But then the second feeling—which comes quickly, thank goodness, before she *does* shatter into a million pieces—is relief. She is being buoyed on the wings of a thousand doves that are lifting her heavenward, away from all the turmoil and pain and threats. She's being carried somewhere Mikhail can't get to her, where his threats mean nothing. The feeling is so delicious—relief she hasn't felt in years—that she can't help herself and she smiles, then laughs, a burble of laughter spilling over her lips. So much happiness that she can't contain it, can't keep it all to herself. She feels free, freer than she has in a long time.

Thank god, it's about to be over. Her long nightmare is about to come to an end.

The smug look is wiped from Mikhail's face. He lifts an eyebrow. "Why are you smiling?"

She understands finally that she doesn't have to answer him. She doesn't have to play by his rules.

She lets out her breath. It feels like she's been holding it forever.

The problem, she sees now, is not her. It was never her. It was all *him*. Things didn't have to get this bad. He could've given her a divorce. She wouldn't have asked for the moon. She never wanted half of everything he owns. That would be grotesquely greedy. She wouldn't even know what to do with all that money. It's his own stupid fault for not getting a prenup. What was he trying to prove? Had he planned from the beginning to play this wretched, useless game with her? He either figured he'd keep her around forever, torturing her, or he'd get her in a bind where she'd ask for the divorce and be left with near nothing, or—easiest choice of all for a powerful man—he'd have her killed.

Poor little Emily Hughes married a shit, an absolute games-playing shit. His only delight in life is to manipulate and twist other people, to torture them, to see how unhappy he can make them. All the more reason to make sure he doesn't get the children. He'd only make them into little carbon copies of himself, make them miserable and train them to think that they had to make everyone else miserable, too. They would be the first two links in endless chain of misery and sadness.

She touches the thing in her pocket again. *God, give me strength.*

Mikhail curls his lip and turns away from her. Back to the suitcase. There are things beside clothing: some papers, thumb drives, a small compact hard drive.

"You should know that I'm going to ask Lynn to come with me. She's quite a wonderful woman. I can see why you were drawn to her. We had dinner together the other night—did she mention that to you?" He is loving this. He thinks he's twisting the knife, wounding her, making her bleed.

Only he's not. She is through bleeding for him.

"I know about your dinner with Lynn. No, she didn't tell me, but it doesn't matter."

He turns to face her. The look on his face is priceless: surprise, confusion. But it's momentary, locked down again in an instant.

"I heard that you've slept with one of Kosygin's women, too. I heard it on the news. If you expect me to be hurt, you're going to be disappointed. It doesn't surprise me in the least. You're so utterly predictable in that way." She tilts her head. "You want me to be upset? To cry and scream and ask why you're stealing my friend from me? I know why you're doing it, Mikhail: because you're a beast, a monster. But also because you're a child. A spoiled, arrogant child."

His eyes squint, like he's drawing a bead on her. He's flushed bright red. No one has ever called him a child before, she's pretty sure of it. No one would dare. He makes the ugly face again, the one she can't stand, only it's much uglier this time. Angrier and uglier, probably because Kosygin has won and he has lost, lost so very much. Not everything, but nearly everything.

The thought brings a smile back to her face, which drives him crazy. "Why are you happy? What have you got to be happy about? I swear, Emily, you're so ridiculously stupid that you don't even know how pathetic you are. You think I'm predictable, do you? Then I suppose you knew that I slept with your sister. Jesamine. We slept together two weeks before the day of our wedding."

His face is one big ugly smile. He stands grinning at her like he's told the most delicious joke while Emily feels the world turn upside down. She's hot hot hot, like she's been set on fire and that feeling of falling is back on her again, like she's been pushed off a balcony. She remembers the days right before her wedding because that's when she had a huge fight with Jesamine. Her sister telling her she can't marry that man, *that horrible man, he's so horrible you don't know.* Tears running down her face like Emily had never seen before. *If you go ahead with this wedding I'll never speak to you again.*

Emily did, and Jesamine didn't.

"I found her fascinating." Mikhail's voice drifts in from somewhere that Emily can't see, like an actor offstage. "She was so young and so smart, so incredibly intelligent for her age. She was eighteen at the time, I think. I really wanted to marry her—think of the children we would've had!—but I knew that would never happen."

"*Of course* it would never happen: she *hated* you."

"Not at first. Then one night she came over to my in-town apartment, and I made her a few drinks and she got very, very drunk . . ."

"She was too young to know what she was doing."

"Oh, come on, a viscount's daughter? Do you want me to believe that she'd never had alcohol?" he asks sharply. "Anyway, she got drunk and one thing led to another. It's a familiar story. I told her it would be for the best if she didn't say anything to you. I don't think she wanted you to know that she was fallible, that she was less than perfect, because you thought so highly of her . . . She couldn't take that. She decided it was better to let you go . . ."

But Jesamine had tried to tell her in the restaurant that night. And now, Emily understands why Jes didn't go through with it: it was because she knew Emily wouldn't take her side. She wouldn't walk away from Mikhail's money.

Jesamine knew her sister too well. She didn't want to have her disappointment confirmed.

He stops—because he sees the gun in her hand. The gun that she slipped out of her pocket and has pointed at him now.

"What *in the world* do you think you're doing?" He is shrill. For the first time in a long time, she sees him surprised. For once, he isn't in control. He doesn't hold the reins. A feeling of pleasure washes over her. She wishes she could hang on to it forever.

"I'm stopping this mad merry-go-round you've had us on." She is careful not to let the hand holding the gun shake. He is so much bigger than her. Not much taller, but heavier. She has no doubt that he thinks he can overpower her and would try it if he sees the faintest sign that she was uncertain.

He draws himself up tall and haughty. "Are you going to *shoot* me, Emily? Do you think you can do it? I know you better than anyone and I don't think you have it in you—"

The sound of the gunshot bounces around the room. So loud. She didn't think it would be so loud. The sound cuts through her like a knife, from top to bottom.

Did she mean to pull the trigger? She knows the answer to that.

Mikhail's hands are clasped to his stomach. Red spreads quickly beneath those hands, turning his crisp white shirt a deep crimson.

She's caught him in the stomach. She should've been more careful with her aim. She's heard stomach wounds can kill you, but they're slow.

My sister, you monster. You took my sister away from me.

You cost me my family, my life.

She lifts the nose of the gun slightly and shoots again.

It's much more satisfying this time. He cringes on impact, his bloody red hands flying up to his chest. He hangs for a millisecond like a tissue caught on a breeze, then drops to the floor.

You've got to hurry. They'll be here any second. Volkov for sure, drawn by the sound of the gunshots.

The first thing she does is lock the door. That should buy her a few seconds. Then she steps over her husband—his hands reaching feebly for her ankles—and sifts through the suitcase. The papers and thumb drives go into her pockets. She lifts the clothing but that's all there is. She prays she hasn't killed him too soon and that she won't miss anything because she didn't give him time to finish gathering things.

Suddenly, she feels a hand encircle her ankle. It's stronger than she would've thought.

She looks down. Mikhail is directly beneath her now, looking up at her. His mouth is full of blood. His eyes are pleading. He's reaching for her. He needs her. If she doesn't do anything to help him, he will die and he knows it. His lips move but she can't hear what he's saying.

"It's too late. You brought this on yourself, you really did." She says this gently, the way she speaks when she puts a Band-Aid on her son's knee.

She aims the gun at the center of his forehead and pulls the trigger one last time. All that time hunting on the heath turns out to be useful after all. It was harder to shoot a deer than the man on the floor.

A huge burden rises off her, those thousands of doves lifting all at once.

There is pounding at the door. Volkov's voice risen in anger and confusion. "What's going on in there? Are you okay, Mikhail? Stand back, I'm going to shoot the lock—"

Emily jumps back from the body on the floor, raising her gun. With

Volkov she has only one chance, she knows. He is a professional. Once he assesses the situation, he won't hesitate. He'll take her out. He won't care if she shoots at him. He'll just do what he has to do.

She thinks of Kit and Tatiana. She'll do what she must, too.

The shot is deafening, so much louder than the pop her little gun makes. The room fills with sawdust and smoke and the smell of gunpowder. Her teeth start to chatter, her outstretched arms turn to jelly. *No. No.* She must keep it together. Just a few minutes more. She has a job to do.

She fires just as the door flies open and catches Volkov in the shoulder. Her second shot goes a little lower and toward the center of the body mass. She's getting so much better at this quickly, it's surprising.

Luckily, the gun fell from Volkov's hand at the first shot. It tumbles to the floor out of its owner's reach

There's a fleeting look of utter confusion on Igor's face as he falls, seeing who it is who shot him. He was expecting another Russian mercenary, a professional sent by Galchev. The feeling of satisfaction is surprising and immense.

His hands flap on the ground as she steps over him. He's alive, then. She tries not to feel bad; Volkov has done plenty of things to deserve a shooting. It's not like she shot the children's nanny. She's heard stories told to visitors during an evening of drinking, Mikhail loving to impress them with tales of his bodyguard's derring-do. How many civilians Volkov had massacred while in the Russian Army. How he'd trained with Israeli specialists, spent a year working for British mercenaries in the hire of African dictators.

Only to be killed by a housewife. The irony.

She's roused from her thoughts by sounds coming down the hall. Feet pounding on stairs. Volkov's men, following their boss by chasing gunshots. She must be almost out of bullets. She hasn't any more.

Galchev only gave her the gun, either not imagining or not caring that she might have to kill anyone besides her husband. Not caring if she survived.

These footsteps are lighter but no less deliberate. Who could it be?

How many bullets are left in her gun? She has no idea but lifts it and takes aim at the doorway all the same.

Only it's Lynn who appears suddenly in the doorway.

Lynn, looking from the two men dead on the floor, the spreading pools of blood, then up to Emily.

Lynn, with a gun in her hand.

CHAPTER 35

Emily, Emily, Emily—what have you done?

There's no need for Lyndsey to ask: all the pieces are right there in front of her. Mikhail is clearly dead. It's less certain for Volkov, though, as Lyndsey thinks she can still see his chest rising and falling, though very slightly.

"Why do you have a gun, Lynn?" Emily asks. From the tone of her voice, Lyndsey knows she's in shock. "Where did you get it?"

Lyndsey's not unaware of the danger she is in. Emily could shoot at any minute. And holding this gun on her isn't helping, but somehow Lyndsey can't make herself put it down. It's a hard, cold calculus: she knows she could wound Emily. She's undoubtedly the better shot—a refresher course right before she got on the plane for London—while Emily is going deeper and deeper into shock.

Though at this close range, Emily would undoubtedly hit Lyndsey. Just not with any control.

"Emily, listen to me very carefully. Put the gun down. You don't want to shoot anyone else."

"You mean, I don't want to shoot *you*. That's a rather self-serving thing to say, don't you think? And maybe I do. Maybe you've given me reason."

"Very shortly, a security detail is going to descend on this house. The police—and MI6. They're coming to take Mikhail into custody."

"He made a deal with the British government. He told me."

"You knew that, and you shot him anyway?"

"The question is, how do you know? Did he tell you? Were you there with him?" Emily's voice trembles. Her hands start to shake.

"You don't want to have a gun in your hands when they get here," Lyndsey offers. "That is an invitation for them to shoot you."

Emily jabs the barrel of the gun toward Lyndsey. "You didn't answer me—how do you know?"

The moment has come to tell Emily the truth. Lyndsey can only hope that the Emily she knows, the rational Emily, is still in there. Shock can do funny things.

She steels herself. Something bad might happen very quickly. She needs to be ready. "You need to brace yourself, Emily. I'm not who you think I am. My real name is Lyndsey Duncan and I'm with CIA."

A long moment ticks by. "You're . . . a spy? You've been spying on me?"

"Spying on Mikhail. Never on you."

Emily's laugh comes out as a bark, abrupt and harsh. "You're a spy."

"Emily, put down your gun. The authorities will be here any second."

But Emily doesn't surrender her gun. Her confession comes tumbling out, as though it is a burning-hot secret that she can't keep any longer. The words come out, a confession made to Lyndsey like she's neither the friend nor the spy, but a neutral party. A priest.

"I made a deal with Oleg Galchev. He swore to take care of me and the children if I told him where Mikhail's money was hidden. Once Kosygin had that, he wouldn't need Mikhail any longer. He said Kosygin would want Mikhail dead. No loose ends, no chance of him trying to claw back his fortune." Her voice wavers on her husband's name. She is pointedly not looking down, not looking in the direction of the body.

Focus, Emily. "And do you have this information? The data?"

Emily barks that inhuman laugh again. "Of course I do, but do you think I would give it to you?"

"You don't want to give it to Galchev. It will only go straight to Kosygin. He'll use it for his wars—and to wage war on the U.K., too. Do your country a favor, Emily, and hand it over to them . . ."

"Don't do that, okay? Don't try to appeal to my sense of patriotism. Where was MI6 all this time, besides putting a spy inside my own house? MI6 doesn't give a damn about me—they made a deal with my husband. My lying, cheating, thieving husband. They were going to separate me from my children." Her voice gets shriller, screechier. "Do you think I give a damn anymore who wins? If Kosygin wins? I just want my children to be safe. That's what this has been about all along—keeping Mikhail from taking my children away from me."

The more Emily speaks, the wilder she gets, the hand holding the gun starting to veer left, right. And Lyndsey is aware that the clock is running down: at any minute, there will be police at the door, police running up the stairs. The other security guards must be close by, too. Listening to the two women shout at each other. Servants running about in a panic, the children upset and crying. Whatever time she has left, it's rapidly running out.

And she knows what Emily wants more than anything.

"Emily, listen to me. *Listen to me.* You must do the sensible thing right now. You're never going to get the data to Galchev. You're not going to make it out of this house. You've got to trust me to take care of you now."

A maniacal laugh escapes from Emily. "You! You were about to run away with my husband. You were on Mikhail's side. You were only using me."

"That's not true, Emily," Lyndsey says quickly. "Think about it. You needed a buffer between you and Mikhail, and that was me. Wasn't I? All those days and nights, it was me and you. I can't help that he was trying to drive a wedge between us, Emily. I never wanted him. He was a target, nothing more. You've got to see that."

Emily says nothing, but the gun sags in her hands.

"Let me help you, Emily. We'll make sure you're taken care of. Galchev won't be able to get to you. Kosygin, either. We'll keep you safe and—just as importantly—keep this fortune out of Kosygin's hands. That's the best revenge you could have."

Emily trembles all over. "You're really going to help me? You won't desert me?" A huge, wracking sob overtakes Emily and she nearly swoons. "He seduced my *sister*. Slept with her—she was only eighteen."

It's a huge risk, but . . . Lyndsey crouches, hands up, to place her own gun on the floor, aware every millisecond that Emily is watching her.

Emily heaves a sigh. And then she follows suit, placing the gun next to her husband's cooling body.

Lyndsey would like to run over and hold Emily tight, until the shaking stops, but she knows there is no time. Because not only will British law enforcement show up soon, but there's a good chance Galchev's men might, too. Now that he's this close to the prize, he's unlikely to take his foot off the gas pedal. Not now. Whether Emily knows it or not, Galchev may not have trusted her to deliver. He may have decided to send the same set of trigger-happy goons over to scoop up the data.

"Emily, go get the twins now. I'm going to call MI6 and let them know of the change in plans. There's no telling what might be outside waiting for us. We're going to need their help." She waves Emily to the door at the same time she pulls her cell phone out of her pocket. The old Emily has returned, the fragile one, and she steps gingerly over the bodies on her way to the door. And then, she is gone, her footsteps echoing down the hall.

Pick up, pick up . . . Lyndsey listens impatiently to the pips. Surprisingly, it is not Davis who picks up but another voice. "Davis Ranford's office," the woman says.

In that surreal moment, Lyndsey wonders if Davis has a secretary. Has she ever met her? "I need to speak to Davis, please. It's urgent."

"I'm afraid he's in a meeting. May I take—"

"Please tell him," Lyndsey interrupts, "there's a change of plans. Mikhail Rotenberg is dead. But we have the package and we need to bring Emily Rotenberg in, and the children, right *now.* We need protection. The police en route need to be told that. And please have someone call me back," she adds.

"Very good," the voice says on the other end before hanging up.

Lyndsey picks her gun off the floor. She checks Volkov's pulse even though there's little reason to at this point: he stopped moving some time ago.

She puts this out of her mind—two men dead in the bedroom, killed by the woman she's about to escort into police custody. *Don't think about it now, not when the finish line is so close. There will be more than enough time to think about it later.*

But where is Emily? Lyndsey exits to the hall and starts walking automatically to the children's wing. She speeds up: Emily wouldn't have left on her own, would she? Tried to slip out with the children. There wasn't enough time . . . She would be easy for Galchev's men to snatch up if they are outside already. Watching the house, waiting.

Oh no, Emily. No.

Lyndsey jogs down the hall. The children's rooms are ahead and it's not exactly quiet. A raised voice echoes off the walls and Lyndsey is trying to place it when Alice Wilkinson runs by suddenly, hands over the ears, her face ghastly white. She glances at Lyndsey but doesn't stop, the rubber soles of her sneakers squeaking against the marble floor.

Lyndsey stops in the doorway to see Arthur Westover with a hand on Emily's shoulder. He's jerking her around like a marionette. In the other hand is a small pistol, a ladies' pistol, the kind of thing you could hide in an evening bag. How ludicrous it looks in Westie's chubby hand, pressed to Emily's side.

The children cling to Emily's legs, crying. What a terrible, terrible day for these poor children, and they don't know the half of it yet.

"Westie," Lyndsey says to get his attention.

Arthur Westover spins around. He's upset and shaken. He looks daggers at her, as though she's nothing more than a small obstacle in his path.

"Get out of our way, Lynn," Westie says, full of self-importance. He still thinks she's Lynn Prescott. He doesn't know. How much does he know? she wonders. Does he know Mikhail is dead and that Emily killed him? Does he know Emily has a deal with Galchev—not that it would matter, if Westie was the one who showed up with Rotenberg's financial information on thumb drives rattling in his hand like dice.

"Where are you going?" Lyndsey demands.

"We're all going to take a little trip. You might as well come with us. No sense leaving behind anyone with a story to tell." He's pointing the little handgun at Lyndsey now. "I never did trust you, you know. I have no idea who you are, but I don't think you're an heiress from Philadelphia. Maybe Galchev will be able to get the story out of you."

Galchev. So that's Westie's plan, to sell the whole lot of them to Galchev. There is no honor among thieves.

What a ridiculous weapon in his hands. It only goes to show that Westie knows nothing about guns, that he chose something like that instead of something practical. The rounds are .25 caliber, at best, unlikely to do much damage even if he manages to hit her some place that matters. He's flustered, he's got multiple targets . . . He's not going to get more than one round off before Lyndsey will have reached him and knocked him to the ground.

She can try to shoot him before he'd get a second round off—but she's not a quick-draw artist and isn't sure how quickly she could get her gun out. It might not go smoothly at all, and then there's no telling how Westie might react.

She decides to scare him. To rattle him.

"You're right, Westie, I'm not an heiress from Pennsylvania. I'm with CIA."

Westie stops fidgeting. He goes pale and looks for a moment like he might faint.

He lets out a little panicked laugh. "You're a CIA agent?"

"That's right. At this moment, the police and MI6 are converging on this house. They're coming for Emily"—who has crouched down to pull her children to her chest, hugging them close—"so you might as well give it up. They're not going to let you out of here."

Westie glances left, then right as though he can see through the walls. "There's still time. I can slip out the back. I'm the only one who has *all* the data, you know. Even Mikhail didn't have all of it, the pompous fool. They were my fail-safe. My get-out-of-jail-free card."

Is it true? Could he have been ready to skip out without having all the trails back to his fortune, to his precious money?

Maybe Westie was going to be his last stop, before heading out.

"Your last chance," Lyndsey says, gesturing to the windows. They can hear cars crunching their way up the drive. No sirens, that's the thing that allowed them to slip in unnoticed. But the authorities are here, there's no denying it. "Surrender them to me, and we'll say you cooperated. It'll keep you out of jail."

Westie wants to look out the window. He glances nervously in the direction of the garage. But Westie isn't thinking *freedom*. He's thinking *money*. A payout for all his years of service. Rotenberg's information has to be worth a lot and he can't imagine letting it go for nothing.

Lyndsey doesn't want to do it, not with the children mere feet away. The twins have just calmed down in their mother's arms, under her patient shushing. She doesn't want to put Emily through any more, either.

But Westie still has his gun, and he's shown no sign of relenting. If anything, he seems more flustered, more upset. Maybe he'll go for a standoff, taking them hostage inside the playroom. Negotiating via cell phone.

Blood thrums in her ears and there's a tightness in her chest. She knows she's run out of time. She feels it . . . This is the last quiet moment before all hell breaks loose, before the police storm the house, unaware that there are hostages.

The chance that someone gets hurt is about to go sky-high. And if it were one of the children who gets hurt, Lyndsey won't be able to forgive herself.

She makes her move when there's a loud noise outside and Westie instinctively turns his head. She doesn't pull her gun out of her pocket: instead, she reaches inside and wraps her hand around it. Her finger finds the trigger guard, then the trigger. The safety is off. She aims, then fires. The impact spins Westie away from Emily and the children and pushes him back against the wall. Lyndsey finishes the job in a sprint; three strides and she's beside him, knocking him to the ground, shaking the gun from his hand. He's howling with pain. She got him in the side, a little lower than she would've liked, but the wound is not life-threatening.

She's kneeling on him, panting. Her ears ring painfully from the barking loud noise in such a small place. Next to her, the children are wailing loudly—their ears will hurt, too—clutching their mother, and she is clutching them in return, holding them against her like she would protect them at all costs, absorb any bullets. She is looking at Lyndsey with a mix of horror and fear . . . and gratitude, too.

"I said I would take care of you," Lyndsey says.

CHAPTER 36

It's a lovely summer afternoon. Lyndsey is in the south end of Hyde Park, near the Diana Memorial Fountain. She stands about a stone's throw from the oval track of burbling water, listening. Waiting. It's so peaceful. Thin crowds pass all around her, talking to each other or absorbed by their cell phones. Only a handful of others are looking at the water feature with her.

Eventually, the person Lyndsey has been waiting for ambles over. Dani Childs. She's subdued today. She wears sunglasses. She's not smoking. The two only nod at each other in recognition and then fall into step as they walk down West Carriage Drive.

"Any word on Ed Martin?" Lyndsey asks.

Dani removes her oversized sunglasses and slides them into her tote. Her fingernails are painted a bright pink. "He's come out of the coma, finally, but he's still in the hospital. They're hoping to send him home in about a week."

"That's a relief."

"Yes. Though I won't be working for Intent any longer. Things seem to have gone sideways there, or maybe the problems became more obvious once Ed was out of commission. I'm not sure what's going on, really." She shrugs, hugging the tote tightly under her arm.

Lyndsey thinks about the things Davis had told her, Martin's reservations. "That's probably for the best. If you want my unsolicited advice, I wouldn't go back if they call."

Dani laughs, though not exactly cheerfully. "Oh, but they were so much fun. So unpredictable. In all seriousness, I thought I could learn a few things from Ed Martin."

"Ed Martin, perhaps. But Ed knew the company was working for Galchev and he's going to need to answer questions about that. There are all kinds of temptations in this business, but whether you're on the inside or out, you can't let yourself be swayed by them. Going over to the dark side in this field . . . well, it's really dark."

Dani doesn't look over at her. She just keeps putting one foot in front of the other. *Well, she didn't ask for my advice*, Lyndsey tells herself.

"How is Emily doing?" Dani asks. "Have you seen her recently?"

"I saw her two days ago. She was being debriefed. I think she's ready for it to all be over, but she's got a way to go. Anyway, she's exhausted but knows that she's lucky, under the circumstances. Vauxhall Cross has gotten the murder proceedings postponed so she can go through psychiatric evaluation. I think her defense will be spousal abuse—"

"God, I hated that man. He deserved what he got."

"Poor Emily. Even if she escapes imprisonment, it's not like she won't pay. She'll be forever scarred by what she did and she'll have to explain to her children someday why she killed their father. She could still lose them to Mikhail."

The two walk in silence for a while. It's such a beautiful day, too nice to talk about bad things.

Dani doesn't speak until they stand in the shade of a flowering tree. "How far have they gotten with the books?"

"Westie's bookkeeping? MI6 analysts are working with various Crown offices to peel back the layers of shell companies and other subterfuge, but it's too soon to tell. The Russian government has seized a few of his assets on the grounds that Rotenberg had cheated on taxes for decades, and to this end petitioned the U.K. government to provide a copy of Rotenberg's books, which the U.K. has so far refused to do. It's a mess."

"Poor Emily. Is she penniless? I would hope her family is helping her out."

"MI6 is taking care of her. To play it safe, they're being housed in a secret government facility for now. Waiting to see if Galchev or Kosygin try something." Lyndsey checks her watch. "I'm afraid I have to make another meeting. Are you staying in town a bit longer or headed back to Virginia?"

"My flight's this evening."

"I was going to say we should get together, but I'm not sure when I'm going to be stateside again. Maybe at the holidays."

"No worries. I know how it goes." They hug briefly, even though Dani doesn't strike Lyndsey as a hugger. It also seems to Lyndsey that neither of them will bother to reach out to the other down the road, that there's a chance this may be the last time they see each other, and this might be a shame. There are things about Dani she has come to appreciate, even admire. Maybe one day she'll find the guts to make a similar move. She has a feeling it might be in the cards.

Dani puts her sunglasses back on and lopes off in the direction of the taxi stand.

Lyndsey turns and walks up South Carriage Drive, toward the Knightsbridge Underground station, not far from Mikhail Rotenberg's apartment. She turns down Wilton Place and keeps walking until she comes to a pleasant if nondescript café. There are tables out front taking advantage of the warm weather. A few of the tables are occupied in twos or threes, people having a pint or a glass of chardonnay or rosé. The tinkle of glassware and silver, low conversations, occasional bright laughter.

Sitting at one of the tables, alone, is Davis Ranford. He is smiling broadly, rubbing his hands together in anticipation.

Lyndsey wends around a stanchion and approaches his table. She drops her tote bag onto an empty chair and takes the seat opposite him.

He lifts an open bottle of pinot grigio from an ice bucket. "Would you like a splash?"

She watches him pour. "They must be pleased with you at Vauxhall Cross to set you free in the middle of the day to drink."

He puts the bottle back in the bucket. "The jury is still out as to whether it would've been better to have Rotenberg, to pick his brains and see what else we can learn about Kosygin's operations. But then we'd have had to deal with him, and he was so damned disagreeable. Not that I need to tell you." He smiles at her. "Whereas Emily is much easier. She's so grateful for everything, even bringing her a lukewarm tea in a paper cup. She's a doll, really."

"She's been controlled within an inch of her life for the past five years." It's typical to have a gallows sense of humor at intelligence agencies. A need to put on a brave front, she supposes. But Davis's jocularity is getting on Lyndsey's nerves. It's to be expected, this touchiness after an operation, being on the front line. She's been keyed up for weeks. It's going to take time to shift gears. To remember that she's not being watched every minute. That her life is no longer on the line.

"But, yes, the powers that be are generally pleased with how the operation turned out. They'll undoubtedly be able to cull a few millions in back taxes from Rotenberg's estate, too, once they finish going over the books. All that unacknowledged money hidden in offshore accounts. So, we even managed to pay for ourselves—which may be a first in the annals of operations." He raises his glass for a clink; Lyndsey grudgingly obliges.

They both sip. Davis eyes her over the rim of his glass. "But I didn't ask you to meet me to talk about that."

"No?" She squints.

He hesitates, suddenly shy, as though all the glibness has drained out of him. He rearranges the napkin on his lap. "I wanted to tell you that I took to heart what you'd said the other day." He looks up, holding her eyes. "If I doubted whether I should be with Miranda because you'd turned up in my life again."

She doesn't want to go through this again. For what reason? To assuage his qualms, make him feel better about his decision? "We've been through this, Davis . . ."

"No, we haven't." There's a hitch in his voice. "You see, once I thought about it, I realized you were right. I wouldn't be happy with Miranda, I'd always be wondering *what if.* And that wasn't fair to Miranda."

Lyndsey draws a sharp breath. *No.*

He doesn't seem to hear and continues. "So—I broke it off. I told her I'd made a mistake. I moved out this past weekend." He reaches for her hands. His are trembling slightly.

Lyndsey's hands are trembling, too, but not for the reason he thinks.

"Aren't you going to say something? You're making me nervous,"

Davis says. "I'd hoped you'd be happy. That maybe you'd want to go out tonight and celebrate."

She should be happy. Or rather, she would be happy if she still wanted to be with Davis. But working with him on this operation was eye-opening. She'd gotten to see other sides to him. She can't stop wondering if the whole thing wasn't a bit of a honey trap from the start. That in Beirut, he'd seen in her an opportunity. *Here's a young CIA agent I can possibly get on a string.* Play it light, play it cool. He'd thought he'd lost her when she'd been recalled, only here she was in London. Opportunity regained.

Maybe Security had been right to call her on it before they suspended her. Maybe everyone had seen something she'd been blind to.

How could she be sure he was even back with Miranda? Lyndsey had never seen them together, never heard anyone else refer to the ex-wife. Maybe the whole thing had been a convenient lie, a way to keep her on that string. Only now he saw that he was losing control and decided to reel Lyndsey in closer again. To reestablish control.

Thinking like this could drive you mad, make you lose all faith in humanity. Make you a perpetual outsider. Was there nothing you could trust, not even a man you wanted to love, someone you wanted to be with?

The trouble was, once you started thinking that way, it was over. It would never be good again. You'd always be wondering.

Lyndsey picks up her wineglass and drains it. "I'm sorry to hear that, Davis. I was hoping you two would be able to make a go of it this time."

He shakes his head, dazed. "What are you saying? I thought you felt the same way. Am I wrong? Don't you want to be together?"

She knows not to speak her mind. Never say never in this business. There's no telling the circumstances under which their paths may cross again. No sense making an enemy of him unnecessarily, not to satisfy a temporary fury. Control: that's what this business is all about. "I think you're a wonderful man, Davis. But there's a reason we were split up. You with MI6 and me at CIA. It doesn't work, not in this business. There will always be suspicions—at Langley, in any case. I know MI6 is more . . . tolerant. But at Langley, I'd always be under a cloud."

"What you mean is that I'm not worth your career." He is either astonished or so upset that he spits the words out.

She reaches for her tote bag and starts gathering her things. "I guess I don't feel that way about—us. Don't be angry, Davis. It's not going to work. We don't have a future together and you know it."

"And your career is your future?" he says bitterly. "Is that what you've decided? Your career comes first?"

A girl's gotta eat, she thinks. "I'm glad we were able to do this one good thing together. Aren't you?"

He looks up, scowling. "Was working together a mistake? Did I do something wrong?"

No, she'll always be grateful for the experience. To have her eyes opened. "No, it's nothing like that, not at all," she lies. "It's something I have to figure out for myself." That part is true.

"I thought I was your future. At least, you gave me that impression in Beirut."

Maybe if you hurry, Miranda will take you back. The thought pops into her head but she's savvy enough not to say it.

"Goodbye, Davis." She's surprised that she doesn't feel even a twinge of regret. She rises, resisting the urge to kiss the top of his head.

Back on the sidewalk, walking briskly toward the high street, Lyndsey feels the phone in her pocket vibrate. The damn thing—there are times when she wishes she could just throw it in the river. Which office needs her attention now, Langley or Vauxhall Cross? Or perhaps it's Tarasenko, yanking her chain again, reminding her that he's supposed to be her number one priority. She has rarely felt such a desperate need to get away.

She lifts the phone to read the black screen. Voice mail. It's from Theresa.

She remembers the last time they talked and her stomach drops.

Why didn't you pick up? I know there's a good reason, but . . . look, I desperately need your help. This man they've sent back to me is not my husband. This man is not Richard.

No one at Langley will speak to me. There's no way to warn them.

Come quickly.

ACKNOWLEDGMENTS

It has been a great pleasure to get to write a second Lyndsey Duncan book. The response to *Red Widow* was overwhelming, particularly from folks who used to work in the intelligence business. Thanks to all who wrote to tell me how much they enjoyed it. It's been an honor to have it so well-received.

Red London was completed and sitting with my editor when Russia attacked Ukraine, which commenced on February 24, 2022, and is ongoing as I write this. That act required a substantial change to the story. I don't mean to trivialize what the people of Ukraine are going through by comparing it to the writing of a book. What Ukraine is enduring is a reflection of what's going on in the world, and has been for some time, writ large: consolidation of power and wealth by the audacious or simply greedy at the expense of those who believe in good for all and peaceful coexistence. It is a time of strong men and mad men, though some of us fail to see the appeal. But it does illustrate the perils of writing about world events during a time of great upheaval. Every writer of spy thrillers I know was caught off guard by the Russia attack. Foreseeing the future is quite difficult, not just for intelligence analysts.

I wish to thank CIA's publication review board for the prompt review of the manuscript. My thanks to historian and author Gareth Russell for helping me understand the finer points of British aristocracy.

I also wish to thank the team at G. P. Putnam's Sons for all their efforts: Sally Kim, for her patience and (as always) magical insight into how to make a story better; and Ivan Held, Ashley McClay, Alexis Welby, Katie Grinch, and Tarini Sipahimalani.

My deepest thanks to Richard Pine and Eliza Rothstein for all their guidance and hard work on my behalf. Without them, there would be no books from me. Thanks to Angela Cheng Caplan for helping me navigate Hollywood. And, as always, thanks to my husband, Bruce, for experiencing this weird second life with me.